CAFFEINE NIGHTS PUBLISHING

PROGENY

Shaun Hutson

Fiction to die for...

Published by Caffeine Nights Publishing 2023

Copyright © Shaun Hutson 2023

Shaun Hutson has asserted his rights under the Copyright, Designs and Patents Act 1998 to be identified as the author of this work

CONDITIONS OF SALE
All rights reserved. No part of this publication may be reproduced, stored in a retrieval system, or transmitted in any form or by any means, electronic, mechanical, photocopying, scanning, recording or otherwise, without the prior permission of the publisher

This book has been sold subject to the condition that it shall not, by way of trade or otherwise, be lent, resold, hired out, or otherwise circulated without the publisher's prior consent in any form of binding or cover other than that in which it is published and without a similar condition including this condition being imposed on the subsequent purchaser.
All characters in this publication are fictitious and any resemblance to real persons, living or dead is purely coincidental

Published in Great Britain by
Caffeine Nights Publishing
Amity House
71 Buckthorne Road
Minster on Sea
Isle of Sheppey
ME12 3RD

caffeinenightsbooks.com

British Library Cataloguing in Publication Data.
A CIP catalogue record for this book is available from the British Library

ISBN: 978-1-913200-28-2

Cover illustration by
Mark Taylor

Everything else by
Default, Luck and Accident

Also by Shaun Hutson:

ASSASSIN
BODY COUNT
BREEDING GROUND
CAPTIVES
CHASE
COMPULSION
DEADHEAD
DEATHDAY
DYING WORDS
EPITAPH
EREBUS
EXIT WOUNDS
HEATHEN
HELL TO PAY
HYBRID
KNIFE EDGE
LAST RITES
LUCY'S CHILD
MONOLITH
NECESSARY EVIL
NEMESIS
PURITY
RELICS
RENEGADES
SHADOWS
SLUGS
SPAWN
STOLEN ANGELS
TESTAMENT
THE SKULL
TWISTED SOULS
UNMARKED GRAVES
VICTIMS
WARHOL'S PROPHECY

WHITE GHOST

Hammer Novelizations
TWINS OF EVIL
X THE UNKNOWN
THE REVENGE OF FRANKENSTEIN

ACKNOWLEDGEMENTS

Doing the acknowledgements and dedication for a novel is usually the most enjoyable part.

Mainly because it's nice to thank those who have helped in some way, shape or form during the writing and publication process and beyond but, also, because you know you can't mess it up. Over the years, the number of names appearing in my own acknowledgements have decreased for various reasons but the ones who are name checked here are present because they deserve to be.

Writing is a solitary thing (one of the factors that makes it so attractive to me, being an unsociable bastard) but it's surprising how many people you end up realizing deserve a mention when you come to this part. This book was particularly dark and parts of it weren't pleasant to write but pain is part of the process I've always thought.

So, pretentious part over, here goes the list. Everyone here should know why they're mentioned but, if they don't, I'm not going to bother explaining. It's my way of expressing my gratitude for anything they've done either directly or indirectly.

Massive thanks to my publisher, Darren Laws, at Caffeine Nights who continues to show great faith in my work, and I will always be grateful for that. Many thanks too to Meg Davis, my agent.

Considering how much of the bloody stuff I drink; I should probably thank Lucozade! But I'll stick to people.

I'd like to thank Matt 'where's my white stick' Shaw. Graeme Sayer who continues to run my website, thanks, mate. Michael Knight, Emma Dark and Mark Taylor.

Everyone at Cineworld in Milton Keynes.

Claire, Dani, Leah, Bruce, Steve, Dave, Adrian, Janick and Nicko. Rod Smallwood.

My daughter, Kelly. Belinda.

The most important people I leave until last as usual and that's you lot. My readers. An author is nothing without their readers. I'm lucky, I've got the best.

Right, that's enough messing about.

Let's go.

Shaun Hutson

DEDICATION

Like everything else I write, this is dedicated to my wonderful daughter.

I've made a living out of using words, but I'll never find the words to describe how much I love her.

PROGENY

By

Shaun Hutson

"I dream; therefore I exist."
August Strindberg

*"What did I see? Could I believe?
That what I saw that night was real
and not just fantasy."*
Iron Maiden

PROLOGUE

"All alone now, except for the memories."
Queensryche.

DESPERATION

Her hands were shaking as she reached for the laptop.

Pushing open the device, she gazed at the blank screen as if hoping that simple act might prompt some outpouring of words.

It didn't.

But then, if the truth be known, she wasn't sure what to write anyway.

And was a laptop the best place to complete this particular task? Surely a piece of paper and a pen would have been more appropriate. Just scribble down a few words and leave the result somewhere clearly visible inside the small room.

She sat back slightly, the wooden chair she was perched on creaking slightly. The method of writing was a problem and so was the content. What the hell did you put in a missive like this? What kind of information? Or did you limit it to an outpouring of thoughts?

Or regrets?

There was a small notepad beside her, and she flicked through it, looking for a clean page that wasn't already unmarked by her scribblings. This notepad was just the latest in a series she had filled over the years with her thoughts and musings. There were dozens of them lined up on the shelf before her, just above her desk. They vied for space with books, lever arch files and all manner of other volumes. Diaries, journals. The description didn't seem important any longer. It was what lay within those pages that mattered.

There were other items on the desk that she had used. A micro cassette recorder for when she was so busy she hadn't the time to scribble down words and could only speak them into the device to be transcribed later.

Beside it lay more files. Brown manilla. Each one crammed with more notes and sometimes photographs too. Colour, black and white. Some taken with digital cameras and printed up. Others snapped with older style photographic devices where negatives were worked up in a darkroom before being viewed. That process seemed archaic now and the woman at the desk smiled slightly as she considered it.

There were even Polaroid's lying on the desk.

It was as if certain sections of the workspace were from another era. One not so advanced. A slower, more sedate one. One she missed and longed to have back but she knew that was impossible.

The woman closed her eyes and bowed her head, trying to drive these whimsical thoughts from her mind. There were other things she needed to consider. More important things.

She gripped the pen in one hand once more and pressed the tip to the paper, trying to begin. Attempting to think of the words she needed to express.

There was so much she wanted to say. So much she needed to convey. But how? She hadn't got a clue where to begin.

She dropped the pen and stared at the blank laptop screen again, her face lit only by the dull white light. She rested her fingers gently on the keys and looked down at them, aware that they were still shaking. She clenched her fists tightly together, her heart thudding hard against her ribs.

In the silence of the room, she could hear sounds drifting on the darkness.

Sounds that she wished she couldn't hear.

Sounds of pain. Of suffering. Of rage.

And others she couldn't identify. Sounds she didn't want to identify.

The hairs were standing up on the back of her neck and, as each new noise filtered through, she tried harder to shut them out and to concentrate on the task before her, the one that had occupied her for the last half hour.

How did you write a suicide note?

PART ONE

"The life of the dead is placed in the memory of the living."
                                            Cicero

ONE

Lauren Davison brought the car to a halt and sat motionless behind the wheel for a moment.

She looked across the huge car park towards the main entrance of St. Michael's Hospital and she couldn't suppress the grin that now spread across her face. And, she thought, why should she try to contain her joy.

This would be her first day as head nurse in the hospital's Maternity Unit. Something she'd dreamed about since she first became a nurse more than twelve years earlier. It had taken dedication, effort and pure hard work but all that had finally seen fruition and, as Lauren glanced at herself in the rear-view mirror, she felt a swell of pride that it was impossible to contain.

The position itself was like an affirmation of her abilities but it also carried a significant salary increase which was very welcome. At thirty-five, Lauren felt that she and her husband were ready to expand in more ways than one. They had already committed to an extension on their house and, if everything went according to plan, that would shortly become a nursery. The extra money would certainly come in handy in more ways than one. Her husband had also just been promoted in his own right and they were basking in each other's reflected glory somewhat. Life was pretty good at the moment, Lauren thought, smiling.

No more secrets.

She hesitated a moment and then swung herself out of the car and sucked in a deep breath. Even the air seemed to taste sweeter today, Lauren told herself, smiling at her own home spun philosophising.

She walked briskly across the car park and through the main entrance of the hospital, waving to several colleagues during her short journey. The Maternity Unit was on the ground floor of St. Bridget's, accessed through a series of doors that could only be opened by staff with the application of four-digit codes changed every day. It was sad that the security had to be so stringent but, as Lauren mused, they were caring for the most valuable possessions that any human being could ever have. Children. A future.

She entered the unit and turned right towards the nurses' station and the small staff room beyond. There were two nurses inside the small room when she entered, both younger than herself and both seated at a wooden table sipping from mugs of tea.

They all exchanged greetings and pleasantries and Lauren gratefully accepted the mug of tea that was handed to her by the older of her two colleagues. Sandra Mackay ran a hand through her bright red hair and retrieved some biscuits from the tin that stood close to the kettle.

The other nurse, Paula Morgan, dabbed at her nose with a tissue, muttering that she thought she might have the beginnings of a cold. The other two women backed away from her theatrically, both laughing before returning to the more pressing matter of their morning tea.

Another ten minutes and Lauren checked her watch against the wall clock and made her way into the New-born room. There were up to fifteen babies inside this room, each one housed in its own little clear plastic sided cot. No matter how many times Lauren saw these small containers and their precious cargoes she smiled. To her it had always seemed as if the babies were being kept in clear sandwich boxes, designed to ensure their tiny inhabitants remained fresh. She smiled once more as she approached the first of the little children.

She peered down at the first child, glancing at the small clipboard that hung from the metal frame of the container. All the necessary information about the child was written there and Lauren ran appraising eyes over the notes before moving on to the next cot. And the next.

She inspected each baby and each set of notes with the same concentration and attention to detail because her job was to ensure that these little people were healthy and well when they were finally taken from here by their adoring parents. She wondered what that must feel like and her smile grew broader as she gazed down at the last of the children.

The child was sleeping, and Lauren watched its tiny chest rise and fall slowly as it lay there, a small bonnet on its head and a pink knitted blanket covering its tiny form.

One of her colleagues walked past the large window that ran the full length of the New-born room and she waved happily as the other nurse passed by, finally returning her attention to the baby before her.

Lauren was still smiling when she reached into the cot and closed one hand firmly around the baby girl's right ankle.

She lifted the child effortlessly, raising her own arm, swinging the baby back over her shoulder the way she would raise a tennis racket ready to strike.

Lauren swung her arm forward with tremendous power, keeping her grip on the baby's ankle and lower leg, her fingers digging into the soft pudgy flesh there.

The little girl's head slammed into the metal bar around the next cot with incredible force.

The impact stunned her because she made no sound as Lauren repeated the movement, raising the child again by her ankle and swinging her down once more with almost gleeful ferocity. The second strike obliterated the face completely. Bones in the cheek and jaw, still soft, simply seemed to dissolve beneath the stunning impact. Blood burst from the child's face and, as Lauren struck it a third time against the metal bar, the head seemed to split from front to back, pinkish-red brain exploding outwards as if propelled from within.

Lauren dropped the lifeless form and moved to the next cot, pushing her hand onto the face of the little boy there. She gripped the head with one hand and, with her other, pushed her thumb against his fontanelle. It pulsed briefly beneath the pad of her thumb then Lauren pushed the digit forward, through the paper-thin flesh and into that still open gap in the skull bones. She drove deeper until she felt the warm, wet brain matter beneath, and blood jetted up her forearm as she held the child before her, her thumb still embedded in its malleable skull.

The third baby she lifted tenderly from its cot, gripped it beneath the chin and at the ankles and merely snapped the body violently at the waist, the spine breaking effortlessly.

She held the child by its neck for a moment, gazing into the lifeless eyes, then she dropped it to the floor and moved on.

It took her less than ten minutes to slaughter every single baby in the unit.

Only as she tore the eyes from the last child with her fingernails did she hear footsteps hurtling towards her from both directions outside the glass fronted room.

By then, it didn't really matter.

TWO

Jake Porter stood motionless for a moment, glancing around into the gloom that surrounded him.

The blackness was impenetrable but for the feeble light of his torch and now he swept that thin beam of light back and forth, trying to carve a path through the dark. To both sides of him there were thick stone walls and, when Jake put his hand out to touch the nearest one, he felt the iciness of the old brickwork. It was as if the stone were sucking all the warmth from him. Absorbing it. He shivered involuntarily and moved on, his footsteps echoing inside the high-ceilinged corridor.

Above him hung strip lights that had been dormant for so many years Jake doubted if they still worked and, when he finally reached a panel of switches, he flicked at them. No light was forthcoming. The overhead lights remained as dark as the rest of the building.

And the cold seemed to be intensifying.

When he exhaled his breath clouded before him and with each fresh inhalation he felt as if he was snorting pure ice. The cold air filled his lungs and made him shiver. The blood in his veins seemed to be the same temperature now, coursing through his body in a freezing torrent. He felt the hairs on his arms and the back of his neck rise but he wasn't sure if that was all a result of the rapidly falling temperatures.

Fear played a part too.

Jake could feel his heart beating a little faster as he moved deeper and deeper into the heart of the building. He had already climbed two flights of wide stone steps and now he was faced with a third. It was up ahead, barely visible in the blackness but, as he took a few more tentative paces towards it, he could see the bottom steps illuminated by the weak beam of his torch.

The light reflected off the bare stone and also something else. Something that was trickling slowly down the steps.

Jake moved nearer. As he did, he could see that the slicks of glistening fluid were what he had first feared. There were two or three rivulets of blood coursing down the stone. For a second it looked as if the very concrete itself was bleeding, but Jake knew that was impossible. The blood was coming from higher up, dripping inexorably from step to step. Puddling on one stair and then overflowing to the next. Making its way down the flight like a slow-moving crimson waterfall.

Jake paused before the first step then slowly began to climb, trying to avoid the blood. When he was halfway up, he shone the torch around him again, but it wasn't his eyes that were alerted it was his ears.

Somewhere inside the building, the sound amplified by the stone walls and high ceilings, he heard something he'd heard before since entering.

It was the unmistakeable sound of a baby crying.

Jake froze on the steps for a second, trying to pinpoint exactly where the noise was coming from. For long seconds it floated on the chill air then died away, but he knew which direction to go now. The sound seemed to be drawing him and he even hurried up the remaining steps, bringing himself out on another landing that spread out in two directions. To his right and his left there were long corridors that snaked away into even more impenetrable darkness but, as Jake was deciding which way to go, he heard the strident sound of the baby's cries once more.

Without hesitating he turned to his left and the direction of the sound.

Jake's footsteps echoed inside the building as he walked but, as he turned a corner into the corridor beyond those same footsteps were suddenly muffled by the thick layers of dust that had accumulated. Years of neglect and absence of cleaning had allowed the dust to grow thick. It was several inches deep in places and it stuck to his shoes as he walked through it, clinging to the material like a living thing. Motes of it turned in the torch beam as Jake advanced, the sound of the crying baby pulling him closer all the time.

And then silence.

Complete and impenetrable silence.

All Jake could hear now was the rushing blood in his ears and the steady thud of his beating heart.

He froze in the corridor, looking around, shining the torch at some of the closed doors that confronted him on either side.

The silence was total, and he stood immobile within it and the blackness. Cocooned by the stillness and gloom. Jake tried to swallow but his throat was chalk dry. He held the torch out before him at arm's length, the beam flickering ominously. The batteries were definitely failing.

Not now. Please.

The light coming from the torch had been pure white when he'd first entered the building but now the beam was a sickly yellow. Just like the walls of the edifice seemed to be sucking the warmth from his body, the blackness and silence seemed equally capable of draining the luminescence from his only source of light.

Just up ahead of him there was a large window set into one of walls but even that allowed very little natural light in. It was a moonless night and that, combined with the thick banks of cloud that were scudding across the heavens, combined to give next to no brightness. The building was a good mile from the nearest road so there was no glinting street lights to help either. Jake paused and glanced out of the window onto the darkened grounds beyond.

Ahead of him he heard the baby once more.

Galvanized by the sound he moved towards it, his heart thumping hard against his ribs.

Only once did he consider that the sound might be drawing him into a trap. Teasing him and coaxing him towards something he had no chance of confronting let alone defeating. But now that thought stuck in his mind and would not shift.

You're walking into a trap.

THREE

Jake tried to push the thought to one side as he continued along the corridor.

The idea was ridiculous.

Wasn't it?

The thought that he had been lured into this situation was insane. As if he'd been manipulated into coming to this place without realizing the possible consequences was madness.

Wasn't it?

As he continued to walk, he found that conviction harder and harder to dismiss. But still he tried. He had come here out of choice. No one had forced him. Nothing had compelled him to drive to this building and seek something within its labyrinthine depths. He had come because he wanted to. Because he *needed* to.

Hadn't he?

The baby's crying had now turned to shrill screams and that sound forced Jake to move quicker through the dark, chilly building. The child's wails now sounded more like entreaties to him. He had to find it.

He shook the torch as he walked, hoping that would somehow reinvigorate the rapidly failing batteries but it didn't. The light that came from the device was barely more powerful than that which might be generated by a candle. Jake held it higher, hoping that simple act too might allow him to see more within the oppressive gloom. It didn't.

He found himself approaching another corner but this time there was only one way to go. The corridor turned sharply to the left, into a stretch of tunnel like stone that was even thicker with dust.

Jake hesitated for a moment, shining the torch over the area before him. As he played the beam across the dust, he saw that it had been disturbed in a few places. He saw the unmistakeable shape of footprints.

Someone had walked along this corridor before him. And recently.

He dropped to his haunches and inspected the imprints in the dust more carefully. The outline of the feet was clearly visible and so too was the fact that those feet had been bare when they'd traversed this dirty, neglected place. The outline of the toes was clear. And whoever had walked through this detritus had possessed small, almost child-like feet.

A little further ahead he saw something else lying in the dust.

Moving closer Jake could see that it was a small teddy bear.

One of the glass eyes was missing and an ear had been chewed, the stuffing was even bulging from a tiny rent in the toy's belly, but it was smiling up at him, nonetheless.

There was blood soaking into most of the stuffed animal and as Jake reached out with one finger and prodded the toy, he could feel that the crimson liquid was still warm.

He wiped the blood on his jeans and got to his feet, moving deeper into the corridor, aware now that there as a closed door a few feet ahead of him.

From behind this door, he heard the cries of a baby once again and this time they were more insistent. Jake moved forward, his hand pressing against the heavy door.

Even the wood felt icy cold and Jake pulled his hand away again sharply as if fearing that the flesh might stick to the freezing surface. However, the small pressure he'd applied to the partition was enough to open it a few inches. The door swung back to reveal more darkness beyond.

However, this new room contained at least some form of illumination because Jake could see the puddle of dull light towards the rear of it. He edged further inside the room and saw clearly now that this light was coming from behind an old pram. How the hell it had got there he had no idea but when he realized that the sound of the crying baby was coming from inside it, he advanced slowly towards the pram.

The room in which it stood was empty but for the battered old conveyance. A single large window was open and allowing the cool night air in but even that breeze wasn't enough to have transformed the temperature into what felt like sub-zero.

Jake swallowed hard and slowed his pace slightly as he saw something lying on the floor just ahead of him. He shone the fading torch beam onto the object and saw that it was a small doll. Jake reached out to touch the little figure, noticing that the clothes it wore were torn and stained.

As he lifted it, he saw the tiny white shapes dropping from it.

Maggots. Hundreds of them.

They writhed and squirmed from the body of the doll, covering the plastic before dropping to the floor.

Jake grunted in disgust and dropped the figure. He stared down at it for a second longer then continued towards the pram.

He was halfway across the room when he heard sounds of movement coming from his right.

The figure that stood there, hidden mostly by the shadows, made no attempt to come any closer. It seemed content to watch from a distance.

The same was true of the apparition on his left.

Both remained in the gloom, visible in the darkness only by their long white robes that fluttered around them as the breeze intensified, fanning the diaphanous material so that it opened like the petals of some huge flower.

Jake could see that both figures were female. Both in their twenties. The one on the right was holding a baby to her right breast and the child was feeding happily from that teat. Or so Jake thought until he looked more closely.

Whatever the woman was holding was not feeding *from* her. It was feeding *on* her.

Jake could see a mouth chewing relentlessly into the soft flesh of the breast, blood coursing down her torso.

And as he stood transfixed the figure to his left moved closer, her legs spread wide as she walked in some mock comic gait, her legs spreading with each faltering step.

The reason for this shambling advance now became visible too.

A head was pushing insistently from between her legs, tearing itself free of her vagina, a look of twisted anger on its face. Because this was not the face of a baby emerging from that most delicate of places, it was the head of a fully grown man. The mouth was open in a silent roar of rage, the eyes bulging wildly in sockets choked with blood.

Jake tried to ignore the two figures, moving closer to the pram instead.

He knew that what he sought lay inside.

As the two figures closed in on him, Jake peered into the pram, the sound of the crying baby now filling his ears.

What he saw inside the pram nearly caused him to vomit but, he fought back the urge and, instead, contented himself with a scream that shook his entire body.

FOUR

Jake Porter sat bolt upright in bed, his eyes wide, his breath coming in short gasps.

The last vestiges of the nightmare slowly slipped away, and he swung himself around, sitting on the edge of the bed, his head bowed and supported by his shaking hands.

It was so vivid. So real. It always was. No matter how many times he experienced the nightmare (and it had been for weeks now in various guises) it was always so believable that he could practically smell it. Jake exhaled deeply and felt the sweat soaking his back and chest. He clenched his fists, digging his nails into his palms as if that would also hasten the departure of the residual images still clinging to his mind.

Only when his breathing had slowed did he wipe a hand through his hair and get to his feet. He wandered from the bedroom through to the en-suite where he turned on the shower, waiting for the water to heat up, wishing that the last fragments of the nightmare would fade a little faster. Perhaps, he mused, the shower would wash them away once and for all.

Beneath the cleansing jets, Jake washed quickly, aware that he was running a little late. Certainly, he'd be at his office by ten, there was never any doubt of that, and his first appointment wasn't until ten thirty, but he always gave himself plenty of time whatever he was doing. If there was one thing Jake was a stickler for it was punctuality. He felt it was a mark of professionalism. He hated lateness. He didn't forgive it in himself and he didn't excuse it in others. He'd always been like that for as long as he could remember. All through his forty-eight years on the planet, time had been a commodity he felt he didn't want to waste.

Life was too short; life wasn't a rehearsal. Jake didn't care which bumper sticker people lived by, but it was difficult to argue. He had never believed in waiting around for things to happen if he could influence them himself and he was careful not wasteful with his time.

He stepped out of the shower and then shaved and dressed quickly, finally inspecting his reflection in the full-length mirror in the bedroom.

Vain? Jake smiled to himself. No. It wasn't vanity. It was just caring about his appearance, wasn't it? He re-adjusted the navy-blue tie he was wearing, wondered briefly about substituting it for a different one but then shook his head and decided he would have to do as he was.

He quickly pulled the duvet over his bed, retrieved his phone from the bedside table and made his way downstairs for a quick breakfast before he left. That was something else he always made sure he did. Breakfast, to coin another cliché, was the most important meal of the day he'd always been told, and Jake always made sure he had something even if it was just some toast and a cup of coffee. At the weekends if he wasn't working, he'd sometimes cook himself a full English on a Sunday morning. But, during the week some cereals and toast and a glass of orange juice did the job.

Jake checked in the fridge and noticed he'd have to go shopping later that day. He hated it but it had to be done.

No one to do it for you now.

He stood motionless in front of the fridge for a moment then closed the door and sat down at the large table. As he was pouring milk onto his cereal, he heard movement outside the front door and then the sound of mail dropping onto the matt.

Jake got to his feet and retrieved the offerings, scanning the envelopes with disinterest.

Circulars. Bills. Junk mail.

And.

The last envelope was larger than the others even though the letter inside didn't require it. Jake swallowed hard as he looked at the franked address on the top left-hand corner.

As he opened it, his hand began to shake slightly.

FIVE

Danielle Grant slipped off one trainer and massaged her right foot.

Too much time standing she reasoned. She'd been working at this job for the last six years, rising gradually to the lofty heights of branch manager but she'd never got used to the amount of time she spent on her feet. She was sure that it was causing back problems too, something she'd feel a lot later in life. She was twenty-nine now and sometimes she felt double that age. To say she hated the job would have been an overstatement but, when the alarm sounded every morning to signal the resumption of another long shift, she wasn't exactly delighted. Dani smiled to herself. Who was? Who actually enjoyed their job? Who actively looked forward to a day's work? If you had a job you didn't. If you had a career it was a different matter. She's read something once to the effect that "if you've got a job you *count* the hours in a day. If you've got a career there aren't *enough* hours in the day."

The job she'd had before was even worse in many ways. She'd worked for a tiny local magazine that specialised in protective clothing and safety equipment. The job itself had been relatively easy but it was the people she'd had to work with that had finally caused her to leave. To this day she was convinced that the woman who ran the magazine was unstable. Given to verbally violent outbursts when things weren't done exactly the way she demanded, she was unpredictable, and Dani wasn't afraid to say that the woman had scared her with her outbursts. Apparently her first husband had knocked her about, and Dani had to confess the only thing that puzzled her was why the guy hadn't killed the shrieking, unstable bitch.

The other staff there had been wary of their demented boss too, but they had learned to cope with her almost psychotic outbursts.

The self-important assistant who thought she was better than everyone else because she had a degree in Creative Writing. The one who always kept the sleeves of her top rolled up just enough to cover the self-harming marks on her arms.

The older designer (a man in his sixties who thought his pony-tail made him look younger and fashionable when all it really did was make him look like an idiot) and a younger girl who was all perma-tan, hair weave and fake fingernails. Dani had hated all of them if she was honest.

Now she slipped her trainer back on and tried to concentrate on the task before her once again.

She was sitting in the staff room at Starbucks, poring over next week's rotas and some other paperwork sent from head office that she had yet to inspect.

The branch of Starbucks where she worked was inside a huge cinema complex that boasted sixteen screens and, at one time, had been the first of its kind in the country. However, it had been somewhat overtaken in the last few years by even larger and more luxurious cinemas both in the same chain and those of competitors. Dani had worked at a few them in her time, but she'd been settled here.

Settled or stagnating? She was never sure.

She sat back from the paperwork for a moment and glanced around the small staff room. The notice boards. The staff rotas. The Employee of the Month awards (each winner received a voucher for a local fast-food restaurant). Dani sighed. It all looked so bloody *ordinary*. For a moment she sat and wondered what it must be like to do something you loved. To get paid for something you'd do for nothing as a hobby. She'd been painting and sketching ever since she left school, with a view to breaking into design on some level but nothing had ever come of it.

She posted many of her designs on Instagram, perhaps in the hope that some studio or publisher somewhere would see them and descend on her, complete with a contract and tons of money but it hadn't happened so far, and Dani was beginning to wonder if it ever would. She sighed and ran a hand through her long light brown hair, pulling gently at her ponytail.

Seconds later the staff room door opened, and Alex Dawson peered inside. He was nineteen, stocky and the t-shirt he was wearing barely covered his heavily muscled chest. Dani glanced at him briefly, trying not to alert him to the fact that she found him ridiculously attractive for a guy ten years younger than herself. He wasn't what she needed right now. Unless it was maybe just for a month or two of completely meaningless, no strings attached sex. Dani smiled to herself, trying to push away the thoughts, momentarily ashamed with herself for entertaining such ideas.

"What is it, Alex?" she asked, returning her attention to the paperwork before her.

"A customer's got a complaint," he told her, still standing in the doorway.

"Can't you deal with it?"

"They're demanding to speak to the Manager, and you *are* the manager, remember?"

Dani sighed, hesitated a moment longer then got to her feet.

"With great power comes great responsibility," Alex said, smiling and stepping aside as Dani came towards him.

"I'm the manager, not Spiderman," she reminded him and they both laughed.

She was about to leave the room when her phone rang and, more out of habit than anything else, Dani glanced at it to see who the message was from.

As she realized she frowned.

CALL ME. The message said. WE NEED TO TALK.

Dani shook her head.

"No, we don't," she murmured under her breath.

It was only a second or two later that the phone went again, and Dani looked at the next message.

Same caller. Mike.

This time there were five words;

PICK UP YOUR FUCKING PHONE.

Dani swallowed hard and pushed the phone back into her pocket, finally edging past Alex into the corridor outside the staff room.

"Anything important?" Alex asked, seeing the expression on her face.

Dani's shake of the head was anything but convincing.

SIX

Jake Porter glanced at the sign outside Paxton Villas Care Home and shook his head gently. The place looked less like a villa than anything imaginable. He wondered what kind of 'brain-storming' meeting had perpetrated that particular title. Once upon a time it might have made him smile but not today. Jake sat behind the wheel of his car for a moment, gripping the leather as if trying to summon the strength to get out and, finally, he found it.

The early morning sunshine was strong, and Jake shielded his eyes as he walked towards the main entrance of the building. It was new. Red brick, grey roof and the kind of characterless edifice that sprang up regularly. Not that any of the residents would have complained Jake mused. Most of them probably didn't even know where they were, let alone the state of the building they called home.

He walked through the reception area, nodding to the large, cheerful looking woman seated behind her computer near the main door. There was no need to check his Id. She'd seen him enough times to know who he was and why he was here.

Jake headed straight down one of corridors that led off from the main reception area, walking past a large day room where several residents were already seated before the large and very loud TV. Jake continued on his way, finally finding the room he sought.

He paused outside the door then knocked tentatively.

When there was no answer he knocked again, louder this time but, when he still received no response, he opened the door and looked inside.

The room beyond was like an overflowing ashtray. It wasn't dirty but it was badly in need of a clean. Just to tidy up the many dropped tissues scattered around like over-sized confetti.

There was a bed in the room, sticks of furniture, some ornaments and a television propped on one of the chests of drawers. It was on now, blaring out and filling the room with the sound of a cheering, clapping audience. Jake looked at the screen and saw that it was one of the interminable daytime TV shows that polluted the networks.

Some appalling discussion show hosted by a man who looked and behaved even more contemptuously than his guests. Jake stepped inside the room and closed the door behind him.

Seated in a high back chair opposite the television was Margaret Porter. She was in her eighties, white haired, frail and with hearing aids in both ears. Neither of which judging by the volume of the TV Jake mused, seemed to be doing much good.

He glanced around, trying to locate the remote and, when he did, he snatched it up and eased the sound down a few decibels.

"Mum," he said.

Margaret continued gazing blankly at the TV.

"Mum," Jake persisted, raising his voice.

At last, she looked around at him and after a look of complete bewilderment for a second or two something flickered across her wrinkled features and she smiled. Jake crossed the room and hugged her.

"I didn't think you were coming today," she told him as he moved back again.

"I thought I'd just nip in and say hello on my way to the office," he told her. "And I had something to sort out here."

"Is something wrong?"

"You tell me. I had a letter from one of the supervisors saying that you hadn't been taking your tablets."

"Oh, that's rubbish, of course I have."

"You have to mum, you know that."

Margaret broke wind loudly and, despite himself, Jake turned away in disgust.

"Are you busy?" she asked, still gazing at the TV.

"Trying to be," Jake told her.

Margaret belched; her gaze still fixed on the TV screen.

Jake sighed and looked around the room, shaking his head slightly.

"You should try and keep it a bit tidier, mum," he said. "They're not here to clean up after you all the time."

"It *is* tidy."

"No, it isn't."

Margaret lifted herself out of her chair slightly and broke wind again. Once more Jake sighed.

"Stella came to see me the other day," Margaret announced.

"Oh, that's good. What had she got to say?"

"Not much."

Silence descended once more until Margaret broke wind and then spoke again.

"Are you seeing Lucy today?" she wanted to know.

"I only see her once a week, you know that" Jake muttered.

"It's not right. A father should see his daughter more often."

"I know that mum but it's not as easy as that."

"Well, I don't know about that."

"If I could see her more often I would," Jake snapped.

"She should be living with you," Margaret insisted.

"I know that but it's not that easy, there are things to consider."

"Like what?"

"I'm not going to sit here and discuss this now."

"A man should be with his children," Margaret went on, stopping only to raise herself up slightly in her chair and break wind loudly. When she'd done that, she began picking her nose, pushing a finger into a nostril deeply.

Jake got to his feet while Margaret continued her chore, finally deciding she would have more luck using a thumb instead of a finger.

"Do you have to do that?" Jake snapped, disgustedly.

She continued without looking at him.

"I've got to go," he said, briskly. "I need to be at the office."

"Oh, all right, dear," Margaret said, happily.

Jake walked across to the door and opened it slightly, hesitating there before looking back towards the older woman. She was looking raptly at the TV screen once more, reaching for the remote to increase the volume. Jake was about to say something else when she belched twice, tapping her chest lightly.

Jake shook his head wearily and slipped out.

COMPULSION

The storm that had been building all evening finally broke with a ferocity that was almost biblical.

For long moments she stood at the window just watching as massive bolts of lightning ripped across the sky, threatening to tear the clouds apart as they slashed brilliant white barbs across the heavens. Huge banks of black cloud scudded across the firmament bringing more of the driving rain that had been lashing the countryside for the last hour or more.

She didn't want to go out into such inhospitable conditions, but she had no choice.

The drive would take her less than thirty minutes she hoped but, in such hostile conditions she was prepared for it to be longer.

But it had to be done.

She patted her pocket, feeling the car keys in there and then she finally forced herself to walk out, hurrying down the steps towards the ground floor of the flats where she lived. She paused for a moment, gazing out again at the driving rain and storm, finally summoning up the courage to dash to her car.

It was only twenty feet from the front door to her car but, by the time she slid behind the wheel of the vehicle, she was drenched. She wiped her face with both hands then started the engine, allowing it to idle for a moment as she flicked on the wipers. Even on double speed they were barely adequate to wipe away the rain hammering onto the glass, but she jammed the car in gear and guided it away from the front of the building towards the road.

There was very little traffic on the road both because of the lateness of the hour and also because of the horrific conditions. Other drivers, she assumed, had decided it was more prudent to stay out of the storm.

She wished she had that choice.

The headache that had been growing steadily worse all evening was now hammering inside her skull, making it feel as if someone inside was trying to break out. She narrowed her eyes, more sensitive to the bright lights of the odd passing car and also to the vehement savagery of the lightning ripping across the heavens. Each massive discharge was followed by a deafening rumble of thunder, so intense it felt as if it was shaking the car.

She drove on, relieved that the headache was easing slightly. She'd taken a couple of tablets for it and now it finally seemed as if they were beginning to act. She switched her lights to full beam as she came to the outskirts of the town.

The roads were less well-lit now, many of them lined with trees and bushes that seemed to suck in the little natural light there was.

Lightning thrashed the heavens once more and she sucked in a startled breath, shocked by how powerful the celestial display was.

The tears came suddenly. Coursing down her cheeks and dripping onto her t-shirt, little circles of moisture widening on the material as they were soaked up.

She drove on, sniffing and sometimes wiping her eyes with the back of one hand, careful to keep a firm grip on the steering wheel. The roads were becoming increasingly covered by water, the rain hammering down and turning some thoroughfares almost impassable. But she drove on, slowing down when she had to, negotiating each expanse of water as carefully as she could. Sprays of water rose on either side of the car as she drove through deep puddles, the car sometimes threatening to stall in the appalling conditions.

She was clear of the town by now. On both sides of the road trees closed in, making it seem even darker.

The storm seemed to intensify but she drove on.

She had to. She knew what would happen if she didn't.

It would be another fifteen minutes before she reached her destination and as she gripped the steering wheel more tightly, she began to shake gently, knowing what awaited her.

SEVEN

Danielle Grant looked at the food in her lunch box and sighed.

Even though she'd packed it herself she was struck by how unappetising it looked.

She'd fought her way through some Miso soup but now the brown rice and tofu she'd also brought were staring back at her like a challenge. She sighed and put down her fork, glancing across the table at Alex Dawson instead.

Stop it. Stop it. He's nineteen. It's practically child abuse.

Dani smiled and tried once again to concentrate on her lunch. Alex was eating his, chewing his way through a sandwich he'd bought using his staff discount.

"You should make your own lunch," Dani observed. "Save yourself some money."

Alex looked at her mid-chew, wondering what she was on about. His own attention had been on his phone and how many matches he had on Tinder. Now he glanced at Dani instead, wiping the corners of his mouth with his thumb and index finger.

"You make your own, but you hardly ever eat it," he observed, nodding towards Dani's lunch box. "Is it Vegetarian crap?"

"No, Alex, it's vegetarian *food*," Dani told him, shaking her head.

"Don't you miss meat? I couldn't go without it."

"Do you want to try some of this?" she asked, pushing the lunch box towards him.

Alex screwed up his face as if she'd just suggested he put his fingers in a waste disposal unit.

"You might like it," Dani insisted.

"You won't even eat it and you're vegetarian," Alex chuckled.

They were both still laughing when Dani's phone rang. She glanced at it then pushed it to one side.

It continued to ring.

"You'd better answer that," Alex suggested. "It might be important."

"It isn't. I just saw who was calling."

"It might still be important."

"It's not. Trust me."

"Who is it?"

"Mike."

"Your boyfriend?"

"He's not my boyfriend it's just that he doesn't seem to understand that."

"Tell him to stop calling then."

"I have. Loads of times."

"He must want you back. He must love you." Alex grinned.

"Oh, shut up," Dani said, trying to sound authoritative.

"So, are you single right now then?" Alex went on.

"Maybe. Why?"

"Just wondered," Alex murmured, shoving more of his sandwich into his mouth.

"What about you?" Dani enquired. "Are you seeing anyone?"

"Not long term."

"Does *she* know that?"

Alex grinned.

"I don't want to get tied down at my age, do I?" he went on.

"So, you're just fuck buddies, right?"

Alex blushed slightly but his grin widened.

"So, who's that old guy who comes in here and talks to you then?" he wanted to know. "You know the one."

Dani's expression darkened slightly.

"He's just a friend," she exclaimed. "I've known him for a couple of years now."

"He's a bit old. He looks more like your granddad."

"He's not *that* old, don't exaggerate."

"So, who is he?"

"I told you. He's just a friend. Does it matter?"

"All right, don't get all defensive. I was just asking."

"I'm not getting defensive but why do people always think that just because two people talk that there's something going on between them?"

"Because there usually is, and you can see the way he looks at you."

"What do you mean?"

"Oh, come on, he's always looking you up and down. He *wants* you." Alex laughed, pieces of his sandwich spraying out of his mouth like edible shrapnel.

Dani picked up a piece of tofu and threw it at her younger companion.

"You are a such a dingus," she chuckled.

"It's true," Alex went on. "You better not let Mike know about him."

"I told you, Mike isn't my boyfriend. It's nothing to do with him."

Alex laughed again.

Dani looked at him and shook her head.

Her phone rang once more.

EIGHT

Jake Porter looked up from his notes when he heard the knock on the office door.

Sheree Fowler edged into the office almost reluctantly, her hands clasped in front of her as if in supplication.

"You've got no more appointments until three, Doctor Porter," she announced somewhat apologetically. "Is it okay if I pop out for lunch?"

"Of course it is," Jake said, smiling.

"Do you want me to bring you anything back?"

"No thanks, I'm going out myself soon."

Sheree hesitated a moment longer then nodded and backed out of the room as if she were facing royalty. Jake smiled and watched as she closed the door behind her. She'd been his secretary/receptionist for the last three years, ever since he moved to this building with his practice, but she still seemed almost in awe of him. Jake had never felt that members of the psychiatric profession like himself should be afforded such deference but there was something strangely agreeable about it he told himself.

He got to his feet and glanced out of his window, looking down into the car park below, watching Sheree cross it as she headed towards the main street and a rendezvous with her lunch.

He was still watching her when he saw the black Audi pull up and glide into one of the designated parking bays outside the building.

Jake continued standing there, wondering who this new visitor was, frowning slightly when he saw a man in his early thirties clamber out of the car and head towards the main entrance of the building.

He wasn't expecting any patients and Sheree had confirmed that before she left. Jake sat down behind his desk again and continued finishing the notes he'd been working on earlier.

However, his heart wasn't in it and he sat back in his chair eventually, gazing at what he'd done but not too impressed with it. He was still considering this when there was a knock on the office door.

Jake wondered if Sheree had forgotten to tell him something before departing but, when he called to whoever was on the other side of the door to come in, he was confronted by someone quite different.

The man who had climbed out of the black Audi was wearing a charcoal grey suit, the tie slightly undone to accommodate what seemed to be an unusually large Adam's Apple. He was a tall, wiry individual with jet black hair and a growth of stubble that looked as if it would resist the sharpest razor. Jake recognised him but that recognition did nothing to dispel the look of surprise on his face.

"Doctor Porter," said the man, advancing towards him and extending his right hand.

Jake rose and shook the offered hand firmly.

"I'm Detective Inspector Raymond Vincent," the tall man said, reaching for some Id to back up his claim.

"I remember you," Jake confessed. "How's your wife?" He gestured towards the chairs that faced his desk and Vincent sat down, glancing quickly around the office as if to reassure himself that he was indeed in the right place.

"She's much better, thank you. She speaks very highly of you," the policeman said, smiling.

"That's good to hear. She had a lot of problems to work through. I'm glad I could help."

Vincent nodded.

"What can I do for you, DI Vincent?" Jake wanted to know. "I assume you're not here to discuss your wife's case?"

"No. I wish I was in some ways. It might be easier."

Jake eyed the policeman warily for a moment.

"I need your help," Vincent went on.

"If I can, I will. I've acted as court appointed psychiatrist a number of times and..."

"This isn't like any of those cases," Vincent interrupted, his face pale. He lowered his gaze momentarily. The words trailed away, and Vincent pulled at the knot of his tie as if it were suddenly choking him. He shook his head gently.

"What does it involve?" Jake wanted to know.

"Children. Babies." Vincent again shook his head, exhaling heavily. Once more he lowered his gaze. "I sent the files to your e-mail before I left the station. As soon as I realized that it was one of your former patients."

Jake nodded and hurriedly checked his inbox.

Sure enough, there was a file, with several attachments, waiting for him.

He opened it.

"Have you eaten yet?" Vincent asked.

"Why?" Jake wanted to know.

"You might need to prepare yourself before you look at those photos," the DI said, nodding towards the monitor.

Jake nodded slowly then clicked on the first attachment.

"Jesus Christ," he murmured, his stomach somersaulting, his eyes moving slowly over the images before him. "When did this happen?" He opened a second then a third attachment. More pictures. More horrors.

"Earlier this morning," Vincent told him. "I've just come from the scene. We've got the perpetrator. She called us herself when she'd finished. As calm as you like. She used to be a patient of yours, didn't she? That's why I'm here."

Jake nodded gently, scanning the other pictures.

"I'm sorry," Vincent murmured. "But I wanted you to see what we're up against."

Jake nodded; his gaze still fixed on the pictures before him. "I need to speak to the...the subject as soon as possible," he said, softly.

"There's no hurry. She's in custody. She's not going anywhere."

Jake sat back from his monitor, minimising the images, removing them from view.

"Has she said much since you arrested her?" he wanted to know.

"Nothing useful. She just keeps saying that she had to do it."

Jake nodded.

"Any theories of your own?" he asked.

"On why someone would kill fourteen new-born babies? Not a clue."

NURTURE

She hadn't seen a house for a good five minutes.

Once she left the outskirts of the town, buildings were few and far between and most of them appeared nothing more than black shadows in the storm lashed night.

Some had lights burning in their windows and they looked welcoming because of that. But once the last of these dwellings had faded into the gloom it seemed as though the only light now was provided by her headlights and the ever-present lightning.

The road narrowed abruptly as she drove through a shallow valley, the land rising on either side of her. Thickly wooded hills added to the gloom and seemed to be closing in around her. She slowed down slightly, aware too of the increasing amounts of water laying on the road. She didn't want to hit some of that and end up aqua-planing. The last thing she needed was to be stranded out here in a storm like this.

And what would happen if she didn't arrive at her destination she didn't dare think of.

She thought about switching on the radio, just for company as much as anything else but then she decided against it, realizing that she needed all her wits about her to concentrate on driving in such conditions. The rain, the lightning and the almost impenetrable blackness seemed to be conspiring against her.

Even with the lights on full beam and the windscreen wipers on double speed it was virtually impossible to see more than five or six yards ahead. The road was awash now, the flashes of lightning that were still cutting through the black clouds periodically reflected in the huge puddles that had formed on the tarmac.

Every rumble of thunder sounded like a twenty-one-gun salute and the car itself seemed to be vibrating such was the intensity of the celestial explosions.

She pulled over into what passed as a lay-by about a hundred yards from the place she sought, peering up at the boiling sky apprehensively.

It would pass. It had to. Even if it only eased up enough to allow her to continue driving another few hundred yards.

So near.

There was a high stone wall marking the boundary of the property, clumps of trees gathered next to this formidable barrier as if for shelter against the elements.

She could hear the wind rattling the branches every now and then.

She sat behind the wheel for a moment longer, peering out into the blackness, her heart beating a little faster.

The rain continued to lash down but then she was sure there was a slight respite. It was enough. She guided the car back out onto the road, surprised when a vehicle passed her going the other way.

She wondered what was forcing the driver of that other car to be out in such appalling conditions.

The dashboard clock showed 12.46.

She rubbed gently at her neck with one hand, the headache that had mercifully receded during the journey now threatening to return.

She winced when a particularly vehement flash of lightning ripped across the sky, shielding her eyes from the cold white explosion.

The huge wrought iron gates that would normally have barred the way into the grounds were open wide enough to allow her easy passage. She was grateful she didn't have to step out of the car into the storm to open them any wider. The passenger side of the car scraped against the metal as she passed but she didn't care. All that mattered now was reaching the building that lay about five hundred yards along the curving driveway.

As she pulled up outside it, a huge series of lightning flashes illuminated it briefly, bathing it in bluish-white light for a second. Revealing it in its full decaying majesty before plunging it into impenetrable blackness once again. It was as if the entire monolithic structure had fleetingly appeared from nowhere, only to shrink back into the darkness seconds later.

She sat behind the wheel for a moment longer then pushed open the door and ran for the main entrance as fast as she could.

As she reached it, she wiped her face with one hand, pausing with her back against the thick wooden door, looking back across the grounds as they were lit up by more lightning.

The grass that had once been carefully manicured lawns was overgrown and weed filled, the topiary shapes that had decorated them now nothing more than amorphous blobs on the landscape. It had been a long time since anyone had lavished any attention upon them. A little like the building itself. It was a monument to neglect.

She turned and pushed gently on the door, not surprised when it opened slightly. As thunder rocked the heavens yet again, she slipped inside.

NINE

The heat that had been so oppressive during the day had dissipated a little with the coming of night, but it was still uncomfortably warm in the bedroom.

Jake Porter could feel the perspiration on his back and forehead as he rolled back to his side of the bed, his breath coming in deep gasps.

Beside him, Danielle Grant lay motionless for a moment, recovering her breath too, laying splay legged on the sodden sheets.

Her hair was plastered to her face and neck and she ran a hand through it to free from her hot flesh where it was stuck as surely as if it had been glued there.

She waited a moment then rolled onto her side, looking down at Jake.

"Not bad for an old man," she purred.

"Cheeky bitch," he breathed, slapping her bare bottom playfully.

They both lay still for a moment, regaining their breath.

"When is this heat going to stop?" Jake murmured.

"We need air conditioning in here," Dani said.

"You want air conditioning? Open the window wider."

They both laughed.

"You should take it easy at your age," Dani said, grinning impishly.

"Oh, shut up about my bloody age," Jake told her. "I'm as fit as a guy half my age."

"If you say so."

"I do. Anyway, age is just a number."

"And in your case that number is fifty-six."

Dani sat up, reaching for something on the bedside table. She lit up a cigarette and blew out a stream of smoke.

"You should give up," Jake offered, watching a single rivulet of sweat running down her back from her shoulder to her buttocks.

"Are you going to lecture me about that as well?" Dani grunted, not turning around.

"It's your life," he reminded her.

"That's right."

"They stunt your growth. If you didn't smoke, you'd be twenty-six feet tall now."

Dani looked briefly at him, shook her head, and then continued puffing away at the cigarette.

"Mike rang me today," she announced. "Eight times."

"I thought he'd got the message."

"So, did I. It looks as if I was wrong."

"What did he want?"

"How do I know? I didn't speak to him."

"Did he know about...about us?"

"God no. It was over between us long before you and I..."

"Then why is he still contacting you?"

"He obviously thinks there's a chance we could get back together."

"And *is* there?"

Dani turned and looked disdainfully at Jake then she took another drag on her cigarette and blew the smoke in his direction.

"Are you jealous then?" she wanted to know.

"Do I have reason to be?"

Dani shook her head.

"We've still got the dog between us, haven't we?" she murmured. "He still likes to see him."

"Let him have the bloody dog," Jake muttered. "If it gets him out of your life for good it'll be worth it."

"I'm not giving him Reuben. I love my dog. How can you say that?"

"Every time you let him come and see the dog you let him back into your life. I've heard of shared custody for kids but not shared custody for dogs."

"We bought him when we were together. What do you want me to do? Just get rid of him?"

"As long as you've got the dog, you'll have Mike pestering you."

"Don't lecture me about that as well, Jake. I get enough of that from my parents."

"They're only trying to help. Just like I am."

"If I didn't have to live with them, I'd be all right."

"So, move out."

"On my crap wage?" She took another drag on her cigarette. "Not much of a life is it? Nearly thirty years old, rubbish job, no prospects of a better one and still living with my parents."

"You could try and do something with your artwork."

"Yeah, right. I've got more chance of winning the lottery."

Dani swung herself out of bed and began retrieving her clothes from the floor, pulling on her knickers and bra as Jake watched. She finished her cigarette and tossed the butt out of the open window, standing there for a moment waiting for a cooling breeze that never came.

"You're not going home, are you?" Jake asked. "I thought you were going to stay the night."

"I can't," she told him. "I've got work in the morning and I need to take Reuben for a walk."

"Your mum or dad will do that."

"Something else I have to rely on them for. Great."

Dani pulled on her jeans and then slipped on her top.

Jake got out of bed and walked across to her, touching one cheek with his fingers.

"Stay," he murmured. "Please."

"I can't."

"You could if you wanted to. You could move in with me if you wanted to."

Dani looked at him questioningly.

"Why don't you?" Jake went on.

"I can't. You know that."

She turned and walked towards the door.

"I'm not going to discuss it now," she told him.

Jake snatched up his trousers and pulled them on, following her out onto the landing and then down the stairs.

"Dani," he called. "We need to talk."

"They all say that," Dani said, smiling back at him as she pulled open the front door.

"Dani," he called again.

And then she was gone.

***

Dani sat behind the wheel of her car, enjoying the slight cool breeze that had sprung up.

She lowered both front windows and prepared to start the engine. Just as she reached for the ignition key the phone rang. Dani sighed, looking at the caller Id for a moment. Mike again.

How many more times?

She stared at the phone, waiting for the electronic buzzing to stop.

When it did, she reached again for the ignition keys only to be interrupted once more by the phone. Dani murmured something under breath and, almost against her better judgement, she answered.

"For Christ's sake, Mike stop ringing me, will you?" she blurted into the phone.

"I just wanted to see if you were okay," said the voice at the other end of the line. "If you won't answer my calls or my texts how am I supposed to know."

"What does it matter to you how I am?"

"Of course it matters."

"Well, I haven't got time to talk now. It's late."

"You've *never* got time to talk." There was an edge to Mike Quinn's voice that Dani wasn't slow to pick up.

"If you only rang up to argue I'm hanging up now," she snapped.

"No, please don't," Mike said, a sudden note of pleading in his voice.

"What do you want?" Dani demanded.

"I just want to talk," he told her. "Face to face. Can I buy you a coffee or something?"

"That's not difficult, I work in a Starbucks."

Mike laughed and even Dani afforded herself a smile.

"Can I come in and see you?" he went on. "Just for half an hour. Just for a little chat?"

"There's nothing else to say, Mike."

"Please."

There was a long silence and then finally Dani spoke again.

"All right," she said, wearily. "Tomorrow. Just for half an hour. My break's at half past one."

"I'll be there," Mike told her.

"I don't doubt that. I'm going now, okay?"

"Okay. Sleep tight."

Dani shook her head and terminated the call. She sat motionless behind the wheel for a moment then started the engine, guiding the car out into the street.

As she pulled away, she never thought to look back towards Jake's house. If she had she'd have seen him looking down from the bedroom window.

Watching.

TEN

Jake Porter wandered into his spare room allowing the light from the landing to spill into the gloom. He moved across to the desk he'd set up in one corner and sat down in front of the laptop there.

He'd set up the spare room as a kind of 'home office' about four years ago and he found that it was more conducive to work when it was separated from the rest of his life. This way he could shut it all away when he was finished. Jake had always believed that there should be very definite boundaries between work and life, and he found it useful to be able to shut the more practical side of his life out sometimes.

Since he'd set up the office, he'd also managed to complete two books (both about aspects of psychiatry) one of which had been published to a small measure of success within his field. The next one was due for publication at the end of the year and Jake had to confess that he was excited about the prospect. The second book was more accessible to a wider audience (so his agent had said) and there was even talk of a promotional tour and interviews. Jake smiled to himself as he sat down behind his desk. He quite liked the idea of becoming a celebrity.

He opened the laptop, glancing at his screen saver for a moment (a picture of Dani) then he went straight to his e-mails.

For what seemed like an eternity Jake sat looking at the pictures DI Vincent had sent him. Still stunned by their savagery, sickened by the pure ferocity of the attacks. There was a report attached and Jake read and re-read the words in it. Finally, he closed the laptop and just sat there in the darkness, knowing he should go to bed but half afraid to sleep.

The nightmares he'd been suffering from lately had taken their toll. He hadn't had a decent night's sleep for a few weeks now and that, combined with the heat, had conspired against him. There were other things on his mind too of course. His mother. His daughter. And Dani.

Always Dani.

He opened the laptop again and looked once more at the screen saver then he clicked on a file marked "Saved Photos."

Mostly culled from her Social Media accounts, there were dozens of pictures of Dani. Hundreds possibly. As Jake scrolled through them slowly, he occasionally focussed on one, enlarging it, adjusting the focus and clarity.

Some of her alone. Others with friends. Some of them were more than ten years old. He'd never told her he'd collected them. He'd never felt the need. She would only laugh at him, give him that disapproving look. He smiled and continued scrolling through the pictures, wishing she'd stayed with him tonight. He finally closed the file and just sat there gazing at the screen and carefully stored items.

There was another labelled "New Folder (2)"

For long seconds Jake let the cursor hover over that file, wondering if he should open it or not. Finally, he decided against it, slamming the laptop shut.

Not now.

He sat at his desk, his breath now coming in short gasps but finally he got to his feet and wandered out of the room once again, locking the door behind him.

Jake made his way across the landing towards his bedroom where he lay down, waving a hand before his face briefly in a vain attempt to counteract the heat. It was, of course, useless. He lay there for another ten minutes then swung himself out of bed again and stalked through to the en-suite bathroom where he turned on the shower, finding a cooling temperature for the spray of water. He finally stepped beneath it, luxuriating in the refreshing streams of water.

When he finally clambered back into bed, he felt pleasingly drowsy and sleep, he was delighted to find, came easily.

ELEVEN

When Dani walked into the sitting room of the house that had been her home for nearly thirty years she was greeted by a withering stare from her mother.

Catherine Grant was a formidable looking woman in her early sixties and the thick glasses perched on her nose made it look as if she was squinting. As Dani entered the room the older woman reached for the TV remote and lowered the volume, re-adjusting her position on the sofa.

"I didn't think you'd still be up," Dani said a little sheepishly.

"I'm not surprised at this time," Catherine grunted, jabbing a finger towards the clock on the mantlepiece. "It's late."

"Mum, I'm nearly thirty, not fifteen," Dani reminded her.

"Where have you been?"

"That's not really your business is it?" Dani said, sitting down in one of the chairs and pulling her shoes off.

"As long as you're living here it's my business," Catherine reminded her.

"I was with a friend," Dani conceded.

"Which one?"

"Jesus, does it matter?"

"A man?"

"Mum..."

"I'm just curious. I like to know what you're doing."

"You're nosey, you mean."

They sat in silence for a moment and then Catherine cleared her throat and announced, "Mike called round earlier."

"Mike? What did *he* want?"

"He wanted to see you."

Dani sighed and shook her head.

"I only spoke to him about half an hour ago," she murmured.

"Nice lad, Mike," Margaret went on. "I like him."

"Then *you* go out with him," Dani murmured.

"He left something for you. It's in your room. Go and look."

Dani looked at her mother then stretched.

"Don't you want to know what it was?" Catherine enquired.

"I'll look when I go up, right?"

Catherine shook her head.

"Where's Reuben?" Dani asked.

"Your dad took him for a walk. He's out in the garden."

"He should be in here. He gets lonely out in the garden."

"Dani, he's a dog for God's sake. You spoil him."

"I like spoiling him. How far did dad take him?"

"I don't know but your dad was worn out when he got back. He's in bed now."

"I don't blame him," Dani announced, getting to her feet. "I'm going to bed too. Goodnight."

Catherine watched her as she walked out of the room and Dani made her way quickly up the stairs to her room, slapping on the light as she entered.

The flowers were lying on the bed.

A small bouquet of red roses encased in clear cellophane.

Dani smiled almost in spite of herself. She walked across to the bed and looked down at the flowers, noticing that there was a small envelope attached to the stems. She picked it up and opened it, shaking her head as she looked at the little card inside. There was writing on it.

I HOPE THEY BRIGHTEN UP YOUR ROOM LIKE YOU BRIGHTEN UP

MY LIFE.

Dani's smile broadened. So cheesy, she thought and yet she couldn't prevent herself from grinning.

She read the card again, glancing at Mike's signature at the bottom of it then she took the flowers and began unwrapping them, freeing them from the grasp of the cellophane.

As she did, her phone began to ring.

TWELVE

Sound carried inside the high-ceilinged corridors of the building and he could hear footsteps approaching long before he saw the man enter the room.

The man was in his thirties. Short, powerfully built but, even in the darkness, his skin looked pale, almost luminescent. His eyes were bulging wide too, as if he had just seen something that he didn't want to witness. Now, he staggered drunkenly into the room, hands outstretched as if to stop himself from falling. He slapped one against a wall, using it to support himself as he walked.

Jake Porter watched the man but did not move. From his position in the room he had a clear view of the figure as he moved cautiously through the darkness. The man stopped for a moment and looked as if he was trying to get his breath. He looked as if he'd just been through some supremely tough physical task. Sweat was beading on his forehead and cheeks.

Jake saw him stumble towards one corner of the room, towards a small figure that was hunkered there.

It was too small to be a child wasn't it?

Little larger than a baby and yet it was standing on bowed legs looking up at the newcomer.

Outside the moon managed to fight its way out from behind the thick banks of cloud and, as it did, silvery white light suddenly flooded the room, illuminating the tableau within.

Jake had a clear view of the small figure in the corner now.

The skin looked shrivelled, as if it had been left in water for too long. The head was bulbous and swollen. But it was the eyes that were the most striking feature of the small form. They were huge, seemingly covering half of the face. Great black and glistening pools that reflected the light. They fixed the man in an unblinking stare and he met that gaze and continued to look down at the small figure.

When it opened its mouth the sound that came forth was muffled, choked by thick phlegm that seemed to have collected in the throat of the tiny form. Dark fluid spilled over its fluttering lips and the man took a couple of steps backwards as if disgusted by this.

The tiny figure also moved back slightly, moving with difficultly on the dusty floor.

It suddenly dropped to all fours, hauling itself along, wanting to be away from this man. Wanting to sink back into the shadows where it felt more comfortable.

The man watched it for a second then followed, reaching inside his jacket for something that Jake couldn't see clearly until the moonlight hit it.

The white light glinted off the long blade and the man held it above his head, finding the best angle, gripping it so hard that his knuckles turned white.

He ducked low over the tiny scrabbling form reaching out with his free hand to grab one of its stunted legs, trying to prevent it crawling any further away from him.

As it turned to look at him again the man wavered, staggering slightly, and gritting his teeth as if he'd just been struck by something invisible. He released his grip on the tiny figure and swayed uncertainly for a second.

Jake could see something dark burst from his nostrils and realized immediately that it was blood.

Droplets fell to the ground, sinking into the dust.

The man staggered again and more of the crimson fluid began to trickle from his ears, welling up there and then overflowing.

He closed his eyes tightly for a second then lunged towards the tiny shape before him once more. This time he used the knife, driving it down towards the soft, almost purulent body, ramming the point deep into the face of the figure.

When he tore it free the tiny creature let out a sound that seemed impossibly loud for one so small. The roar of pain and shock reverberated inside the room with such incredible volume that the windows themselves shook.

Jake gritted his teeth against the sound, watching mesmerised as the man struck again, this time burying the knife in the chest of the little form, tearing it downwards and opening a huge rent in the body. Intestines spilled from the gaping gash, coated with thick almost black blood, they pulsed gently as the man used his free hand to pull them from the open cavity. He struck again and again, each blow opening a fresh wound, causing more rancid fluid to flow from the tiny body.

Even after it stopped twitching the man continued to drive the knife into it, only stopping when he was too exhausted to continue.

As he straightened up, Jake could see that his face was coated with blood but also stained with tears. The man was sobbing quietly as he backed away from the pulverized body, the knife still fixed in his hand as if it were a part of him.

He turned towards Jake; his eyes blank. He looked as if he was in a trance, moving purely instinctively.

And now, from outside the room, Jake heard more footsteps approaching. Dozens of them it seemed. Growing louder.

The man too was aware of the sound and this seemed to spur him to greater action. He advanced towards Jake with the knife held before him, his teeth gritted. His lips were moving but Jake couldn't hear what he was saying. All he seemed to be able to focus on was the man's eyes.

Blood was now running freely from the corners of them both. Coursing down his cheeks and dripping into the dust below.

Jake tried to move but he couldn't, and the man just kept coming, waving the knife around wildly now. The blade descended towards him and Jake knew he could not avoid it.

He began to scream.

THIRTEEN

"It tastes revolting but it's better than nothing."

DI Ray Vincent put the plastic beaker of coffee on to the desk before Jake Porter then sat down, nursing his own drink.

Jake smiled and sipped at the brown fluid, nodding.

"You're right," he smiled. He swallowed another mouthful then sat back in his chair, blinking myopically, gently rubbing his forehead with four fingers.

"Are you okay?" Vincent wanted to know. "You look a bit...under the weather."

"I haven't been sleeping lately."

"The weather?"

"Nightmares. They seem to be getting worse."

"You should see a psychiatrist."

Jake smiled.

"I appreciate you coming, Doctor," said Vincent.

"I hadn't got any more appointments today, it seemed sensible," Jake told him. He let out a long breath. "And I'll learn more from talking to her face to face than I will from any amount of files and photographs."

"When you were treating her was there nothing that might have indicated this kind of behaviour?" the policeman wanted to know.

"Nothing."

Vincent nodded and got to his feet again. Jake followed him out into the corridor beyond and down that same walkway towards a single door. Above it was the legend;

INTERVIEW ROOM 1

"Do you want me to come in with you?" Vincent asked.

Jake merely shook his head, gazing straight ahead, waiting as the DI opened the door and ushered him in.

Lauren Davison was sitting at the small wooden table in the interview room, looking at the wall opposite her. Even when Jake entered, she didn't look up but merely kept her eyes fixed on the wall as if she were studying every detail of the whitewashed surface. Jake sat down across from her and laid out his notes on the tabletop.

Lauren didn't turn her attention from the far wall.

"Hello, Lauren," Jake began. "My name is Jake Porter. I'm a psychiatrist. I don't know if you remember me?"

Only now did she look at him but there was no emotion in her grey eyes.

"I just wanted to talk to you," Jake went on.

"About what?" Lauren wanted to know.

"Different things," Jake said, smiling. He scribbled a couple of things on a piece of paper in front of him and then looked more intently at Lauren.

"About the children?" she asked, clasping her hands together on the table in front of her.

"If that's what you want to talk about."

"I had to do it."

"Why?"

"I *had* to."

She looked at him imploringly. Wondering why he didn't understand. She reached out one hand and gently touched Jake's arm.

He hissed through his teeth and dragged his arm away as if he'd just been jabbed with a cattle prod.

What the fuck was happening?

He grabbed for the part of his arm that Lauren had touched, kneading it with the fingers of his other hand, feeling the numbness there beneath his probing digits. A feeling of intense heat seemed to fill his body, radiating from that single place where Lauren had touched him until it seemed to fill his veins. He felt suddenly faint and beads of sweat popped onto his forehead and top lip. Jake sucked in a deep breath, trying to steady his breathing and his heartbeat which also seemed to have increased alarmingly.

He glared at Lauren wondering what she had done to him, his head still spinning.

When he looked at her again, she was smiling.

Wasn't she?

"It isn't the first time you've killed a child is it?" he said, his voice cracking.

If she had been smiling it faded rapidly to be replaced by a look of concern.

"Is it?" he persisted, sitting forward, jabbing an accusatory finger at her. "How old were you when you had the abortion? Seventeen?"

Lauren shook her head gently.

"How did you know?" she asked.

Jake glared at her but didn't answer.

Lauren moved back slightly, the legs of the chairs scraping noisily on the floor of the interview room. Her face was pale and against that milky whiteness, the trickles of blood that ran slowly from her nostrils now looked even more vivid. She murmured something under her breath, looking at Jake.

He was still gazing fixedly at her when she passed out.

FOURTEEN

The shopping centre was huge. Jake wasn't sure how many acres it covered but it was a lot. When it had first opened it had been revolutionary. Ground-breaking in its concept but now most major cities in the country boasted the same kind of soul less, generic shopping mall. With every store and shop jammed together under one roof, shopping centres might not be aesthetically pleasing but, as Jake told himself now, people came shopping for goods, not artistic enlightenment.

He smiled to himself, amused by his own sudden attack of pretentiousness then he glanced at his watch once more. She was late.

A quick look at the sea of faces passing him was equally unrewarding. Jake was seated on one of the benches in the shopping centre, stationed outside a shop that boasted *"Olde Worlde Confection."* Or, in other words, lots of sweets no one had seen since their childhood, sold from jars instead of packets. There was a kind of pleasing packaged nostalgia to it and Jake himself had popped into the shop to purchase some Aniseed twists before seating himself where he was now.

Waiting.

He wasn't the most patient man in the world and punctuality was important to him. If someone said they were going to be at a certain place at a certain time, then Jake thought it wasn't asking too much to expect that. He tried to balance that against the fact that the person he was waiting for was young. A teenager. And time seemed to be less important to them.

When he looked up again, he was relieved to see her, and he got to his feet and began walking towards the slight young girl with the shoulder length blonde hair who was traipsing along with her phone pressed tightly to her right ear.

Jake smiled broadly at his daughter, but the gesture wasn't returned.

When he was four or five feet away from her, he could hear her speaking.

"I know, I know," she said. Then her tone darkened slightly. "Look,

I've got to go. I've got to meet my dad. I'll call you later."

She terminated the call as Jake moved closer, opening his arms to embrace her.

Lucy Porter just about responded, allowing her father to put his arms around her but doing very little to mirror the action.

"Hello, gorgeous," Jake beamed. "Are you okay?"

"Not bad," Lucy told him, barely smiling.

"I thought we could get something to eat," Jake offered, gesturing to the Sushi restaurant just behind them.

"I can't stay long," Lucy told him. "I've got to meet Sam."

"Couldn't you meet her another day?"

"It's important."

"So is *this*."

"Yeah, to *you*."

Jake wasn't slow to catch the edge in her voice and his smile slipped a little.

"If you couldn't make it you could have let me know," he said.

"I'm here aren't I?" Lucy snapped. "I just said I can't stay too long."

Jake nodded and they both walked towards the main entrance of the eatery, choosing a table close to the window. It wasn't very crowded, and the waiter ambled over to take their order, smiling a practised smile. When he left Lucy sat back in her seat and gazed past her father towards the people milling about outside the restaurant.

"We could have gone somewhere else if you liked," Jake offered.

"Like where? It's either here or sit in your car for two hours."

An uneasy silence descended finally broken by Jake.

"How's your mum?" he asked.

"She's alright."

"How's work?"

"I hate it."

"You should have stayed on at school."

"Why? I hated that too."

"I know but with a better education you could have got a better job and..."

Lucy cut across him. "It's a bit late for that now isn't it? Anyway, I'm going to hand my notice in. I hate that fucking place and I hate the fucking people I work with."

"Language," Jake murmured reproachfully. He could see the two women at the next table glancing their way when Lucy swore.

"Oh what? I'm eighteen, not eight," Lucy snorted. "And *you* swear."

"I'm your dad."

Lucy raised her eyebrows then began prodding the food that the waiter had returned with. Jake looked at her for a moment then set about his own food. "You need to get yourself sorted as soon as possible, find something you really want to do," he went on. "I worry about you."

"Why?"

"Because I'm your dad."

"If you'd been that worried you wouldn't have walked out on me and mum."

The words hit him hard and Jake sucked in a deep breath.

"Lucy, I'm not going to go over that now," he told her, quietly.

"Why not? Why can't we talk about it?"

"This isn't the time."

"There's *never* been a time," she snapped.

The two women at the next table both glanced across once more and Jake tried to control his embarrassment.

"If you want to know what happened ask your mum," he said, quietly. "She's the one who asked for a divorce. Not me."

"Because *you* were cheating on her."

Lucy reached for her phone and began scrolling through it. She finally found what she was looking for and presented it to Jake as if it was some kind of accusation. He looked at the device and saw a picture. It showed himself and Dani. He reached for the phone to take a closer look, but Lucy pulled it away again.

"Who is she?" Lucy wanted to know.

"Where did you get that picture?" Jake enquired.

"Instagram. She follows me. I checked out her account and found that."

"She's a patient of mine."

"Yeah, right," Lucy said, dismissively.

"She was to begin with. She had a few problems."

"What? She was a patient to start with and now you're fucking her?"

Jake shot his daughter an angry glance.

"How old is she?" Lucy persisted.

"Twenty-nine."

"Jesus, she's only ten years older than me then."

"It's not what you think."

"Like it wasn't anything with the last one? She was even younger, wasn't she? God, you're pathetic."

Jake wanted to say something but restrained himself.

"Why did you finish with the other one?" Lucy went on. "Did the NSPCC come and collect her or something?"

"She moved away."

"So how long have you been seeing this one?"

"A few months. You'd like her."

"Oh, don't say that," Lucy sneered. "I don't have to like her. I'm never going to meet her, am I?"

"You could if you wanted to."

"No thanks. I don't want to meet some sket who thinks she's going to be my stepmother."

"That's enough," snarled Jake.

Lucy got to her feet.

"Sit down," Jake urged.

"No," she told him, defiantly. "I've got to go. I've got to meet Sam."

"Can't it wait?"

"No, it can't. You see the difference is, I actually *want* to be with her."

She turned and hurried out, watched by Jake and at least half a dozen of the other people inside the restaurant.

Jake glanced down blankly at his plate, unwilling or unable to look anywhere else.

FIFTEEN

As Danielle Grant and Mike Quinn walked slowly through the park, they both glanced around them at the other people who had come to the vast green expanse on such a warm day.

Mostly children, some of whom were kicking a small plastic ball around while others played on the swings and slide nearby. Two or three old people out for their constitutionals, Dani mused to herself. A woman walking her dog.

The park was just across the road from the large complex where Dani worked, and she was happy to be free of it for an hour at least. Mike had arrived about ten minutes earlier and she had suggested they take a walk. Perhaps, she reasoned, the air would clear her head.

There was a small man-made lake (although the term large pond might have been more accurate) at the centre of the park and it was towards that they now headed. Other children were gathered around the water here, some of them throwing bread to the ducks that sailed effortlessly across the shimmering surface.

One of the children waved happily in Dani's direction and she smiled.

"He must be a fan," Mike said. "I don't blame him."

Dani sighed.

"What did you want to talk about, Mike?" she said finally.

"Us," he said, flatly.

"We've already talked."

"You told me what you were thinking, that's not quite the same thing. What if I don't agree?" He aimed a kick at a nearby can that had fallen from a waste bin. "I miss you; you know."

"Even my mood swings?" Dani said, smiling.

"Even those," Mike assured her.

Just ahead of them there was another small playground which, for some reason, was not filled with small children. They walked towards the swings and Dani sat down, rocking back and forth gently on one of them. Mike chose the one next to her and he too sat down.

"Couldn't we try again?" Mike asked.

"It's not as easy as that."

"Why? It's not like I hit you or anything like that. We didn't argue. Not much anyway."

They both laughed.

"A fresh start would be good for both of us," Mike persisted. "I just want another chance. With you. With *life*."

"Very philosophical."

"Whatever I've done wrong, I want to put it right." Mike assured her.

Dani continued to swing gently back and forth.

"It's complicated," she said, allowing the words to trail off.

"There's another guy isn't there?"

"Sort of."

"Are you in love with him?"

Dani looked disdainfully at him and shook her head.

"Were you in love with *me*?" Mike wanted to know.

Dani didn't answer but merely kept swaying gently back and forth, gripping the metal chains of the swing. Despite the heat of the day, they felt cold.

"What do you say?" Mike asked. "One more chance."

SIXTEEN

Jake Porter glanced around his mother's room and shook his head almost imperceptibly.

She was gazing fixedly at the TV screen, apparently unworried by the fact that the volume was making it possible to hear what was happening throughout most of the building. Tiring of the thunderous sound, Jake leaned forward and reached for the remote, easing the noise down to more manageable levels.

Margaret looked at him and then back at the TV.

"What are you doing?" she wanted to know.

"Turning it down," Jake told her. "It's deafening."

"I've got to be able to hear it."

"You'll have people complaining about the noise. If your hearing aid isn't working, tell them about it."

"It's working."

"No, it isn't."

Margaret broke wind loudly and Jake sighed, disgusted by her actions.

"How's Lucy?" the older woman wanted to know.

"I told you, she's fine."

"I wish she'd come and see me. I might not be around for much longer."

"Oh, don't start that again, mum. You're not going anywhere."

Margaret belched and continued gazing at the TV. Jake got to his feet and crossed to the window, looking out.

"What's it like out there?" Margaret wanted to know.

"The same as it was when I told you five minutes ago," Jake said, wearily.

"I didn't hear you."

"You didn't hear me because your bloody hearing aid isn't working."

"You should speak up. You speak too softly. You always have."

Jake shook his head.

"How's Lucy?" Margaret went on.

"I just told you," Jake snapped.

"I forgot. I forget things."

"I noticed," Jake sighed.

He turned and walked back to his seat, settling himself just as Margaret again broke wind. Jake pointed at the TV screen.

"Isn't that the guy from that soap opera?" he mused.

"I don't know," Margaret said.

"You've been watching it for the last ten minutes. His name's on the screen. Look!"

"I can't see that" Margaret murmured then she belched loudly.

Jake sucked in an angry breath and got to his feet.

"Where are you going?" Margaret wanted to know.

"I just want to have a word with someone about something," he said, heading for the door. "I'll be back soon."

"Where are you going?" Margaret went on.

"I'll be back in a minute," Jake snapped, barely able to control his irritation. He pulled open the door of the room and stepped out into the corridor beyond, taking another deep breath then he set off through the building, his jaw set in hard lines, his heart beating a little faster.

He found the office easily enough and hesitated a moment before knocking. The voice from inside told him to come in and Jake stepped into a small, cramped room dominated by a desk piled high with files and books. The walls were covered with various notifications, some in different colours to make them more striking. The woman seated behind the desk was in her forties but looked older. She smiled efficiently at Jake.

"Can I help you?" she asked.

"I'd like to talk to you about Margaret Porter," he said. "I'm her son."

"Sit down," the woman said, motioning to the chair opposite her desk.

Jake picked up some of the paperwork on the chair, slid it onto the desk and then sat down.

He glanced at the name plaque on the woman's desk. It read; PAULA WEST. SENIOR ADMINISTRATOR.

"How can I help you, Mr Porter?" she asked.

"I'd like you to keep a closer eye on my mother, please," Jake said.

"Your mother is cared for the same way all our residents are, Mr Porter. What exactly is your concern?"

"I think she's losing it."

Paula raised her eyebrows.

"I thought a man in your profession would have chosen his words more carefully, Mr Porter," she said, disdainfully.

"You know what I mean," Jake snapped. "I tell her something and five minutes later she's forgotten it. My dad was the same before he died. I think it might be an idea to do some tests on her, just to confirm whether or not she has Alzheimer's."

"There are certain steps that can be taken, you know that."

"I don't know if she can't hear properly can't see properly or if she can see and hear but things just aren't registering."

"She does have problems with cataracts."

"I'm aware of that. And she can't walk properly. Yes, I know all that. That's why she's here. She was housebound for nearly a year before she came here." He exhaled deeply.

"I don't know what else you expect us to do, Mr Porter."

"Just your job. Nothing more. I realize I don't pay enough to merit better care for her."

"If you're unhappy with the quality of care your mother is getting, you're free to put her somewhere else. I appreciate that."

Jake shook his head.

"But to be honest, Mr Porter," Paula West continued. "You won't find better care for your mother anywhere around here. Not considering her condition."

"What's that supposed to mean?" Jake snapped.

"The deficiencies in her vision, her hearing and her mobility are related to her age, not necessarily to any condition she might have."

"You mean she's old."

Paula raised her eyebrows.

"It happens to us all one day, Mr Porter," she said, softly.

Jake nodded.

"Tell me about it," he murmured.

SEVENTEEN

Bloody kids.

That was all Dani Grant could think as she stood gazing out over the huge foyer area of the cinema that enveloped the Starbucks where she worked. She watched four small children running frenziedly back and forth on the far side of the open area, gazing on as one of them crashed into one of the standees that dotted the foyer. It was a life size model of Tom Cruise and it toppled effortlessly as the child crashed into it.

Dani watched as two of the other children looked on aghast and two women, who she assumed were their mothers, rushed over to inspect the carnage. Uniformed members of staff were also converging on the area, one of them holding a mop on the assumption that someone, somewhere, must have spilled something.

Dani looked at the little tableau for a moment later then finished collecting up dirty mugs, wiped the table down and retreated behind the counter.

It had been a busy morning (the first day of the school holidays when there was always a huge influx of people) but now it was beginning to slacken off a bit she was delighted to say.

As she headed for the staff room, she saw a couple of the staff busily mopping up some spilled coffee. Alex stood back slightly watching them, smiling at their predicament. Dani thought about saying something but then she decided to leave them to it. She had stuff to do and she wanted the relative peace and quiet of the staff room to do it. When she walked in, she was relieved to find that it was empty. She sat down at a table in the corner and checked her phone for messages.

A couple from Jake.

Two from friends.

Two from Mike.

Dani read them all briefly and then sat still for a moment, collecting her thoughts for a moment before she turned her attention to the paperwork, she'd abandoned about an hour ago. She knew it had to be done but she had already put it off as long as was humanly possible.

Finish it and it's out of the way, she told herself and she sighed and cast her eyes over the rotas for the following week.

She had barely begun when Alex walked in.

"Are you busy?" he said, grinning.

"Take a wild guess," Dani grunted, motioning towards the paperwork in front of her.

"Have you got a minute?" Alex wanted to know.

"I just said..."

"There's a delivery for you. The guy said you had to sign for it."

"A delivery? For me?"

Dani looked puzzled.

Alex hesitated in the doorway.

"What is it?" Dani wanted to know.

"I don't know," Alex told her. "Come and have a look and you'll find out, won't you?"

Dani hesitated again and then got to her feet and followed him out of the staff room.

The UPS man was standing near the counter glancing at the pastries and sandwiches arrayed within.

"You've got a package for me?" Dani said, moving closer to him.

He smiled and nodded, pushing the electronic pad towards her.

"If you're Danielle Grant, then yeah," he told her.

She glanced briefly at the small oblong object he had in his left hand, but it was too heavily wrapped for her to be able to discern what it might be. She quickly scribbled something on the screen and took the package from the man.

The two staff members behind the counter both moved towards Dani, anxious to find out what she'd received.

"What is it?" one of them asked.

"I don't know," Dani said, feeling a little embarrassed by all the attention.

"Open it," the other one said.

Dani inspected the package more closely.

"Who's it from?" the first girl asked.

"There's no card," Dani told her.

"Open it," the second girl persisted.

"It might be private," Dani grinned.

"Maybe someone's sent you a vibrator," Alex chuckled.

Dani shot him a withering glance, but she couldn't help but smile as she pulled at the thick tape sealing the package, her own curiosity now beginning to overwhelm her.

She finally managed to get the package open and she lifted the lid slowly, peering inside to inspect the contents.

"What is it?" Alex wanted to know.

Dani just smiled.

It was a chocolate heart and just beneath it she could see the corner of a card which she gently pulled free, scanning the message on it.

YOU'VE ALREADY GOT MY HEART.

Dani shook her head and continued to smile.

"Who's it from?" Alex persisted, moving closer, trying to get a look at the card.

Dani merely moved away and smiled.

EIGHTEEN

The restaurant was quiet, there were barely a dozen people in it including Jake and Dani.

They were seated at a window table that gave them a view of the street beyond, but Jake was looking nowhere other than at his companion. She looked stunning, her long blonde hair brushing her bare shoulders when she turned her head. Encased in a tight black dress and perched on high heels (even though Jake thought she'd be more comfortable in jeans and trainers) she had attracted gazes from other diners all night. How many of those were due to her appearance and how many were because of the age gap between the two of them he had no idea. If he was honest, it didn't bother him, and he did feel a little smug thinking that there were men in the restaurant envying him.

Or are they laughing at you?

He pushed a forkful of food into his mouth and looked across the table at Dani once again, noticing that her wine glass was empty. He picked up the bottle and re-filled it.

"You don't have to do that," she told him.

"I know. It's called good manners."

"You know I hate all that romantic shit like pulling out chairs and opening doors and that."

"I was re-filling your glass, not proposing." He took a sip of his own drink. "Just because your other boyfriends didn't do it..."

"You're not my boyfriend," Dani interjected.

"Isn't that the term they use these days? What am I then? Your fuck buddy?"

They eyed each other irritably for a moment then Dani picked at the last remnants of her food.

"What's put you in a bad mood?" she wanted to know. "Did you see Lucy today? You're always in a bad mood when you've seen her."

"It isn't Lucy's fault." He pushed his plate away from him and sipped his drink again. "Why didn't you answer your phone when I rang you this afternoon?"

"It must have been turned off."

"You never turn your phone off. It's like another limb to you. You're lost without it."

"It must have been on silent then."

"You'd have felt it vibrating."

"I must have been busy."

"You'd still have known it was ringing."

"Jesus, what is this?" Dani snapped, annoyed at his persistence. "I can't be at your beck and call twenty-four hours a day."

"I'm not asking you to be but how long does it take to answer a call or an e-mail? Ten seconds?"

"I'm sorry, right? If I'd known it was going to cause so much trouble, I'd have answered it." Dani put down her knife and fork and dabbed at the corners of her mouth with her napkin.

"Do you want something else?" Jake asked.

"I think I want to go," she told him.

"Just because I asked you about your phone?"

"No. Because I've got to be up early in the morning. I've got a big regional meeting in London tomorrow at nine."

"We could have stayed in London tonight; you'd have been right on the spot."

Dani shook her head and pulled on her jacket. Jake watched approvingly, smiling to himself.

"You look stunning tonight," he said, quietly.

Dani rolled her eyes, and he wasn't slow to see it. She hated him speaking like this. She wasn't comfortable with compliments no matter who was supplying them.

"I'm just saying," Jake went on. "That dress is beautiful."

"Jake..."

"Right, I know, I get it. I'll shut up. Didn't any of your other boyfriends ever compliment you?"

"Stop asking about my other boyfriends," she insisted. "You're always asking about them."

"I'm just curious."

Dani got to her feet.

"Can we leave?" she said, ignoring the looks from the other diners.

"I've got to pay the bill first," Jake reminded her. "Sit down. You're making an exhibition of yourself. People are looking."

"I don't give a fuck who's looking," she said through clenched teeth.

"Dani, sit down," he insisted.

She hesitated for a moment then flopped down in her seat once again, her face set in hard lines.

"You say *I'm* in a bad mood, you've been like a bear with sore back all night," Jake reminded her. "Did you have a bad day at work or something?"

Dani shook her head.

"Can you please just pay the bill?" she went on.

Jake sighed and called the waiter over. Ten minutes later they were in the car. But the change of setting did little to ease the tension between them. Jake glanced across at her a number of times, seeing that she was gazing fixedly out of the side window.

"Are you going to tell me what I did that was so wrong?" Jake said, finally.

"You really don't know do you?" Dani sighed, still more concerned with the scenery passing them outside the car.

"If you'd answered your phone it would have been okay," he joked.

"I'm not your daughter, Jake. You don't own me. And if you want to know why I didn't answer this afternoon it's because I was with Mike."

"Your ex?"

"He thinks we deserve another chance and I agree with him."

"Is this your way of telling me it's over between us?"

"It was only ever going to be a short-term thing, you said that yourself. You said I should enjoy it while it lasted but that there was no future in it. What the hell was I supposed to think?"

"I did say that you're right."

"Then what's your problem?"

"My problem is that I'm getting old, Dani. I've got more years behind me than I have in front of me, and it scares me. Sometimes I sit and think about that and it frightens the shit out of me. When I'm with you I don't think about things like that."

"So, you're only with me because you can't stand to think of yourself getting old?"

Jake shook his head.

"We can still be friends," Dani went on.

"Oh, keep your clichés to yourself," he sneered.

The remainder of the drive was made in silence, Jake finally bringing the car to a halt outside her house. He left the engine running, staring out of the windscreen now.

"I didn't think you'd be like this," Dani offered. "I thought you'd be more...grown up about it."

"Just get out," he snapped, without looking at her.

Dani reached down and pulled off her shoes, shoving open the door and stepping out onto the pavement.

"What are you doing?" he wanted to know, watching as she dropped the high heels onto the passenger seat.

"I never *could* walk in these," she told him. "I only wore them because you bought them for me."

She slammed the door and walked away, ignoring the cold concrete beneath her bare feet.

Jake sat watching her for a moment longer then he stepped on the accelerator and drove away.

NINETEEN

A severed human head weighs approximately nine pounds. Of that weight, the bulk of it is made up, naturally, of particularly dense bone but also of the mass of the brain. This can weigh up to three pounds, but size is no indicator of intelligence of course.

The brain of an idiot can weigh more than the brain of a genius. Size and volume are not necessarily indicators of intellect.

Removing the brain from the skull is almost impossible unless performed with the finest of medical equipment and in controlled surroundings. The chances of taking a brain from the skull cavity using only a hammer, sharp knife and fingers are slim. In horror films, the brain invariably slides whole from the cranium into a receptacle when required. In real life this would be an impossibility. The brain is secured inside the skull by various veins, arteries, and muscles not to mention the spinal cord, held firmly in place to prevent any damage from excessive movement or impact.

Removing pieces of a human brain from a shattered human skull is somewhat easier. If there is no need or desire to keep the brain intact, then it doesn't matter if it is damaged during the removal from the cranial cavity.

The head laying on the floor of the room had been severed by several powerful blows, the most effective of which had separated it from the neck just below the jaw line.

It had been cut off hours before so the blood coming from the stump of the neck was negligible. Just the odd drop every now and then dripped from the torn ends of veins and arteries.

The eyes were partially open, rolled upwards in the sockets. Some of the blood vessels in one of them had burst so the orb on the right looked swollen and red as it glinted in the socket.

The flesh on the face was cut in places too, injuries sustained during the initial assault. The head had been cut off later, after the victim was dead from other wounds.

The hair on the head was thick and black and the features, despite the damage sustained, were unmistakeably those of a man in his late twenties.

But the sex of the victim wasn't important to the four figures inside the darkened room.

The largest of them picked up the head and moved slowly across the room towards the trio of shapes that watched from one corner. He dangled the head before him, using it as someone might use a lure to tempt a dog from a hiding place. None of the other three shapes moved, they remained shrouded in the impenetrable blackness, watching. Waiting.

Only when he dropped the head in front of them did they move towards it.

And now, as he knelt over the bloodied object, he began to whisper something softly. Words of encouragement.

He reached inside his jacket and pulled out the claw hammer, flipping it so that the curved metal was facing away from him. As he did the three shapes moved nearer.

He struck the head three times at the side of the temple, shattering the sphenoid bone and causing fresh blood to dribble from the rents in the skull. Each impact reverberated inside the room, throbbing in his ears as he struck the skull. Then, using the curved ends of the metal, he dug into the bone more deeply, pulling at the splintered fragments, ripping them apart until the brain itself was exposed.

It welled up through the splits in the bone and the largest figure struck the skull again. Four more heavy blows smashed more bone, and he used his fingers to pick the pieces free, tossing them aside, eager to expose more of the brain.

The three shapes were close now, excited by the sight before them.

They watched as the larger figure used his hands to pull away more of the shattered bone and then he dug one hand into the brain matter and scooped it free, holding it in his hand, allowing the three shapes to see it more clearly.

One of them moved towards him and the man felt its soft lips close around his fingers as it tried to suck some of the slippery brain into its mouth. He tilted his hand slightly, allowing the jellied matter to slide into the gaping maw.

As he watched it chewing, the man smiled, wiping portions of sticky material from its misshapen chin, pushing more of the gelatinous mess towards it. Encouraging it. Nurturing it.

The second shape also fed straight from his hand but the third and smallest of the apparitions made straight for the open cranium, digging both its tiny hands into the mass of brain within the obliterated skull.

The man smiled lovingly as he watched.

Jake Porter screamed.

And he was still screaming when he woke.

TWENTY

The house was a small red brick dwelling in a street of many other identical properties.

The only difference was that there were several large Union flags displayed on the side of the building and also one flapping noisily from a pole in the back garden which was clearly visible as Jake Porter pulled up.

He sat behind the wheel for a moment, massaging the bridge of his nose, his eyes tightly closed. The beginnings of a headache were gnawing at the base of his skull and he decided to take a couple of pain killers if it got any worse. Lack of sleep always did that to him and now he sat behind the wheel preparing to swing himself out onto the pavement as the sun continued to beat down.

Jake hurried across to the door of the house, pushed the envelope he took from his jacket through the letterbox then retreated to his car.

He was just about to start the engine again when he heard his name being called. He turned towards the sound and saw a small, slim woman in her mid-forties advancing towards him.

"Jake. Jake," she called. "Have you got a minute?"

"I'm just on my way to the office," he told his ex-wife.

"It won't take long," Claire Conlan informed him.

"I just pushed your money through."

"Yes, I know. It was that I wanted to talk about. I can't manage on what you give me."

"Oh Christ, Claire, I haven't got time for this now."

"You never have. It isn't enough, Jake."

"You work, your boyfriend works. You're not exactly struggling, are you?" Jake looked at the flags flapping outside the house and pointed to them, smiling. "He's obviously patriotic."

"Don't start."

"Flags aren't cheap, are they?" Jason chuckled.

"I don't expect you to like him."

"I don't *have* to like him, Claire. I'm not the one sleeping with him.

That's your business."

"I don't want to rely on Jason. He pays his way already."

"So do I."

"I need more."

"Don't we all."

"Why can't you spare it? Have you spent it all on your new girlfriend?"

"For God's sake."

"Lucy told me about her."

"There's nothing to tell. We split up last night."

Claire raised her eyebrows.

"Why?" she wanted to know.

"Does it really matter?" Jake sighed.

"She sounded like an improvement on the last one. How old was she? Eighteen? Nineteen?"

"It isn't your problem, Claire."

"They only want you for your money you know."

"Like you did?"

"You had nothing when we first met."

"And I'll have nothing *now* if I don't get to work." He started the engine.

Claire leaned closer to the car, running appraising eyes over her ex-husband.

"You look terrible," she said.

"Thanks for the vote of confidence," Jake murmured.

"Are you okay?"

"I'm not sleeping well and, when I do, I've been getting terrible nightmares."

"About what?"

"It's hard to describe...it...terrible things...really horrible."

"Like you used to have?"

Jake nodded. "They seem to come periodically," he said, quietly. "But this time it's more vivid. Much more."

"You should see a psychiatrist," Claire said, raising her eyebrows.

"Very funny, Claire, I thought I'd get some sympathy from you." He stepped on the accelerator, revving the engine.

"That money is for Lucy too you know, she's still your daughter," Claire reminded him.

"Lucy couldn't give a shit about me, she makes that obvious every time I see her," Jake said.

"Do you blame her?"

Jake hesitated a moment then stepped on the accelerator again.

"No," he said, sadly. "I don't blame her at all."

He pulled away, leaving Claire standing at the roadside. As she watched the car drive off, she shook her head slowly.

TWENTY-ONE

your disgusting
you make me sick
hanging around with young girls.
Your pathetic.
Sick fucker.

It didn't take long to write the note.

A few scribbled words on a piece of white paper.

Once it was done the paper was folded and pushed into a white envelope, Crisp, gleaming paper.

No need for a stamp. It could be pushed through the door when the time was right.

When no one was looking.

Easy.

TWENTY-TWO

When he heard the doorbell ring, Jake Porter's first instinct was to look at his watch.

It was late, that much he knew. He'd already dropped off in front of the TV a couple of times, the second time dropping the book he'd been reading with such a loud thump that it had shocked him into wakefulness. He'd been considering going to bed when he heard the two-tone electronic sound.

Who the hell was calling at 11.15, he asked himself, getting to his feet to answer the door. He walked through the hallway, rubbing his eyes in the process, hoping it wasn't bad news. His mind began to race as he reached for the door handle.

He wasn't prepared for what he saw.

Danielle Grant merely looked at him and raised her eyebrows as he gazed at her.

"You know that offer you made about moving in with you?" she said, forcing a smile. "Does it still stand?"

"I thought it was all over between us," Jake said, puzzled.

"If you let me in, we can discuss it," Dani suggested, lifting her suitcase into view.

Jake sucked in a deep breath, taken completely unawares both by her appearance and by her words. He finally stepped back, ushered her inside and closed the door behind her. She followed him into the sitting room, putting down her case.

"Do you want a drink?" Jake asked.

"I'd better not," Dani grinned. "I'll never stop." She sat down, perching on one end of the sofa.

Jake also sat down, running appraising eyes over her.

"If this is...inconvenient, I can go," Dani offered.

"No, no. You just took me by surprise. I didn't expect to see you. Not like this."

"I was thinking. I've been thinking a lot and then I had a fight with my mum. A bad one. I just thought it was time to get out...I didn't think you'd mind."

"What did you tell your parents?"

"I just said I was going to live with a friend."

Jake raised his eyebrows and smiled.

"Like I said, if this is inconvenient," Dani went on.

"No, it's fine," Jake interrupted. "I wouldn't have offered if I hadn't meant it. But I'm still a bit confused. One minute you're telling me you want it to be over between us, the next you're moving in." He smiled.

"I've never lived with anyone before. You'll have to give me time to get used to it."

"Not even with any of your other boyfriends?"

Dani shook her head.

"I'm losing my co-habiting virginity with you," she said, smiling. "Have you lived with anyone other than your wife?"

Jake hesitated a moment then nodded.

"A girl called Rhiannon," he said, quietly. "She was here for about nine months but..." He let the words trail off. "Listen, I'd better let you unpack. I'll take your case up for you."

"No, it can wait," Dani protested.

"What about the rest of your stuff?" Jake asked. "That can't be it." He pointed towards the solitary suitcase.

"I'll get the rest once I've settled in," Dani told him. They sat in silence for a moment then Dani finally exhaled deeply. "I think I will have that drink," she announced.

Jake nodded and disappeared into the kitchen for a moment, returning with a large glass of wine that he handed to Dani. She sipped it appreciatively.

"So, who was this other girl then?" she said, smiling.

"Does it matter?" Jake said, sharply.

"You haven't talked about her. I'm just curious. Who was she? What was her name?"

"Her name was Rhiannon. She was nineteen. She worked at my publishers. Is that enough for you?"

She wasn't slow to catch the edge in his voice.

"It was all completely inappropriate," Jake went on.

"You've never mentioned her. I..."

"It isn't important," Jake interrupted.

"What happened?"

"Just drop it will you?" he snapped. "It's over. It's been over a long time. She moved away. Can we change the subject?"

They sat in silence for a moment then Dani got to her feet.

"I'll go and put my stuff away if that's okay," she said.

"You know where the bedroom is," Jake murmured. "Use the wardrobe nearest the bathroom door."

Dani nodded and disappeared out of the room.

Jake sat motionless for a moment longer, then he got to his feet and followed her.

***

From where he sat, he could see the lights in Jake Porter's house clearly.

The glow from the sitting room and then from the bedroom at the front of the house.

He watched silently, sitting behind the wheel of his car, taking occasional drags on his cigarette.

As the sitting room light went off too, he started the engine. When the bedroom light was extinguished, Mike Quinn drove off.

TWENTY-THREE

Jake woke to beams of watery sunlight pushing their way into the bedroom. Beside him, Dani was still sleeping.

It took a second or two for him to realize that he wasn't alone, and he propped himself up on one elbow and looked down at her briefly, taking time to move some long strands of hair from her cheek.

He swung himself cautiously out of bed, not wanting to wake her yet. It was still early (the electronic digits on the alarm clock were showing 6.56) so he switched off the device on the bedside table. Moving as surreptitiously as he could, he took some clothes from the drawers and wardrobe and then walked quickly and quietly out of the room, heading for the main bathroom.

Only when he was washed and dressed did he finally move back towards the bedroom where Dani was still sleeping soundly.

Jake turned and headed for the stairs, cursing under his breath when one of them creaked loudly as he put his weight on it.

He was halfway down when he saw the single envelope lying on the matt below the front door.

It was far too early for the postman wasn't it? Too early, also, for people to be delivering circulars surely.

Jake picked it up and saw that there was no stamp or post mark on it and also that the envelope wasn't even sealed.

He opened it and took out the note inside, scanning the scrawled words on the piece of paper within.

ENJOY YOUR NEW YOUNG SLUT
WHAT HAPPENED TO THE LAST ONE?

Jake frowned as he read the words, his hands beginning to shake slightly.

He read the words again. And again. Then he crossed to the door and opened it, gazing out into the early morning, wondering if he might see someone. Possibly whoever had pushed this note through.

The street was deserted as it usually was at this early hour and Jake wandered to the end of the path, gazing both ways up and down the road.

One solitary car drove past but he couldn't see who was behind the wheel.

Whoever it is, chances are he didn't push that note through.

Jake sucked in a deep breath and glanced down at the note once more. It might not even have been pushed through this morning. It could have been left late last night. Any time between when he went to bed and when he finally discovered it. Seven hours or more. He took one last look up and down the street and then headed back into the house, closing the door behind him.

Dani was at the top of the stairs when Jake looked up from the hallway.

He hurriedly stuffed the note into his pocket, not wanting her to see it.

She padded down the stairs wearing just the large t-shirt she'd pulled on the night before.

As she passed him, she kissed him lightly on the cheek.

"What time are you going in to work?" Jake asked.

"I'm not going in today," she told him.

"Why not?"

"I need to get myself sorted. I've got plenty of holiday left."

Jake nodded, watching as she disappeared into the kitchen, returning a moment later with a glass of water.

"You go back to bed then," he said. "I'll bring you up a coffee or something."

"I think I'd rather go back to sleep," she confessed.

"Do *that* then," Jake offered smiling.

Dani nodded and retreated back up the stairs. He could hear her footfalls on the stairs as she climbed.

Jake waited a moment then took the note from his pocket once again, scanning the scribbled words once again.

When he folded it up once more, he noticed that, as before, his hands were trembling.

TWENTY-FOUR

Once his five appointments for the morning were taken care of, Jake decided it would be more useful to return home to continue his work.

The house had been silent when he'd returned and he'd headed straight for his office, not stopping to check in the bedroom to see if Dani was still sleeping. If she was, he didn't want to disturb her. Instead, he had seated himself at his desk and begun to sift through several files and cases that he felt needed more immediate attention.

When those had been taken care of, he had turned his attention to the opening chapters of his new book, and he'd been delighted to find that he'd added several pages to his manuscript almost effortlessly. Now he sat back slightly, re-reading what he'd written, making minor adjustments here and there.

When he heard the door open, he glanced up.

Dani walked in, smiling broadly and seating herself on a chair near his desk.

"Hi," she said, happily.

Jake closed the window on the laptop and sat back in his seat.

"If it's porn you don't have to cover it up," Dani chuckled. "I like a bit of porn."

"It isn't," Jake said, flatly.

Dani got to her feet and moved towards him; her gaze fixed on his laptop screen.

"Go on, show me," she insisted.

"It isn't porn," Jake told her again, a stern tone to his voice now. "What did you want?"

"I heard you come in, I thought I'd see what you were doing," she told him.

"Working," he said. "Or *trying* to. What did you want?"

"Oh, charming," Dani exclaimed. "I just wondered what you were doing. You don't have to bite my head off."

"Sorry, but I'm not used to...company when I'm working. You'll have to give me chance to get used to you. It'll be fine once you go back to work."

"I've been thinking more about that. I think I'm going to leave. I hate it there. It's not what I want to do."

"How many people do jobs they *like*?"

"I don't care about other people. I'm talking about me. You said I should give my artwork a chance."

"You need a job too. Anything creative is so hit and miss. Give it a go by all means but you need something else as a backup."

"I could use one of your spare rooms as a studio."

"I just think you need to concentrate on your job at Starbucks for now."

"I've been concentrating on that for the last five years. And where's it got me? I'm no better off than I was when I started. It's not like I can get any higher up the ladder there."

"You're a manager."

"Of a fucking Starbucks." She sighed. "If I could just get someone to look at my artwork."

"You post it on social media, don't you?"

"Yes, but I haven't exactly been inundated with offers to go and work for Marvel or DC."

"Things like that take time. I haven't got that much time."

"Dani, you're twenty-nine. You've got your whole life in front of you."

"Nearly a third of it is gone already."

They sat in silence for a moment then Jake sucked in a deep breath.

"I've got to go out later," he announced. "Work related things."

Dani nodded.

"What time will you be back?" she enquired.

"I don't know," he told her. "You could get some more of your stuff from your parents while I'm out."

Again, she nodded then she stood up.

"I'll let you get on," she murmured, turning towards the door.

Jake thought about saying something but then changed his mind.

GROWTH

The words sounded as clear as if they'd been spoken in her ear by someone standing directly beside her.

Soft but full of strength.

Strength that seemed to reverberate inside her head, making it throb. As if every word was bumping gently against her brain.

She put both hands to her head, wincing slightly. The words stopped momentarily, and she let out a long, grateful breath.

There was silence for a moment and then the words began again. Loud and insistent, reverberating inside her head. She nodded, wanting to make it clear that she understood, wanting the sounds to stop.

She felt cold, shivering inside the large empty room. Sometimes she would cross to the window to peer out into the gloom, squinting to make out shapes in the night beyond.

Words inside her head asked if she was followed.

She shook her head.

"I made sure no one saw me," she added.

More words inside her head told her that was good. Warned her that no one must know where she went and what she did.

"No one knows," she said.

There was silence for a moment and then she turned to look into the corner of the room again.

"What do you want me to do?" she enquired, her mouth dry, her hands shaking slightly.

Words inside her head told her she would have to help. Have to continue to provide shelter and warmth. And food.

"I can't keep coming back here," she protested. "People will find out and..."

It felt as if someone had struck the back of her head with a heavy object.

She staggered, thought for a second she was going to pass out. It felt as if her brain was swelling, filling the cavity of her skull until it pressed hard against the bone casing. She gasped loudly and once more put hands to her head.

She was told that no one must find out. No one must discover this place or what was in it.

"I could take you out of here," she said, falteringly.

Words inside her head wanted to know where to.

"I can hide you somewhere else," she offered.

The voice seemed to grow in volume. The words throbbed like living things. Parasites digging ever deeper into her brain.

She was reminded that no one must know.

She nodded.

More words formed. Words that told her what would happen to her if this secret was discovered.

"I know," she whispered. "I understand."

She sat down heavily; her eyes closed. From the far side of the room she heard movement. Like something being dragged across the bare floor. Hidden by the darkness of the night and the gloom inside the room, it crawled across the dusty expanse towards her.

She gritted her teeth, fighting back tears.

And inside her head, whispering, like the wings of dozens of moths.

It was close to her now, hauling itself across the floor with determination and single-minded intent.

She reached for it. Embraced it.

TWENTY-FIVE

The pub was the kind of generic, plastic hostelry that was so popular because of its cheaper prices. Combined with the fact that it served food too (also fairly cheap) made it popular and one of the busiest watering holes in the area. However, this particular evening it was quieter.

The music coming from the speakers was as characterless and bland as the beers on offer or the menu on display. In a dining area, reached by climbing four wooden steps, people were eating. In the area immediately around the bar there were others gathered in groups, couples or singly, all sipping their chosen beverage. A constant low murmur of conversation filled the air. Outside, the low rumbles of thunder that they'd heard earlier had finally subsided but been replaced by rapidly falling rain. It hammered against the windows for a few minutes then it too died away.

Danielle Grant and Mike Quinn were sitting at a table in one corner of the bar.

Dani prodded the ice in her glass with one slender index finger before taking a sip of the Vodka and Coke. Mike watched her, cradling a pint of cider in his large hand.

There were several empty glasses on the table from earlier and Mike pushed them carefully away, wondering why no one had collected the empties. He took a sip of his drink and looked at Dani.

"When are you going to say something to him?" he wanted to know.

Dani shrugged.

"When the time's right," she told him.

"And when is that?"

"How the hell do I know?"

They sat in silence for a moment then Mike swallowed more of his drink.

"I thought it would be easier than this," he mused, watching as two drops of condensation raced each other down the side of the glass.

"Nothing in life is easy is it?"

"Very profound," he grunted, downing more of his pint.

"Perhaps we're doing everything too quick," Dani murmured. "Maybe we should take our time."

"We haven't *got* time."

"We've got the rest of our lives, Mike."

"This isn't much of a fucking life is it? If we can change it why not do something about it?"

Dani nodded slightly and took a sip of her own drink. Noticing that Mike was smiling.

"What's so funny?" she wanted to know.

"I was just thinking about the first time we met," he told her.

Dani rolled her eyes.

"That was some party," Mike went on. "I wanted you as soon as I saw you."

"You mean you wanted to fuck me?"

"Was it that obvious?"

Dani smiled more broadly.

They sat in silence for a moment then she exhaled deeply.

"What if this doesn't work, Mike?" she said, her voice catching slightly.

"It will. Why shouldn't it?" he assured her.

"Because he's not a stupid man."

"He's infatuated with you. He'd do anything for you."

"I just think we should give it time."

"You're not going to bottle this are you?" Mike snapped.

"I'm the one sleeping with him. It's all right for you." She downed more of her drink.

"This was your idea."

"I know but...I...I don't want to hurt him."

"He'll survive."

Dani ran the tip of her index finger around the rim of her glass.

"What time is he back tonight?" Mike wanted to know.

"Late. He's got a case to go over. A complicated one."

"He says he's going over a case, you don't know where he is or who he's with. He could be with another woman."

"He's not like that."

"His marriage broke up because he cheated didn't it?"

"Yes, but he wouldn't cheat on *me*. I know he wouldn't."

"What would he say if he knew you were cheating on him?" Mike smiled and there was something in the gesture that Dani found distasteful. It smacked of gloating.

"He'd throw me out," she murmured.

Again, silence descended, Mike finishing his pint and bringing the empty glass down onto the tabletop with a crack that made the three people sitting near them look around.

"You're not going to bottle this?" he said, softly.

"You've already asked me that."

"So just tell him. Tell him you're pregnant."

TWENTY-SIX

"I knew they were dangerous."

Lauren Davison's words seemed to echo around the inside of the interview room.

"Don't ask me how, I just knew," she went on. She looked down at the tabletop, rubbing two fingers over a part of it that bore a blemish.

Jake Porter eyed her impassively.

"They were babies, Lauren," he said, softly. "How could they have been dangerous?"

"I just knew."

"Dangerous to you or to others?"

She didn't answer but just sat gazing blankly at the tabletop, her breathing low.

"Was that why you had an abortion when you were younger?" Jake asked. "Did you think the child you were going to have was going to be dangerous too?"

Lauren didn't answer him. She lowered her head a little more, determined not to make eye contact with him.

"How did you know I had an abortion?" she asked. "There was no record of it anywhere."

"There must have been. The hospital where it was performed would have..."

"It wasn't done in a hospital," Lauren snapped, cutting across him.

Jake eyed her warily.

"Where was it done then?" he wanted to know.

"I was fifteen. I daren't tell my father. He would have killed me. My mum knew that too," Lauren said, her voice barely audible.

Jake moved his chair closer, anxious not to miss her mumbled words.

"So, what happened?" he asked.

"My mum had a friend who said she could help. She'd helped other girls in the area. My mum took me to see her."

"And she did the abortion?"

Lauren nodded.

"How advanced was the pregnancy?" Jake wanted to know.

"Four months," Lauren told him, her head still lowered. "When she'd finished...I... she didn't really know what she was doing. She...damaged me down there."

"Can you still have children?"

"The doctors said yes but..."

She let the words fade away. They seemed to be swallowed by the deep shadows at the edges of the room.

"What did you think those children you killed were going to do?" Jake asked, tapping his pen gently against the tabletop. "How did you think they were going to hurt you?"

Lauren merely shook her head.

"You had so much in your life," Jake persisted. "Your husband. Your job. You had so much to look forward to and yet you threw it all away when you hurt those children."

"I had no choice."

She snarled the words at him, hissing through clenched teeth and, for a second, he saw something savage behind her eyes. A fury and anger that made him move back slightly.

"Now tell me how you knew about my abortion," she rasped, rising out of her seat and glaring at him.

"Sit down," Jake said, flatly.

She hesitated a second and then did as he instructed, settling herself once again.

"How could you know?" she breathed. "No one knew."

Jake held her gaze.

"There's no way you could have known," Lauren insisted. "There was no evidence. Nothing. You *couldn't* know."

Jake pushed his pen back into his inside pocket and got to his feet, retrieving his briefcase from beside the table.

"I think we've talked enough today, Lauren," he told her. "I'll come back and see you tomorrow."

As he made for the door she leapt to her feet, her lips drawn back like a snarling dog.

"I want to know how you knew," she roared at him, but Jake ignored her outburst and took another step towards the door. Just before he reached it, it swung open and the uniformed policeman who'd been standing outside the interview room stepped inside.

"Are you all right, sir?" the uniformed man asked. "I heard shouting."

"We were just talking," Jake told the man.

The uniformed man looked at Jake again and then at Lauren who was sitting down again, her head lowered.

Jake looked at her once more then headed out into the corridor beyond.

As he ran a hand through his hair, he noticed that his hand was shaking.

TWENTY-SEVEN

Dani looked at the front door key resting in her hand for a moment before inserting it into the lock.

It seemed strange having the key to someone else's house as well as her own family home after all these years. Jake hadn't thought twice about giving her keys to the front and back door of his home. It was like a certificate of approval she mused. She remembered getting her first house key when she was eighteen (her mother had insisted she didn't achieve this rite of passage before she was that age). It had been like some kind of silent acknowledgement. Now, as she turned the key in the lock of Jake Porter's home, she felt the same way.

The house had been in darkness when she pulled up and now, as she stepped into the hallway she was enveloped by the silence and she realized that he still hadn't returned from wherever he was. In some ways she was grateful for that. She didn't want to try and explain where she'd been, and she didn't feel particularly chatty if she was honest.

Guilt?

She pushed the thought to one side and closed the front door behind her.

She slapped on a couple of lights and turned immediately towards the stairs, making her way up, pulling her jacket off as she climbed. Once inside the bedroom she hung up her jacket and then decided to have a quick shower before she went to bed. There was no point sitting up waiting for Jake because she had no idea what time he was getting in and she felt tired so a soothing shower and then a decent night's sleep would do her good.

She turned on the shower and began to undress, tossing her clothes onto the bed.

Dani suddenly hissed in pain as she stubbed her toe heavily against something beneath the bed.

Muttering to herself she sat down on the bed, massaging the injured toe, wondering what the hell she had kicked. She dropped to her knees and lifted the duvet away from the floor so she could see the offending object.

It was a suitcase. A cheap black plastic case that looked dusty and had several scratch marks on its stiffened lid. Dani frowned and pulled it out from beneath the bed, casting appraising eyes over it. One of the locks was broken she noticed and, almost without thinking, she opened the other and gently lifted the lid.

The case was full of clothes. Stuffed to the brim with all manner of items. Jeans. Blouses. Shoes. Knickers. All of them small, petite. Striking colours. The kind of thing a young person would wear. For a moment Dani wondered if the clothes belonged to Jake's daughter but, she reasoned, why would they be here? Why would a case full of his daughter's clothes be under his bed?

Dani lifted some of the items out and saw that there were more below them and there were also photographs. Dozens and dozens of photographs.

She picked up the first of them and saw that it featured a pretty blonde girl in her late teens or early twenties. She was looking sheepishly at the camera, one hand entwined in her long hair. There were more of the pictures showing her lying on a bed, barefoot, sometimes in just jeans and a vest top. Again, she was sporting that slightly awkward expression.

Dani looked more closely at the pictures and noticed that the duvet the girl was laying on was the same pattern as the one that was currently on the bed.

The blonde had been pictured laying on this same bed by the looks of it.

Dani sifted through more of the pictures. More of the blonde and again in varying states of undress. Several of them showed her in just a bikini, stretched out in a garden somewhere, again gazing towards the camera with that now familiar awkward expression. The next one showed her posing before a mirror in a short black dress.

Reflected in the mirror Dani saw a familiar figure.

Jake Porter was standing there, holding a camera, gazing raptly at the young blonde.

Dani swallowed hard and dropped the pictures back into the case, closing the lid and pushing it back under the bed.

She waited a moment then got to her feet, padding through into the bathroom where the shower was still spitting warm water. Dani stepped beneath the soothing streams, for some reason suddenly feeling as if, after having looked at the photographs, she needed to cleanse herself.

Twenty minutes later she was still standing there.

TWENTY-EIGHT

He sounded as if he was in pain.

She heard him murmuring. Heard some half-recognised words punctuated by low groans and laboured exhalations.

At first she wondered if she was dreaming when she first heard the sounds but then, as Dani rolled onto her side, she realized that they were coming, not from some corner of her subconscious, but from Jake.

He was laying on his back beside her, the duvet pushed down as far as his waist. She could see sweat glistening on his skin, gleaming in the early morning sunlight. His body was shaking slightly, and, for a moment, Dani considered waking him. If he was having a nightmare, which seemed likely, then perhaps he would be better off being woken. She was about to do that when she remembered the old cliché about never waking a sleepwalker.

Was it the same kind of thing?

Jake grunted and then lay still, his breathing settling rapidly. Dani watched the slow rise and fall of his chest, satisfied that he was calming down. She pulled her hand away from him, waited a moment longer then swung herself out of bed.

As she made her way down the stairs she coughed, trying to mask the sound in case she woke him.

She hurried into the kitchen and retrieved a glass from a cupboard, filling it rapidly and gulping down several mouthfuls.

Jake hadn't returned until after midnight the previous night and he'd slipped into bed quietly, trying his best not to disturb her. For a moment she'd thought about mentioning the suitcase beneath the bed and what was in it but had eventually thought better of it. Why start an argument? He obviously had his reasons for keeping the clothes and the photographs and they didn't affect her, did they? That was all in the past.

She swallowed more water, the ticking of the wall clock loud in the stillness. She looked up and saw that it was just after six. Dani wondered about staying up but then decided that another couple of hours in bed was preferable. Carrying the glass, she made her way back out into the hall.

The single white envelope was lying on the mat at the front door.

Dani crossed to it and picked it up, turning it over in her hand, inspecting the front of the white paper.

There was no stamp. No postmark. No address.

It wasn't even sealed.

Dani opened the flap and saw that there was a single sheet of A4 paper inside which promptly fell out.

As she retrieved it, she saw the words scrawled on the paper;

I SEE THIS ONE IS A BIT OLDER.
YOU GETTING FED UP WITH THE LITTLE GIRLS PICKING OLDER ONES NOW?

DIRTY FUCKER.

Dani frowned as she read the words.

Where the hell had this come from?

Again, she scanned the scribbled words.

Who would write something like that?

Dani turned and looked up the stairs, towards where Jake was still sleeping.

Why *would someone write it?*

She folded the note again and stuffed it back into the envelope, putting that back on the mat just the way she'd found it.

Dani stood gazing at the envelope for a second longer, then she headed back up the stairs.

He was awake when she walked back into the bedroom.

Should she mention the note?

"Did I wake you?" she asked. "I just needed a drink of water."

Jake shook his head.

She decided not to tell him about the note. He'd find it when he got up anyway wouldn't he?

"I was dreaming," he sighed.

"I could hear you," she grinned, slipping back into bed beside him.

"Bad dreams," Jake breathed. "They're *always* bad dreams."

"What about?"

He shook his head. "I can barely remember now. I've suffered with them all my life. Always the same kind of thing. Sometimes are worse than others."

"Can you remember them?"

"Sometimes I can, sometimes I can't. I suppose there's a bit of irony about a psychiatrist being plagued by bad dreams isn't there? I wonder what Freud would make of it all."

They both laughed.

"They say that what you dream about is something that's happened in your life," Dani offered.

"I hope not," Jake told her. "I *really* hope not."

TWENTY-NINE

He'd been downstairs for more than half an hour when Dani finally slid out of bed.

She knelt, reaching underneath, her hand closing on the plastic handle of the cheap black suitcase. She pulled it into view then flipped the lid open, digging beneath the layers of clothes, searching for the photographs she'd found before. Dani selected three of them. All showing the same blonde teenager. She closed the case and put it back where she'd found it then she pushed the photographs into her handbag.

She dressed quickly and made her way downstairs where she found Jake seated at the kitchen table, sipping a coffee, and chewing on some toast. He was reading the newspaper and only looked up briefly when she entered the room.

"People read the papers online now, old man," she said, smiling.

Jake raised one middle finger in her direction and smiled.

"Are you going out?" he said, noticing that she had a jacket with her.

"Just to see a mate," she told him.

"But it's the weekend. I thought we could spend a bit of time together."

"We can later. I won't be that long."

"Go on then. Abandon me," he said, smiling.

She kissed him lightly on the top of the head and made her way to the front door, picking up her car keys.

The blazing sunshine of the last few days had given way to some rain and Dani pulled her jacket over her head as she sprinted towards her car. Once behind the wheel she dug in her pocket for her phone.

It only took a second to find what she was looking for.

Dani scrolled through the pictures and words impassively then she started the engine and guided the car out into the road.

The journey took her less than fifteen minutes and she finally found a parking space and clambered out, once more running the gamut of the swiftly falling rain until she reached the main entrance of the shopping centre.

It was busy inside, crammed full with shoppers and, in some cases, people who had ventured inside merely to escape the rain.

Dani moved quickly through the throng of people, checking her phone every now and then and finally reaching her target.

There weren't many people inside the sushi restaurant, so she had little trouble spotting her quarry.

Lucy Porter was sitting at a window table munching happily through a bowl of noodles.

Dani slipped inside and made straight for her table, seating herself opposite Lucy who glanced at her with an expression of concern on her face.

"Do I know you?" she said.

"You're Lucy, right?" Dani exclaimed.

"Who wants to know?"

"I'm a friend of your dad's. I'm..."

"Oh God, are you Dani?" Lucy snorted, indignantly.

The older woman nodded.

"So, you're his girlfriend, are you?" Lucy grunted.

"You could say that" Dani admitted.

"So, what do you want with me?"

"I wanted to talk."

"Why? And how did you know I was here?"

"You've been posting pictures from here on Instagram for the last twenty minutes, it wasn't hard."

"So, you're a stalker as well as a gold digger?" Lucy sneered.

"I didn't come here for a fight, Lucy," Dani told her.

"Why did you come here then? I've got nothing to say to you."

"I wanted to ask you some questions."

Lucy sucked in a deep breath. "Do I hate my dad for breaking up his marriage? Yes. Do I think he's pathetic for getting with a girl more than twenty years younger than him? Yes. Anything else?"

"Did you know his last girlfriend?"

"The one that was younger than me? No."

"Did you ever meet her?"

"I saw her a couple of times. Why?"

Dani dug in her handbag and pulled out the pictures of the blonde teenager. She spread the pictures out on the tabletop and jabbed an index finger at each one in turn.

"Is this her?" she enquired.

"Could be."

"Well, have a closer look and make your mind up will you?" Dani snapped, her patience wearing thin.

Lucy caught the edge in her voice and nodded.

"Yes, that's her," she said. "Where did you get those? Has my dad got her pictures displayed all around the house?"

"What was her name?" Dani wanted to know.

"Rhiannon. Rhiannon Morton or Norton. Something like that."

"Where did she go after her and your dad split?"

"How do I know? Lucy shrugged.

"There are still some of her clothes at your dad's house. I wondered why he might have kept them."

"Perhaps he's still in love with her," Lucy sneered.

They sat looking at each other for a moment then Dani spoke again.

"He loves you, you know," she said, softly. "He's always talking about you and how proud he is of you. Maybe you should cut him a bit of slack."

"And what? Forgive him? Forget that he ruined my life?"

"You can't be angry with him for the rest of your life, Lucy. He doesn't deserve that."

"Doesn't he?"

"No. And neither do you. You've got to move on. All this anger isn't helping you."

"Did you come here to find out about my dad's last girlfriend or to psychoanalyse me? My dad's the psychiatrist you know."

"I was trying to help. Anger is a bad thing. It hurts everyone."

"Well, if I ever decide to live my life by bumper stickers, I'll get in touch but, until then, I'm going."

Lucy got to her feet, threw a ten-pound note on the tabletop to cover her bill and walked out.

Dani sat immobile at the table, watching the younger woman as she hurried out of the restaurant then she gathered up the photographs she'd laid out and stuffed them back into her handbag.

THIRTY

Jake Porter stood in the bay window gazing out into the street beyond, his eyes moving slowly back and forth.

The other houses in the street looked so "normal" (he couldn't think of a more apt word). And yet he knew that there were so many stories unfolding behind the facades of each one.

So much hidden.

For most of his working life, Jake had been paid to find whatever was hidden within his patients. Helping them to unlock things within themselves that they preferred to keep hidden. There was a certain irony to the whole thing he mused. However, the slight smile on his face faded rapidly as he looked down at the handwritten note he was holding.

YOUR OLD ENOUGH TO BE HER FATHER
YOU SHOULD BE ASHAMED.
DIRTY FUCKER
JUST LIKE THE LAST ONE.

Jake exhaled and once more scanned the other houses in the street.

Had the notes come from one of those? Was there someone in this very neighbourhood who hated him enough to send him such missives? All of them had been pushed through by hand, that much he was sure of. It must be someone close by.

He was still pondering these facts when Dani walked into the room.

"Anything interesting?" she asked, pointing at the note he was holding.

Jake shook his head, pushing the sheet of A4 hurriedly into his pocket.

Dani seated herself on the sofa and began scrolling through messages on her phone.

"Does anyone else know you're living here?" Jake wanted to know. "Anyone other than your mum and dad?"

"No, why?" Dani mused; her attention fixed on the phone.

"You haven't told friends?"

"No. Why do you ask?"

"I just wondered," he said, dismissively.

"What about you? Do your wife and daughter know I'm living here?"

"It's none of their business," Jake insisted.

"Your daughter will have to know eventually."

"Why? It's not like she lives here is it?"

"I'd like to meet her."

Jake smiled thinly. "I don't think she'd...approve of you," he said, quietly.

"Didn't she approve of your last girlfriend? You know the younger one who lived here?"

Jake didn't answer.

"What was her name?" Dani persisted.

"Does it matter?" Jake snapped.

"I was just asking," Dani countered, all too aware of the anger in his voice.

They sat in silence for a moment then Dani spoke again. "What would I have to do to make your daughter approve of me?"

"Oh, Christ, do we have to go through this now?" Jake sighed.

"All right, calm down, I was just asking. Why do you always get so sensitive about stuff that happened in the past? It's over. Forget about it."

Jake shot her an angry glance and shook his head.

Another heavy silence descended. Dani eyed him warily and the only sound in the room came from the TV. The canned laughter of the audience seemed even more incongruous in the stillness.

"What time are you leaving tomorrow?" Dani enquired.

"Before you get up probably," Jake told her, the edge leaving his voice. "You should come with me."

"To your publishers?"

"No. To London. I'm booked into a nice hotel too."

"You've got meetings all day, haven't you? I'd get bored."

"You could go window shopping. Have a look around some museums. We could go out for a meal in the evening."

"I hate window shopping when I've got no money. Anyway, I've got shit to do."

"Like what?"

"Personal stuff," Dani told him.

Jake smiled and moved closer to her on the sofa.

"I'm sorry for snapping earlier," he said. "I just don't like talking about..."

"Your last girlfriend?" Dani said, smiling.

Jake nodded; his eyes fixed on something ahead of him.

"You don't have to be ashamed of her, you know," she told him.

Jake lifted his gaze slightly, but he didn't speak.

"Did it end badly?" Dani persisted.

"She moved away," he said, quietly. "That was it." Jake looked at her. "Is that enough for you?"

They both smiled but as he got to his feet.

"And you're definitely staying in London tomorrow night?" Dani went on.

"I've got *stuff* to do too," he said, smiling.

THIRTY-ONE

The journey had taken longer than he'd have liked.

Delays on the train followed by a bomb scare on the tube had forced him to return to street level and find a taxi. Jake Porter was already more than a little irritated when he finally managed to hail a cab, clambering into the back seat, and flopping down.

The driver was a talkative type which was fine because Jake didn't really feel like chatting, he was quite happy to let the man ramble on about different things. He had warmed to his subject when he'd got to Brexit and Muslim terrorists (Jake didn't think there was a link, but he'd listened anyway).

Now, as the taxi pulled up outside the achingly new and dazzlingly glass building on the banks of the Thames, Jake fumbled for his wallet and pulled out the cost of the fare.

The driver thanked him and drove off, almost colliding with a despatch rider who roared past on a motorbike.

Jake ran a hand through his hair and looked up at the building before him. The headquarters of Caxton Press was an imposing looking edifice and Jake couldn't help but be impressed as he headed towards the main doors. The security guard standing just inside the foyer nodded affably as he passed, and Jake made his way over to the reception towards the young woman in the charcoal grey two piece who sat there smiling efficiently.

She asked him who he wanted to see and issued him with his laminate, ensured he signed the visitors' book and checked he hadn't got a car registration that he needed to enter. Once the preliminaries had been attended to, Jake was pointed towards a bank of glass sided elevators that served all fifteen floors of the building.

As he walked towards them, he could see that there were posters for some of the books that Caxton had published recently framed on the walls. They also did fiction which supported their academic arm (of which Jake was a part). Needless to say, the fiction was considerably more successful in commercial terms but the sales of more learned tomes to universities and other seats of learning ensured that Caxton were one of the most successful publishers in the country in their chosen fields.

Jake pressed the 'call' button of the elevator and stepped in when it arrived. He rode it to the third floor, glancing down at his visitor's laminate occasionally. When he reached the third floor he stepped out and headed down the carpeted corridor towards the office he sought.

There were small offices to his right as he walked and a larger open space containing more computers and workers and Jake could hear a steady babble of conversation rising from the figures to his left, some of whom glanced in his direction wondering who he was. He finally reached the office he sought and tapped lightly on the door.

The voice inside instructed him to enter and he stepped inside, a smile spreading across his face.

As Jake entered, Robert Leighton, got to his feet, smiling broadly. Leighton was in his late thirties but was grey around the temples and prematurely balding. He was dressed in a pair of jeans and a white shirt, attempting the smart casual look, and wanting it to look effortless. He gestured towards a chair in front of his desk and Jake sat down.

Leighton had been his editor on his books and the two men got on well. It had been he who had suggested that a promotional tour might widen the appeal of what had previously been thought of as purely academic works. Leighton had pointed out that most daytime TV shows employed a psychiatrist of some description and that Jake might be well suited to such a role. It was indicative of how even the role of an author had changed, Jake thought. They needed to be as visible as possible nowadays if their books were to achieve the kind of figures everyone hoped for.

The two men chatted happily, and Jake stood beside the large windows of the office gazing out at the sun glinting on the Thames.

Leighton showed him some promotional material they'd been working on for his next book and Jake's mood lightened considerably.

By the time they walked out of the office to get some lunch, he was feeling much better.

The sunlight was strong, and it warmed him as they walked, heading through back streets and a couple of narrow alleyways until they came to the restaurant. It was used by several people from Caxton Press (those with expense accounts anyway) and Leighton waved happily to colleagues or stopped at a table to chat before they finally seated themselves at their own table.

They ordered their food and drink from the waitress and settled themselves.

Jake placed his mobile phone on the tabletop close to him.

Just in case.

THIRTY-TWO

Dani scanned the Instagram account, her gaze flicking back and forth over the photographs there.

A young girl, late teens, long blonde hair, very slim. Dani glanced at the top of the account.

RHIANNON MORTON

Beneath it there were a series of emojis. Smiley faces. Dogs. Flowers.

The usual rubbish.

Dani looked at the most recent post.

October 18th a year earlier.

Nothing since. And yet before that, Rhiannon Morton had posted two, sometimes three pictures every day. She's been happy to show off herself and the parts of her life she wished to share with the world. And then. Nothing.

Dani checked the same girl's Facebook account.

Same thing.

Lots of pictures until October 18th and then nothing.

Dani glanced at the pictures once again. Most of them had been posted on both accounts but every so often there were some different ones (usually on the Instagram account). More pictures. Some Dani recognised. At least she recognised the backgrounds. These had been taken at this house, no question of it. There were some in the bedroom. Several in the sitting room and a number in the garden. In the photos the sun was shining brightly, and Rhiannon was in a bikini in most of them. Dani sat forward as she looked at one of the pictures.

It showed Rhiannon standing with her back to a green painted wooden door. A flap that looked as if it led to a flight of steps beyond and below.

Stone steps that led down below ground level.

A cellar?

Dani didn't remember seeing the doorway before but then again, she reasoned, she had never been out there looking for it. She enlarged the photograph, gazing more closely at it. Staring fixedly at the picture, she took a sip of her coffee, her mind racing.

Another moment and she got to her feet, hurrying out of the room and through the house to the back door.

She stepped out into the garden, bare feet sinking into the long grass as she made her way between the two tall privet hedges that marked the boundaries of the property. There was a wooden shed at the end of the garden, and it was towards this that Dani advanced. Could the trap door be inside she wondered?

The door wouldn't open when she pulled it, but she was relieved to find that it was because the wood was swollen and sticking rather than because the shed was locked.

Dani peered inside. It smelled musty in there and it was full of garden tools, many of them hanging on individual hooks. *Very neat.* There was a petrol mower. A leaf blower. Long lengths of hose pipe.

But no trap door.

Dani turned and headed back towards the house.

She was halfway up the garden when she saw the dark green area ahead of her. Half hidden behind some old garden furniture; it was almost invisible to anyone not expecting to find it there.

Dani pulled the chairs away from the hatchway and saw that there was a padlock on the chain that secured the dark green doorway. She pulled at it with one hand, wondering where the key was.

"It's a coal cellar."

The words made her spin around and she turned to find their source.

The man standing at the hedge gazing over at her was Ted Brady. He was a thick set man in his late forties, but his heavy jowls made him look older. That combined with his thinning hair didn't help him. He ran appraising eyes over Dani and jabbed a finger towards the trap door she'd exposed.

"Lots of the older houses around here had them," he went on. "Most people had them converted or just walled up. I don't know what your boyfriend did."

"He's not my boyfriend," Dani said, flatly.

"They all say that" Brady grinned, again looking her up and down.

Dani was aware of his gaze and felt a little uncomfortable under it.

"He's padlocked the door, so he obviously doesn't go down there," she said, pointing at the lock and chain.

"I've seen him go down there," Brady offered.

"When?"

"When I've been looking out of my window." He sniffed loudly, wiping his nose with the back of one hand before returning his attention to Dani. "You're older than his last one."

She frowned.

"His last girlfriend," Brady went on. "She was younger than you. A right little cutie."

"Did you know her?"

"I saw her out here a few times. She used to sunbathe in her little bikini." He laughed. "Sometimes her friends used to come around too. They all liked sunbathing." A lecherous smile spread across his face.

"Did you speak to her?" Dani wanted to know.

"Just hello. You know how it is? Just being friendly." Again, he looked Dani up and down. "She looked a bit like you. Slim. Pretty. Sexy. I don't know how he does it, your boyfriend. You girls seem to love it."

"Love what?"

"Whatever he's got that makes him so attractive to young girls."

"I'm sure you've got it too," Dani said, ensuring that he caught the sarcasm in her voice.

"Tell my ex that," he said, laughing. It was a hollow sound.

"Well, I'd better go," Dani announced.

"It's okay, I'm not busy," Brady told her.

"*I've* got stuff to do."

She turned to walk away.

"Her parents came round here a couple of times you know," Brady went on. "They didn't like her staying with him."

"How do you know they were her parents?"

"I could hear from what they were saying. I was out here doing a bit of gardening. I couldn't help but overhear. You know how it is."

Dani nodded.

"Why didn't they want her here?" she asked.

"They knew what your boyfriend was like. They didn't want their daughter mixed up with him."

"What do you mean?"

"Reckons himself a bit, doesn't he? Thinks he's better than everyone else."

"I can't say I've noticed."

"Well, I have. I know *people*. I was in sales for twenty years. I know what I'm talking about. He's an arrogant bastard. He needs bringing down a peg or two."

Dani shook her head and, again, turned to walk away.

"Nice to have met you," Brady said, grinning. "I'm sure we'll talk again."

"Can't wait," Dani said, wearily.

"Maybe your boyfriend moved that little blonde out so he could move you in. You should ask him."

Dani nodded.

"Thanks for the advice," she grunted, finally heading back towards the back door, anxious to be away from Brady.

He watched her as she left, his eyes fixed firmly on her backside.

"Fucking whore," he murmured under his breath.

THIRTY-THREE

"I ordered you a brandy to go with your coffee."

As Jake Porter seated himself, he saw the glass of amber liquid before him and smiled.

Bob Leighton sipped at his own wine, watching as Jake swirled the brandy around in its glass, inhaling the aroma approvingly.

The restaurant was almost empty by now. The waiting staff were clearing and cleaning tables and a couple of them had already glanced impatiently in the direction of Jake and his editor, but the two men were untroubled by the looks. Jake sipped from his glass nodding appreciatively.

"I'm not sure if it's ethical for a psychiatrist to drink at this time of the day," he mused.

"Psychiatrist *and* writer," Leighton added, also smiling. "You'd better get used to that title, Jake."

"Do you really think there's a chance that side of it could take off?" Jake asked.

"With the right kind of promotional campaign, the sky's the limit."

"But it's a specialized area."

"So is cosmology. So is natural history but most people have heard of Professor Brian Cox and David Attenborough, haven't they? It all depends how it's packaged. And those two are always on TV too which is a massive help to their book sales."

Jake raised his eyebrows.

"What are you doubting, Jake?" Leighton went on. "Your own ability in front of a camera?"

"I've never done anything like that before," Jake reminded him.

"You talk to people every day in your practice. You encourage them to talk, you make them feel at ease. Just think of the camera as a new patient."

They both laughed.

"But none of this is set in stone is it?" Jake said.

"We've got a very good publicity and marketing department," Leighton told him. "They've got some great contacts with the major

TV networks and there are so many of the smaller channels looking for this kind of expertise. You'll be in demand, Jake, trust me."

"I'm a psychiatrist, not a TV personality. I never wanted that."

"It could be a very nice additional revenue stream," Leighton said, smiling and raising his glass in salute. "I'm sure your new...companion will be very impressed."

Jake grinned and shook his head.

"My new companion," he mused. "That's one way of putting it I suppose."

"Am I going to meet her?"

"One day perhaps."

"What's her name?"

"Danielle. Dani to her friends."

"How did you meet?"

"It sounds like the worst kind of cliché, but she was a patient."

Leighton laughed.

"I know, that sounds terrible and I'm sure it was breaking every kind of ethical consideration, but we weren't seeing each other while she was my patient."

"You don't have to justify yourself to me, Jake," Leighton assured him, smiling. "If she's half your age it's a wonder you've got the strength to write *and* carry on with your practice." Again, he smiled broadly and raised his glass in salute.

"Your last...companion was much younger, too wasn't she?"

Jake nodded.

"I think you'll fit right into the world of celebrities, Jake," the editor grinned.

Jake shook his head.

"How's your mum?" Leighton wanted to know.

"No better," Jake told him. "But she's in the best place."

"It must have been hard for you."

"I made the choice that was best for her. I couldn't look after her myself." He sipped slowly from his glass then set it down gently on the gleaming white tablecloth. "I visit as often as I can but...I'm ashamed to say it, Bob but I can't wait to get out of there when I visit. I know it isn't her fault but sometimes she drives me mad. I just look at her and I think how pointless her life is."

"I'm sure there are lots of people like that."

"I know and I know I've got no right to even think things like that."

"You can't help the way you think, Jake."

"But it's wrong."

"Why?"

"I feel bad about it. About the whole situation."

"But you can't change anything."

"I know and that's what makes it worse. I get angry about the way she is. As if it's her fault. And then I feel guilty for having thoughts like that. Perhaps if she was my real mother I'd feel differently."

Leighton looked puzzled.

"What do you mean?" he asked.

"My mum, the woman I call mum," Jake explained. "She isn't my birth mother."

THIRTY-FOUR

Leighton looked perplexed for a moment. A little unsure how to react to the information he'd just received.

"I didn't realize that" he finally said.

"Why would you?" Jake offered. "It's not the sort of thing you put on your CV is it?"

Leighton sipped at his drink, sitting forward slightly.

"Do you know your birth mother?" he asked.

Jake shook his head.

"I have no memory of anything in my life until I was about ten or eleven," he said, quietly. "I was brought up in children's homes and foster care until I was adopted by...by my mother. The woman I've been calling mum for the last thirty-five years."

"No memory at all?"

"Nothing. I've looked into it, in a professional capacity." He smiled. "I've analysed myself more thoroughly than any patient I've ever treated but it's no good. If there are memories there, I can't unlock them. I even had a series of consultations with a colleague, but she couldn't help me either. Whatever is locked away is buried too deep." He took a sip of his drink.

"Does that mean it's too much for you to face?"

"It's possible but it's unusual for there to be no traces of memory at all, not unless the sufferer has sustained some kind of head injury and I didn't. At least not that I know of."

Leighton nodded, intrigued by the conversation.

"Have you ever tried to find your birth mother?"

"No. I couldn't see the point. If she'd have wanted me then she wouldn't have put me in care, would she?"

"You don't know the circumstances?"

Jake shook his head.

"If she'd have wanted me that much, she'd have found a way, wouldn't she?" he murmured.

"You don't know that Jake. She could have been a teenage mum. Something like that. Couldn't cope."

"You're probably right. I've buried my head in the sand a little, if I'm honest. I don't want to know everything. I'm afraid of what I might find." He smiled. "Maybe I was just a horrible little bastard and she couldn't put up with me."

"What age were you put into care?"

"I haven't a clue."

"Have you ever looked into it?" Leighton continued. "Tried to find out about your past?"

"I was more concerned about why I had no memory of my early life. Most people can remember things from when they were four or five, sometimes earlier but I have no recollection of that at all."

"And you only remember things from the time you were adopted?"

"It seems like that. It's as if the adoption went through and a switch was thrown in my mind." Jake smiled. "The mind shuts down sometimes. Blocks out incidents and events it can't face. I don't know if that was what was happening to me during the first ten years of my life but if it was then the events must have been serious. My subconscious obviously felt it needed that protection."

"From what?"

"I have absolutely no idea."

"But there must be records. Something you could use to trace your early years. If you were in care, then it would be on file somewhere. The families who fostered you would be listed somewhere..."

"I told you, I never *wanted* to look into it," Jake snapped.

Leighton wasn't slow to pick up the irritation in his voice. He sat back slightly, his hand reaching for his wine glass. He could see that Jake's expression had darkened somewhat.

"I can only think that something particularly traumatic happened during those early years," Jake finally said. "Something that caused my mind to shut out the memories. Something that still can't be unlocked."

"You must be curious," Leighton offered.

"Of course I am, but perhaps some things are best left alone."

"Sleeping dogs?"

"Exactly," said Jake, his smile returning. He finished what was left in his glass and set it down gently.

"Do you want another?" Leighton asked.

"I'd better not," Jake told him.

"I'm the one who should be laying off the booze. I've got an editorial meeting when I get back. I'll be dropping off."

"That interesting is it?"

"Books about Economic theory, the history of concrete and another about veganism. How does that sound to you?"

Jake smiled. "I see what you mean. So, there won't be huge publicity and marketing campaigns launched around those?"

"We don't see them as having as much potential as you, Jake," Leighton told him, turning his empty glass between his thumb and forefinger.

"And you're serious about me getting involved with the media?" Jake said.

"Deadly serious. It's a no-lose situation. If we can get you onto some TV and radio shows, then the sky's the limit."

"I'd better not tell my ex-wife. She'll be chasing me to give her more money."

"Is she still after you?"

Jake nodded.

"If I could afford to, I'd give it to her," he said.

"My ex was the same," Leighton told him.

"I didn't realize you'd been married."

"We were young. It was a mistake. Thank God there were no kids involved. It all ended quite amicably to be honest. But I know lots of splits can be messy."

"Tell me about it," Jake sighed.

The two men sat in silence for a moment then Leighton spoke again. "What are you doing for the rest of the day?" the editor enquired.

"I'm staying in London overnight. I've got some jobs to do while I'm here."

"Anything interesting?"

"Nothing worth talking about."

Jake drummed his fingers gently on the tablecloth.

"And then back to your new muse?" Leighton joked.

"I wouldn't call her my muse," Jake said.

"Give it time. What's she doing while you're here?"

"I haven't got a clue," Jake confessed. "I'm sure she'll find some way of amusing herself."

They both laughed.

THIRTY-FIVE

Mike Quinn sat up, his breathing gradually returning to normal.

Beside him, Danielle Grant was laying on her back, trying to regain her composure, her whole-body tingling. She gently stroked his spine as he sat there, reaching for his cigarettes that were on the bedside table.

There was still sweat trickling down his broad back, testament to the ferocity of their love making. A single bead of perspiration ran down between Dani's breasts and she smiled as she leaned forward and kissed his broad shoulders.

"You shouldn't smoke in here," she breathed. "He'll smell it."

"Fuck him," Mike grunted. "It'll be gone by the morning."

He looked around, nodding approvingly.

"Nice place isn't it?" he murmured. "He must earn a fucking fortune."

"He writes books as well as being a psychiatrist you know," Dani explained.

"Clever cunt," Mike said, dismissively. "Is he famous then?"

Dani shook her head.

"I always wanted to be famous when I was a kid," Mike grinned.

"Famous for what?"

"I don't know. Just famous. Rich. Like a celebrity, you know. There has to be more to life than working twelve hours a day, six days a fucking week." He drew on his cigarette and got to his feet, walking around the room slowly, untroubled by his nakedness. Dani watched him, a smile spreading slowly across her face.

"Once we get the money we can start again," Mike mused, pulling open the door of the wardrobe he stood in front of.

"How much do you think it will take?" Dani wanted to know.

"Fifty grand? More."

"He's not going to give us that much. He knows it doesn't cost fifty thousand for an abortion. He's not stupid."

"Then tell him something else. Whatever it takes."

"He won't fall for it..."

"He will if we do this right," Mike snapped, interrupting her. "But you can't bottle this, Dani. Not now. He'll pay up, I'm telling you." Mike reached into the wardrobe and lifted out a shirt, holding it up against himself. "Not my colour is it?" he chuckled.

"He *is* twice your age," Dani reminded him.

"Yeah, I know," Mike sighed, replacing the shirt with the other clothes hanging there. "How the fuck do you do it? How do you sleep with him?"

"Don't start that again."

"I'm curious."

"Why? Are you worried he's a threat to your masculinity? Worried he's better than you?"

"Is he?"

"He has his moments."

Mike looked at her and grinned crookedly.

"Dirty bitch," he grunted.

"That's why you love me," Dani told him, also smiling.

Mike grinned.

"He was married, wasn't he?" he said, looking at more items in the wardrobe.

"For eighteen years."

"What happened?"

"He had a couple of affairs."

"Dirty bastard. You wouldn't think it to look at him, would you?"

"Never judge a book by its cover. The last girl he lived with was only nineteen."

"No way," said Mike, turning to look at her, a look of bewilderment on his face. He watched as Dani slid out of bed and knelt, reaching under the frame of the bed to pull something free. He walked around to join her and saw that she had pulled the cheap black suitcase into view. Mike watched as she flipped it open and dug inside. He could see clothes in there and then Dani produced a couple of photographs.

"That's her," she announced, holding up the pictures of Rhiannon Morton.

"Fuck, she's hot," Mike breathed, scanning the images before him. He reached into the case and pulled out several more of the photographs. "And these are her clothes?" He picked up a tiny pair of knickers, pressing them to his nose and sniffing loudly.

"You fucking pervert," Dani chuckled, punching him playfully.

"Why would he keep her clothes?" Mike wanted to know.

"Perhaps she just left them here when she left?"

"Why did she go?"

"I don't know. He never talks about her."

Mike pulled some more photographs from the case, scanning each one carefully.

"This is a different girl isn't it?" he murmured, pushing the picture towards Dani. She looked at it and nodded.

"The guy next door said her friends used to come round here sometimes," she said.

"The guy next door?"

"He's a bit nosey. I don't think he likes Jake."

"Jake probably got those girls to put on a show for him. I bet he's got the videos all over his computer." He laughed.

"Oh shut up," Dani sighed, shoving the pictures back into the case.

"I'm serious," Mike went on. "I bet he's got loads of videos of her and her mates on his computer. Where is it?" He got to his feet.

"What are you talking about?"

"Show me his computer," Mike said, his face impassive. "Show me where he works."

THIRTY-SIX

It was late when he got back to the hotel.

After midnight.

Jake Porter walked slowly through the foyer, nodding amiably at the night Porter and then at the uniformed receptionist who was busying herself behind the marble topped desk in the centre of the foyer.

He was relieved to find that he was the only one in the lift and he rode it to the fifth floor, fumbling in his pocket for his phone as he stepped out into the immaculately decorated area beyond the sliding doors. As he walked, he found Dani's number and pressed "call."

There was no answer.

Jake sighed, slid the key card into the electronic lock and waited for the green light to glow. When it did, he pushed the door open and walked in, trying Dani's number again.

Still no answer.

He dropped the phone onto the bed and turned irritably towards the mini bar, selecting a bottle of vodka. He emptied it into a glass and then topped it off with some lemonade, swallowing a large mouthful. Again, he tried her number.

Again, no answer.

Jake cursed under his breath and finished his drink then made his way into the bathroom where he turned on the shower. He tried Dani's number once more before he got beneath the soothing jets but there was still no response. Ten minutes later when he got out of the shower and walked back into the bedroom he tried again.

When there was no answer this time, Jake sucked in a deep breath and held it, trying to control his growing anger.

What the hell was she doing?

He put the phone on the bedside table and turned again to the mini-bar. As he poured himself another he switched on the TV, trying to ignore the phone but he couldn't stop glancing at it, willing it to ring. He flicked channels, moving past a political conversation, some stand-up comedian, a programme about the Vikings and the inevitable pointless celebrity garbage. Jake was just settling himself to watch a documentary about Venice when his phone finally rang.

He snatched it up without even checking the caller id.

"About time," he murmured. "Where the hell were you?"

The caller said they had been busy.

"Obviously," Jake grunted. "I left a message yesterday and you ignored that too."

The caller assured him they hadn't ignored it.

"I need to talk to you," Jake went on. "Tomorrow? About one? Where I said?"

The caller said that was okay.

"I'm sorry, I'm just a bit tired," Jake breathed. "It's been a long day."

There was a difficult silence then Jake terminated the call. He sat for a moment gazing at the phone then replaced it on the bedside table before wandering over to the mini-bar once more. He always had trouble sleeping in hotels and he figured that four or five vodka miniatures might help. It was an expensive insomnia cure, but Jake decided it was worth it.

He lay back on the bed, raised the TV volume and continued to drink.

It was another two hours before he fell asleep.

THIRTY-SEVEN

The only light in the room came from the monitor. A dull, cold light that illuminated Mike Quinn as he sat at Jake Porter's small desk. He was scanning the desktop items, looking for anything that stood out or caught his attention.

Beside him, now wearing just a long vest top, Dani watched impassively.

"We shouldn't be doing this," she breathed.

"Who's going to know?" Mike asked.

"It's not...right," Dani offered, hesitantly. "Anyway, he's not going to store dirty pictures or videos on his desktop, is he?"

"Of course he is but I bet he's got them in some hidden file or something," Mike suggested. "He's got some secret name on them that only he recognises."

"Is that how you keep yours then?"

Mike grinned. "Of course it is."

Dani shook her head and moved closer, also peering at the screen.

"I'll check his history," Mike said.

"We really shouldn't be doing this," Dani reminded him.

"You could be living with a paedo, I think we need to do this."

"He's not a paedophile. What guy doesn't like a younger girl?"

Mike raised his eyebrows and continued glancing at the files on the computer.

Dani turned and began scanning the titles of the books on one of the overstuffed shelves. She moved from those to the nearest cabinet, sliding open drawers and checking the contents. Envelopes of all sizes. Packets of printer paper. Cartridges.

Notebooks. All the paraphernalia of a home office.

And the pieces of A4 with scribbled writing on them.

Crude, scrawled words almost carved onto the paper.

Dani picked up two of them and realized there was something horribly familiar about them.

They were like the note she'd found on the door mat only a few days ago.

Same tone. Same venomous words.

She frowned and handed three of the single sheets to Mike.

"What are these?" he wanted to know.

"Jake's been getting them," she said, quietly. "Someone's been pushing them through the door."

"Maybe he is a paedo," Mike suggested. "Perhaps someone knows the truth. Maybe they're trying to frighten him."

"He's not a paedophile," Dani snapped. "It's just someone who doesn't like him that's doing it."

"Like who?"

"How the hell do I know?"

"It's either someone who doesn't like him or someone who knows him really well," Mike offered, returning his attention to the computer screen.

Dani merely shook her head, snatching the notes from him and slipping them back into the drawer she'd originally taken them from. As she did, she heard Mike draw in a sharp breath and turned to see what had elicited that reaction. He was sitting closer to the screen, leaning towards it now.

Dani moved towards him, intrigued by what he was looking at.

"Have a look at this," he urged, pointing to the screen. "It was in a file marked 'Special'."

Dani looked, her eyes widening.

"Jesus," she murmured under her breath.

THIRTY-EIGHT

There were four severed heads in the corner of the room, all in various stages of decomposition.

All had been smashed open like hard boiled eggs, the contents scooped out and disposed of so that the gaping craniums were revealed as empty.

In one of them maggots were writhing slowly.

As they were in the eye sockets and mouths of two of the other heads.

The stench was appalling.

A fetid, cloying aroma that clogged in the nostrils and was almost palpable when the room was entered. The weather had been unseasonably warm lately so the smell from the rotting appendages was even more acute.

As he walked slowly around the room, he paused occasionally to look at the heads, sometimes prodding them with one finger, watching the maggots' cascade from the orifices they had filled. They were like moving confetti. Twisting, writhing shapes that sometimes crawled across the dusty floor in search of more carrion on which to feed.

Sometimes he would pick one of them up and push it into his mouth before moving on.

But not this time. He stood looking at the heads for a moment longer and then made his way across the room towards the door.

As usual it was locked. There was no way out.

She always locked it behind her when she left. He would have to ask her why. Tell her to leave it open. He didn't like being kept prisoner like this. There was no need for it.

Not now.

He walked to the door and gripped the handle, surprised when it twisted in his grip.

She hadn't locked it.

He paused and gently pulled the door, hearing the hinges squeal in protesting. But all that mattered was that it opened. He stood at the threshold, peering out into the corridor beyond, allowing his eyes to become accustomed to the gloom. When he could see he took a couple of steps outside the room.

On both sides of him the walls rose towards the high ceiling. Walls cracked in places and occasionally discoloured by mould or damp. Years of neglect had caused the damage. It was as if the building was decaying as surely as the heads in the corner of the room behind him. He walked on, glancing up at the doors on either side of the corridor, wondering what lay behind them. He tried a couple of the handles and found they were locked.

The corridor stretched away before him and he moved slowly along it, finally tiring of his explorations, retreating into the room that he knew so well instead.

The woman would be arriving soon he thought.

She always came at night.

And outside, the sun was sinking, spilling dark red colour across the sky. Banks of cloud were gathering in the heavens, blocking out the glow. Soon it would be dark. He could see birds silhouetted against the clouds as they hurried to return to their nests.

In the overgrown grounds of the building, visible from the window where he stood, he could see something moving, disturbing the tall grass as it ventured towards the edifice.

As it emerged close to what had once been an ornamental fountain, he saw that it was a cat. A skinny looking tortoise shell animal that hopped up on the low wall surrounding the centre part of the fountain, licking its paws and glancing around, its eyes drawn to a couple of birds that had landed not too far away.

He watched it from the window as it ceased its ablutions and began creeping towards the birds, but they saw it and fluttered into the air leaving the cat to watch they go, watching them soar heavenward into the rapidly darkening sky.

The cat jumped back down into the long grass and disappeared once again.

The wind was growing stronger, bending the tall stalks of grass and large weeds almost vertical sometimes when a particularly powerful gust came.

He saw that all from his vantage point, watching silently.

Waiting.

She would be here soon. She had to come. She knew what would happen to her if she didn't.

THIRTY-NINE

The sound of the key in the lock woke her.

Dani was normally a heavy sleeper (especially if she took a sleeping pill which she often did) but the noise coming from the hallway alerted her.

She sat up quickly, realizing immediately what was happening. She shook Mike who was lying on his side facing away from her.

"Wake up," she hissed, pushing him.

He rolled onto his back and looked up at her, a smile spreading across his face.

"Not again?" he said, sleepily. "You're insatiable." He tried to grab her, but Dani pulled away.

"Get up," she snapped. "Jake's back."

Mike sat up rapidly, swinging himself out of bed, grabbing for his clothes and pulling his jeans on.

"You've got to hide?" Dani said, advancing towards the bedroom door, listening as the sounds from the hallway grew louder. She heard the front door open, heard Jake entering. "Get in there," she snapped, pointing to the wardrobe on the other side of the bed. "I'll get rid of him."

And now she heard footfalls on the stairs and realized that Jake was climbing slowly.

Mike snatched up the last of his clothes and eased himself inside the wardrobe, pressing himself against the back of the structure, trying to control his breathing. He too could hear the sound of approaching footsteps now and realized that Jake was close to the bedroom. There was a small crack where the wardrobe doors didn't close properly and through it, he could see Dani clambering back into bed.

Seconds later Jake Porter walked into the room.

Dani turned towards him, stretching as if she'd just woken up. She pretended to yawn, hoping the pretence would work.

Jake dropped his overnight bag beside the bed and crossed to her, snaking his arms around her.

Inside the wardrobe, Mike watched intently.

"Hey, you," Jake said, kissing Dani gently on the lips. "Sorry if I woke you."

"I wasn't expecting you until lunch time," she said, faking another yawn.

Jake sat down beside her on the bed.

"The care home called and said my mum had a slight fall," he said. "I thought I'd better come back and check on her."

"Oh God, it's not serious is it?"

"No, just a couple of bruises." He reached for his overnight bag and began taking clothes out.

"I'll do that for you later," Dani offered, glancing towards the wardrobe where she knew Mike was watching. "Why don't you go and make us some coffee as a sort of sorry for waking me up." She laughed convincingly enough.

"I'm sure there's another way I could apologise," Jake said, leaning forward to kiss her. He slid a hand along one of her slender thighs, but Dani moved back.

"Easy tiger," she chuckled. "Go and make me a coffee first."

Jake smiled and backed off nodding.

"I tried to call you last night, but you weren't answering," he said.

"I must have had it switched off," Dani explained. "I didn't feel too good. I had an early night."

"You okay now?"

"I'll be better when I've had a coffee," she told him, smiling.

"Right, I get the hint," Jake announced, getting to his feet, and turning towards the bedroom door. "Do you want anything to eat?"

"Some toast would be nice."

As she spoke, she glanced to one side and noticed that Mike's phone was still lying on the bedside table.

Dani swallowed hard and prayed that no one chose to ring him. She slid gently towards the offending device, trying to block it from Jake's view.

"Toast and jam," Dani said, her voice catching.

Jake raised a hand in acknowledgement and then made his way out of the room. Dani waited until she heard him descending the wooden steps then she jumped out of bed and ran across to the wardrobe, pulling it open, almost dragging Mike from inside.

She pulled him towards the window and opened it, motioning to the heavy wooden trellis that covered the wall beneath the window.

"You can climb down that," she whispered, pushing his phone into his hand.

"It'll never take my weight," he protested, also keeping his voice low.

"What else are you going to do? Walk out the front door?" Dani snapped.

She glanced anxiously towards the bedroom door and then pushed Mike again towards the open window.

He swung his leg through and got a foothold on the trellis, slowly easing himself out, clinging to the wood. Dani watched as he climbed down, cursing when one of the narrower trestles snapped under his foot but he clung on, gradually reaching the bottom. He looked up and then darted off across the garden, clambering effortlessly over the fence.

Dani let out a long sigh, feeling her heart slowing a little. She turned towards the bedroom door.

FORTY

When she walked into the kitchen, Jake was sipping at his coffee and glancing through the paper.

As Dani sat down opposite him, he pointed a finger towards a mug of coffee and some toast on a plate before her. She thanked him and began spreading butter on a piece.

Jake continued glancing at the paper, but he didn't speak. Dani chewed thoughtfully.

Did he know? Had he sensed something was wrong?

She sucked in a breath. He couldn't know. How could he possibly know that Mike had spent the night with her?

"So, your mum is okay then?" Dani offered.

"Just a slight fall, the home said," Jake informed her. "Even they said it was nothing to worry about."

"That's good." She chewed more toast. "So, when are you going to see her?"

"Are you trying to get rid of me?" Jake chuckled.

Dani shot him a glance.

Does he know?

"I'm just saying," she countered.

He's playing it cool, but he knows, doesn't he?

"Have you got anything planned for today?" he wanted to know.

"I might go back to bed."

"Want some company?" he said, smiling.

She returned the gesture.

"So, what happened last night?" Jake wanted to know.

"What do you mean?" Dani asked, chewing more slowly.

"I tried to ring you a few times but there was no answer."

"I told you, I didn't feel too good. I was probably in bed."

Yes, with Mike.

Jake nodded.

"How did you meetings go?" she asked, wanting to change the subject.

"Very productive. You should have come with me. It would have been fun."

"Maybe next time."

Again, Jake looked her up and down, his gaze lingering on her crossed legs. He smiled at her.

"What?" she wanted to know.

"I'm just looking. That's okay isn't it?"

She shook her head and ate more toast.

"Your neighbour's a bit of a weirdo, isn't he?" she offered, again anxious to change the subject. "The guy there." She jabbed a finger in the direction of Ted Brady's house.

"Why were you talking to *him*?"

"I was out in the garden, he started chatting."

"About what?"

"Nothing interesting. He just saw me out there and came out."

"If he tries it again just come back inside."

"Yes *dad*," Dani chuckled.

Jake glared at her for a second.

"He's a dickhead," he snapped.

"He talks very highly of you too," Dani said, smiling. "What's the problem between you two?"

"He's nosey. Stay away from him."

"Is that what you told your last girlfriend?"

Jake fixed her in an unblinking stare.

"What are you talking about?" he asked, his voice low.

Dani shuffled uncomfortably on her seat.

"Just saying," she told him.

"Did he mention her then?"

Dani shook her head.

"He needs to mind his own fucking business," Jake rasped, reaching for a piece of toast. "By the way, have you got a new phone? I thought I saw one on the bedside table earlier."

He knows. He definitely knows.

Dani shook her head, trying to give herself time to think.

"No, it belongs to a friend of mine," she lied. "I said I could get it fixed for her. There's something wrong with the reception or something."

Jake chewed his toast slowly, his eyes still on Dani.

"I didn't think you'd be interested," she went on. "You hate technology."

Jake smiled.

"That's true," he conceded. "I just wondered. I didn't think it was a secret." His smile broadened. "I don't like secrets."

FORTY-ONE

Margaret Porter broke wind loudly.

Jake sighed and continued gazing out of the window, disgusted by the sound.

"So, you're sure you're okay?" he asked at last, turning to look at her as she dug her fork into the food on her plate.

However, several pieces of it fell from the utensil and dropped onto her blouse. She didn't bother to remove it but just continued eating.

"Be careful what you're doing," Jake said, irritably, watching as some of the cottage pie slid down her top.

Margaret broke wind again by way of an answer.

"Do you think I can't hear that?" Jake snapped.

She continued pushing food into her mouth, holding the fork in her right hand, chasing some portions around the plate.

"Use your knife as well," Jake told her. "You're not American. Use your knife *and* fork."

She looked blankly at him then belched.

He shook his head and sighed again.

"I've got to go, mum," he said. "I've got patients to see."

"What?" she said, pieces of food still in her mouth.

"I've got to go," he repeated.

She suddenly reached for a piece of tissue and spat some food into it, wrapping it up like a small parcel.

"That is disgusting," Jake hissed.

"What did you say?" Margaret said.

"It doesn't matter. Just get those hearing aids fixed, will you?"

"They're fine."

"No they're not. You're stone deaf."

He watched as she knocked a piece of food onto the floor but immediately reached down, picked it up with her fingers and pushed it into her mouth.

"That is really disgusting," Jake snapped. "What are you doing? And you should change that blouse, it's filthy."

He'd barely finished speaking when Margaret began pulling at the buttons of the blouse.

"Not while I'm here," he told her, angrily. "Stop it. I'm your son, that's not right."

"It doesn't matter."

"Yes it does. Don't do that in front of me."

"Oh shut up."

"And don't tell me to shut up."

"And stop shouting."

"I have to shout; you can't hear me."

"I can hear if you speak up. You've got a soft voice."

Jake rolled his eyes.

"You don't have much patience with me, do you?" Margaret said.

"I'm going," he told her, flatly. "You finish your lunch."

She broke wind loudly.

Jake hesitated beside the door then pulled it open.

"See you soon," he said.

"Pardon?" Margaret grunted.

"Never mind," Jake sighed, and he walked out, closing the door behind him. Glad to be away.

For a moment he stood with his back to the closed door then he walked briskly out, heading towards his car. When he slid behind the wheel he sat there in silence for a moment, finally reaching for his phone.

There was no answer from the number he rang so he started the engine and pulled out into traffic.

By the time he reached his office there was still no answer.

Jake glared at the phone momentarily, as if he blamed the device personally for not being able to connect him with the person he wanted to speak to but then he hauled himself out of the car and headed into the building.

Detective Inspector Ray Vincent was sitting in reception waiting for him when he walked in.

Jake extended a hand in greeting and the policeman shook it.

"I would have called," Vincent announced.

"Come through to the office," Jake told him, turning towards Sheree Fowler. The receptionist looked expectantly at him. "Can you hold all my calls, please?"

Sheree nodded, watching as the two men disappeared inside Jake's office.

"What can I do for you?" Jake asked.

"It's Lauren Davison," Vincent told him. "She was found dead in her cell two hours ago."

FORTY-TWO

The tall youth who gently bumped into the back of the chair apologised and held up a hand in supplication.

Jake told him it was no problem and returned his attention to his phone, glancing at the array of photographs displayed there but careful not to allow any prying eyes to see them.

They weren't for sharing.

He finally let out a long sigh and put the phone down, glancing instead out of the window of the Starbucks where he sat. It was a smaller branch than the one where Dani worked, placed in the centre of the shopping mall, sandwiched between a book shop and a place that sold scented candles and crystals.

Jake looked at his watch and then peered out of the window again wondering where the hell his companion had got to.

When Claire Conlan finally walked in, she weaved her way past the other tables and customers and flopped wearily into the seat opposite him.

"I hope this is important," she said, exhaling deeply. "I've only got an hour for lunch. How come you're not working?"

"I am," he corrected her. "I only had a couple of consultations this morning and I've got business at the hospital later."

"What is it?"

"I can't say."

Claire raised her eyebrows.

Jake pushed a mug of coffee towards her and smiled.

"I got you a de-caff latte," he explained.

Claire turned her nose up.

"De-caff's no good," she sneered. "I need that caffeine boost."

"Well drink it anyway," Jake told her.

"You're not ill, are you?" Claire wanted to know. "You didn't get me here to tell me you're dying or something like that?"

Jake shook his head.

"Would it bother you if I was?" he asked.

"Of course, it would. Just because we're divorced doesn't mean I don't care what happens to you. You said you were due at the hospital later so..."

"I'm not ill. Not that I know of." He smiled, cutting her short.

"So, what's so important?"

Jake reached into his pocket and pulled out some pieces of paper that he laid in front of Claire. She picked up the first of them and scanned it, her brow furrowing. He heard her suck in a breath as she read another of the hastily scrawled missives. She read another then put them back on the tabletop, moving back from the letters as if they were dangerous to her.

"Where did you get those?" she wanted to know.

"They were pushed through my door. I wondered if you knew anything about them."

Claire shook her head.

"I've got better things to do with my time and my life than send you abusive notes about your love life," she said.

"Like you had better things to do than throw a stone through my window?"

"That was just after we broke up. I was angry."

"You're *always* angry, Claire. It's your default setting."

"Do you blame me? You were the one who broke up our marriage. You were the one who cheated. I had a right to be angry."

"I didn't ask you here to go over all that again."

"We never went over it. We never discussed it."

"And I'm not going to do it now."

"You just wanted to know if I've been sending you abusive notes?"

"I thought it was worth asking."

"Am I the only suspect or will you be interrogating others during the course of your investigation?"

"If you sent them just tell me the truth."

"Don't flatter yourself. You don't figure in my thoughts that much any more."

"What about your boyfriend? Did he send them?"

"He's even less interested in you than I am."

"He didn't like you speaking to me though, did he? What's he afraid of? That you're going to want me back?"

Claire eyed him across the table for a moment then shook her head gently.

"You are a pompous bastard sometimes," she said under her

breath. "Why would I want you back? So, you could put me through what you put me through before? No thanks. Anyway, you wouldn't want me now, would you? Not after your...young girls. I'm a bit of an old crock, aren't I?" She got to her feet. "Good luck with your investigations. I hope you find who sent those." She jabbed the notes with her index finger.

"Sorry," Jake murmured. "I had to know."

"So, you're sorry for accusing me but not sorry for breaking up our marriage. Ruining my life and Lucy's?"

She turned and walked out.

Jake watched her go.

FORTY-THREE

Dani stretched on the sofa then picked up her iPad again and glanced at what she'd already done earlier in the day.

There were two or three sketches. A large black crow breaking out of a cage, the bars twisted and bent. A coffin with a girl laying on top of it looking raptly into a mirror, the glass of which was cracked, distorting her image. And a large clawed and purple hand holding a heart that looked as if it had just been ripped from a chest and was still dripping blood.

Dani ran appraising eyes over her work and decided it was time for a coffee.

She was about to get up when she heard the doorbell sound.

Dani hesitated for a moment, wondering who was calling during the early part of the afternoon. For a second, she thought about ignoring it but when the bell was pressed once again, she swung herself off the sofa and padded through into the hall to answer it.

She was surprised to see the person standing on the doorstep.

Ted Brady nodded affably and looked her up and down.

"Not disturbing you, am I?" he said, smiling.

Dani shook her head.

"Could I just come inside for a minute?" Brady went on, stepping across the threshold.

Dani, almost in spite of herself, stepped back and allowed him into the hallway.

However, he didn't remain there but headed for the sitting room, Dani trailing in his wake. He stood by the door, glancing around, taking in every detail of the room.

"Very nice," he murmured.

"Would you like to sit down?" Dani wanted to know, settling herself on the far end of the sofa, watching as Brady took the other end, glancing down at her iPad, inspecting the sketch that was on show.

"You a bit of an artist then?" he enquired.

"It's a hobby."

"Do you sell any?"

"Just enough to keep me working at Starbucks," Dani said, smiling. "Look, Jake's not here. I don't know when he's getting back..."

"I didn't come to see him," Brady cut across her. "I came to talk to you." He glanced down at the iPad again. "You do any self-portraits or anything like that?"

"I couldn't stand to look at myself long enough for that," Dani told him.

"Any nudes?" He grinned crookedly.

She shook her head, beginning to feel a little uncomfortable. Speaking to him outside had been a different matter. She'd had the option of walking away. Here she didn't. Dani pulled her knees up to her chest, her back pressed against one arm of the sofa.

Brady looked down, his gaze settling on her bare feet.

"Very nice," he breathed. "You've got really pretty feet. It looks like you take care of them. Nails nicely trimmed and no varnish. I like that. No blemishes. Nice toes. They look really soft and smooth. Lovely."

Dani swallowed hard and tried to move back further on the sofa, finally swinging her legs off the cushions. She suddenly wanted this man out of the house. She wanted to be away from him. Brady wasn't slow to see her reaction.

"Sorry," he said, smiling. "I've got a thing about sexy feet. That's all. Some guys are leg men, some boob men. I love pretty feet." He winked at her then he pointed at her face or, more particularly, at the small silver nose ring she wore.

"Did that hurt?" he wanted to know.

Dani shook her head.

"And you've got tattoos as well," Brady went on, indicating the designs on both her arms. "Those must have hurt."

"You get used to it after a while," Dani explained.

"You like a bit of pain, do you?" He grinned.

"What did you say you wanted?" Dani asked, wanting to change the subject.

Porter reached for his phone and held it up in front of her so she could see the screen.

"I wondered if you could explain what's going on here," Brady told her, gazing at her as she watched the video he'd set in motion.

Dani recognised it instantly as she watched Mike Quinn

clambering from the bedroom window, trying to get a foothold on the wooden trellis, climbing down until he reached the ground and then bolting away, hauling himself over the fence.

She swallowed hard.

"You took that?" she challenged.

Brady smiled, lowering the phone. "I had a good view from my bedroom window," he told her. "Who is he? Because he's certainly not your boyfriend, is he? Well, not the boyfriend who's house you're living in." He drew in a deep breath. "The guy in the video is about your age, isn't he? Much younger than Jake. I bet the guy in that video gives it to you like you really want it doesn't he?"

"Will you leave please?" Dani asked, her voice catching.

"Don't be like that," Brady countered. "I'm just curious. What's a young guy doing climbing out of your boyfriend's bedroom window just after your boyfriend gets home?"

"Get out," snapped Dani.

"Go on, tell me. It'll be our little secret."

Dani sat up, the hairs on the back of her neck rising.

"So, you were sitting in your bedroom spying on this house, were you?" she rasped. "That's how you got that video?"

"I was minding my own business, looking out into my garden when I saw this guy climbing out of your boyfriend's house. I thought he might be a burglar escaping so I thought I'd film him; in case it helped the police." He smiled, broadly. "He looked as if he was in a right hurry."

"If you don't get out, I'll call the police," Dani assured him.

"And tell them what? I'm not doing anything wrong. I just came round to show this video. I was just trying to help."

"Yeah, right," she sneered.

She could feel her heart beating more rapidly now. She was angry with this man. Intimidated by him but disgusted by him too, aware that his gaze was constantly straying to her feet and legs.

Fucking weirdo.

But she didn't want to provoke him. After all, he was the one in the position of strength here. As long as he had that video in his possession, he held all the cards. Dani sucked in a deep breath, clenching her fists momentarily as she eyed Brady once more.

He held up the phone and set the video running once again, smiling as they both looked at the screen.

"He's a well-built lad, isn't he?" Brady murmured. "Big. Is he big down there too? I bet he is. I bet you love it big, don't you?"

Dani got to her feet and walked to the door.

"You need to get out," she snapped, trying to ensure there was an edge to her voice.

"All right, all right," Brady chuckled. "No need to be rude. I was just trying to help. Just keeping you in the loop as it were. I thought you had a right to know I'd seen what happened. You can't fool me like you fool your boyfriend you know." He winked at her and the gesture repulsed her.

She held the door wider.

"Please go," she said through gritted teeth.

"I bet Jake thinks you're a real catch, doesn't he?" Brady breathed. "Sexy young girl who'll do whatever he wants. Dirty bastard. You're young enough to be his daughter." He raised his eyebrows. "And now this guy turns up too. Getting a bit complicated isn't it?" Again, he smiled.

"Tell me what you want," Dani insisted.

"I haven't decided yet," Brady informed her, getting to his feet. He walked across to where she was standing, pushing his face towards her. "Why? What are you offering?" He looked her up and down then laughed. Dani shot him a furious glance, stepping back as he brushed past her, heading for the front door.

"I'll keep this video," he added. "Just in case I need it." He smiled and reached for the front door handle, pulling it open. "I wish I had a video of what went on before he climbed out of the window. I bet that was really worth watching. Maybe next time."

He laughed and walked out, closing the door behind him.

Dani crossed to the window, watching Brady as he made his way back to his own place.

It was only a second later that she reached for her phone, her hand still trembling.

FORTY-FOUR

Jake Porter shivered involuntarily.

It was much cooler in the basement of the hospital, a marked contrast to what felt like the perpetually raised temperatures on ground level and above. As he walked along the corridor towards the morgue the temperature seemed to drop even further. Jake could hear his footsteps echoing in the high-ceilinged walkway and the noise seemed intrusive. He slowed his pace slightly as he reached the reception area, relieved to find that Detective Inspector Ray Vincent was waiting for him there.

Vincent had told him there was no need for his presence, but Jake had waved away the suggestion with a slightly shaking hand and insisted on helping if he could, although even he wasn't sure how he could contribute.

The two men shook hands and Vincent told him they had to wait for the coroner before they could view the body of Lauren Davison.

There were two doors leading off from the reception area, one leading into the mortuary itself and the other into a small vestibule where identification could be performed by family members or those unfortunate enough to be chosen to perform such an unthinkable task. It was from the first doorway that the coroner emerged. He was a tall, grey haired man with a neatly trimmed beard and huge eyebrows. He shook hands with Vincent and then with Jake who followed him through two doors to a small area just outside the morgue.

Jake pulled on the green overall that was handed to him although that simple act made him even more nervous than he had been before. He tried to hide his growing apprehension, but it was becoming increasingly difficult.

When the coroner led them through into the morgue itself, Jake felt a bead of perspiration pop onto his forehead, despite the chill in the air. What also struck him was how bright it was inside the huge room. The lights were dazzling. Gleaming white fluorescents that made him wince such was the intensity of their cold glare. They seemed to reflect off the white tiled floor and the array of white and steel storage cabinets that made up one wall. A storehouse for sightless eyes, Jake thought, glancing at the large doors.

There were three stainless steel topped work benches, two of them empty to reveal the scrubbed metal.

The third was occupied by a body covered with a thin, white nylon sheet.

As he walked nearer to it, Jake could make out the shape and outline of the figure beneath and, as he moved to the head of the slab, he noticed dark hair protruding from beneath the sheet.

He tried to steady his breathing.

"Are you okay?" Vincent whispered to him, leaning close to his ear. Jake nodded.

"The preliminary autopsy was completed about four hours ago," the coroner said, reaching for one corner of the sheet. When he pulled it back, Jake was relieved that he only lowered it far enough to expose the face and shoulders of Lauren Davison.

"And?" Vincent murmured.

"I still can't believe it," the coroner said, quietly.

"How did she die?" Jake asked. "And keep it simple." He smiled awkwardly.

The coroner returned the smile and nodded.

"Massive blood loss," he announced. "Internal bleeding."

"How did it happen?" Vincent wanted to know.

"If I didn't know better, I'd put it down to an ectopic pregnancy," the coroner said. "But the extent of the damage to her fallopian tubes make it look as if the pregnancy was at least three months advanced which is impossible."

"A foetus wouldn't remain in the fallopian tubes for that long would it?" Jake offered.

"Exactly," the coroner added. "But there's more than that. She's exhibiting the signs of a fallopian rupture, but she wasn't even pregnant."

Vincent and Jake both looked fixedly at the coroner.

"I found no evidence at all that she was pregnant," the other man said. "No foetus. Nothing."

***

Jake hadn't felt right since he first arrived at the hospital and what he'd heard inside the morgue hadn't helped.

As he sat in his car, his head still spinning slightly, he sucked in a deep breath, trying to process the information he'd heard earlier.

He was still considering the seemingly impossible catalogue of facts when his phone vibrated. Jake reached for it, reading the message before him.

GOT OPTICIAN APPOINTMENT TOMORROW AT 10. COULD YOU
TAKE ME?

The message was from his daughter.

Jake sighed, wishing that he could take her, but he knew that was impossible and sadly he sent a message back;

I CAN'T TOMORROW. SORRY.

He sighed as he sent the message.

CAN DO ANOTHER DAY.

He added the next message as quickly as he could and waited.

One came back and Jake let out a deep breath as he read it.

FORGET IT.

And that was it.

Nothing more.

Jake continued to stare helplessly at the phone.

FORTY-FIVE

Jake brought the car to a halt outside his house and switched off the engine, sitting with his head bowed for a moment. He finally sucked in a deep breath and swung himself out of the car, retrieving his briefcase from the back seat.

As he walked towards his short driveway, he realized that Dani's car wasn't parked outside and, briefly, he wondered where she might be. She hadn't told him she was going out.

She doesn't have to tell you everything you know.

Jake dug in his pocket for his front door key, turning slightly when he heard a low swishing sound.

He turned to see that Ted Brady was sweeping his front path with a brush.

"Hard day?" Brady said.

Annoyed that he hadn't made it into the house without avoiding his neighbour, Jake merely nodded, still heading towards his front door.

"Mind you," Brady went on. "The work you do isn't really hard is it? Not like normal people do. Not like sitting behind a till at Sainsbury's for twelve hours or sorting stuff in a warehouse somewhere."

"I'd better get in," Jake told him.

"You're lucky, aren't you?" Brady went on. "Good job. Nice house. Sexy young girlfriend."

"You've got a nice house too," Jake sighed, already tired of the conversation.

"But I have to get by on my disability pensions. I haven't got money to burn like you have. Money to spend on some young hottie." He laughed.

"I really haven't got time for this," Jake told him.

"*Make* time."

There was a darker tone to Brady's words now that hadn't been there before, and Jake slowed his pace and looked at him.

"Did you have something to say to me?" the psychiatrist asked.

"Apart from reminding me of what a privileged lifestyle I have?"

If Brady heard the sarcasm in Jake's words, he ignored it.

"I'm just saying," he continued. "You're a lucky man. Getting paid shit loads for doing next to nothing."

"I did have to study for my psychiatric qualifications. I didn't get them from a cereal box."

"Whatever. Coming home to a nice, sexy young girlfriend. You must love it."

"I really must go in." Jake insisted.

"She's not in," Brady told him. "She went out a couple of hours ago."

"I gathered that when I noticed her car was gone."

"She looked really good. Tight black jeans, black vest top. Very nice. Do you know where she was going?"

"She doesn't have to report to me, you know."

"Cool. As long as you know where she is. It's all about trust isn't it? As long as you know what she's up to."

He smiled and continued brushing the path.

"What do you mean?" Jake snapped.

"Just saying," Brady mused. "She's a sexy young woman."

"So you *keep* saying," Jake hissed.

"She might not be satisfied with just what *you've* got to give her," Brady leered.

"It's nothing to do with you, is it?"

"It is when you flaunt your little girlfriends around here. It's not right. People don't like to see things like that. An old guy like you with some young girl. It's sick. That last one was even younger, wasn't she?"

"You've obviously got a lot to do," Jake snapped, turning away. "I'll leave you to it."

"How old was that last one? Eighteen? Nineteen? You certainly know how to pull them. Amazing what a bit of cash can do."

"If you spent more time living your own life instead of sticking your nose into mine then you might be happier."

"You lot are all the same. Rich bastards. It's like a little club."

"Not that it's any of your business but I probably don't earn as much as you think and what I earn I work hard for."

"Yeah, right." The contempt in Brady's voice was almost palpable. "Money for old rope. And then you use that money to impress these young girls and get them to sleep with you."

"You're an idiot."

"They only want your money; they don't want you. They don't care about you."

Jake turned on his heel.

"Why did she leave you? Couldn't you keep up with her? Or didn't you buy her enough to keep her happy? I saw her. I saw her and her little friends out in your garden. That little blonde you had. That little eighteen-year-old. And now this one. Another blonde. A bit older but still young enough to be your daughter. And I bet you trust her, don't you?" Brady laughed and it was a dry, hollow sound. "Where did that last little blonde go? Did she run out on you? You should be ashamed."

"Fuck you," hissed Jake and finally he did walk away, pushing the key into the front door, letting himself in and allowing himself to be swallowed by the welcoming silence inside the house.

Outside, Ted Brady glared at the door, his hands clamped tightly on the broom handle.

"Cunt," he snarled.

FORTY-SIX

Mike Quinn sat silently for a moment, the veins on his temple bulging, his jaw set in hard lines.

More than once he looked as if he was about to speak but then he seemed to think better of it. It was as if he wasn't going to utter a word until he knew exactly how he wanted to express himself, but Dani knew better than that. Now, as she watched him, she could see the thoughts flickering behind his eyes. She could almost feel the tension building inside him.

"He won't show anyone," he finally hissed. "He's bluffing."

"He's got the video of you climbing out of Jake's bedroom window," she protested. "He *showed* it to me."

"Just because he showed you doesn't mean he'll show it to Jake." Mike shook his head. "He's got nothing. Me climbing out of a window. Big fucking deal."

"Climbing out of Jake's bedroom window. How many times do I have to say it. If Jake sees that he'll throw me out."

"No he won't. He's not that stupid."

They sat in silence for a moment, both of them occasionally glancing out of the car windows, watching people walking past. Everyone passing, it seemed to Dani, was smiling. Perhaps, she mused, they all had better lives. Something to smile about. She closed her eyes for a second and the moment passed.

"We should just concentrate on getting the money out of Jake," Mike said, softly. "Fuck that dickhead and his video."

"There won't *be* any money if he shows that video to Jake," Dani snapped. "There won't be *anything*."

"Can't you talk to him? See what he wants?"

"It's pretty obvious what he wants, Mike. He's blackmailing us."

"Blackmailing *you*."

"I'm not the one on the video, am I? He's blackmailing *both* of us." She sat back, letting out a long and laboured breath. "You've got to love the irony I suppose."

Mike merely shook his head.

"It isn't money he wants is it?" he breathed.

"What do you mean?" Dani enquired.

"He knows you're not loaded, what's the point in him trying to blackmail you for money?"

She looked at him quizzically.

"What are you saying?" she asked.

Mike let out a long almost painful breath.

"I don't fucking know," he sighed. "You'll have to talk to the guy. See what he wants. See what we've got to do to stop him showing that video to Jake. We've got to keep him quiet."

Dani considered his words, sitting back in her seat. She gripped the steering wheel tightly for a moment then banged it with one fist.

They sat in silence for a moment then Mike spoke again.

"How old is he?" he wanted to know. "This neighbour."

"Late forties."

Mike nodded.

"And he lives alone?" he added.

Dani nodded this time.

Again, the silence descended.

FORTY-SEVEN

After she dropped Mike back at the garage where he worked, Dani drove aimlessly for about thirty minutes.

She didn't know where she was going, she just drove, hoping that the apparently pointless journey would clear her head and enable her to focus more clearly.

As she drove the image of Ted Brady kept seeping into her mind.

Brady standing holding the mobile phone.

The video of Mike climbing out of the window running incessantly on the small screen.

Brady smiling triumphantly at her.

Licking his lips.

She pulled over, jammed on the brakes, and sat silently for a moment, gazing out at the overcast sky, watching as the first tiny droplets of rain spattered the windscreen. When she finally drove on, she was no clearer in her thoughts, no more certain of what her course of action should be, but she was now sure at least of where she was heading.

Dani stopped the car across the street from the house she'd called home for so many years, turned off the engine and set off towards the front door. The street was deserted apart from an older man who was busily washing down two of his wheelie bins. He glanced in her direction as she headed up the short path towards the front door but then seemed more concerned with his task.

Dani fumbled in her purse for her front door key but, before she could find it, the door swung open.

"Hi, Dad," she said, looking up.

"Are you okay?" Martin Grant asked, and Dani thought how tired he looked.

"I just wanted to pick up some more of my things," she explained. "I didn't think anyone would be here at this time of the day."

Martin stepped back and ushered her in.

"Is mum here?" Dani wanted to know.

He shook his head.

Dani stepped across the threshold a little more enthusiastically than she might have had the answer been in the affirmative.

"I was just passing," she said. "I thought I'd pop in."

"Mum will be sorry she missed you. She's gone shopping."

"I don't think she'll be *that* sorry," Dani said, forcing a smile.

"It's not the same without you here," Martin told her.

"I had to move out some time, dad."

"Do you want a cup of tea while you're here?"

"No. I can't stay long. Like I said, I just wanted to pick up a couple of things."

Martin nodded and they faced each other in silence for a moment then the older man spoke quietly.

"Is he treating you well?"

Dani nodded.

"He'd better be," Martin offered. "Or he'll have me to answer to."

They both smiled then Dani headed towards the stairs.

"I'd better get what I came for," she continued.

She was halfway up the steps when she heard his voice again.

"If you want to come back any time you know you can," he told her, his words hanging in the still air. "This will always be your home. No matter what happens."

Dani nodded but didn't turn to look at him.

"It's not the same without you, you know," he said.

"It's quieter you mean?"

"Your mum *does* miss you."

"Oh, come on, dad, we were always at each other's throats. You know that."

"That doesn't take away from how much she loved you."

Another silence descended, finally broken by Martin.

"Your mum says he's a lot older than you, this new man," he murmured.

"Age is just a number isn't it?" she mused.

"He'd better look after you."

"Dad, it's the twenty-first century. I can look after myself."

She hesitated a moment longer on the stairs then walked up the remaining steps, crossing the landing to her bedroom.

As she walked in, she felt a sudden surge of emotion sweep over her.

Sadness? Relief?

It had only been a short time since she moved out and yet there was something that made her feel as if she hadn't set foot inside this room for an age. It felt strangely alien to her. A place that had always been a sanctuary suddenly seemed unwelcoming. She sat down on the edge of the bed for a moment, looking around at the interior of the room. At the bare walls (she had even taken some of her posters and photographs with her) and the furniture, the drawers all emptied of clothes and belongings when she made her exodus. She crossed to the wardrobe and opened it, scanning the items she'd left hanging there. Mostly older garments she never wore anymore. She ran her fingers over the clothes and shook her head.

In one of the drawers, she found some sketchbooks, all full of drawings and illustrations she'd done over the years. She decided to take those with her, and she pushed the drawer shut again, sighing as she did so.

When she returned to the ground floor of the house, she could see that her father was now seated on the sofa in the sitting room.

Dani poked her head around the door.

"I'm going now, dad," she announced.

Martin got to his feet and, as he did, she saw him wince slightly.

"Are you okay?" she asked, frowning.

"Just my back playing up, you know I get trouble with it sometimes," he told her.

"Have you seen the doctor?"

"No need. It'll pass."

"Dad..."

Martin smiled and gently touched her cheek.

"Oh, shut up, stop worrying about me," he said, dismissively. "I'm fine. Are you sure you're not going to stay and say hello to your mum?"

Dani shook her head.

"I'd better go," she said.

They walked to the door together and then she hugged him tightly, unaccountably emotional as she stepped away from him and headed down the path towards her car.

Martin watched her as she climbed into the vehicle, waving as she drove away.

He stood there for a long time. Even when the car had disappeared around a corner he was still standing in the doorway.

FORTY-EIGHT

Jake Porter hurried into the hospital reception, glancing in first one direction then the other.

He was trying to control his breathing as he walked through the crowded area, avoiding patients who were stretching their legs or visitors coming and going within the huge building.

The hospital was a monolithic structure that had been built in the early seventies and had been cutting edge then but now looked as if it needed a good coat of paint. Jake walked across to the reception desk where a large woman with her grey hair in a bun was speaking on the phone while tapping away at the keyboard in front of her. Despite her tasks she still managed to smile at him as he leaned over the desk. She raised one finger to her ear, indicating to Jake that she was listening to someone and, as soon as they'd finished, she lowered the finger and smiled even more broadly at him.

"Hello," he said. "I'm looking for Mrs Margaret Porter. She's my mother. The lady on the main reception told me to come here."

The woman with the bun glanced at her screen, her fingers flying across the keyboard.

"She's in room eight," she explained, waving her hands around as if they were semaphore flags. "Down that corridor and it's the last room on the left."

Jake nodded by way of thanks then set off in the direction the woman had indicated.

He passed rows of curtained off areas, occasionally glancing in to see what was happening behind the diaphanous partitions. He saw a man in his fifties being hooked up to an ECG machine. A woman in her thirties groaning as a doctor examined her leg.

Just another day in a busy hospital, he thought.

The door of room eight was closed when he arrived and Jake pressed his face to the narrow window, peering inside to see his mother laying motionless on the gurney inside.

He tapped gently on the door and then walked in.

"Mum," he murmured. "Mum. It's me."

She didn't stir and, for one horrible moment, Jake wondered if she was dead.

He crossed to her and looked down at her thinking how pale and how old she looked.

Her skin looked like wax, thin flesh stretched so tightly over bone it looked as if it might tear and reveal the wasted muscles beneath.

"Mum," he whispered again.

Still, she didn't move, and Jake realized that she wasn't wearing her hearing aids.

He could have whispered all day and night and she wouldn't have heard him.

"Mum," he said more forcefully.

She turned to look at him but there was only blank incomprehension in her rheumy eyes.

"Fred?" she murmured.

"No mum, it's not dad, it's me, Jake," he told her.

"Where's Fred?" she wanted to know.

"Dad's not here."

"He said he'd come and see me."

Jake exhaled wearily, feeling angry with himself for feeling that way. She couldn't help it if she was confused, he told himself. Even so, his feelings of annoyance didn't subside immediately.

The door opened and a nurse walked in, looking briefly at Jake and then at Margaret who had now closed her eyes again and was laying motionless once more.

"I'm her son," Jake explained before the nurse had time to ask. "Is she okay?"

"She had a fall," the nurse told him. "Nothing serious but the care home thought she should be checked over. She cut her arm when she fell but that's been dressed."

Jake nodded.

"What made her fall?" he wanted to know.

"She's just unsteady on her feet. Not surprising at her age. All the tests have been clear though. She's a tough one. The doctor just wants to do an E.C.G and then she can go home tomorrow morning."

"An E.C.G. Is something wrong with her heart?"

"It's routine at her age. We just want to make sure everything is clear before we discharge her."

Jake nodded again.

"The doctor is coming in soon if you'd like to have a word with him," the nurse went on.

"No, that's all right. There's nothing I want to ask him."

The nurse looked a little surprised.

"I might as well go," Jake added. "There's nothing more I can do is there?"

"You can sit with her if you want to."

Again, he shook his head, glancing down at his mother whose eyes were firmly closed.

No point in staying.

"She knows your here you know," the nurse insisted. "Even if she's asleep."

Jake doubted that.

He slipped out.

FORTY-NINE

The house was silent when Dani walked in.

She wondered where Jake was but a quick wander around the rooms on the ground floor revealed that he wasn't in. At the office she pondered. She wandered back into the kitchen, got herself a glass of water and then walked slowly upstairs to the bedroom carrying the small holdall she'd brought from her home earlier.

Inside the bedroom she took out the various items she'd collected, put them away with her other belongings and then decided to stow the holdall beneath the bed.

She dropped to her knees, pushing it under the bed.

As she did something caught her eye.

It was a silver hoop earring.

Dani held it up, inspecting it more closely. It certainly wasn't one of hers and she didn't remember seeing anything like it in the house before. She looked again, her brow furrowing. The cheap black plastic case that had been under the bed was also gone.

She exhaled deeply wondering why Jake had moved it but more concerned with the earring.

Where the hell had it come from?

She slipped it into the pocket of her jeans and stood up, walking out of the bedroom and across the landing towards the door of Jake's office. Almost out of habit she knocked lightly before poking her head inside the room.

She hesitated a moment then stepped across the threshold, crossing to the desk. Dani sat down, glancing at the blank computer screen. She sat there motionless for a time, her gaze flitting over the items on the top of the polished wood. Notebooks. Pads. Pens.

Dani looked down at the desk drawers and, almost despite herself, she pulled the bottom one open and checked the contents.

Printer paper. Envelopes.

She felt slightly awkward as she slid each of the drawers open, realizing that she had no right to be checking up on him and sifting through the contents of the desk, but she continued.

What do you think you're going to find?

There were more envelopes in another drawer. Paper clips. A stapler.

A packet of photos.

Dani looked at it as if she'd just discovered some ancient artefact. A yellow and black folder stuffed with pictures that had been developed at a chemist's years before. To her it was like looking at an antique. She smiled thinly then flipped the container open, gazing at the pictures within.

They looked innocuous. Holiday snaps by the look of it. Taken at some English seaside resort. A fun fair. The beach front. The pier. She squinted more closely at one of the snaps that showed the pier entrance. Welcome to South Walmsley Pier the sign above it proclaimed. Dani had never heard of it.

Where the hell was South Walmsley?

As she flicked through more of them, she found more and more shots of these almost cliched sights. It was only as she had almost tired of gazing at the old snaps that she saw some figures in the ones remaining.

A woman in her thirties holding a baby.

The same woman sitting on the sea front with the baby in a push chair. More of the same woman holding the child up as she paddled happily in the sea.

Dani wondered who the woman was, who had taken the photos. She looked through more of them, trying to find some distinguishing features on either the people in the shots or of the landscape itself. She spread about a dozen of the pictures out on the desk top, peering more closely at each one. From the way the woman was dressed and the attire of the people in the background she could tell that these were not recent pictures.

There were more shots taken in a garden somewhere. A large garden that was surrounded on three sides by a high privet hedge. There were well kept flower beds too and a small pond that was surrounded by a waist high wooden fence. Two weeping willow trees stood near to the pond, their branches trailing close to the shimmering surface. In some of the other shots a small child was standing close to the fence surrounding the pond.

The same child as the one in the other pictures? Perhaps a few years older?

Dani compared pictures of the baby with ones of the child, but it was impossible to make that connection.

She knew these pictures weren't of Jake's child because the youngster in the photos was unmistakeably a boy. Dani flipped through more of the images wondering why there were so many of a large, monolithic building constructed of dark stone that looked more like a stately home. The place was huge. It had been snapped from quite a distance away, from beneath some gates and a high wall judging by the shadows visible in the photos.

The same woman from the seaside snaps only this time posing before the gates of the dark building.

Beneath a metal sign that arched over the gates.

It read; EXHAM PSYCHIATRIC HOSPITAL.

The sign was rusted in places, testifying to its age.

Dani slid her phone from her pocket and took a couple of shots of the images before her then she gathered up all the photos she'd taken from the yellow and black folder and replaced them, pushing them carefully back into the drawer where she'd found them.

FIFTY

A Reality TV show. A quiz. An old film. A gardening programme.

Jake jabbed the button of the remote control, sighing each time he changed the channel and found nothing worthwhile.

A cartoon. A documentary about cancer. A drama. Another Reality TV show.

Jake shook his head and kept on pressing.

Dani was seated at the other end of the sofa gazing at her phone, aware of the constant channel changing.

She glanced at Jake and then at the TV screen.

Jake closed his eyes momentarily but continued pressing the channel change button.

"Do you want to go out?" Dani asked.

Jake shook his head and continued with his channel changing.

A film. A programme about fishing. Another Reality TV fiasco.

"Jake, for Christ's sake," Dani gasped.

"Sorry," he murmured. "You wouldn't think that with so many channels there'd be so little to watch."

Dani raised her eyebrows.

"Put it off, we could talk if you want," she suggested.

Jake shrugged.

"How was your mum?" she wanted to know.

"She's okay. She's coming out tomorrow."

Dani nodded.

Jake continued changing channels.

"Anything else you want to talk about?" Dani persisted.

"Like what?" Jake enquired.

She reached into her pocket and pulled out the silver hoop earring.

"Like this, maybe?" she offered.

Jake looked in her direction and saw the object she was holding. He frowned then moved closer to her, trying to look more intently at the piece of jewellery.

"Where did you get that?" he wanted to know.

"In our bedroom," Dani told him. "I wondered how it got there.

It isn't mine."

Jake moved closer, reaching out to take the silver hoop from her. He laid it on his palm, inspecting it.

"How did it get there?" she asked. "Did she leave it behind after you finished fucking her?"

"What the hell are you talking about?"

"I told you, that isn't my earring. Who left it in our bedroom? Is there something I should know?"

Jake sighed.

"Well, what's going on?" Dani continued. "If you wanted another girl you only had to say. You didn't have to go behind my back."

"There isn't another girl."

"Then who does that belong to?" She pointed at the earring.

Jake let out another pained breath.

"Don't take me for an idiot, Jake," she snapped.

He sighed, lowered his gaze, and finally managed to force out some mumbled words.

"It belonged to Rhiannon," he said, flatly.

"The girl who lived here before me?" Dani said but it was more a statement than an expression of surprise.

Jake nodded.

"It must have been in the suitcase," he went on.

"Suitcase?"

"I had a suitcase with some of her clothes in, some of her belongings. It must have fallen out of there when I moved it."

"Why the fuck would you keep her clothes?"

"I don't know...I..."

He shook his head.

"Where's the suitcase now?" Dani persisted.

"I put it in the cellar. Out of the way."

"But why did you keep her clothes...?"

"I loved her," he snapped, angrily. "There. Happy now?"

Dani saw the anger on his face. She could hear the desperation in his voice.

"I know she was only nineteen. I know I'm a pathetic old man," he went on. "I'm sorry."

"You don't have to apologise," Dani said.

"I was stupid. She was young. I enjoyed the attention I suppose."

"Is it the same with me?"

"No. You're different." He managed a smile. "You're older for a start."

Dani looked at him, not sure if she should feel sorry for him or feel angry that his feelings for this girl had persisted as strongly as they had.

"Did she leave you?" Dani wanted to know.

"Her father came round here one day, shouting and screaming about how wrong it was between us. He was a bloody halfwit. He didn't listen to what either of us had to say. He'd got a job somewhere. He wanted her to go with him. Start again. He was using that as an excuse to get her away from me."

"But imagine how you'd have felt if it was Lucy living with a guy that much older than her," Dani offered.

Jake raised his eyebrows.

"Why couldn't Rhiannon have stayed?" Dani asked.

"Her father would never have allowed it. He was an animal. I had to let her go. He'd hit her before and..." The words trailed off as if the memory itself was painful. "I couldn't bear the thought of him taking her away. I felt so useless because I couldn't help her. I wanted to protect her." He lowered his gaze, lost in his own thoughts.

"So that's why you kept her clothes? You felt guilty?"

"I should have done more to help her." He cleared his throat and tried to force a smile. "You don't want to hear this."

"I just want to know that you're over her," Dani breathed.

"Are you worried I might go looking for her?"

"I just don't like seeing you like this."

"Not what you signed up for, eh?"

They sat in silence for a moment longer then Dani spoke.

"If you want to talk about her any time..." she began.

"That's enough," Jake interrupted.

"I mean it. If..."

"Enough," he shouted.

Dani eyed him warily for a second, surprised at the vehemence in his tone.

"I'm going to bed," Jake told her, getting to his feet, and heading towards the door.

"I'll be up soon," Dani offered.

"No hurry," he said, wearily.

And he was gone.

***

Dani drew gently on her cigarette as she walked around the back garden of the house.

The grass felt cool beneath her bare feet and she could smell the fragrance of the flowers on the still night air.

As she glanced up, she saw the light on in the bedroom and, for a moment she saw Jake pass by. Seconds later the light went out.

But now she was aware of another glow nearby.

It was coming from one of the upper windows of Ted Brady's house.

Was he watching?

She tossed her cigarette butt away and headed back towards the house.

As she did, the light inside Brady's house went out.

FIFTY-ONE

Jake hadn't slept much the previous night and that, combined with the warm sunshine pouring through the large windows of his office, was making him feel drowsy. He looked at the computer screen before him, changed a couple of lines of the report he was writing and yawned.

Kim Jackson. Thirty-eight years old. Married. She'd been referred to him by a local hospital who thought she might benefit from more intensive psychological investigation.

Two suicide attempts in the last eight months. One with a razor blade (she'd cut one wrist) and one with an overdose.

Cries for help?

The cuts that she'd inflicted had been made *across* the wrist, not down from the elbow and the overdose had been taken about thirty minutes before she knew her husband was due home from work.

Playing at it?

Jake had only been seeing her for three weeks and so far the sessions had revealed little apart from some childhood problems involving her older brother. Jake suspected that she had more than the usual feelings for her sibling and that those feelings had overcome her not just earlier in life but also more recently. Only time would tell if those incidents were related to the suicide attempts. He suspected that they were, and that guilt was the primary driving force behind them.

He moved on to another patient report.

Marcus Holding. Forty-three. Married.

He also had a record of childhood abuse involving a family member but this time it had been his father.

Holding had been a patient for nearly eighteen months and seemed to enjoy his sessions for their social value rather than their psychological worth. He was a personable enough man and Jake didn't dread their sessions the way he did with some of his patients. There were some who he felt could never be reached or helped and those made him feel useless. He felt that his primary purpose was to help those who visited him and, when that couldn't be achieved, it made him question the validity of his own skills and sometimes of his entire profession.

Jake sighed and sat back from his desk.

He found another file on his computer and opened it somewhat tentatively.

Danielle Katherine Grant.

She'd been twenty-five when they'd first met. The attraction had been instant. It had from his point of view anyway. There had been that indefinable quality about her that attracted him. A dynamism and enthusiasm that was infectious. She wasn't conventionally beautiful, but Jake had been struck by how attractive she was from the very first time she walked into his office.

Her vulnerability only served to add to that he thought, feeling slightly ashamed that he must have contravened God knows how many ethical rules by falling for a patient.

Was it lust or love?

Even now he wasn't sure exactly what his feelings for Dani were, but he was more than happy to let their relationship continue until he did work it out one way or the other.

Is love too strong a word?

It had been a relief to Jake that the attraction was reciprocated. It had also been something of a surprise. He was, after all, almost twice her age but it was something he'd never stopped to analyse too closely. He was just grateful that their relationship had blossomed into something much more than just doctor and patient. He was only too aware of the age gap, only too certain that some thought him sad and pathetic for pursuing a woman so much his junior in years, but Jake had learned to cope with the derision of others during his and Dani's time together.

It hadn't always been easy, he hadn't expected to be, but he found it hard to contemplate his life ahead without her being a part of it.

As he heard the light knocking on his door, Jake closed the file and looked towards the sound.

"Come in," he called.

Sheree Fowler slipped inside and walked slowly towards his desk; her eyes downcast. As she approached him, Jake thought she looked a little pale.

"Bad news," she murmured.

Jake looked blankly at her.

"Kim Jackson's husband just rang," Sheree went on. "She was rushed into hospital this morning about nine."

"So he rang to cancel her appointment?" Jake offered, smiling slightly.

Sheree didn't return the gesture.

"She died an hour ago," she continued.

"Oh, God," Jake breathed. "That's terrible. She was only young, wasn't she?"

"My age," Sheree reminded him.

"What was it?" Jake asked.

"It was an ectopic pregnancy."

FIFTY-TWO

Dani parked her car on a double yellow line but before she jumped out, she flicked on the hazard lights.

The ruse had worked before and she only intended being five minutes or so inside the shop. She knew what she wanted, and she wanted to get in and out as quickly as possible.

It was a small chemist. Not part of the usual chains but independent as the sign above the door proudly proclaimed.

She ran inside, found what she wanted more or less straight away and hurried to the counter to pay for it.

Unfortunately, there were two other customers waiting to be seen by a woman who appeared to be doubling as pharmacist and shop assistant.

The first customer, a woman in her sixties, was asking about antiseptic cream and Dani sighed impatiently as the pharmacist ran through the list of which creams they stocked, and which one might be best for her needs.

The man waiting was a little younger but seemed to be suffering from a cold. That at least was the reason he kept sniffing and coughing; Dani assumed. More than once he sneezed loudly, not attempting to cover his mouth and it was all Dani could do to avoid the explosive effects. She took several steps away from him, glancing theatrically at her watch as if that simple act would encourage the pharmacist to speed up.

It didn't.

She heard words like oozing. Heard others like scab. And sore. It turned her stomach and she glanced irritably at both the older woman and also at the pharmacist.

The man looked at her, sniffed and then sneezed again.

Dani sighed once more, aware that someone else was about to join the queue.

Didn't they have any other tills open?

Dani checked the price on the item she was holding and then dug in her handbag for her purse. She had more or less the right price and this waiting was driving her nuts. She dropped some money on the top of some packets of condoms, attracted the Pharmacist's attention and informed her she was in a hurry and had left the cash. The pharmacist said something about giving her a receipt, but Dani was already heading back down the aisle towards the exit.

She left the chemist's shop and sprinted back to her car, clambering behind the steering wheel.

For a moment she sat motionless then slowly she glanced down at the item she'd just bought.

The pregnancy testing kit promised to give immediate results. Dani picked it up again and read the instructions on the box, her heart beating a little faster now. It was almost as if the act of physically holding the test suddenly made its purpose more pressing.

She was still considering that when she glanced up and saw a traffic warden walking slowly down the street.

Dani started her engine, flicked off her hazard lights and guided the car back out onto the road.

As she turned a corner the pregnancy testing kit slid towards her on the passenger seat. She batted it away the same way she would dismiss a fly.

FIFTY-THREE

Ted Brady was dozing off when he heard the knock at his front door.

He grunted, rubbed his eyes, and then hauled himself out of the chair, wincing when he felt pain from his lower back. It was always the same place. Always across the small of his back. He rubbed it with one hand and made his way to the door just as it was knocked again.

"All right, all right," Brady called, reaching for the handle. "I'm coming. Hold your horses."

He opened the door and his irritation disappeared quickly when he saw Dani standing there.

"Hello," Brady said, smiling. "You got the wrong house or something?" He laughed. "You live next door you know."

Dani attempted a smile, but it appeared more like a sneer.

"I wanted a quick word," she said.

Brady motioned her in, closing the door behind her. He pointed towards the door of the sitting room, following her through into that room, his eyes fixed on her buttocks. Brady smiled.

"Have a seat," he offered, flopping back down into his chair.

"No thanks," she said. "I'm not stopping."

"That's a shame. I can make you a cup of tea if you like."

"I want to talk about that video."

"Which one?"

"You *know* which one," Dani snapped.

Brady smiled.

"Oh, *that* one," he chuckled. "Nothing unless I have to."

"What's that supposed to mean?"

"Let's just call it a little...leverage." Again he smiled and the gesture made Dani even more angry. As he did, he looked her slowly up and down. "As long as I've got it, you're going to listen to me, aren't you? Just in case I show it to your boyfriend. The one you're living with, I mean. Not the one who fucked you and then climbed out of the window." His grin broadened.

"If you're trying to blackmail me, you're wasting your time," Dani snapped. "I haven't got any money."

"I don't want your money, love."

"What *do* you want then?"

Brady raised his eyebrows.

"I've got a bit of a hobby. I've done it for years. Never professionally but I know what I'm doing."

"Just get to the point, will you?"

Brady got to his feet and wandered across to the nearest wall, indicating the framed pictures that hung there.

"I took those," he said, pointing to the pictures. There was one of a countryside scene. Another of a seaside panorama. More of cityscapes and two of open fields skirted by woods. "I might not be Lord Lichfield, but I've got a decent eye, don't you think? I wanted to be a film cameraman when I was growing up but that never happened." He raised his eyebrows. "I still carried on with my little interest though. I like to photograph things. I like to immortalize some things on film."

"Meaning?"

Brady took a step towards her and Dani moved back.

"That's what I want from you. I want to take some pictures of you. And maybe some films."

The colour drained from Dani's cheeks.

"Maybe you and that guy who climbed out of the bedroom window. He looks like a fit guy in more ways than one. He'd look good on film with you." Brady smiled again.

"You're fucking sick," Dani hissed.

"No, no," he said, shaking his head reproachfully. "I just want some pictures of you. Just for personal use, you understand. I wouldn't share them."

"And if I say no?"

"Then I'll show this video on my phone to Jake Porter. He'll know you're cheating on him. He'll throw you out. Then what will you do?"

Dani looked furiously at him. The sense of anger was as powerful as the feeling of helplessness.

"He'll never believe you," she snapped. "He hates you. Why should he believe what you're saying?"

"Well then I'll just show him the video and he can decide for himself. How's that? You want to call my bluff?"

Dani realized that she couldn't intimidate him. She clenched her fists at her side and glared at Brady who continued to smile.

"What kind of pictures would you want to take?" she said, finally.

"Just tasteful ones," Brady grinned. "You know the sort?"

"I can imagine."

"Maybe some that aren't quite so tasteful. Just for me."

"You fucking pervert."

"Now, now. No need to be like that. I told you, I like to immortalize beautiful things by photographing and filming them. You should be flattered."

"So, if I do what you want, you'll delete that video?"

"Scout's honour."

"Do you think I'm stupid? You'll delete the video, but you'll still have photos of me."

"Why would I share those?"

"You might want more than just photos."

"All you need to worry about is what I do with this video." He held up his phone, tapping gently on it with one index finger. "Now, you just run along. I'll be in touch when I want you to come round. And when you do, wear something sexy." He smiled once more.

Dani turned and headed for the front door. Brady heard it first open and then slam shut behind her.

He blew a kiss, his laugh filling the air.

FIFTY-FOUR

The envelope was heavy. Stuffed with thick paper, Jake thought as he picked it up from the mat next to the front door.

He glanced quickly at the other mail and saw that it was just circulars and junk, but this last white A5 envelope intrigued him. The thick vellum paper felt expensive, almost like parchment. As he turned it over in his hand, he saw that it bore an embossed name and address in the top left-hand corner.

WHITELY AND HIND
SOLICITORS.
3 VERNON AVENUE,
WALMSLEY

Jake frowned. The name didn't look familiar.

He carried the letter into the kitchen where Dani was already seated at the table chewing on a piece of toast.

"Anything interesting?" she asked, watching as Jake sat down opposite her and tore open the envelope.

"If it is it'll make a change," he said, smiling, unfolding the first sheet of paper, and scanning it.

Dani watched as the expression on his face changed from one of mild interest to something approaching concern. His brow furrowed and he put one hand to his mouth as if to stifle a sound. When he finally put the letter down, he glanced at the other items that had been in the envelope. The first one looked like instructions from an Estate Agent. Jake eyed the sheet and then sighed.

"Anything wrong?" Dani asked, getting up and walking around the table to where he was, peering over his shoulder to glance at the contents of the envelope.

She too saw the address, and something suddenly struck her.
Walmsley.
Why did that name look familiar?
She frowned and looked more closely.
Walmsley.
The photos she'd found in the bottom drawer of Jake's desk when

she'd been looking in there the other day. The woman she'd seen in the photos had been posing outside South Walmsley Pier.

And now this.

"Where's Walmsley?" she wanted to know.

"East of England," Jake informed her. "I'm not sure exactly where it is."

"So, what's in Walmsley?"

"A house."

Dani looked puzzled.

"This letter," Jake held it up. "It says that my mother left me her house in her will."

"Your mother. But your mother is in a care home in..."

"Not my *birth* mother," Jake corrected her. "I never knew my birth mother."

Dani reached for the other sheet of paper, glancing at the photos of the property.

"It looks like a nice place," she said, noting the large front garden and the back garden with...

With high privet hedges on three sides of the lawn.

The realization hit her suddenly. This was the place that had featured in some of the pictures she'd looked at too. Was the woman in those photographs Jake's birth mother? Was the child in the photos him?

"What are you going to do?" she wanted to know.

"I suppose I should go and at least look at the place," he offered.

"And you had no idea about this?"

"I can't even remember my real mother. I've never been in contact with her, not since she gave me up for adoption when I was little." He sucked in a deep breath, still shaken by the news. "The solicitors are acting for my mother's estate. They say that I can go and look at the property any time I like."

"So, what are we waiting for?"

"I can't go now, Dani. I'm too busy and..."

"You can re-arrange your appointments, can't you?"

"Well, yes but..."

"You need to see that place, Jake. There might be information there about your early life. Stuff you need to know."

"Like what? Why my mother abandoned me?"

"She didn't abandon you. She gave you up for adoption because she obviously couldn't cope. She thought enough of you to want you to have a better life. A life she thought she couldn't provide."

"She didn't give me up due to lack of money by the look of the house," Jake mused.

"You need to know what happened. And if you don't want the house you can always sell it. It looks like you'll make a fortune out of it."

Jake sighed again.

"If I go," he murmured. "Will you come with me?"

"Definitely. A couple of days away will do us both good. When do we leave?"

PART TWO

"We have to distrust each other. It is our only defence against betrayal."
                    Tennessee Williams

FIFTY-FIVE

There are few more depressing places than a seaside resort in the off season, Dani thought.

Hotels and Guest Houses closed. Amusement arcades not in operation, many with metal shutters now at their doors and windows. Sea front attractions empty and abandoned until the season begins again.

As Jake drove slowly along the main road that ran the length of Walmsley sea front, Dani glanced to her left and right, surprised by just how quiet and deserted the area was. The stretch of beach that ran from a large cinema called The Aquarium all the way up to a small fun fair was, like so many other sea front panoramas, called The Golden Mile. It consisted of crazy golf courses, cafes, a couple of indoor swimming pools, a boating lake and a model village on one side of the street (the side that led to the beach) and, on the other, a row of hotels, guest houses, restaurants, pubs, bingo halls and amusement arcades that were soul crushingly similar in appearance.

All seemed abandoned and unwanted now due to the time of year. There was a collection of buildings that passed for a town centre and many of those shops were also closed due to the huge drop off in business that occurred once the tourists stopped visiting. Dani tried to imagine how vibrant and alive the place must be when it was in the middle of the busy season but even her imagination was struggling as she looked at the endless array of businesses that were not currently operating.

There were a handful of people walking about, moving sluggishly up and down the front, some of them even chancing a walk along the sea front itself. Their attempts to ignore the strong wind failing miserably.

Three or four of the sea front cafes were open and it seemed that most of the people who had ventured out were seeking shelter and warmth within their confines.

The only thing missing seemed to be tumble weeds.

Jake slowed down a little, also peering to his right and left. He drove up as far as the fun fair (also closed) and then turned the car around and headed back towards the town centre.

As he waited at a set of traffic lights, Dani pointed at one of the buildings to his left.

Royal Hotel the neon blue sign above its entrance proclaimed.

"That one's open," she said, watching as two people walked out of the building.

Jake nodded and noticed a side street close to the hotel. When the lights changed, he swung the car into the street, finding a parking space straight away.

Jake took the small overnight bag from the boot then locked the car and they walked back up the front towards the main entrance of The Royal.

The reception was small. Just a dark wood desk with a computer propped on top of it. There were leaflets spread out on the surface advertising the attractions that would have been busy during the season. The model village. The funfair. Even a circus. Dani looked at the leaflets while Jake peered towards the door that opened out onto the reception.

There was a bell almost hidden behind a dying pot plant, so he tapped it gently, the tone echoing inside the silent reception.

A moment later a middle-aged man with pock marked skin and a large moustache emerged from the room behind reception. He raised a hand warmly to Jake and Dani and wiped his mouth, brushing crumbs from his lips.

"Sorry," he said. "Just grabbing some lunch." He wiped his mouth again and clapped his hands together. "What can I do for you?"

"We'd like a room please," Jake told him. "Just for the night."

The moustached man nodded and checked something on the computer, nodding enthusiastically.

"Number five is free," he said. "A nice front room with a lovely view of the sea front." He turned to the array of keys behind him and plucked down the key to room five. "If I could just take an imprint of your card, that would be lovely."

Jake reached for a credit card and pushed it across the reception desk.

"Will you be having dinner tonight?" the moustached man wanted to know.

"Is anywhere else open?" Dani asked, smiling.

Moustache man looked at her blankly for a moment then shook his head.

"We're about the only ones," he confessed. "The whole place grinds to a halt in the off season."

"Why do you stay open?" Jake enquired.

"There's always someone who needs a room," the man replied. "Like yourselves." He smiled broadly again. "Have you come far?"

"It took us about three hours," Jake informed him.

"Have you ever been to Walmsley before?" the man wanted to know.

Jake shook his head.

"I've got business here," he said, quietly. "With Whitely and Hind, the solicitors. Do you know them?"

"Yes. They've got an office in the main street. You can't miss it."

Dani was now looking into a large room off to the right that was full of sofas and chairs.

"That's our lounge," the man told her, noticing our interest. "You can sit in there at night and have a drink before bedtime. It's a nice place to chat with other guests."

"Are there any other guests?" Dani wanted to know.

"Well, there are just two at the moment," the man said. "But...normally."

Dani smiled.

"Things are jumping, are they?" she chuckled.

The moustached man nodded. "Shall I take your luggage up for you?" he asked but Jake shook his head and picked up the overnight bag.

"We can manage," he explained.

"The lift is behind you," the man told them, pointing to the metal doors on the other side of the reception. "You're on the first floor. Just turn right when you get out of the lift. You can't miss it."

Jake nodded and he and Dani made their way across the reception to the waiting lift where Dani hit the 'call' button. The door slid open immediately and they stepped into the cramped space within, rising slowly to the first floor.

"Not exactly Las Vegas is it?" Dani chuckled.

Jake smiled and shook his head.

"Let's dump this," he said, lifting the overnight bag slightly. "Then we'd better find the solicitors."

FIFTY-SIX

The main street of Walmsley was almost as deserted as its sea front.

Jake and Dani walked along the wide pavement unobstructed and passed by less than half a dozen people as they made their way towards the office of Whitely and Hind.

Many of the shops were closed and not just because it was off season. There were a couple of covered shopping areas but, glancing through the large glass double doors that led into them, they looked as unfrequented as the rest of the town.

"How the hell do they make a living?" Dani mused, glancing at the deserted shops.

Jake didn't answer, he was gazing blankly ahead.

"Even during the season, it can't be that busy here," Dani added, walking ahead to look in the window of a clothes shop.

Jake walked on.

"Are you okay?" she asked, a little perturbed by his silence.

He nodded almost imperceptibly and walked on, his head turning to the right and left as if he was taking in details that only he could see.

There was a crossroads up ahead, branches of it leading off towards the sea front, another towards some houses. Straight ahead were more shops. Jake paused for a moment then shot out a hand to steady himself. Dani moved swiftly across to him, supporting him.

"Are you sure you're all right?" she asked, anxiously.

"I just felt a bit dizzy," Jake told her, still looking around. He sucked in a deep breath.

Dani kept one hand against his back as if fearing that he might topple over if she removed it.

"Do you want to sit down?" she enquired.

Jake shook his head and sighed again.

"I know this place," he murmured, gaze flicking back and forth.

"Have you been here before?"

"Not that I can remember but...parts of it look familiar. I don't know why."

"Maybe you came here as a kid."

Jake stood motionless for a moment then stepped out into the road. The van that roared past missed him by inches.

Dani grabbed his arm, pulling him backwards, almost causing him to fall but he recovered his balance and his composure, glaring in the direction of the fleeing vehicle.

"Fucking idiot," Dani hissed. "Couldn't he see you?"

Jake again inhaled deeply.

"Come on," Dani urged, pulling him towards a nearby cafe. "We should have a sit down for a minute."

"I'm okay," said Jake, smiling. "Really. Let's just get to the solicitors and get this over with."

Dani hesitated for a moment then nodded and they walked arm in arm up the main street, finally seeing a small white sign outside a red brick building that proclaimed.

WHITELY AND HIND.
SOLICITORS.

Jake pushed open the door and led the way inside.

There was a narrow staircase leading up to the first floor and they both made their way up it, footsteps echoing inside the small space.

The steps ended at a small vestibule with a glass door on one side. The name of the firm was stencilled on the glass in white and, beyond that door Jake could see a receptionist working away busily at her desk. He and Dani walked in and the woman looked up and smiled.

"Can I help you?" she asked.

"I'd like to see Mr Whitely or Mr Hind please," Jake told her, and he handed her the envelope he'd received through the post.

The receptionist pulled the letter free and scanned it then she nodded and got to her feet, heading towards another door. She disappeared inside for a moment then emerged again, her beaming smile even broader.

"If you'd like to come in," she said, stepping back, ushering them inside this new office.

There was an overweight man in his mid-forties in the office and he introduced himself as Marcus Hind. When Jake had explained who he and Dani were, Hind invited them to sit down and the receptionist hurried off to make tea for them while the usual pleasantries were exchanged. Only when the door closed firmly behind her did Hind clear his throat and turn his attention to the envelope that Jake had shown him.

He spread out the letter and the estate agents' instructions on his desk and peered myopically at them.

"Firstly, can I say how sorry I am for your loss, Mr Porter," he said, his voice low. "It isn't the way one wants to acquire property is it?"

Jake shook his head.

"And the manner of your mother's death must have made it harder if that's possible," Hind went on. "I am very sorry."

"What do you mean? The manner of her death?" Jake mused.

"The loss of any loved one is hard but to lose them to suicide must be even worse."

FIFTY-SEVEN

Jake could feel the colour draining from his cheeks as Hind spoke and when the other man mentioned the word suicide, he sat forward, raising a hand to halt the solicitor.

"My mother committed suicide?" Jake murmured.

"Yes, I'm very sorry, I..."

"How?" Jake gasped.

"I don't know that, Mr Porter," Hind went on, his words faltering. "I just assumed you'd been informed." He looked embarrassed.

"The first I knew about her death was when that letter arrived from your office," explained Jake. "We weren't close. She gave me up for adoption when I was very small."

Hind nodded, feeling a little awkward.

Dani too shifted uncomfortably in her seat, the leather creaking beneath her. She reached out and gently touched Jake's arm, trying to offer reassurance.

"I'm very sorry," Hind said again.

"It isn't your fault," Jake reminded him. "Perhaps it would be better if we just got this business cleared up. The quicker it is, the quicker I can get away from here."

Hind nodded.

"Well, as you are aware, your mother left you her house and all its contents," he explained. "What you do with the property and those contents is, of course, your prerogative, Mr Porter."

"What usually happens in these cases?"

"It depends on the individual of course. Some people retain the properties they're left. Others sell them. It's very much a matter of personal choice and..."

"How well did you know my mother?" Jake interrupted.

"I didn't know her," Hind said apologetically. "Her relationship with this firm was purely professional."

"When did she instruct you to act as executors?"

"Five years ago, when she came in to make her will." He smiled. "She seemed a very nice lady. Very friendly. We chatted for quite a while when she was here."

"What about?"

"Oh, this and that. The usual things. Work. Life. Family."

"And she *had* no other family?"

Hind shook his head.

"What did she do for a living?" Jake went on.

"As far as I know she was a psychiatrist. I know she'd worked at hospitals in other parts of the country, she mentioned that when we spoke."

"Whereabouts?"

"The Home Counties from what I could gather. She mentioned a place called Exham, do you know it?"

Dani frowned slightly.

Exham.

Her mind went back to the photos she'd found in Jake's office.

The woman standing before the main entrance of Exham Psychiatric Hospital.

Jake's Mother?

"Do you know anything about her life before she came to Walmsley?" This time it was Dani who asked the question.

"As I said, we only chatted about her will when she was here," Hind told her. "I don't know who you'd go to for that kind of information."

Dani nodded.

"Would it be possible to see the house?" Jake enquired.

Hind nodded and got to his feet, reaching into his desk drawer for a bunch of keys that he held up as if he'd just found a long-lost treasure.

"I can drive if that helps," the solicitor told them. "It isn't that far."

Jake and Dani got up and followed Hind out of the office and down the stairs to street level. There was a small car park at the rear of the building and the solicitor ushered them towards a green Peugeot which they slid into, Jake seating himself beside the other man who started the engine and guided the car out into traffic.

"How long have you lived in Walmsley?" Dani wanted to know as they drove.

"All my life," Hind told her. "I love it around here."

"It's a bit quiet," Dani countered.

"Well, everywhere around here is quiet in the off season," Hind told her. "You learn to adjust."

"What do people do for excitement?" Dani went on.

"They go and live somewhere else if they want excitement," Hind chuckled.

Dani also laughed but the sound died abruptly as she felt her phone vibrating in her pocket.

She pulled it free, saw that the caller was Mike and hurriedly switched the phone off, glancing at the two men ahead of her but neither of them had noticed her dismiss the call.

Jake looked fixedly out of the windscreen as the solicitor drove, glancing at the houses with their well-kept gardens. The further away from the sea front and the town they got, the less like a seaside town Walmsley looked. He wondered what had brought his real mother to this place to begin with. How had she found it? What had attracted her to it?

He was still turning those thoughts over in his mind when Hind stopped the car.

The solicitor looked almost apologetically at Jake then motioned towards the house close by.

"This is it," he said.

FIFTY-EIGHT

It was Dani's turn to take a deep breath.

As she swung herself out of the car, she looked at the house, surrounded as it was by a high privet hedge and she realized that this was definitely the place she'd seen in the photographs from Jake's desk.

His childhood home.

As they all walked through the wooden gate and headed up the path towards the front door, she noted the weeping willows and the pond, other items she remembered from the photographs. The house itself didn't look much different to how it had in the pictures. Imposing. Well-kept and maintained. She wondered how much it was worth.

Jake slowed his pace slightly as they approached the front door and Dani reached out to hold his arm, sensing that he needed some support and reassurance. He smiled at her then returned his gaze to the front of the building, his eyes taking in all the details even though nothing looked familiar to him.

Why didn't it?

You were here for years, why can't you remember it?

Hind unlocked the front door and then took a pace back, ushering Jake forward. The hallway beyond was gloomy and Jake hesitated before stepping over the threshold. As he did, he thought he was going to faint. He shot out a hand to steady himself, his head spinning.

Again, Dani moved to his side, seeing his face grow whiter.

"Are you all right?" she whispered, and Jake merely nodded, sucking in a deep breath as he walked further into the house.

Hind didn't notice the reaction and followed them inside, glancing around at the hallway and the doors that led off from it.

"There are three bedrooms," the solicitor said. "Sitting room. Kitchen. Large back garden."

Jake merely nodded.

"Well," Hind said, clearing his throat. "You don't need me to do my Estate agent bit do you? Perhaps I'd better leave you to look around on your own," he offered. "You might like a bit of privacy." He held out the keys which Jake took. "If you call me when you're ready to leave I can pick you up."

"That's very kind of you," Jake told him, considering the keys.

Hind hesitated a moment longer then turned and walked out, closing the front door behind him.

Jake listened to his footsteps receding away down the path then glanced around the hallway once again.

"Are you sure you're all right?" Dani asked again.

Jake nodded and moved towards the nearest door, walking through it into a sitting room.

"We might as well start in here," he said.

"And you can't remember anything about this place?" Dani wanted to know.

"Nothing. I thought that something might have come back to me once I got here but..." The words trailed off. He sat down on the large sofa and let out a long breath. "Why would she commit suicide?" he murmured. "What the hell was so bad in her life that she needed to end it?"

Dani also sat down, wishing she could offer some kind of comfort but knowing she couldn't.

"I didn't know your mother was a psychiatrist," she said, conversationally. "Is that why you became one?"

Jake shrugged.

"I had no idea what she did," he confessed. "My choice of career wasn't influenced by her."

"Weird coincidence though."

He raised his eyebrows, less impressed by the similarity in their career choices.

As he sat, he looked around the room. Like everything in the house, it appeared to be neat, tidy, and well maintained. Books on shelves filled one wall. A small fireplace with a gas fire stood before them and, above it, some framed photos on the wall. Jake didn't recognise anyone in the pictures either. Several were of his mother.

Mother. Even the *word* sounded alien to him.

Two mothers. One real. One adoptive. One dead from suicide, the other in a home. Not a very good batting average.

Jake got to his feet and wandered around the room slowly, not even sure what he was looking for. There were several small bureaux and cabinets in the room too and he slid open the drawers of these as he reached them. Each one contained piles of papers it seemed. Documents. God alone knew what. It would take time to sift through all of these, checking for their importance. And the other rooms might be the same. The task of going through the house, he decided, could take days. Jake let out a long breath.

"I should just call a firm of house clearers," he said. "Get them to take everything away and dump it."

"But there could be something important here?" Dani protested.

"Like what? Something that's going to help me find out why my mother killed herself? Something that's going to help me remember the first ten years of my life?"

"But there might be something that you want. Something that means a lot to you. Something that meant a lot to your mother."

"Something that meant a lot to the woman who gave me away as a child and never contacted me for the rest of her life, you mean?" He shook his head. "I don't want anything she had, Dani. It isn't *my* life. It was *hers*."

"But it was your life when you were growing up here."

"A life I don't remember a single thing about. My life started when I was adopted by the only woman who has ever been a *real* mother to me. And I should be back home now, checking she's okay, not hanging around here looking for clues to a life I don't even care about."

He continued sorting through the drawers.

"Are you going to get rid of the house then?" Dani wanted to know.

"What's the point of keeping it? It means nothing to me."

He walked out of the room; Dani heard his footsteps in the hallway. She waited a moment then followed him.

As she did, her phone rang again.

FIFTY-NINE

It was late by the time they got back to the hotel.

One of the illuminated blue letters spelling out ROYAL HOTEL above the building was broken and it flickered every now and then. It seemed to reflect the whole town, Dani thought. Everything was either broken or on the verge of breaking.

Dani had suggested a walk back up the sea front and Jake had agreed but had made the journey in silence, his mind elsewhere it seemed. Occasionally he would stop and gaze out to sea, watching the cold water that looked black in the night. A cold breeze was blowing in from the shore and Dani shivered as they walked, wishing she'd never suggested this late evening stroll.

A few people passed them coming in the other direction but, for the most part, the sea front was deserted.

A discarded plastic bag blew across the beach below them like some multi-coloured tumbleweed before a particularly strong gust of wind sent it flying skyward.

They finally cut across the large open area that separated the sea front from The Golden Mile and headed towards their hotel.

"Shall we get a drink before we go to bed?" Dani suggested. "Might warm us up a bit."

"I'm tired," Jake said, apologetically. "And we've got another long day tomorrow sorting through the crap in that house."

"Just a quick one," she urged, smiling, and squeezing his arm.

Jake returned the gesture and nodded and the two of them walked through reception towards the small bar of the Royal.

The wooden floor beneath them creaked loudly as they entered the room. Jake glanced around, looking first at the row of optics behind the brightly lit bar. There were mirrors running the length of the wall behind them and he could see himself reflected in the polished glass. On the walls there were horse brasses, framed photos of Walmsley sea front when things had been much busier and some fishing nets and seashells, as if they were trying to remind themselves that people had once made a living from the sea.

There were three or four tall bar stools arranged before the counter and a fruit machine at one end. The lights on it were flashing and it looked somewhat incongruous in the silent confines of the room. The heavy dark blue curtains were drawn across the windows to shut out the night, or maybe the world. The bar looked as if it came from another time. A more sedate and relaxed era.

There was an open fireplace, but it was displaying nothing but a small electric fire, one bar glowing red to keep the chill away.

Dani walked across to it and warmed her hands while Jake stepped over to the bar. There was a small bell on top of the counter with a small plastic sign that read, PRESS FOR SERVICE.

Jake did as the sign instructed and the moustached man who had checked them in earlier that day emerged from a small room at the far end of the bar.

He smiled happily at them.

"Ah, a night cap, eh?" he beamed. "I don't blame you."

Jake smiled.

"Have you had a good day?" the man continued.

"Busy," Jake told him.

The moustached man nodded again.

"What can I get you?" he wanted to know.

"White Russian and a sparkling mineral water, please," Jake said.

The moustached man looked puzzled.

"A White Russian?" he mumbled, quizzically.

Jake smiled and Dani joined him at the bar.

"That's for me," she announced, smiling. "It's vodka, Kahlua and cream but I'll just have a vodka and orange if that's a problem."

"Sorry," the barman said. "We don't usually get requests for such exotic drinks."

He busied himself getting the order and set the glasses down on the counter. He hesitated for a moment but then saw Jake take the glasses across to the fireplace. Deciding he wasn't needed any longer, the moustached man retreated back into the room behind the bar.

Jake sat in one of the high-backed chairs while Dani settled herself in the one opposite, sipping her drink.

"Do you think we'll finish going through all the stuff in the house tomorrow?" she asked, glancing at Jake.

"What we don't go through I'm just going to dump," he murmured.

"But there could be something important in there."

"Like what?"

"I know this must be hard for you, Jake, but..."

"It isn't hard it's just inconvenient," he snapped, cutting across her. "I just want to get this over with. The woman who lived in that house meant nothing to me."

"She was your mother, Jake."

"We've got different definitions of that word then. My mother is in a care home. That woman who died just gave birth to me. She was nothing else to me."

Dani eyed him for a moment then nodded.

"If that's the way you feel," she intoned.

"It is." He took a large swallow of his drink then put the glass down. "To hell with this, I need something stronger." He got to his feet and walked back to the bar where he ordered a large brandy. Dani watched him as he wandered back to the fireside, the glass gripped in his hand. He considered the alcohol for a moment then downed half of it with one gulp.

"I've never seen you drink alcohol before," she murmured.

"Stick around," Jake grinned. He raised his glass in salute and then sipped more of the brandy.

He and Dani were still laughing when the newcomer walked into the bar.

SIXTY

She was a tall, dark haired woman in her late thirties, and she looked immaculate in a pair of black jeans and a cream-coloured sweater.

She glanced across in their direction as she made her way to the bar where she ordered a glass of white wine. The woman seated herself on a bar stool, her back to Jake and Dani.

Jake finished his drink and got to his feet to fetch re-fills for himself and Dani. As he stood at the bar the woman glanced in his direction and smiled.

Jake returned the gesture.

"Can I get you another?" he asked, nodding towards her glass.

"I've only just ordered this one," she chuckled.

Jake shrugged.

"But thanks for offering," the woman went on. "You're staying here too, are you?"

"We checked in yesterday," he announced, gesturing towards Dani. The woman eyed her for a moment then nodded approvingly.

"Quiet isn't it?" she went on. "This town is like a bloody graveyard in the off season."

"Why are you here then?" Jake enquired.

"I'm working," she told him. "I sell cutlery. I've been into some of the restaurants around here." She sipped her drink then extended her right hand. "Heather Lawson." She smiled. "I'd give you a business card, but I've left them in my room."

Jake smiled, shook her offered hand, and introduced himself and Dani. "Would you like to join us?" he added.

Heather accepted the invitation and pulled up a chair near the fireplace close to Dani.

"Don't people buy things over the internet these days?" Jake enquired.

"Not things like cutlery," Heather informed him. "Lots of customers still want to look at the merchandise, feel it in their hands before they buy it."

"It sounds interesting," Dani offered.

"It's as boring as hell," Heather chuckled. "But it's a living. What about you guys? What brings you here? It must be a good excuse."

"Just tying up some loose ends," Jake told her.

"Family business," Dani added. "Well, *his* family anyway."

Heather nodded.

"Are you two married then?" she enquired.

"God, no," Dani said a little too swiftly.

"I don't blame you," Heather offered. "I tried it twice and it didn't work."

They all laughed.

"I know the feeling," Jake added. "Not twice but..."

"Marriage is overrated," Heather said. "If I were you two, I wouldn't even *think* about it."

"We're not," Dani told her and, once again, her response was almost unnaturally swift. She was aware of Jake looking evenly at her. He continued to watch her until he got to his feet and fetched more drinks.

Dani lost track of the time as they sat before the electric fire knocking back their alcohol. The conversation flowed easily, probably because of the amount of booze they were consuming but she was glad to see Jake relaxing a little more. She knew that the events of the last day or two had weighed heavily on him. She liked Heather. The woman had an openness about her that was refreshing. Dani found herself laughing easily and often as they all spoke. Even some of her own problems and concerns began to recede and for that she was grateful.

"How long have you two been an item then?" Heather wanted to know, glancing at Jake then at Dani.

"We've known each other for a couple of years," Jake said. "On a professional basis to begin with."

"That sounds ominous," Heather told him, smiling.

"I'm a psychiatrist," Jake announced. "Dani was referred to me for some CBT."

"Nothing serious," Dani added. "I'm not crazy or anything."

They all laughed.

"I've always thought I'd like to go to a psychiatrist," Heather explained. "Just for a good old heart to heart."

"We're there for a bit more than that," Jake told her, grinning.

"You said you were married," Dani said, looking at Heather. "Have you got any kids?"

"I never really wanted them," Heather announced as they continued.

"I've got a daughter," Jake said.

"How old?" Heather enquired.

"She's twenty-two. She's a good girl," Jake murmured.

"Every father says that about his daughter," Heather chuckled.

"She *is* a good girl," Jake repeated. "I just wish I saw more of her."

His expression darkened slightly, and Dani realized that she would now have to guide the conversation in a different direction before it was too late.

"I wouldn't want kids at my age," Dani said.

"How old are you?" Heather wanted to know.

"Twenty-five," Dani told her.

"There's a bit of an age gap between you then?" Heather observed, impishly.

"More than twenty years," Jake admitted.

She nudged Dani playfully. "I hope he can keep up with you."

Dani blushed a little.

An uneasy silence settled over the trio broken once more by Heather.

"Twenty-five is too young to have babies. You need to enjoy yourself a bit first. Kids tie you down."

"How would you know if you've never had any?" Jake said, a slight edge to his tone.

"I like my freedom," Heather grinned. "I don't want to have to think about a child's needs before I have a bit of fun." She raised her glass in salute and smiled. "I know that sounds a bit selfish but who cares?"

Dani grinned.

Jake didn't.

"Don't you get lonely," Dani wanted to know. "Being...on the road a lot of the time? Moving from hotel to hotel?"

"No," Heather told her. "It can be fun. I get to meet people like you. You'd be surprised how friendly people get when they're in a hotel bar on their own."

"Tell us more," Dani chuckled.

"I can't tell you my secrets," Heather insisted, a smile on her face.

"We wouldn't judge," Dani assured her.

"You haven't heard all my stories yet," Heather told her, sipping her drink.

Jake kept his gaze fixed on the dark-haired woman; his eyes narrowed slightly.

"You didn't want kids," he said, quietly. "Is that why you had an abortion?"

SIXTY-ONE

Heather swallowed hard as she heard the words.

She looked at Jake who held her gaze, his eyes unblinking.

Dani shifted uncomfortably in her seat glancing from one to the other as if she was waiting to see who spoke first.

"What did you say?" Heather murmured.

"You said you didn't want kids," Jake told her. "I asked if that was why you had an abortion."

"How do you know I had an abortion?" Heather went on.

Jake didn't speak but he continued to look fixedly at her.

Dani moved in her chair again, aware of the atmosphere that had settled around them.

"It's true isn't it?" Jake finally breathed.

"It's none of your business," Heather told him, defensively.

"How old were you?" Jake persisted. "Thirty?"

Heather got to her feet.

"You can keep your theories to yourself," she blurted, wagging an accusatory finger in Jake's direction. "You've got no right..."

"No right to what?" Jake snapped.

Heather looked at him for a moment longer then turned towards the door that led out of the bar an expression on her face that was a combination of shock and anger.

Jake watched her as she stalked off.

"How did you know she'd had an abortion?" Dani wanted to know.

"Does it matter?" Jake grunted. He reached for his glass and downed what was left in it. He held up the empty glass for a moment then brought it down so hard on the table that he almost cracked the cheap crystal. The moustached man behind the bar looked across but said nothing.

"We'd better go to bed," Dani said, leaning nearer to Jake.

"Why? It's still early. Let's have another drink."

"I think you've had enough, Jake."

He shot out a hand and grabbed her wrist, pulling her closer to him.

"Don't tell me I've had enough," he hissed. "I'll decide when I've had enough." He let go of her arm, sitting back in his seat.

"Well, *I'm* going to bed," Dani announced.

Jake dug in his pocket and produced the room key, holding it before him tantalisingly. Dani made a grab for it, but he pulled it away from her reach, a smile spreading across his face.

"All right, all right," he sighed. "You're probably right. It's bedtime. Happy now?" He got to his feet, swayed a little uncertainly and then sucked in a deep breath. "Lead the way," he went on, gesturing towards the doorway leading out of the bar.

Dani looked at him then set off, Jake a couple of paces behind her. They walked to the lifts in the reception and got in, riding the small, cramped car to the first floor. As they stepped out onto the landing leading to their room, Jake grabbed her again, pulling her around to face him.

"If this is you when you've been drinking, I can see why you don't touch it that often," Dani grunted as Jake pushed his face close to hers.

She pulled away from him, watching as he opened the door of the room and stumbled inside. Dani hesitated a moment then followed him, closing the door behind her. As she stood with her back against the wooden partition, Jake moved swiftly towards her, pinning her against the door. He kissed her hard. Almost angrily.

Dani was surprised at the strength he displayed and a little unnerved by it. She struggled slightly as Jake pushed up against her, feeling his erection pressing against her. Almost despite herself she allowed one hand to glide towards the stiffness, tugging at his trousers, pulling them open while he continued to kiss her, his tongue pushing past the hard white edges of her teeth and into the warm moistness of her mouth.

As he slid one hand up inside her t-shirt she winced slightly, feeling his fingers close tightly over her left breast. He used his thumb to rub her stiffening nipple, pushing his groin more urgently against her as she continued to pull at his trousers.

She freed his erection and closed her slender fingers around it, almost surprised at how hard it felt. And now she felt his other hand tugging down her jeans, pushing them as far as her thighs.

Dani helped him, her back still against the door. She shrugged the jeans down, kicking off her shoes, stepping awkwardly out of her jeans so that one leg at least was free.

As her thighs opened further this seemed to inflame Jake and he dragged his own trousers down as far as his knees, his erection now rubbing between Dani's legs, the tip rubbing against the material of her knickers.

They broke their kiss but remained only inches from each other, eyes locked. They were both breathing heavily, the passion and the exertion causing them to gasp. When he tried to kiss her again, she gently bit his tongue causing him to recoil slightly but this only served to provoke him and he crushed her once more against the door, feeling her head move towards his neck. She bit him lightly again, her body quivering.

She rubbed his stiffness, guiding him towards the increasingly slippery warmth between her legs, rasping that pulsing erection against her swollen clitoris. She gasped again and arched her back, feeling him push towards her. He clawed at her knickers and dragged them down, one hand forcing its way between her legs, feeling the swollen and wet lips of her sex. He forced his stiffened organ towards that cleft.

Jake felt the moisture on his tip, and it spurred him on. He sank deeply into her, inch by inch, sliding as far as he could go until she gripped his buttocks and held him there. Each thrust slammed her against the wooden door, but Jake didn't care, just as he didn't care that her nails were scratching his back savagely as he filled her.

He kept up his rhythm, looking deeply into her eyes, their foreheads touching as he continued to thrust, his fingers now digging deeply into the flesh of her waist where he held her so tightly.

She raised one leg, curling it around his thighs, allowing him to push more deeply into her. He didn't ignore the invitation and she heard his breaths grow more frantic as he pumped in and out, every thrust taking him closer to release.

As he reached his climax he grunted loudly, finally slowing his frenzied movements.

He held her tightly for a moment longer then pulled out, looking at her blankly.

As if he'd never seen her before.

She watched as he stumbled over to the bed where he sat down heavily, his trousers still around his thighs. There was something in that expression she didn't like. Something that made her uneasy.

Dani was struggling to regain her composure, shaken by the suddenness and ferocity of what had just happened. She didn't know whether to pull her jeans and knickers back up or take them off and climb onto the bed with him.

Jake glanced at her once more then closed his eyes and slumped backwards.

SIXTY-TWO

Heather Lawson lowered the book she was reading when she heard the gentle tapping on the door.

She hesitated a moment, wondering if she'd imagined the light rapping on the wood but, when it came again, she swung herself out of bed and padded across to the door, pressing her eye to the small spy-hole there.

Heather saw the figure on the other side of the door, and she frowned, waiting a second before she unlocked the door and pulled it open.

Dani smiled at her.

Heather looked her up and down.

Dani had changed into a pair of loose jogging bottoms and a black vest top and she stood there a little awkwardly while Heather looked on, wondering what she wanted.

"I'm sorry to bother you," Dani began. "I hope I didn't wake you up."

"How did you know which room I was in?" Heather asked.

"You're the only other guest here. It wasn't hard to find you," Dani said, smiling.

Heather nodded and ran appraising eyes over Dani once again.

"What did you want?" she asked.

"I came to apologise," Dani said, flicking her long hair away from her face, her hand quivering slightly. "For Jake. For what he said. I think he was a bit drunk and he doesn't normally drink and..."

"So, when he drinks, he says stupid things? Join the club."

Dani smiled.

"You seemed upset about what he said. About the abortion." Her voice softened slightly. "I just wanted to say sorry if he made you feel uncomfortable."

"Do you want to come in for a minute?" Heather enquired, pulling the door a little further open.

Dani smiled once more and nodded, stepping over the threshold.

Heather closed the door behind her and ushered her towards a chair near the window.

"I don't want to keep you up," Dani told her, seating herself. "Like I said, I just came to say sorry."

"Why didn't he come himself and apologise?" Heather wanted to know.

"He's flat out. He really did drink too much."

"So, you came to do his dirty work?"

Heather perched on the end of the bed; one leg drawn up beneath her.

"I don't know what made him say that" Dani went on.

"How did he know?" Heather enquired. "How *could* he know?"

"I don't know. A lucky guess?"

"It's a hell of a subject to make a guessing game of. And what were his chances of being right? I'm not offended he said what he said I just want to know why he said it."

Dani could only shrug.

"How could he know I had an abortion?" Heather persisted.

"I don't know," Dani protested. "I didn't come here to explain *what* he said, I came to apologise if he offended you."

Heather nodded.

"I'm sorry," she murmured. "It isn't your fault." She sighed. "Shall we have a drink and forget all about what he said?" She smiled and raised her eyebrows, reaching over to pull open the bedside cabinet. From within she produced a small bottle of whiskey that she brandished, as if it were some kind of trophy.

Dani chuckled.

"I should get back to Jake," she said.

"Fuck him," Heather grunted. "Have a drink with me before you go. Anyway, you said he was flat out. He won't even know you've gone." She held the bottle a little higher. "Just a quick one."

Dani laughed and nodded. "Just a quick one," she echoed.

Heather used the toothbrush glasses for the whiskey, handing one to Dani who sipped tentatively, wincing as she felt the amber liquid burn its way to her stomach.

"Do you always carry a bottle of whiskey with you when you go on the road?" she wanted to know.

Heather grinned. "It's an essential," she admitted, settling herself close to Dani. She raised her glass. "Cheers."

They touched their glasses together, both smiling.

"When you go back to your room just tell him he's a dickhead," Heather said, smiling.

"Sorry again," Dani murmured.

"It isn't your fault. Is he always like that when he's had a few?"

"He doesn't normally drink. He had some problems with it when he was younger."

"What kind of problems?"

"He was almost alcoholic in his twenties."

"Did you know him then?"

Dani shook her head.

"You could do better you know," Heather told her.

Dani shrugged, took another sip of her drink then got to her feet.

"I'd better get back," she offered.

"Sit down," Heather protested. "Finish your drink."

Dani shrugged again.

"If I drink any more of that I'll be drunk," she insisted.

"So what?"

Heather also stood; her eyes fixed on Dani now. She reached out and gently touched her cheek.

"You should leave him to sleep it off," she murmured, her fingers still tracing a path across the smooth skin of Dani's cheek. The younger woman stood motionless as Heather used one index finger, trailing it gently across her bottom lip before stroking the other cheek.

Dani sucked in a breath and took a step back, turning towards the door.

"If you change your mind come back," Heather told her, watching as she opened the room door.

"I will," Dani breathed, hesitating a moment longer.

She stepped back out into the corridor, her heart thudding hard then she made her way back to the room, slipping the key from her pocket and easing back inside, into the enveloping darkness.

When she stepped back into the room, she closed her eyes. Something was different. She couldn't hear the harsh, deep breathing she'd heard when she left.

It took her a second to realize that Jake was gone.

SIXTY-THREE

He moved slowly and quietly through the house, hidden by the gloom within.

Walking from room to room, occasionally glancing out of a window to see if any other householders nearby had noticed that there was movement within the building.

But it was late. There were very few lights burning in any of the other houses nearby. Anyone with any sense was fast asleep in bed by now. Not preoccupied with what was happening in one of the houses in their street.

Jake Porter sat in one of the armchairs in the living room, his head tilted backwards, his eyes closed. He listened to the silence for a moment longer then got to his feet and headed upstairs.

There were three bedrooms and he walked slowly from one to the other, the boards beneath his feet creaking once or twice. The first two were sparsely decorated and furnished. Both contained just single beds and rudimentary chests of drawers or wardrobes. In the last room he stood beside the bed, gazing down at the pure white duvet.

Your mother's room.

Mother.

He put a hand to his forehead, a sudden stab of pain and dizziness sweeping through him. Jake moved back out of the room, pausing at the small window on the landing to look out into the front garden. The breeze was moving the arms of the weeping willow trees, causing them to brush over the ground like leafy tentacles. Fallen leaves rattled across the lawn every time the wind blew.

At the top of the stairs he paused, holding onto the wooden rail there as if fearing he might fall if he released his grip. The trees outside the house rustled again as a breeze blew through them and Jake turned slowly as he heard a tapping on one of the windows. It took him a second to realize that it was just the branches clicking against the glass like bony fingers. Dead men's hands.

He turned to look back at the door of his mother's room.

Mother.

How often had he been in there when he was growing up in this house? What had she said to him in there? In the rest of the house? What had she taught him? How often had she told him she loved him?

Mother.

Had she *ever* told him she loved him? Had he known he was wanted? Or had she always been cold towards him? Could a woman who would give her child away for adoption even know what love was?

He descended the stairs slowly and made his way to the kitchen, pausing beside a framed picture of his mother. She was dressed in a long gown and holding a scroll. Jake realized it must have been taken the day she graduated. He reached out and touched the picture gently.

Lovingly?

Again, that stab of pain hit him between the eyes, and he swayed drunkenly in the narrow passageway that led into the kitchen. He shot out a hand and steadied himself against the wall behind him, the feeling passing quickly. Jake sucked in a deep breath and moved on.

He sat at the wooden table, gazing blankly at the wall before him. Finally, he got to his feet again and moved towards it, running his fingers across the smooth surface like a blind man reading Braille.

Jake pressed his forehead against the cold plaster, his eyes now closed tightly.

He shuddered, his whole body quivering as if he'd been subjected to an electric shock. His eyes snapped open and he continued to glide his fingertips over the wall, tracing a pattern like a rectangle.

He dug his nails into the plaster until pieces of it began to flake away. Fragments fell to the floor and Jake continued to pull at the wall, pausing for a moment when he dug so hard, he bent a nail back.

Hissing with pain he pulled his hands away and stood looking at the wall, a part of his mind wondering when he would wake from this latest nightmare.

He was still standing there when he heard a sound behind him. He realized that it was coming from the direction of the front door.

And he realized he wasn't dreaming.

SIXTY-FOUR

A key in a lock. The front door opening.

"Jake."

He recognised the voice and turned to face Dani as she walked in, a look of concern on her face.

"What the hell are you doing here?" she wanted to know, crossing to him, putting her arms around him.

Jake stood motionless as she embraced him, his mouth open, his head spinning.

"How did you get here?" she asked.

"I don't know," he murmured. "I don't remember a single thing since we walked out of the hotel bar."

Dani urged him to sit down and she seated herself next to him, grabbing for one of his hands, holding it tightly. She saw the white plaster beneath his nails and frowned, glancing at the wall that he had dug those nails so ferociously into.

"You'd passed out," she told him. "I left you sleeping."

Jake could only shake his head.

"You were drunk," she went on.

He sat forward, putting a hand to his forehead.

"Can't you remember anything?" Dani persisted.

"I remember having a drink in the bar," Jake breathed, shaking his head again. "After that..." He allowed the words to fade away.

"Why did you come here?"

"I don't *know*," he snapped. "I had to. I...I couldn't help myself."

Dani looked at his face and then beyond him to where the wall had been scratched and damaged. She got to her feet and crossed to it, inspecting the marks on the plaster.

"What is it?" she asked, drawing her fingertips over the gouged wall.

"There's something behind it," Jake told her.

"How do you know?"

Again, Jake did nothing but shake his head slowly, unable to furnish her with an answer.

"Can you remember it from when you lived here?" Dani offered.

"It *must* be that" he conceded. "Some...buried memory. Something..." He put a hand to his forehead again, closing his eyes tightly. "Being here again it must have brought that memory forward."

Dani began pulling at the cracked plaster, peeling portions of it away.

She dug away at a particularly large piece, jumping back as it fell to the ground, portions of white plaster skittering across the floor. Jake spun around when he heard the sound.

"It's a door," Dani breathed, looking at what she'd exposed.

Jake got to his feet and joined her, inspecting the damage to the wall once more but, behind the broken plaster he could see something darker. Something that looked like rusted metal. He put out his hand to touch it, feeling the coldness beneath his fingertips.

"There's a cellar," Jake told her, his eyes fixed on the door.

"Can you remember it?"

He nodded.

"What else can you remember?" Dani asked, excitedly.

"I remember...darkness. Being in darkness a lot of the time."

"What was in the cellar?"

"*Me*," Jake murmured.

Dani looked horrified.

"Your mother kept you in the cellar?" she gasped.

Jake began pulling more of the plaster away, anxious to expose the door behind it more fully. Dani eagerly helped him, the crumbly white material now raining down upon the floor as they tore at it.

The entire metal partition was finally exposed, and Jake moved towards it, putting out a hand to touch the rusted iron.

"When we first came here, she kept me in there," Jake breathed. "She was trying to protect me."

Dani looked incredulous. "From who?" she demanded.

Jake merely swallowed hard, unable to give her an answer.

"Where are the keys?" Dani wanted to know. "There were other keys on that ring that the solicitor gave you."

Jake fumbled in his pocket and pulled out the key ring, looking at each key in turn. He finally selected one and pushed it into the door lock. It was stiff with age, but it eventually turned and there was a dull clang as the lock slid free. Jake hesitated a moment then pushed the door slightly. It swung back, the hinges squeaking loudly. Jake couldn't imagine the last time they'd tasted oil.

Dani put out a hand and gripped his arm.

"Are you okay?" she wanted to know.

Jake nodded. "If this helps me remember, it's worth it," he told her, his voice low.

Dani fumbled inside the door, trying to find light switches. When she did, she flicked them on.

Dull yellow light bathed the subterranean room below them.

"Jesus Christ," Jake gasped, looking down the flight of stone steps that led downwards.

SIXTY-FIVE

Dani hissed and brushed a particularly thick cobweb from her face as she descended into the cellar.

The stairwell was narrow, and she could feel the walls on either side of her against her elbows as she followed Jake down into the subterranean depths.

"The solicitor obviously didn't know about this room," she said, waving a hand before her to remove more of the cobwebs that had been spun across the stairwell. She glanced down occasionally, looking at the bare stone steps, careful not to lose her footing on the gleaming surfaces. An earwig scuttled across one of the steps and Dani screwed her face up as she saw it retreat into a gap in the stone. She wondered what other insects or vermin might be lurking in the depths of the house. Judging by the amount of cobwebs there was obviously no shortage of spiders down here. She shuddered involuntarily and brushed her shoulders, hoping nothing had dropped onto her from the ceiling above.

Ahead of her, Jake moved on, further down the steps until he reached the bottom of the flight. Then he glanced around.

The room was small. The walls and floor bare stone. There were storage boxes piled against two of the walls and, on a third, there was what looked like a large dresser. Parts of it were dark with mould and one of the doors was hanging off the hinges. There were a couple of wooden crates too, both sealed. Jake moved towards them, placing his hands on the nearest one, his gaze still moving around the cellar.

The lid of one box was open and inside it he could see clothes. Child's clothes.

His clothes.

He reached in and pulled out a small blue jumper, lifting it into view for a second before dropping it back into the box.

"Why would your mother keep you down here?" Dani murmured, pulling at the broken door of the dresser. "That's terrible. You said she was trying to protect you. Protect you from what? What kind of mother makes her child live in a cellar?"

Jake moved deeper into the subterranean room, trailing his fingers over the surface of boxes and crates as if that simple act would trigger the memories hidden so deeply within his mind.

"I slept there," he muttered, gesturing towards one corner of the room. "There was a mattress on the floor."

"But why?" Dani insisted.

"I don't know," Jake whispered, still gazing around the cellar.

Dani pulled open the drawers of the dresser too, looking inside. There were several books inside. Large, A4 size tomes with plastic covers. Dani lifted one free of the drawer and opened it, the spine creaking. It was a photo album. There was an image on the cover showing a sunrise while two people walked along a riverside path, hand in hand. As Jake continued to wander slowly around the cellar, Dani concentrated on the tome before her.

The pages were filled, not with photographs but with newspaper cuttings. They had been taken carefully from papers and stuck evenly on the pages, preserved. Dani scanned the ones on the first few pages. The headlines on the stories stood out starkly.

HOSPITAL TO CLOSE.

INSUFFICIENT FUNDS CAUSES HOSPITAL TO SHUT DOWN.

Dani glanced at the stories, wondering who had stuck them into this scrapbook and why. Surely it hadn't been Jake himself.

More cuttings. More headlines.

Some of the stories were only nine or ten lines but, as she turned more and more of the pages, she found larger cuttings.

LOCAL RESIDENTS FEARS.

HOSPITAL CLOSURES MIGHT CAUSE SECURITY PROBLEMS.

Dani glanced at the heading, trying to find the source of the cuttings. One of them said *The Exham Chronicle* in small fading letters.

Exham. That name again.

Dani continued leafing through the scrapbook then she returned her attention to the dresser and saw that there were several other volumes hidden in the drawers. She removed those too and flicked hurriedly through them.

More cuttings. All of them carefully and fastidiously stuck onto the plastic covered pages. The newspapers had yellowed in places, the typeface had faded but it was still possible to make out the stories.

"This is pointless."

Jake's voice echoed inside the subterranean room.

Dani looked up to see him standing close to the farthest wall, his fingers gently touching the bare bricks there.

"I'll never remember what happened here," Jake went on. "Perhaps I shouldn't. Perhaps I wasn't meant to. Maybe I've blocked it out. That's why I can't remember. I don't *want* to remember."

"Shall we go back to the hotel?" Dani asked.

Jake nodded.

"There's nothing here for me," he insisted. "I'm going to get someone to clear the house and I'm going to sell it."

Dani nodded gently, watching him as he continued to walk slowly across the bare floor, his footsteps echoing within the confines of the room. She picked up as many of the scrapbooks as she could carry, stuffing them under her arm.

"There could be something in here that helps," she told him.

"Does it matter? I need to concentrate on *now*. On the future. Not on the past. Not on a past that I don't even want to know about."

"But if you could remember..."

"I can't remember for a reason, Dani," Jake interrupted, cutting across her. "My mind has obviously shut out those memories to protect me."

"Just like your mother was protecting you by keeping you down here?"

He shot her an angry glance.

"I wasn't down here all the time," he countered.

"I thought you couldn't remember."

"I can remember *that*."

"So, you can remember she kept you here, but you can't remember anything about *her*?"

"Just drop it will you?" he snapped.

"The answer might be in these scrapbooks."

"I don't care. I don't care what happened here. I don't care about her."

"She was your mother, Jake. You need to know."

"No, I don't."

He walked briskly across the bare floor towards the flight of stone steps.

"If you want to stay down here sorting through this rubbish then that's up to you," he snapped. "I'm going back to the hotel."

Dani hesitated a moment then she followed him, the scrapbooks still wedged under her arm.

She was at the top of the steps when her phone rang. She grabbed for it, one of the scrapbooks falling from her grip. Dani dropped to pick it up noticing that the incoming call was from Mike. She ignored it and pushed the phone back into her pocket.

If Jake heard the phone, he didn't comment on it. As she walked into the kitchen he was sitting at the table, his gaze lowered.

"If you want to go..." she began.

Jake nodded.

"I've seen all I want to see of this house," he told her.

"You go back to the hotel and rest," Dani told him. "I'll finish looking around here."

"I don't want to keep anything," Jake told her again.

"I understand."

Jake hesitated then nodded. He reached out and touched her cheek with his fingers.

"Thank you," he murmured, turning towards the door.

Outside, the first rays of dawn sunlight began to filter across the sky.

SIXTY-SIX

The headache had begun within minutes of Jake leaving the house.

A dull crushing pain that began at the base of his skull and slowly enveloped his head until it felt as if someone had put his cranium in a vice and was slowly tightening it.

He sat in the back of the taxi, eyes closed, and head lowered, one hand pressed against his forehead.

The taxi driver glanced into his rear-view mirror occasionally, seeing how pale his passenger looked. More than once he thought Jake had passed out but then a movement would tell him this wasn't the case.

"Rough night?" he finally asked.

"You could say that" Jake murmured; his eyes still closed.

The taxi driver glanced at him again in the rear-view mirror and decided any further attempts at perfunctory conversation would be wasted. Jake glanced out of the window, watching as the houses, shops and hotels sped past. He let out a low murmur of pain and rotated his head gently on his shoulders, hoping that would alleviate some of the discomfort. It didn't.

As the taxi reached the sea front, Jake leaned forward and tapped the driver on the shoulder.

"Stop here," he said.

The driver looked puzzled for a moment but brought the cab to a halt.

"The Royal is another half a mile," he said but Jake was already pushing money into his hand.

"I know that," he announced. "I need some fresh air."

The driver was fumbling for change when Jake stepped out of the cab, slammed the door behind him and headed off across the wide pavement towards the sea front. The taxi driver waited a moment longer then drove off.

Jake walked across the wide, open paved area, between the path and the walkway that led along the top of the sea wall. The wall itself was less than five or six feet above the sand below and that stretched out a good six or seven hundred yards until it reached the grey waters of the sea. Jake could smell the salt in the air as he gazed towards the waves. There was a strong breeze coming in off the water and it washed over him like invisible spray. He started walking, realizing with delight, that the pain in his skull was diminishing.

Up ahead of him was one of Walmsley's piers. There were amusement arcades and several other buildings upon it including a whitewashed structure that, during the summer months, housed a variety show. Jake passed under it, struck by how dark it was in the shadows there. The path dipped sharply down as it passed beneath the pier and Jake stepped carefully, avoiding the puddles that had accumulated there.

Away to his left he saw a figure moving across the sand and realized that it was someone walking their dog. The animal bounded about happily before finally heading down towards the water, its owner in hot pursuit.

Jake walked on, emerging from the other side of the pier. He had travelled another thirty yards when the wave of dizziness hit him.

He swayed uncertainly and headed straight for one of the wooden benches that lined the beach front walkway, sitting there until the feeling passed.

The breeze that was blowing in from the sea seemed to be intensifying and this helped him fight off the unsteadiness. He sucked in several deep breaths, got to his feet, and walked on.

He estimated it took him another twenty minutes before he reached the Royal.

He could see it across the road away to his right. Jake paused, seating himself on another of the wooden benches, his attention once again drawn to the sea. The waves were getting larger, fanned by the increasingly strong wind. He could see someone down by the water skimming stones across the dark water. Jake watched for a moment then headed towards the hotel, glancing up at the facade as he reached it. He thought he saw someone standing at one of the other windows looking out onto the front but the shadow there vanished as quickly as it had appeared.

Jake slowed his pace slightly, feeling another bout of dizziness hit him. He clenched his teeth hard and shot out a hand to steady himself as he passed through the main entrance.

He could smell food. Breakfast was obviously being prepared for the small rota of guests, but the scent only made him feel sick. He walked on, anxious to reach his room now.

As usual there was no one at the reception desk so he walked across to the lift and jabbed the 'call' button.

The door slid open immediately and Jake stepped inside.

As he stepped out again on the first floor, he saw one of the doors further down the corridor open a fraction and then close again. Inside he heard floorboards creak.

He got to his room and walked in, slumping on the bed, and closing his eyes immediately. It was like throwing a switch.

Jake was fast asleep in minutes.

SIXTY-SEVEN

"I don't give a fuck."

Dani held the phone away from her ear slightly as Mike Quinn ranted angrily on the other end of the line.

"When are you coming back?" Mike persisted. "You've been gone for fucking ages."

"Mike, it's only been two days," Dani reminded him.

"What the fuck is he doing anyway?"

"It's complicated."

"It's not your problem. It's his. You should come back. Let him sort things out."

"I told you, I'll be back soon."

There was a long silence at the other end of the line then Mike finally spoke again.

"You having fun with him?" he sneered.

"What the fuck is that supposed to mean?" Dani snapped.

"You know what I mean."

"You're like a child sometimes."

Another long silence.

"I had to go with him," Dani explained. "This is a big deal for Jake."

"Yeah, for *him*, not for you. Not for *us*."

"When he sells his mother's house, he'll have extra money to play with. He's going to feel more like giving some of it away when the time comes."

"I suppose you're right," Mike admitted, some of the vehemence leaving his voice.

"I *am* right," Dani insisted.

"What's the house like?"

"It's nice. His mother was a psychiatrist like he is. It must have paid well."

"But he can't remember anything about living there?"

"Only bits and pieces. It's weird."

"I told you there was something wrong with him."

"It's not his fault he can't remember his childhood, Mike."

"So, when are you going back to the hotel?"

"I told him I'd have a look around here then I'm going back."

"What are you looking for?"

"I'm not even sure. Just some clues about his childhood. About his mother."

"What does it matter?"

"It's interesting."

"Why? What the fuck does it matter to you?"

Dani sighed and shook her head.

"Look, I'll let you know when we're heading back, right?" she told him, sharply.

"You've got shit here to sort out," Mike reminded her.

"What do you mean?"

"That old bastard who lives next door to Jake. He's not going to stop until we sort something out."

"Don't worry about him. I'll take care of him."

Another silence.

"Mike, I've got to go," Dani went on. "I'll let you know when I get back."

He grunted something unintelligible and terminated the call.

Dani glanced at her phone for a moment then pushed it back into her pocket. She walked slowly around the pond in the front garden (she'd come outside to take the call in the first place because the reception was better beyond the confines of the house), looking down into the murky depths. There were dead leaves floating on the surface and any fish that had once inhabited the pond had long since died. Dani finished her cigarette then walked back into the house, closing the door behind her.

In the kitchen she stood looking at the door leading down into the cellar as if mesmerised by it.

She had an overwhelming feeling of sorrow. For Jake. For what he'd gone through as a child. If she could do anything to help him, she would.

While stealing his money?

Dani tried to push the thought from her mind.

She sat down at the kitchen table and looked at the pile of scrapbooks she'd taken from the cellar.

There were six of them, all bearing similar banal covers like sunsets or cuddly animals and as far as she could tell, they weren't in any particular order.

Were they?

From what she had seen already some of the cuttings and assorted paraphernalia contained details about Jake's mother. Margaret Ford. Better known as Maggie Ford.

His birth mother and his adoptive mother were both called Margaret.

There were cuttings from newspapers. Some handwritten letters and notes. One from a friend congratulating her on passing the exams necessary to allow her to attend university in Cambridgeshire. A birthday party invitation. Gig ticket stubs. Some photos from University years. Wedding invitations. Saved Birthday cards. All sorts. The detritus of a life. Nothing telling or significant it seemed.

Not until Dani got to the second scrapbook.

SIXTY-EIGHT

In the dream someone was pulling at his arm. Someone had hold of it and was tugging hard.

Jake groaned and tried to resist the probing fingers.

He moved slightly to one side but the hand that had grabbed him continued to hold him and to shake him. He tried to push them away, but it was useless. He turned his head in that direction and, as he did, he realized that he wasn't dreaming.

Jake grunted and opened his eyes, looking up at the figure above him.

Dani looked down at him, still shaking him.

"All right, all right," Jake gasped, panting loudly. He finally managed to focus on her, blinking myopically as he looked. He held up a hand to try and prevent her continuing with her shaking.

"Christ, I thought you were dead," Dani told him. "I've been trying to wake you for ages. Did you take a sleeping pill or something?"

"No. I didn't take anything, I just...I must have passed out when I got back. I remember laying down on the bed and then...nothing."

He sat up slowly, propping himself against the headboard, feeling tentatively at the back of his neck, relieved that the stiffness there had dissipated. Any lingering traces of a headache had also vanished. Jake accepted the glass of water that Dani handed him, sipping gratefully. He rubbed his eyes, noticing that it was approaching dusk outside. He crossed to the windows and gazed out, shivering slightly. The trees on the other side of the road were bending slightly as the increasingly strong wind battered them. The sky above the sea was nearly as gloomy as the grey waves themselves. Jake looked at his watch, surprised to see that it was almost four thirty pm.

"How long have you been back?" he wanted to know.

"Half an hour," Dani told him. "Maybe more. I've been trying to wake you for most of that time."

Jake rubbed his eyes. "I didn't realize it was that late. I must have been flat out since I got back."

He swung himself off the bed and walked to the bathroom where he splashed his face with cold water. He straightened up, looking at his reflection in the polished glass. Not particularly impressed with what he saw. His skin looked pale and waxy, dark rings beneath his eyes made it look as if he hadn't slept for days.

"Did you find anything interesting at the house?" he called.

"More scrapbooks, I've put those in the car."

"Nothing else?"

"You didn't want to keep anything anyway, did you?"

Jake shook his head and splashed more water on his face, keeping his eyes closed as it ran down his cheeks in rivulets.

When he looked at himself in the mirror again some of the colour seemed to be returning to his cheeks. Or so he thought.

"None of the furniture or ornaments?" Dani persisted.

"Nothing," Jake assured her, supporting himself on the sides of the white porcelain sink.

"When they come to empty the house, they'll make an inventory, if you change your mind about keeping anything you can..."

"I don't want *anything* from there," Jake snapped. He sucked in a deep breath and sat down on the edge of the bath.

"Feeling better?" Dani asked, appearing in the doorway.

"A little," he told her. "Just so groggy. It can't still be a hangover can it?" He managed a smile.

"You did drink *a lot* last night," she reminded him.

"I don't know why I did."

"You were trying to relax."

"And look where it got me."

"I think all the stress about your mother and the house just got to you."

Jake raised his eyebrows by way of an answer.

"And you obviously needed to sleep," Dani went on. "I just can't believe you managed to sleep through all the commotion," she said.

Jake frowned.

"What commotion?" he wanted to know.

"People have been coming and going since I got back."

Again, he could only offer a puzzled look.

"What people?" Jake enquired, rubbing his face with a towel.

"The police for one."

He looked at himself in the mirror and then at Dani once more.

"They were here when I got back," she went on. "An ambulance too. Heather Lawson, that woman we were talking to last night in the bar, she was found dead in her room this afternoon."

SIXTY-NINE

Jake slept for most of the journey back from Walmsley.

He clambered into the passenger seat and drifted off almost as soon as they left the hotel. Dani waited ten or fifteen minutes then switched the radio on, keeping the volume low so she didn't disturb him but needing the company of the voices and music that came from the speakers. The chatter was inane and most of the music was the usual generic, manufactured garbage that seemed so popular but, Dani reasoned, it was better than driving in silence.

She muttered to herself when some spots of rain hit the windscreen but, fortunately it didn't last long, and the majority of the journey was completed before the droplets became more plentiful.

Dani was happy to find that the roads were quiet leading away from the holiday resort and, only when they got to within thirty miles of their destination did they become busier again.

She pulled into a petrol station on the way back and hurried to the bathroom, leaving Jake sound asleep in the passenger seat. She had returned to find him still sleeping soundly. More than once she'd squeezed his arm, just to make sure he could feel it.

Just to make sure he wasn't dead.

The journey took less than two hours, and she was relieved when she pulled the car to a halt in front of Jake's house. He woke easily and looked across at her, smiling.

As they walked to the house, they saw the light in one of Ted Brady's bedrooms flicker on.

It stayed on for a moment then went out again.

There was two days' worth of mail lying on the doormat as they walked in, but Jake was relieved to see that none of the letters were important. Dani took the bag full of scrapbooks into the sitting room and put them beside the sofa. Jake wandered upstairs to check his e-mails.

Normality it seemed, had returned.

Dani gave him twenty minutes then she went up and knocked lightly on the office door, stepping inside when he told her to.

"Do you feel better?" she asked.

"Much better, thanks," he told her, smiling.

"I've got to pop out for a little while," she said.

Jake nodded.

"I might have an early night," he told her.

"You looked as if you needed it."

"Where are you going?" he wanted to know.

"Just to see a friend. She's having boyfriend trouble. She wants to talk," Dani said, making sure she didn't stumble over her words. "She messaged me when we were on the way back. You know how it is."

"Not really," he said, smiling. "But, if you've got to go, you've got to go."

"I'll be as quick as I can. You go to bed."

Jake nodded.

Dani hesitated a moment longer then turned and headed off down the stairs. Jake heard her footfalls on the stairs and then the front door opening and closing. He watched from the office window as she drove away then he turned back to his computer screen. He glanced at his e-mails for a moment longer then reached for his phone, finding the number he wanted immediately.

He pressed the phone to his ear and waited.

"Hello, Jake," the voice at the other end of the line said.

"Ray, I'm sorry to bother you so late," Jake announced.

"It's okay, I'm still at work," DI Ray Vincent told him. "What can I do for you?"

"I need a favour."

"Go on."

"I need some information about a woman called Heather Lawson."

"What kind of information?"

"Cause of death."

There was a long silence then Vincent spoke again.

"When did she die?" he wanted to know.

"Earlier today in a hotel in Walmsley. It's a seaside resort."

"Why do you want to know?"

"I met her last night, talked to her. If it's a problem..."

"No. It's not. I'll see what I can do. Give me a few more details."

"I can't tell you too much about her, I only met her last night as I said. I can tell you the address of the hotel and things like that."

"Go on."

While Jake did just that he continued to glance at his computer screen, scanning his e-mails once more and then opening another window.

"All right," Vincent said. "I'll make a couple of calls. See what I can do."

"Thanks Ray, I appreciate it," Jake told the policeman.

He terminated the call and returned his attention to the screen, his face lit only by the glow coming from it.

It was another hour before he finally made his way to the bedroom.

SEVENTY

Dani gasped as she felt Mike Quinn's hands part her legs. She raised herself up on her elbows slightly, looking down at him as he lowered his face between her slender thighs.

When his tongue pushed between her slippery lips and then flicked at her swollen clitoris, she arched her back and reached for his head, wanting to hold him where he was while he licked at her.

As the pleasure grew, she pushed her hips down towards his questing tongue, sighing when Mike kissed his way up her body, using his tongue to trace a path over her flat stomach to her stiff nipples. He kissed those hard buds and then her face and mouth and Dani shuddered when she felt the tip of his penis rubbing against her wetness.

Mike slid into her with one deep thrust and she felt him swell inside her as he built up a steady rhythm.

She locked her legs around his back, drawing him in more deeply, running her fingers through his hair.

He lifted himself up on his powerful arms, looking down at her body beneath him, gazing at his own erection as it slid back and forth between her legs. Again, Dani arched her back and, as she did, Mike drove particularly deeply and powerfully into her. The feelings that spread from between her legs seemed to envelope her entire body and she slipped one hand down there to hasten the release, her own fingertips gliding over and around her clitoris, but Mike suddenly pulled out, kneeling before her so she could see every inch of his throbbing penis.

Dani was about to protest when he rolled her onto her stomach, gripping her hips and raising her pert buttocks before him.

He kissed each of her taut cheeks briefly and then knelt behind her, guiding his stiffness into her once again.

His thrusts were even more urgent this time and Dani felt his fingers digging into her skin as he increased his pace, as anxious for release as she was.

She gripped the sheet beneath her hands, clenching the white cotton tightly as the sensations built quickly inside her. She moved one hand back between her legs again, fingers working expertly until she felt that glorious pleasure building once more.

Dani climaxed, pushing back against Mike's deep thrusts, her breath rasping in her throat. She was still shuddering when Mike gripped her hips so strongly, he almost broke the skin. She heard him grunt, felt him shoot his hot liquid inside her and that seemed to push her over the edge again. They both slumped forward, gasping for breath, his erection still inside her.

He moved her long hair away from her ear and neck so he could kiss them gently, his erection softening and finally slipping free of her wet, clasping centre. When he rolled off her, she flopped onto her back, still breathing heavily.

"Did he know you were coming here?" Mike breathed.

"Yes Mike," she said, sarcastically. "I said I'm just nipping around to Mike's flat so he can fuck me." She looked at him. "What do *you* think?"

He smiled, reaching for his cigarettes. He lit one and took a long drag.

"I don't know what you tell him," he answered. "I don't know anything about your relationship, do I?"

"Do you want to?" she challenged.

"Not really," he grunted. "You can tell me about what happened while you were away with him though. Tell me about the house. About his mother."

"It was a nice place. Expensive looking."

"So, he should get a decent price when he sells?"

Dani nodded, sipping from the glass of water beside the bed.

"And he couldn't remember anything about the place when he saw it?" Mike went on.

"Not to begin with," she explained. "The only thing he seemed to remember was the cellar."

"He's got a cellar under his house, hasn't he?"

"Maybe that's why. Perhaps he subconsciously picked a house with a cellar because it rang some kind of psychological bell."

Mike grunted and laughed.

"What?" Dani asked, seeing the dismissive expression on his face. "It's possible."

"If I was you, I'd stick to working in Starbucks. Forget about the amateur psychiatry."

She slapped him on the arm indignantly.

"What about his mother?" Mike went on.

"She killed herself."

"Shit. Why?"

"No one seems to know."

"They say people who top themselves are cowards, but I think they must be pretty brave. Imagine having the balls to take your own life. How did she do it? Pills? Razor? Hanging?"

"I didn't ask," Dani murmured, rolling her eyes.

"She must have been really fucked up."

"Or had some really bad problems."

"But she was old, wasn't she? Old people don't normally commit suicide. They just wait to die."

"Whatever made her do it, she obviously couldn't face it any more. Couldn't cope."

"And he can't remember anything about her or about his childhood?"

Dani shook her head.

"I brought some scrapbooks back from there, but he says he doesn't want to go through them," she explained.

"What's in them?"

"Pictures. Lots of photos. Of him. Of his mother. Of places he used to live but he won't look at them. He just wants to leave all that in the past."

"I wonder what he's hiding," Mike chuckled. "Maybe he was abused when he was a kid or something. I think abused kids sometimes try and shut out bad experiences, don't they?"

"It's possible but he's a psychiatrist, he'd know how to deal with that kind of stuff wouldn't he?"

"Depends how bad it was."

He leaned across and kissed her cheek, turning her head to kiss her lips.

Dani responded fiercely, one hand reaching for his penis. She squeezed it gently as they kissed, satisfied when she felt it begin to stiffen again.

"You really did miss me, didn't you?" Mike grinned, looking down to watch her hand moving up and down his rapidly hardening shaft. "What time is he expecting you back?"

"Not for a while," Dani told him.
As she spoke, she lowered her head towards his growing erection.

SEVENTY-ONE

Jake turned the key in the ignition once again, groaning when the engine started, whirred for a second then died.

He sat motionless for a moment then tried again.

Same thing. The whine of the engine and then nothing. Jake swung himself out of the car and walked around to the front of the vehicle. He looked reproachfully at the vehicle for a moment then turned as he heard Dani's voice behind him.

"What's wrong?" she asked, walking across to join him as he continued to glare at the recalcitrant car.

"Christ knows," Jake grunted. "And there's no point me looking under the bonnet because I haven't got a clue what I'm looking for anyway. I'll have to call the RAC."

"That could take hours. It might be okay. I heard it start a couple of times."

"I don't want to chance it."

"Take my car. You won't be long, will you?"

"I was going to see my mother."

"Are you going into the office today?"

"Not today. I called earlier and my appointments have been shifted to tomorrow."

"I can drop you if you're just going to see your mum."

"Car trouble?"

They both turned as they heard the third voice.

Ted Brady walked to the end of his path; his gaze also fixed on the stranded car.

"What the fuck does he want?" Dani murmured under her breath.

"They're a bloody nuisance, aren't they?" Brady went on, jabbing a finger in the direction of the car. "Unpredictable. Like women." He looked at Dani and smiled. "You should call the AA."

"Wow, you think so?" Dani grunted.

"Thanks for the advice, I was just going to," Jake replied, not attempting to hide the sarcasm in his voice.

"A mate of mine is a mechanic. He'd have a look at it for you. For a price," Brady offered.

"Thanks," Jake replied. "I'll get it looked at."

"You should," Brady continued. "You never know what could go wrong. They can run for months and you never know there's a problem until it's too late. You can't trust them. Just like women." Again, he smiled as he looked at Dani.

She met his gaze with an angry look.

"It was obviously all right while you were away," Brady went on. "Where did you go? A little holiday? I noticed you'd been away for a couple of days."

"Yeah, I bet you did," Dani murmured. "Nosey fucker."

"Where did you go then?" Brady went on. "Just nipped off for a dirty weekend, did you?" He laughed.

"It wasn't the weekend," Jake reminded him.

"No," Brady growled. "And you don't need to go away for a bit of fun, do you?"

"As ever it's lovely chatting with you," Jake told the other man. "But we'd better go."

"I'll drive you," Dani told him, and Brady watched as they walked towards her car. He stood at the bottom of the path watching as the vehicle pulled away. As it did Brady smiled and waved.

Dani glanced at him disgustedly as they drove past.

"He's a fucking creep," she hissed.

"I agree," Jake answered.

"He probably did something to your car," she went on. "He probably messed with the engine. That's why it won't work."

"Why would he do that?"

"Because he's a dickhead. He knew we'd been away, didn't he? I bet he's been at his window watching until we got back."

Jake raised his eyebrows. "You might be right," he said, smiling.

Dani drove on.

When they finally reached Paxton Villas, she stopped the car outside the Care Home and watched as Jake prepared to get out.

"Your mum will be pleased to see you," she offered.

"My real mum you mean?" Jake mused.

"Are you going to say anything to her about...you know...the house? Your birth mother?"

"What's the point? She wouldn't know what I was talking about anyway."

"My mum's sister was the same. She had Alzheimer's too. Sometimes when they see a new face it can help."

"Do you want to come in with me then?"

"It couldn't hurt."

"I wouldn't recommend it."

"You're not going to be long, are you?"

Jake shook his head and smiled. He reached out and squeezed Dani's hand.

"Thank you," he murmured.

SEVENTY-TWO

The silence inside the room was almost oppressive.

Jake shifted uncomfortably in his chair, watching as his mother once again ran appraising eyes over Dani.

Margaret Porter glanced at the TV and then at Dani again before she leaned forward slightly and broke wind loudly. As she settled herself in her seat, she began picking her nose.

"So, you're all right then?" Jake said, wearily, looking away as she pushed her thumb deeper into one nostril.

"Is it warm out there?" Margaret wanted to know.

"I told you when we first got here," Jake reminded her.

"It *is* warm," Dani interjected.

"Where's Lucy?" Margaret wanted to know.

Jake sighed.

"Lucy's not here, mum," he explained.

"Lucy's his daughter," the older woman told Dani. "Lovely girl."

Dani smiled.

"And who are you?" Margaret went on.

"This is Dani, mum, she's a friend of mine," Jake offered.

Margaret belched loudly.

There was an awkward silence then Dani spoke again.

"Jake said you had a fall," she began. "Are you feeling better now?"

"I'm all right," Margaret said.

"You have to be careful," Dani went on.

"Where's Lucy?" Margaret enquired again.

"She's not here," Jake snapped. "I told you that." He couldn't hide the impatience in his voice.

"It was such a shame when Jake and Claire divorced," Margaret persisted. "I felt so sorry for Lucy. No child should have to go through that."

"All right, mum," Jake sighed. "I don't think Dani is interested in my divorce."

"He only sees Lucy once a week. That isn't right is it?" Margaret continued, shaking her head.

"All right, mum," Jake snapped. "That's enough."

"Father's should be with their children," Margaret insisted. "Not just seeing them once a week. It's not right."

"For Christ's sake drop it will you?" Jake shouted.

Margaret broke wind loudly. Jake looked at Dani and shook his head then he returned his attention to the older woman.

"We've got to go," he announced. "I need to get to the office."

Margaret looked at Dani again and leaned forward slightly in her chair.

"What do you do?" she wanted to know.

"I work at Starbucks," Dani told her. "It's a coffee place. They sell coffee. I'm the manageress."

Margaret looked blankly at Dani.

"We really must go," Jake repeated, motioning to Dani to join him as he headed for the door.

"Has Lucy got a job yet?" Margaret wanted to know.

"Not yet," Jake sighed then he looked at Dani again, holding the door open.

"It was lovely to meet you," Dani told Margaret.

Margaret belched loudly.

"For Christ's sake," Jake shouted. "You're fucking disgusting. Stop it."

Dani looked at him, surprised by the vehemence in his tone.

Jake lowered his gaze, his breath coming in ragged gasps.

"Tell Lucy to come and see me," Margaret muttered.

Jake glanced at the older woman for a moment longer then walked out closing the door behind him.

SEVENTY-THREE

Dani could see the frustration and something darker on Jake's face as he slumped into the passenger seat of her car, his eyes gazing straight ahead, wanting only to be away from Paxton Villas.

As she started the engine and guided the car away from the front of the building she reached across and squeezed Jake's arm.

"It's her age, she doesn't know what she's saying," she said.

"Not all of it," Jake snapped. "There's no excuse for some of the things she does. I don't care how old she is. She's disgusting sometimes. Belching and breaking wind like that. It's not right."

"At least she's being looked after," Dani insisted.

They drove a little way in silence and then she spoke again.

"She certainly seems to miss Lucy, doesn't she?" she murmured. "Does she ever visit?"

"What's the point?" Jake grunted. "My mum can't hear properly. She can't see very well. Lucy wouldn't be able to talk to her even if she did visit her."

"Have you changed the way you think after finding out about your birth mother?"

"No. Like I've said before, the woman back there in that home, the woman sitting around and waiting to die, she's my *real* mother. That woman in Walmsley was nothing to me."

Dani nodded slowly.

"You need some good news to cheer you up," she offered.

"Anything."

"What would you say if I told you I was pregnant?"

Jake froze. He slowly turned his head to look at her, the colour draining from his cheeks.

"You're pregnant?" he murmured.

"I'm not sure yet. I need to do another test."

"When did you do the first one?"

"About a week ago."

"And it was positive?"

"Is the news that bad?"

"It isn't what I was expecting."

"I thought you might be happy."

"Maybe I would have been...twenty years ago."

"I'm sorry it's such bad news for you," she breathed.

"It's just a bit of a shock," he admitted. "Do you want to keep it?"

"After your reaction I'm not sure."

"If you decide to get rid of it..."

"I haven't thought about this, Jake," she interrupted. "Do you want me to get an abortion then?"

"We should discuss this later."

"Or shall I just drive straight to the abortion clinic now?"

"You've never mentioned wanting kids. I just assumed you were on the pill."

"I was. It's not one hundred per cent you know, and I did have that spell of sickness last week. That might be when it happened."

Jake sighed.

Dani glanced at him.

"Kids aren't exactly top of my wish list you know," she said, quietly.

"Then surely your choice is obvious."

"It should be but it's not that easy, Jake. I haven't thought this through yet. You've got to give me some time."

He nodded.

"What do you want me to say?" she asked. "That I'm sorry?"

"I can't be a father again at my age, Dani," Jake protested. "It wouldn't be fair on you or.... the child."

"Perhaps now you know how your mother felt. Your real mother."

"What the hell is that supposed to mean?"

"She must have considered what to do with you and realized she couldn't cope. Do you still think she was wrong to give you up for adoption?"

Jake shook his head incredulously.

"Oh, come on," he snapped. "That's a completely different situation. I was ten for Christ's sake. If she was going to get rid of me then she should have done it earlier. *Much* earlier."

"Perhaps she tried but just couldn't manage."

"So, you're defending her now?"

"I'm just trying to make you understand that circumstances alter things."

"Don't try and lecture me, Dani," he snapped. "We need to talk about this later. Not now."

"What's the point? You're not going to change your opinion, are you?"

Jake tapped gently on his thigh. It was hard to disagree.

SEVENTY-FOUR

The sunlight that flooded the office did little to raise Jake's spirits. He was sitting at his desk gazing distractedly at his computer screen when there was a gentle tap on the door.

He quickly closed the window on the screen pertaining to abortions and looked in the direction of the door.

Sheree Fowler bustled into the room, smiling as usual.

"Your four o'clock appointment cancelled," she announced. "I've re-arranged it for tomorrow at eleven if that's okay. You had a gap there."

Jake smiled.

"Thank you, Sheree," he said, his eyes still fixed on the computer screen.

She turned to leave but then hesitated.

"Doctor Porter, I hope you don't mind me asking but is everything all right?" Sheree enquired.

"What makes you ask?" he wanted to know.

"You just seem to have been a bit...I don't know...distracted, distant since you got back. Was the trip worthwhile?"

"I don't know if that's the right word," Jake said, smiling. "But it was necessary. It's a chapter of my life I can close now."

Sheree nodded.

"Your daughter popped in while you were away you know," she went on. "It was nice to see her. She's grown into a lovely girl, hasn't she?"

"Lucy came here. Why? What did she want?"

"She said she wanted to talk to you. She said she'd tried phoning you, but you hadn't answered. I told her you were busy."

"She didn't say anything else?"

"Well, we chatted about this and that. You know, girls together and all that." Sheree laughed.

"She never normally comes here. Was she okay?"

"She seemed fine. She stayed for a cup of tea. It was really nice chatting to her. You must be so proud of her."

Jake nodded slowly.

"I bet you still think of her as your little girl, don't you?" Sheree told him. "I'm the same with my daughter. I think all parents are like that. It doesn't matter how old your children get they're always your little ones aren't they?"

Jake smiled as convincingly as he could and nodded again.

There was a long silence and then Sheree turned.

"Well, better get on," she said, heading towards the door. Jake watched as she closed it behind her, moving back into the outer office where her desk was. Silence filled the room once again. He glanced across his desk, looking at the framed photo of Lucy on one corner. Almost unconsciously he reached out and touched it.

When his phone rang it startled him. He looked down at it then grabbed it, noting who was calling.

The conversation with his publisher took longer than he'd anticipated but, when he finally put the phone down, Jake did feel as if his spirits had been lifted a little. The last few days had been a catalogue of surprises (most of them not particularly welcome) and revelations that had unsettled him to say the least. Jake liked routine. He didn't like surprises. He didn't like being out of control and the last few days had made him feel as if he had very little control over his life at this precise moment in time. It wasn't a feeling he enjoyed.

He was reading through a case file when his phone rang again.

Once more he snatched it up.

"Hello," he said.

"Jake, it's DI Vincent, I hope I'm not disturbing you," the voice at the other end of the line intoned.

"No. You're not."

"I made some calls about what we talked about," Vincent informed him. "That woman you met in Walmsley."

"And?"

There was a moments silence and Jake was about to speak again when Vincent broke that silence.

"Did you know the woman who died?" the policeman enquired.

"No. We met in the hotel I was staying in. We chatted over a drink. That was it. Why?"

"So, you didn't know anything about her?"

"No."

Again, that lingering silence.

"I spoke to the coroner down there at Walmsley," Vincent went on. "He was very helpful. He was also a little puzzled."

"Why?"

"Heather Lawson died of an ectopic pregnancy."

"Why was that so puzzling?"

"Because there was no sign of a foetus. She died of an ectopic pregnancy or all the symptoms associated with one, but she wasn't carrying a child. How the hell can someone die of an ectopic pregnancy without even being pregnant?"

SEVENTY-FIVE

"When are you leaving?"

Dani put the phone down next to one of the scrapbooks and switched it to speaker.

"Tonight, as soon as I pack a bag," Jake told her. "My publishers said they couldn't fix another date because of schedules. The person they want me to meet is flying off to America to do some work. It's the only time they can manage for the next two weeks and the publishers want to get things rolling."

"When will you be back?" she wanted to know.

"Tomorrow afternoon. Sorry it's short notice but the publishers say it's important. They want me to meet someone who's going to be doing publicity for my next book. They think that this person will be able to get me on TV as well."

"Talking about your book?"

"No, as a guest psychiatrist," Jake chuckled. "They have them on daytime TV sometimes apparently."

"Cool. You could become a star," Dani said, smiling.

"I'm not holding my breath but if it helps sales of the book then that's good. Are you sure you don't mind me going? You could come with me if you wanted to."

"No, I'd better not. I'd just cramp your style." Again, she laughed. "It's a great opportunity, Jake."

"That's what I thought. It could be very profitable."

Dani raised her eyebrows.

"Do you want me to pick you up from your office?" she asked.

"No, it's okay. I'll get a taxi back when I finish then I'll drive my car to the station."

"*Your* car? It's a wreck."

"It'll get me to the station. I'll leave it in the multi-storey then take it to the garage tomorrow when I get back."

"If you say so."

"Sorry again for leaving you on your own tonight," Jake told her.

"No problem. I've got things to do."

They chatted a little longer, then Jake terminated the call.

Dani went back to the scrapbooks.

***

With his last appointment of the day cancelled, Jake left his office around half past three.

Sheree was happy to finish early too. She had something to do she told him. Something about a builder and an extension that was taking too long. Jake didn't really hear what she said but his expression when she was telling him was genuine enough.

He walked the half a mile or so to the shopping mall, moving through the throngs of people and finally finding a window seat in a cafe.

He'd sent the message earlier, just before he left his office. Now it was just a matter of waiting. He ordered a cappuccino and sipped it as he waited, unable to prevent himself glancing at his watch every few minutes. He didn't like waiting around but, in this case, he was willing to make allowances.

However, half an hour later he was beginning to feel irritable. How much longer would he have to wait? He'd made everything clear enough in his message, hadn't he? Location. Time.

It was another ten minutes before he saw her heading towards him through the throngs of people.

Jake waved excitedly but received no acknowledgement of his gesture. She just walked on, slowly and unhurriedly. No urgency in her step.

As she walked into the cafe, she cast him only a cursory glance.

Jake smiled warmly but the gesture wasn't reciprocated.

She sat down opposite him and looked questioningly at him.

"Hey you," he said, smiling.

"What do you want?" Lucy Porter said, flatly.

SEVENTY-SIX

Jake looked at his daughter warmly, but he saw none of that warmth returned in her stern expression.

"I got your message earlier," he said, smiling. "I like your hair. Have you dyed it?"

"It's been this colour for the last month," she reminded him.

Jake nodded.

"Can you drive me to my interview then?" Lucy wanted to know.

"I would, but my bloody car is playing up."

"Why are you here then?"

"I was on my way to the station. I thought it might be nice to have a coffee with you before I left."

"So, you can't take me?"

"I wish I could."

"How am I going to get there then?" There was a note of desperation in her voice but also a touch of anger that Jake picked up.

"Can't you get a train?" he offered. "It isn't that far."

"I wanted a bit of company before I went in. You know I get nervous."

"You'll be fine." He reached out to touch her hand, but Lucy pulled hers away.

"So, you got me to come in here just to tell me you couldn't take me?" she grunted. "What was the point of that?"

"I was heading for the station, like I said. I just thought it would be nice to catch up."

"With what?"

"With you." He smiled warmly but, again, it wasn't reciprocated.

"Why are you going to the station?" she asked. "Going to see your girlfriend?"

"No. I've got to go and see my publishers. I've got a meeting about..."

"Is your girlfriend going with you?" Lucy demanded, cutting across him.

"No."

"Did she tell you we chatted?"

Jake looked puzzled.

"No," he murmured. "When?"

"About a week ago. Maybe more. I didn't keep a note. I wonder why she never mentioned it. Does she always keep things from you?" Lucy smiled but there was no warmth in the gesture.

"What were you talking about?"

"Not much. She was just chatting shit. She wanted to know about your last girlfriend. Is she the jealous type?"

He sat forward slightly. "Dani wanted to know about Rhiannon. What was she asking?"

"What she was like. Why she left you. That kind of thing."

"She never mentioned your chat to me."

"Oh, dear," Lucy grinned, the sarcasm in her tone almost palpable.

"What did you tell her?" Jake wanted to know.

"I didn't tell her Jack Shit. I don't know what your last girlfriend was like, do I? I don't care." She took a deep breath. "Why *did* she leave you?"

"Does it matter?"

"I personally couldn't give a fuck, but Dani obviously could."

The people at the next table glanced across briefly then continued with their own conversation. A silence descended between Jake and Lucy as he gazed down at the tabletop, lost in his own thoughts. He wondered, briefly, about mentioning his trip to Walmsley but then thought better of it. What would be the point? She had no interest in his life anyway. Why bring it up? When he finally spoke again there was a weariness to his tone.

"I went to see Grandma earlier," he told her. "She's always asking about you."

"Isn't she dead yet?" Lucy grunted.

"Don't say things like that," he snapped.

"That's what you want isn't it? Then you wouldn't have to pay for that home you put her in."

"I didn't *put* her there. She had to go into that place because I couldn't look after her."

"You keep telling yourself that if it helps your conscience," Lucy sneered.

Jake glared at her, genuine anger rising within him.

Struck a nerve, has she?

Lucy got to her feet.

"I've got to go," she said, tonelessly.

"Listen, I'm sorry I can't take you to your interview," Jake protested.

"Don't worry about it," she snapped.

He fumbled in his pocket and pulled out some money, pushing it across the table towards her. Lucy looked contemptuously at it.

"Get yourself a taxi," Jake said.

"It's all right, you don't have to pay me for my time," Lucy snorted. "I'm not a whore like your girlfriend."

And she was gone.

SEVENTY-SEVEN

Dani had been through three of the scrapbooks and her head was beginning to ache.

She wondered if she needed new glasses. Sitting on the sofa in the living room she massaged the bridge of her nose between her thumb and forefinger and kept her eyes closed for a moment before she returned to the thick tome on her lap.

As with the other scrapbooks it consisted of mainly newspaper clippings going back as far as the 1980's. There were also flyers, photographs, ticket stubs and other memorabilia carefully collected and mounted within the pages of the books, some of which had been used as diary pages. The actual pages had been written on and then preserved beneath the thin plastic sheets that covered all the leaves of the scrapbooks. Most of those clippings concerned Doctor Margaret Ford and her progress from school to University, how she had fared in those institutions and what she had done while there.

Dani wondered if the books had been compiled for Jake. Had his mother done this with the intention of presenting them to him so he could see what her life had been like? It was a theory but one she didn't hold out too much hope for.

What exactly did she know from her examination of these books of memories she asked herself smiling?

Margaret Ford had been an only child who had done brilliantly during her academic career first at school and then at Loughborough University. From there she'd gone on to work in the psychiatric department of two hospitals in the Midlands before finally moving to Exham Psychiatric Hospital where she had become head of her department.

Dani kept returning to photographs of this woman. Elegant, dark haired, attractive.

Try as she might she could see very few physical resemblances between Jake and his mother.

Maybe he'd inherited his looks from his father, she reasoned. And it was then that the thought struck her again. No one had mentioned his father in all of this. There was enough mystery surrounding his dead mother, but no one had even mentioned the man who had helped bring him into this world. Dani could only assume that he had never been a part of Jake's life. Perhaps he disappeared before he was even born. Perhaps Margaret didn't want him in her life.

Perhaps. Perhaps.

There were so many imponderables, unanswered questions, and mysteries in Jake's early life that Dani was beginning to see why he'd never bothered unravelling them.

Page after page of the scrapbooks was devoted to Exham Psychiatric Hospital.

It's history. It's place in the community. Patient intake. Methods of treatment. After about fifteen pages, Dani tired of that and flipped forward. Yet more about the hospital but now the cuttings were about its impending closure. Where would the patients go? How would they cope? Were they all safe to be released into the community?

Dani decided she needed some help.

She retrieved her laptop and typed the name of the hospital into the search engine.

There were lists of psychiatric hospitals in England. When they had closed down. How many beds they had possessed? Staffing levels and every other thing. Dani ran a hand through her hair, no longer even sure what she was looking for. This was something of an information overload. She decided to see if her research was made any easier by a cup of coffee and padded through into the kitchen to make herself one.

As she stood by the work top watching the kettle she switched on the radio, tiring of the silence inside the house.

However, the inane rambling of the DJ and the even more irritating generic pop music being spewed out seemed even less tolerable than the solitude. She changed channels but talk of politics, gardening and antiques were even less appealing. She switched the radio off and made her coffee, taking a sip before she even left the kitchen. She found some bars of chocolate in a cupboard and munched on one of those before making her way back towards the sitting room.

She spotted the envelope as she entered the hall.

Plain white. Unsealed. No address on it. No stamp. No post mark.

She put down her coffee and opened the envelope, finding just one single sheet inside.

Dani opened it up and scanned what was written on the paper there.

In basic, almost childish scrawl, she saw the words;

YOUR DISGUSTING

I KNOW WHAT YOU DID

YOU CAN'T HIDE IT.

SICK FUCK

Dani swallowed hard, looking again at the letter.

She folded the single sheet and pushed it back into the envelope.

SEVENTY-EIGHT

Ted Brady unlocked the room and stepped inside.

The sun was sinking low outside and it was dark inside, so Brady flicked on a light, gazing around the spare room at the clutter within.

A single bed which, he reminded himself, he should change. Unchanged sheets could get damp when not used often. He didn't know how but that seemed to be the way and Brady couldn't remember the last time this particular bed was used. He couldn't remember the last time he had company. Not that he was bothered by that. It was good having a couple of rooms spare where he could store things and this second guest room had very much become a storage room.

Piles of books, some older VHS videotapes stuffed into boxes, more unopened cardboard boxes containing God alone knew what but the detritus in the room was dominated by some metal boxes. Flight cases. Leather holdalls. Brady crossed to the closest of these and unzipped it.

Inside there were two cameras.

They were expensive pieces that he'd purchased more than five years ago but they were still superb items of equipment and he raised one to his eye, squinting through the viewfinder. In another case there were lenses. Filters. Cleaning equipment for the cameras and their accessories. In other, larger boxes there were tripods, diffusers and all the paraphernalia any amateur photographer would require.

Brady went through it all lovingly, admiring the equipment, holding it up to inspect it, dusting it when he felt it was necessary.

There was a small attaché case, and he opened that next.

The photographs inside were too numerous to count.

All sizes and shapes.

Brady picked up the first of them and ran appraising eyes over it.

Fucking gorgeous.

It was Dani. She was standing in Jake Porter's back garden smoking a cigarette. She was dressed in a pair of tight jeans that hugged her backside and legs perfectly. There were more shots like that which he'd enlarged. Another of her seated on the wooden bench in the back garden, slim legs stretched out before her.

It was a particular favourite of his because it had been taken during particularly warm weather and she was barefoot in it. There was something about a pair of shapely feet and she had them.

Sexy fucking bitch.

More of Dani in the garden. Getting out of her car. Getting into her car. So close he could touch her.

Brady grinned. *The wonders of telephoto lenses.*

He scanned more of the pictures

Some of her leaving work (she hadn't seen him sitting in his car). Some of her going out at night (a nice one of her in black leggings and Doc Marten boots and a leather jacket). So many showing that gorgeous tight little arse, Brady thought, flicking slowly through the pictures. He could feel his erection growing as he looked, his mind racing now.

His heart was beating faster.

Anticipation?

He sat there for more than an hour looking at the photos, finally pushing them all back into the attaché case. He would keep those he told himself but, very soon, he would have new ones, better ones. Taken in good light and up close. Brady smiled.

Before he closed the case, he reached for another set of pictures.

Older ones.

He'd taken those with a telephoto lens too. Hidden. Happy to observe and watch. And preserve the images for himself.

She had been beautiful.

Young. Slim. Long blonde hair that reached as far as the small of her back. Pretty little face, almost angelic. Brady held the photo before him, running lecherous eyes over the image.

Little whore.

He smiled again.

The girl in these pictures was Rhiannon Morton.

He wished he had some better ones of her but, as with those of Dani, he'd been forced to take them from a distance and without being spotted. Also, he thought, he didn't have the leverage that he had with Dani. Nothing to force Rhiannon into an impromptu photo session for him. Dani was a different matter. She owed him. The video he had was his insurance. His way of manipulating her. He picked up a picture of her and held it alongside one of Rhiannon.

Perfect. If only he could have got those two little sluts together. Told them what to do. Instructed them.

He thought about masturbating but then decided against it. He'd wait until later. When the time was right. When the opportunity presented itself. Brady smiled more broadly and reached for his phone.

SEVENTY-NINE

Jake closed the door behind him and stood with his back against it for a moment, sucking in a deep breath and glancing around the hotel room.

Peace and quiet at last, he thought, smiling.

He loosened his tie and walked across to the mini-bar, pulling out a bottle of sparkling water and a glass.

Nothing stronger.

He sat down on the end of the bed and drank most of the water, surprised at how tired he felt.

The meeting had been both successful and enjoyable. The restaurant where they'd eaten had been busy and loud, but the food had been excellent, and Jake rubbed his stomach as he recalled his own meal. He had been impressed with the PR company he'd been introduced to and enthused by what they'd had to say. They had an exhaustive list of contacts all of whom could be used to benefit him and his work. All they required of him, they'd said, was his enthusiasm and his expertise. Jake felt that was a fair exchange.

He drank more of the water, undressed, and then wandered into the bathroom

where he showered quickly, walking back into the bedroom in one of the hotel's thick white bathrobes.

Seating himself at the writing desk in one corner of the room where he'd placed his laptop, he glanced at the screen and noted that he had a couple of e-mails both of which had arrived while he was out at dinner.

There was one from his publisher saying how much they hoped he'd enjoyed the meeting and the meal and another from Dani.

There was no message heading but there were four attachments Jake noticed. He opened the e-mail and read it.

I HOPE THE MEETING WENT WELL.

SEE YOU TOMORROW.

DO ANY OF THESE LOOK FAMILIAR? I FOUND THEM IN THE SCRAPBOOKS.

DANI XXXXX

Jake opened the attachments, looking at the contents of each one carefully.

There were photographs of Exham Psychiatric Hospital, particularly of the imposing entrance with its wrought iron gates and towering archway over the driveway that led up to the main building itself. The main building was an imposing looking structure of dark stone. A huge monolithic edifice that looked as though it had been carved from one massive block rather than being assembled brick by brick.

There was also an article from a local Exham newspaper, The Exham Comet, dated November 1983.

Jake opened it, saw it was a longer article than he'd anticipated and decided to get himself another drink from the mini-bar to keep him company while he read it.

He glanced at the spirits but then decided against it and retrieved another bottle of sparkling water then he sat down again, leaned a little closer to the screen and began to read. The headline screamed;

THIRD DEATH REPORTED

And below it, the story;

A local doctor has expressed his surprise and dismay concerning a series of deaths in Exham. Three women have now succumbed to the same cause of death in as many weeks. All of them in their twenties or thirties and all of them with identical symptoms. Each of the women was known to have undergone an abortion and yet, within weeks of the procedure, they each died

of an ectopic pregnancy.

Jake sat back slightly. The words stuck out like a sore thumb. *Ectopic pregnancy.* The same thing that had killed Heather Lawson and Lauren Davison. He took a large swallow of his drink then continued reading.

The mystery surrounding the deaths was increased because during autopsies on the three women no traces of a foetus was found. Ectopic pregnancy occurs when the foetus becomes stuck in one of the fallopian tubes and continues to grow which can cause rupturing of the tubes, internal bleeding and, in the worst cases, death.

Jake frowned and read on, taking in the facts of the story as best he could, wondering why Dani had even sent him this particular cutting. Only when he reached the last paragraph did it become clearer.

In rare cases, women who have undergone abortions can continue to exhibit the signs of pregnancy despite not carrying a child said psychiatrist Margaret Ford. Doctor Ford stressed that this was extremely unusual.

Jake raised his eyebrows in surprise at the sight of his mother's name. He reached for his phone and found the number he wanted immediately.

He waited while it rang.

And rang.

EIGHTY

Ted Brady paused for a second before he opened the front door, partly to compose himself but also to control his breathing. He'd been waiting for this moment and his heart was already beating hard with anticipation.

As he opened the door, he saw Dani standing on the doorstep, her face already fixed in an expression of angry resignation.

"You got my message then?" Brady said, still grinning.

"Let's just get this over with," Dani snapped.

He ushered her in, looking her up and down again.

Blue and white top, tight black leggings, trainers.

Very nice.

Brady closed the door behind her.

"When's Jake back then?" he wanted to know. "I saw him leave. I thought he was away when I clocked the overnight bag."

"Tomorrow morning," she told him, cutting across him.

"So, you don't have to rush then?" Brady chuckled.

"Look let's just get this done, right. I don't want to be around you any longer than I have to."

"Now, now, no need to be hostile. Do you want a drink?"

"No. I just want to get this over with."

Brady nodded.

"Come on," he said. "Upstairs. First room on the left."

Dani hesitated for a moment then began climbing the stairs. Brady followed a few paces behind her, his gaze fixed on her taut buttocks as she ascended. When they reached the landing, Dani paused. Brady walked past her towards the closed door.

"Where's your phone?" she wanted to know.

He tapped the top pocket of the shirt he was wearing.

"And you'll delete that video as soon as we've finished?" Dani persisted.

"Scout's honour," Brady said, grinning. Then he pushed the door open, ushering her forward.

She stepped across the threshold, looking around the room with the same expression a condemned man reserves for the execution chamber.

The bed and much of the floor had been covered by white sheets. There was white vinyl hung behind the bed and two spotlights and a diffuser box had been set up. The whole bed and centre of the room was bathed in cool white light. The room was pleasantly warm, and Dani could see that the single radiator had been turned up to maximum.

"You did this?" Dani murmured.

"I told you, it's my hobby," Brady exclaimed, proudly.

Dani gently touched the bed, running her fingers over the sheet.

"I hope it's warm enough for you," Brady offered, watching her. "I didn't want you to get cold when you took your clothes off."

"You have got to be fucking kidding," Dani snapped.

Brady winked at her and picked up a camera, snapping off some quick shots of her.

"Fuck off," she hissed.

"This is what you're here for, remember? I know what I'm doing you know."

He took more pictures, the sound of clicking reverberating inside the small room.

"Yeah, I bet you do," Dani grunted.

"Just sit on the bed," he instructed.

She did as he asked.

"Have you ever done this before?" he wanted to know, still snapping away.

"What? Been blackmailed into letting a pervert take pictures of me? No."

"Now, now, no need to be like that. I mean have you ever posed for a photographer before."

"You're not a photographer. You're a weirdo with a hobby."

Brady took more shots and moved closer to her. She glared at him.

"And what are you going to do with the pictures when you've finished?" Dani wanted to know. "Keep them and blackmail me with those too?"

"You don't trust me, do you?" he muttered.

"I could go to the police you know. Tell them you blackmailed me."

"But you won't," he chided.

"How do you know?"

"Because you're more worried about your boyfriend than you are about me. I mean the young guy, not Jake Porter by the way." He winked at her.

"So, when you've got the pictures you want, you're just going to wank over them are you, you sad bastard?" Dani snapped.

"They'll serve a purpose," he grinned, still taking pictures.

"Fucking sicko."

"You should be flattered to think I find you sexy."

"It makes me feel sick," she sneered.

Brady lowered the camera.

"Take your trainers off," he said, quietly.

"Why?" Dani asked.

"I like bare feet. Now take them off."

For the first time she heard a hard edge to his voice, and it frightened her. She reached slowly for the laces of her trainer, pulling them open. Brady watched as she slipped first one then the other off. She dropped them onto the floor then quickly pulled her socks off too.

Brady moved closer; his eyes fixed on her bare feet.

"Nice," he breathed. "No blemishes. You look as if you look after them. I like that you don't wear any nail varnish."

"Glad you approve," Dani grunted, sarcastically.

He took more pictures, this time just of her feet, focusing on the gleaming nails and her toes. He knelt beside the bed, zooming in on the small appendages. She could hear his breathing growing more ragged and, when he straightened up there was a bulge in his trousers. Dani hated him even more.

"You really are a fucking perv, aren't you?" she hissed.

"Just because I appreciate a sexy foot?" he grunted. "Feet are very underrated you know. If a girl looks after her feet, then chances are she looks after the rest of her body too." He raised his eyebrows. "Have you ever had your toes sucked?"

Dani shook her head slowly.

"You don't know what you're missing," he growled. "Now take off the leggings."

EIGHTY-ONE

Dani froze for a moment as she heard his words. But it wasn't so much what he said as the way he said it. There was a threatening edge to his tone that hadn't been there before. If this had all begun as a bit of a joke, then Dani felt it was descending rapidly into something much darker.

"No way," she said, defiantly.

"Take them off," he insisted. "Who's going to know?" He grinned and peered through the viewfinder, taking more pictures.

Dani still hesitated, her heart thudding faster now, her mouth dry. When she tried to swallow, she couldn't.

"And what if I don't?" she asked, her face pale. "Are you going to hurt me?"

"Why would I do that? As long as I've got that video, I don't *need* to hurt you, do I?"

Still Dani waited.

"So, you've never posed like this before?" Brady went on. "Not even for your boyfriend? I mean the one I saw climbing out of the window. Not for Jake Porter?"

Dani shook her head.

"Just because it happens in porn videos doesn't mean it happens in real life you know," she told him.

Brady laughed.

"You think I watch porn?" he grunted. "You do, don't you? I bet you think I spend most of my day hunched over a computer watching girls get fucked."

"Well, don't you?"

"I've...indulged a few times. Who hasn't? I bet your boyfriend has. Even though he's fucking you, I bet he still watches porn." He looked directly at her. "You could be in porn you know. You're sexy enough. I'd love to see you getting fucked by a big hard dick. Next time you come here bring your boyfriend and I'll film the two of you fucking."

"There won't be a next time," Dani hissed.

"Won't there? We'll see about that."

"Is that why your wife left you? Did she get sick of your perverted ways?"

"She didn't understand me," Brady said, grinning. "Now, take off the fucking leggings before I get mad."

Dani looked closely at Brady. He might be overweight and out of condition, but he was a big man. If it came to a physical struggle, she wasn't sure he'd be quite the push over she thought at first. His face was set in hard lines now, his eyes cold.

"Take them off," he snapped, his voice rising in volume.

Dani swallowed hard then hooked her thumbs in either side of the leggings. She slid them down as far as her thighs, exposing the small blue panties she wore beneath. As the knickers were exposed, she heard Brady suck in a breath.

"Pull them down further," he rumbled, his gaze now fixed on her knickers. "Imagine you're taking them off for your boyfriend."

Dani pulled agitatedly at the leggings, lowering them more.

"No, not like that," Brady snapped. "Make it sexy. Do it like you're trying to turn me on."

Dani's cheeks flushed and she closed her eyes momentarily. She was having trouble breathing. Her chest felt tight, as if someone was gradually closing a huge, invisible vice around her torso.

"Take them right off," Brady panted, watching as Dani pulled the tight-fitting material free of her legs. She dropped them on the bed beside her, looking at Brady who was staring fixedly at her panties and the gap between her legs. "You're a fucking sexy bitch. Does Jake tell you that? I bet he loves fucking you, doesn't he? Getting his cock inside that tight young cunt. Does he get you really wet? I bet the young guy does. I bet he makes you fucking drip, doesn't he?"

Dani swallowed hard, trying to avoid making eye contact with him. It was bad enough hearing his words.

Sick fucking bastard.

"I bet he makes your clit swell, doesn't he?" Brady went on, his voice barely more than a hoarse whisper. "Does he push his tongue inside you? Does he fuck you hard? Does he shoot his load inside you? I bet he does. I bet you cum like a fucking train on his cock, don't you?"

Brady took more pictures, then he dropped to his knees next to the bed looking up at her almost in supplication.

"Give me your foot," he breathed.

Dani sat motionless for a moment then slowly raised her right foot towards Brady's outstretched hands.

He took it gently in his thick fingers, using his thumbs to stroke the sole of her bare foot. Then he brought her toes close to his lips. She could feel his hot breath on them.

She wondered if she drove her foot forward hard enough if she could knock his teeth down his throat.

Brady opened his mouth and pulled her toes closer. Dani felt the warmth of his saliva on the tips, then his tongue flicked out, probing between each toe in turn, gliding between them before he began sucking gently on her big toe the way a baby feeds from its mother's breast. He did the same with each toe, biting down gently on the edge of her nails. When he pulled her toes from his mouth he was breathing heavily and as Dani sat forward, she could see the erection pressing against the inside of his trousers.

Fucking weirdo.

She sat rigidly on the bed as he repeated his actions with her left foot. Then he licked gently from the ball of her foot to her heel then over the arch of her foot, lapping his way back to her toes.

When he'd finished, her toes were glistening with saliva.

Brady smiled up at her. Again, she felt the overwhelming urge to kick him in the face. She wiped his saliva from her feet as best she could, using the sheet, smearing the fluid on the material beneath her. She felt as if she needed to step into a red-hot shower to wash away all traces of him. To purify herself and expunge every trace of him on her.

He held her foot in one hand, inspecting it with the same reverence a jeweller reserves for a perfect gemstone. He gently kissed the tips of her toes again, letting his tongue trail over them and with his free hand she realized he was undoing his trousers. Dani felt a shiver run along her spine.

She looked down to see that he had freed his penis and was kneeling before her with it sticking up looking almost painfully hard. He lowered her foot towards his engorged organ.

"No," Dani gasped, both shocked and revolted. "You said just photographs."

Brady smiled; his breathing ragged.

"You're a beautiful girl," he grunted. "With beautiful feet." He laughed and the sound made her skin crawl. "It won't take me long.

You just lay there. You don't have to do anything."

Dani clamped her teeth together so tightly it made her jaws ache. She felt the tip of his penis brush against the arch of her right foot.

"No," she yelped, trying to pull her foot away again but Brady gripped it tight.

"Keep still," he hissed. "If you're having second thoughts just imagine what Jake Porter is going to say when if he sees that video on my phone. Imagine how he'd react to some of these pictures I've taken."

Dani glared at Brady.

"You fucking scumbag," she snarled.

"Shut your mouth," Brady sneered, pulling her feet back towards his throbbing penis. "Like I said, this won't take long." He pushed her feet against his shaft, sandwiching it between them and Dani winced as she felt the warmth against the soft flesh of her arches. Seconds later, when she felt him ejaculate, it was all she could do to stop herself vomiting.

He looked down at the oily white fluid and smiled.

"All we need now is another girl to lick it off," Brady told her, his breathing still ragged. "Like that little slut Jake had before you. I bet she'd have done it too. She looked like she'd have done anything." He chuckled. "I don't know how he does it. He seems to attract girls like you and her without even trying. Has he got a big cock? Is that it?"

Dani glared at him, trying to contain her anger and her revulsion. Brady merely reached for his camera again and took several shots of her semen spattered feet. When he'd finished, he sat back, resting against the wall, seemingly exhausted by his exertions.

"You can go," he told Dani, flatly, watching as she tried to wipe the slippery fluid from her feet with the sheet. "I've finished. Until next time." The smile that spread across his face raised the hairs on the back of her neck.

EIGHTY-TWO

Jake Porter couldn't sleep.

He rolled over in bed almost angrily, annoyed that he couldn't drop off. It took the average person between seven and twelve minutes to fall asleep he told himself. Why did *he* have to be different? He lay on his back gazing at the ceiling for a moment longer then squinted at his watch.

Quarter past two.

Jake told himself that one of the reasons he couldn't sleep was excitement. The meeting earlier in the evening had left him genuinely thrilled. Enthused by the prospect of what he could achieve in his career and how that career might grow and expand. He swung himself out of bed and walked to the window, glancing out at the city beyond.

Far away a siren sounded. An ever-present accompaniment to the stillness of the night here in the capital. Jake looked down into the street and saw two men stumbling drunkenly along the pavement on the other side of the road. It looked as if someone else had had a good evening Jake thought, smiling. He remained by the window for a moment longer, gazing at the night sky and the myriad lights sparkling in the blackness. Streetlights, illumination from inside buildings or on the front of shops and stores, they all glowed in the gloom.

Jake wandered back to the bed and sat down on the edge of it. He switched on the bedside light and looked down at his phone.

He'd tried calling Dani again before he got into bed but there'd been no answer. He wondered what she was doing. Normally she always had her phone with her.

Maybe, he reasoned, she had just managed to find the oblivion of sleep a lot easier than he had. He glanced at the room service menu. Perhaps some warm milk might help him sleep. It had when he was a child.

Who gave you that? Your real mother or the woman you put in a care home?

Jake sighed, the thought coming into his mind both unbidden and unwanted.

He reached for the receiver on the bedside table and pressed the room service number. Warm milk. Anything was worth trying wasn't it?

***

Dani had no idea how long she'd been in the shower.

It could have been an hour.

All she knew was that the hot water striking her skin felt like tiny lashes on her flesh, as if each spurt of liquid was flagellating her. She was sitting in the cubicle, her back pressed against the tiles, the water spurting unceasingly from the shower head. Dani watched as the rivulets ran down her body, concentrating particularly on those that drenched her feet.

She had washed them, scrubbed them, more times than she could imagine since getting beneath the cleansing spray. At times she had rubbed the flesh so vigorously she feared she might tear it off, but she'd persevered, desperate to wash away every last trace of Brady. As she sat there now, she reached for the soap again, making lather and smearing it over her toes and insteps, working the foaming matter over her skin once more. She took an age with her ablutions and then rinsed the lather away, inspecting her feet once more.

Would they ever be truly clean?

She sucked in a deep breath and flexed her toes.

You should have known he'd want more than just pictures.

Dani slammed one fist against the wall of the shower, her anger growing once more. She wished the clenched hand had been connecting with Brady's face. His smug, smirking face.

She had thought about ringing Mike when she got back from Brady's house but what would she have told him? What could he do now to alleviate the feelings that had enveloped her? Feelings of disgust. Of anger? Of shame? She was angry with herself for believing him. For being stupid enough to think that he would be satisfied with some photographs of her. He had kept the video.

Of course, he had.

But now he had much more than just that video to blackmail her with. He had all the pictures he'd taken. He'd even taken shots of her feet when he'd finished. Her toes and insteps spattered with his semen.

Dani closed her eyes, trying to drive the images from her mind but they persisted. Fragments of a waking nightmare. What would he demand next time?

(there would be a next time, she was certain of that). How far could he go when she was at his mercy the way she was now she'd surrendered so much of herself to him?

She struck the wall again. The anger she felt was for Brady but also for herself. She had been naïve. Easily duped. And it hurt.

Fucking bastard.

She got to her feet, switched off the shower and wrapped herself in a bath towel, looking at her reflection in the large mirror opposite. Her image stared back with disdain.

You're stupid. He got you. He won.

She dried herself and went and got into bed, but it was a long time before she slept.

EIGHTY-THREE

The knocking on the bedroom door woke him finally.

Jake sat up with a start, the sound reverberating inside his head and inside the room. For a moment he wondered if he was dreaming but then realized that the sound had a very real source.

"Housekeeping," a voice from the other side of the partition called and the door began to open.

Jake hauled himself out of bed just as the woman walked in.

"Morning," he said, smiling.

"Oh, I'm sorry, sir," the housekeeper offered.

"It's my fault, I overslept. If you could come back in about an hour that would be great. I should be out of your way by then. Sorry."

The housekeeper nodded, turned on her heel and disappeared.

Jake shook his head, surprised at how long and how deeply he'd slept. He rubbed his eyes and was about to wander through into the bathroom when he glanced towards his laptop over on the desk. There were a couple of new e-mails and he opened them, feeling more refreshed and rejuvenated by sleep than he had done for a long time.

The first message was junk. Did he want online security? Did he want peace of mind? Jake deleted it and opened the second one. It was from his publishers. Could he possibly call into their offices later in the day? They had some more good news for him that they wanted to give him face to face.

Jake smiled and replied immediately, telling them he'd be in about noon. That done he headed off towards the bathroom.

He already had his back to the laptop screen when the next message arrived.

***

Dani guessed she'd had barely two hours sleep during the night. Now she dressed hurriedly, pulling on the first things she laid hands on. She didn't want to spend the next few hours in the house. She felt she had to get out. Get some air. Clear her head if that was possible. Images from the previous night were still clogged inside her brain like rotting food in a plughole. She sighed. She could even remember the smells. The odour of damp in that spare room. The way the air itself had become heated the longer the spotlights were left on. And, of course, the unmistakeable musky smell of Brady's semen when he had finally sprayed her feet with his thick liquid. She put a hand to her mouth as if even the recollection was enough to provoke a reaction.

You thought you could handle him, didn't you? And you were wrong.

As she moved towards the front door she glanced through the open door of the sitting room. She'd left the scrapbooks open and scattered around the room but, as she passed the door and glanced in at them, she decided to tidy up when she got back. She had more pressing things on her mind.

Dani slipped her leather jacket on, checked she had her car keys and then walked to her car.

She didn't see but rather *felt* the eyes on her.

As she unlocked her car she turned.

Ted Brady was standing in the bedroom window. As he saw her, he slowly raised one hand and waved, a smile plastered across his face.

Dani clambered into her car and drove off, the rear wheels spinning momentarily on the tarmac. Brady was still smiling as he watched her pull away.

EIGHTY-FOUR

Mike Quinn took a last drag on his cigarette and dropped it beside the door with the other butts that had accumulated there. He wasn't the only smoker among the seven people who worked at the garage and all of them retreated to this one place to enjoy their smoke break.

From the open back doors of the garage, he could hear vehicles being worked on and the loud music that perpetually blasted out from the speakers that were suspended inside the building. As everyone who worked there seemed to have such individual musical tastes the day was divided up into different quadrants (as the boss like to call them). The first two hours were for R&B, the next two were for pop, two more were set aside for Talk Radio and the last two were given over to rock. It was an arrangement everyone seemed to be happy with and probably the only compromise as the ages of the employees at the garage ranged from eighteen up to sixty-three.

Mike tapped his fingers along to a song for a moment longer then walked back through the garage towards the main exit, preparing to head off for his lunch hour.

When he got back there was an Audi that needed a new exhaust and a Peugeot that was due for an MOT but that would wait until he'd finished lunch.

The rain that had been threatening to fall for most of the morning finally began as a thin drizzle, the wind blowing it like a shimmering curtain across the open forecourt at the front of the building.

There was a small cafe about a hundred yards away where Mike usually got his lunch and he headed towards it now, pulling up his collar against the elements. He dug his hands into his pockets and jogged towards the cafe, anxious to be out of the rain.

He was about fifty feet away from the entrance when Dani's car pulled up.

She hit the hooter a couple of times and Mike smiled and ran across to climb into the passenger seat.

"What are you doing here?" he wanted to know.

"I thought I'd surprise you," Dani told him, kissing him lightly on the lips. "I was out and passing so I thought why not?"

"I'm glad you did," Mike told her.

"I've brought provisions," she informed him, jabbing a finger towards the front parcel shelf where there were two packs of sandwiches, a couple of Mars Bars and some crisps. "Where shall we go to eat it?"

Mike shrugged. "You're driving," he said, smiling. "Your choice."

Dani swung the car off the forecourt and guided it along several roads until they came to a modern looking church that was on a low hill overlooking a cemetery.

"Very cheerful," Mike said as she parked the car.

"At least it's quiet," Dani offered and shut off the engine.

They both selected some sandwiches and began eating.

"When's Jake back?" Mike wanted to know.

"He's staying on for another night," she told him. "He messaged me earlier. He's got more business with his publishers."

"More business? More money you mean. Rich fucker."

Dani chewed on her sandwich and glanced at Mike.

Tell him about what happened with Brady.

She let out a long breath and continued eating.

"Want some company?" Mike asked. "I mean, if he's not coming back until tomorrow." He raised his eyebrows and smiled, lecherously.

"Maybe."

"What do you mean *maybe*? What else have you got to do that's so important?"

"I'm still going through the scrapbooks I brought back from Walmsley."

"The ones his mother put together. Why?"

"Because there might be something in there that gives a clue to Jake's early life."

"Who gives a fuck about that?" He looked irritably at Dani. "This guy is supposed to be our cash cow. Our way out. We should be figuring out a way to get him to part with some of his fortune, not working out how he spent his early years."

"The more I can find out about him the more leverage it gives me."

"Bollocks. You should just tell him that you're pregnant. Tell him you want the money for the abortion. Tell him you're leaving him."

"Just like that?"

"Why not? That was the plan right from the beginning wasn't it?

Has he sold his mother's house yet? You said he should get a fair price for that."

"Not yet."

"Fuck it. He's got enough money anyway. He can afford to give us what we ask for."

"And how much is that?"

"I've been thinking about it. I reckon a hundred grand should do it."

"He'll never give us that much."

"A hundred grand should get me a garage of my own and it will pay for us to rent a nice place too. Especially when you start working again. We'll be minted."

"Why would he give us that much?"

"I'm still working on that."

"An abortion costs about eight hundred pounds, not a hundred thousand."

"I told you," he snapped. "I'm working on it."

"We could always go to the place where he was born. See what we could find out ourselves."

"Where was he born?"

"A place called Exham."

"Where the fuck is that?"

"Somewhere near London. We could leave tomorrow. We could find a B&B to stay in or a Travel Lodge. There's always a Travel Lodge."

Mike nodded.

"Yeah, I could get time off work," he murmured.

"We have to go," Dani insisted.

"But what is that going to do? How's it going to help us get the money out of him?"

"He can't remember anything from the first ten or eleven years of his life, right? He says that something might have happened when he was growing up that was so traumatic his mind just...shut down. If we can find out what happened, what made him lose his memory then...then we've got more...leverage against him. We can tell him we know how to help him, but he'll have to pay for that help."

"A hundred grand's worth of help? He'll never go for that."

"This is a big deal for him, Mike. It's driving him nuts wondering what happened back then. Trying to figure out where he came from.

Trying to fill in the details. We could find something out that could unlock that. Then he really *does* owe us."

Mike raised his eyebrows.

"If you had no memory," Dani went on. "How much would *you* pay to have it back?"

EIGHTY-FIVE

The train was busy, and Jake couldn't find a seat, so he ended up standing in the space between two carriages, trying to ignore the man opposite him who was noisily shoving a sausage roll into his mouth, fragments of it falling to the floor with every bite he took.

His visit to his publishers had been very worthwhile and their plans for his promotional tour had been another fillip for him. Jake felt as good as he'd felt for a while as he stood looking out of the window at the swiftly passing countryside. He'd contemplated staying in London for another night but had then decided that he wanted to get home. He wanted to share his good news with Dani. He'd messaged her to tell her he was returning but, so far, she hadn't acknowledged his text.

It was almost dark now, banks of black cloud filling the sky and, occasionally, Jake caught sight of his own reflection in the glass.

When his phone rang, he pulled it free, noting that the message was from Lucy and that pleased him but, as he read it, his brow furrowed.

YOU PROBABLY DON'T CARE BUT MY CAT DIED TONIGHT. JUST THOUGHT YOU'D LIKE TO KNOW.

Jake sighed, knowing how close Lucy had been to the old ginger Tom.

He sent a message back.

SORRY TO HEAR THAT. IS THERE ANYTHING I CAN DO?

He sent it and waited, expecting her to reply instantly.

She didn't.

Jake let out another long breath and tapped out another message.

IF YOU WANT TO TALK LET ME KNOW. I'M ALWAYS HERE.

Moments passed but no reply was forthcoming. He wondered why. But his initial disappointment gave way to irritation. How long did it take to send a text? Seconds. Mere seconds. Why didn't she reply?

Dani seemed to be no better. She still hadn't replied to the message he sent earlier. What was the point of having a mobile which you always carried with you if you weren't going to use it? Jake shook his head, his own question rattling around inside his mind.

He stood gazing at the phone as if that simple act would somehow magically cause a reply to materialize. Needless to say, it didn't.

Jake slipped the phone back into his pocket and decided he needed to stretch his legs. The buffet car was a couple of carriages away, so he picked his way along the narrow aisles, past the other tightly packed passengers and joined the queue that led to the small counter where a harassed looking red-faced man was serving.

Apparently, the till was playing up and the man was having to add up orders and dispense change with the aid of the antiquated looking calculator he'd propped on the counter next to him.

"They're bloody useless," grunted the man in front of Jake who was clutching two cans of beer that he wanted to pay for. "If the trains aren't late then there's something wrong when you get on the bloody things."

Jake raised his eyebrows by way of comment.

"And they've always got an excuse," the man persisted. "Leaves on the track. No staff. Always some kind of bullshit."

Jake nodded this time.

"It's not like the fares are cheaper or anything," a voice behind him chimed in and he looked to see another man who was standing there with a pack of sandwiches and a bottle of Coke. "They should give us all some kind of discount every time they mess up."

The man with two beer cans agreed.

Jake nodded, not wanting to seem as if he disagreed.

The train began to slow down a little and the man holding the sandwiches turned to peer out of the window.

"What now?" he groaned.

"Perhaps they've run out of fuel," the man with the beer cans offered.

"It's a station coming up I think," Jake offered.

"The bloody thing isn't supposed to stop yet," the man with the beer cans said.

"There's probably something on the line," the man with the sandwiches suggested. "Idiots."

It was then that a voice drifted from the PA system.

"This is your conductor speaking," said the voice. "I'd just like to apologise and tell you that we will be making an unscheduled stop at the next station. This is to allow passengers to board."

"No shit," grunted the man with the beer cans, moving closer to the counter. He paid for his drinks and disappeared into another carriage.

Jake stepped forward.

"Tea, please," he said, noting that the large man with the red face behind the counter now seemed even more crimson in appearance. Jake had exactly the right money and laid it on the counter, watching as the man counted it out and nodded. Jake then retreated towards his seat, almost spilling his tea when a woman got to her feet without looking and collided with him. She glared at him as if he were to blame and then continued with her task of retrieving something from the overhead rack.

Jake returned to his position between the carriages and sipped his tea, nearly burning his lips with the searing hot liquid.

He decided to replace the lid for a moment to let it cool down a little.

As the train slid to a halt, his phone vibrated in his pocket and Jake reached for it, seeing who the message was from.

He frowned.

EIGHTY-SIX

Dani felt her heart beating faster as she knocked on the door and dropped her hands to her sides, the fists clenched.

She stood on the porch waiting, aware that lights were on inside the house itself. The occupant was in.

He was always in. Always there. Always watching.

When Ted Brady finally opened the door, Dani saw him smile at her.

"Back again already?" he chuckled. "You just can't keep away, can you?"

Dani clenched her fists more tightly.

"I didn't tell you to be here tonight, did I?" Brady said.

"I came to tell you I'm going away for a day or two so your sick little game will have to wait, right?"

"All right, don't be like that. I'll still be here when you get back. Where are you going?"

"None of your business."

"You really should see someone about your temper you know," Brady said, smiling. "Have a word with Jake. He's a psychiatrist. He should be able to help you with your anger management."

"Fuck you," Dani sneered, turning away.

"Any time, darling," Brady told her.

He watched as she walked up the path, his gaze fixed to her tight buttocks.

"By the way," he called. "You don't decide these things, I do."

Dani thought about saying something but just kept walking, anxious to be away from him.

"When you come next time," Brady said. "Wear something sexy."

Dani heard the door close. She kept walking, the anger filling her.

It was another thirty minutes before Mike Quinn arrived to pick her up. She hurried out to the car and clambered into the passenger seat, pushing her overnight bag onto the back seat.

The drive to Exham would take two hours, maybe longer.

"What did you tell Jake?" Quinn enquired.

"I just said I was going to stay with a friend for a couple of days," Dani explained.

"And he swallowed it?"

"Why shouldn't he? He trusts me."

"Twat," Quinn grunted.

"Besides, he's away at some conference for a couple of days when he gets back from London so he's not going to miss me."

They drove with nothing but music for much of the journey, Dani content to flick through the scrapbooks she'd brought with her from the house.

"So why did his mother keep those?" Quinn asked, pointing at the books.

"I don't know," Dani confessed. "I don't think she kept them for Jake. You know sometimes parents keep scrapbooks of what their kids have done to show them when they grow up?"

"No," Mike said, blankly.

"Didn't your mum do that?"

"My mum was too busy trying to find the money for her next fix," Mike laughed. "Did your mum do shit like that then?"

"I never did anything that was memorable enough to stick in a scrapbook," Dani admitted, sadly.

"So, what's in there then?" he asked, tapping one of the pages with his finger. "Is it all stuff about Jake?"

"No. That's the weird thing," Dani explained. "It's about his mum and about the places she worked."

"Maybe she wanted him to know about her and what she'd done."

"But it's not just about her. There's stuff in here about all sorts of things. The history of Exham. How the town was built. How it was used as a military base during the English Civil War. Why it was used to house evacuated kids during the Second World War. There's even cuttings in here about some murders that happened there thirty years ago."

"What about them?"

Dani turned several pages, scanning the cuttings for what she sought.

"Here it is," she murmured, her finger tracing a path across the articles. Most had been taken from local Exham newspapers but there were one or two smaller pieces from Nationals like The Daily Mirror and the Express. The first article Dani settled on was one from the Exham Comet. It was dated December 1983.

"Some guy killed five people and cut their heads off," she read. "They found the bodies but not the heads."

"Fuck," Mike chuckled. "Did they catch him?"

"Eventually."

"Perhaps that was Jake's dad," he laughed.

Dani shook her head, unamused by Mike's words.

"Why would Jake's mum keep things like that?" she muttered.

"Perhaps she was just a weird old bastard. Some people keep things to do with murders, don't they?"

"Yeah, nutters do."

"You're interested in serial killers, people probably think you're a nutter too," Mike laughed.

"I'm just interested in them. I don't keep a scrapbook about their exploits, do I?"

"No, but you read books about them. Isn't that worse?"

"No. It's how their minds work that interests me. Not what they did to their victims."

"That's what you say."

Dani threw him an irritated glance.

"If she was living there at the time it must have been interesting to her," Mike went on. "Must have been a bit scary too."

Dani turned a couple more pages.

"They finally found the murderer hiding out in the abandoned psychiatric hospital where Jake's mum used to work," she said, quietly. "It had been closed down and this guy used to be a patient there. He was hiding there."

"That must be why she kept those cuttings, because the murderer was hiding in a place where she used to work," Mike offered.

Dani didn't answer.

They were less than fifty miles from Exham when Mike swung the car off the road and into a service station. He parked as close to the complex of buildings as he could, muttering when he saw that it had begun to rain. As they hurried inside, the first low rumbles of thunder began to fill the air.

EIGHTY-SEVEN

When Claire Conlan heard the doorbell, the first thing she did was glance at her watch.

It was after eleven and she wondered who was calling so late. She hesitated a moment then got to her feet when the two-tone chime sounded again.

When she reached the front door, she peered through the spyhole, but the porch light wasn't working, and she could see only darkness through the small gap. Nevertheless, she slipped on the chair and opened the front door a crack.

Jake Porter smiled as he saw her and Claire visibly relaxed.

"What's wrong?" she asked.

"Does something have to be wrong?" Jake wanted to know.

"It's late."

"I wanted to talk to Lucy."

"Why?"

"About her cat. I thought I'd pop by and offer my condolences. She might appreciate it." He smiled.

"She told you then. Poor old thing. Mind you, he was pretty old. It was hardly a shock."

"Is Lucy okay? I know how much she loved that cat."

"She's fine. She's not here though. She went to see one of her friends. She shouldn't be too much longer. If you really want to see her you can go up to her room and wait for her."

"You don't mind?"

Claire stepped back, ushering him in.

"Be my guest," she said.

Jake accepted the invitation, stepped over the threshold, and stood a little awkwardly in the narrow hallway.

"Do you want a cup of tea while you're waiting?" Claire enquired.

"No thanks," he said, shaking his head. "It's okay. It's a bit late for her to be out isn't it?"

"She's not a little girl any more, Jake."

"I know but..."

She cut across him.

"Did you only come round here because her cat died?"

"Why else would I come? I thought I'd just have a word with her. I'm away for a couple of days at some bloody conference so I won't get the chance to talk to her."

"Where's that then?"

"Just outside London."

"What's it to do with?"

"It's a psychiatric conference to discuss the merits of new methods of treatment."

"Sounds boring."

"Well, it probably won't be to me or the other psychiatrists there."

"And you always did like your little trips away from home didn't you, Jake?"

He sighed.

"Not now, Claire," Jake murmured. "It isn't the time or place."

As they stood there, the door of the sitting room opened, and Jake saw a balding head poke out inquisitively. It belonged to Mark Ross. He was in his late forties. A pudgy faced man in a dark sweatshirt and jeans that looked too big for him.

"Who was that Claire?" he asked then glanced at Jake.

They looked awkwardly at each other, then Ross nodded by way of greeting.

"All right?" he asked, looking briefly at Jake who also nodded. Ross hesitated a moment longer then ducked back into the sitting room out of sight.

"Sorry if I'm interrupting," Jake murmured.

"You're not," Claire assured him. "Lucy's room is upstairs on the left. You can't miss it."

Jake nodded and set off up the stairs. Claire watched him for a moment then she too retreated inside the sitting room again.

On the landing, Jake looked to his left and saw that one of the white painted doors had a small plaque on it that stated, LUCY'S ROOM. Next to it was a more crudely drawn sign that proclaimed; FUCK THE TORIES. Jake couldn't suppress a slight grin as he walked towards the door and pushed it gently open.

The room was small and seemingly crammed from floor to ceiling with books, vinyl, DVDs and assorted other collectibles. Most of the space on the floor was taken up with clothes that should more properly have been hung up or put in drawers and some of them were quite grubby Jake noted but he picked his way around the room, glancing at the small cage on one side of the room that contained a tiny hamster. It looked quizzically at him for a moment then hid itself in some plastic tubing.

There was also a small glass bowl containing a goldfish that was swimming around happily among the plants and the plastic shipwrecks on the bottom of the bowl. Jake tapped the glass lightly, watching as the fish cruised slowly back and forth.

He stepped back, almost tripping over some discarded Doc Marten boots. It was difficult walking without stepping on something Jake noted, moving closer to a chest of drawers. There was a single wooden chair next to the storage unit and he decided it might be best to just sit down there and wait. As he seated himself, he glanced down at one of the half open drawers and saw some pieces of paper, some notebooks, some envelopes, and some marker pens inside.

Some of the sheets had been written on in a large, spidery hand that looked strangely familiar.

Jake pulled the drawer open further, reached in, and took out several sheets of paper, scanning the words there.

YOUR DISGUSTING.

He felt his heart beating faster.

LEAVE THE YOUNG GIRLS ALONE. YOUR SICK.

And now he felt a cold feeling deep in the pit of his stomach. The understanding began to hit him harder.

DIRTY FUCKER.

YOUR PATHETIC.

Like the ones pushed through the door.

Jake sucked in a breath and it seemed to stick in his throat. As he held the notes his hand was shaking. In that second of unbearable realization, he knew that it was Lucy who had been sending him the anonymous notes and that knowledge washed over him like an unstoppable, unbearable tide.

He got to his feet, feeling faint, swaying slightly. Then he blundered out of the room and down the stairs.

As he reached the hallway Claire Conlan joined him, wondering why he looked so pale. Wondering why he was hurrying towards the front door, anxious to be out of this place.

"I thought you were going to wait for Lucy," Claire said.

"No," Jake murmured. "I've got to go."

He pulled open the door and stumbled out, slamming it behind him.

EIGHTY-EIGHT

The hotel was called The Post House and it was one of the many generic modern hostelries so prevalent in towns and cities. No character. No charm. Expensive. But it was all they could find at short notice and the only one that would let them book in without a previous reservation.

The room was small, consisting of a large double bed that completely dominated the floor, some wardrobes and chests of drawers, a TV and a kettle with cups and tea bags, sachets of coffee and hot chocolate (there were even some biscuits).

Mike sat on the bed flicking channels on the TV while Dani washed her face in the tiny bathroom.

"This had better be worth it," Mike called, sitting back, propping himself against the headboard, his eyes still fixed on the TV screen.

Dani didn't answer. The only sound from the bathroom was that of running water.

"Why couldn't we have done this research online?" Mike called.

"You can't do everything online," Dani told him, appearing in the doorway. "I just thought actually being here and looking around would be more useful."

"And more expensive," Mike grunted. "Ninety quid a night," he continued, looking around the room. "For *this*."

"The quicker we find something the quicker we can get out," she reminded him. She padded across to the bed picking up a couple of the scrapbooks on her way. As she opened one of them Mike glanced across at it, his gaze running over the cuttings and pictures.

"Where the hell do we start looking?" he murmured. "Do we even know what we're looking for?"

"Anyone who knew Jake's mother would be a good place to start," Dani told him. "Anyone who lived near her. Who worked with her?"

"But you said the hospital where she worked had closed down."

"It has but there must be some records somewhere. We need to find a list of staff, addresses. That kind of thing."

"This isn't a TV drama, Dani, things don't just happen like they do in films and plays, do they? And what are we going to tell people? Why should anyone help us? Who the fuck are we?"

Dani glanced at him for a moment then returned her attention to the scrapbook.

"We could say we were looking for long lost relatives," she suggested. "People are usually helpful if someone says something like that."

"But most of the people who lived here when Jake's mother lived here are probably dead by now."

Dani shook her head.

"She moved away from here about thirty years ago," she said. "It's not that long."

"It's longer than either have lived."

Dani smiled and had to admit he was right. She turned a page and found more cuttings, all seemingly about the same subject. Small pieces about three women. All three had died of ectopic pregnancies.

"Why the fuck would she save something like that?" Mike grunted. "A bit morbid isn't it?"

Dani had no answer. She merely kept flicking through the scrapbook, her gaze travelling slowly over the saved articles and other material. More cuttings about the murders. Some new ones about the police investigation. Pictures of the detective in charge. He was or had been, a man called Louis Randall apparently. There were more pieces about Randall's career prior to his arrival in Exham. Then other items that seemed completely incongruous among the plethora of darker news.

A menu from a restaurant. The label from a perfume bottle. Polaroids of the detective in charge of the murder investigation. And one of Maggie Ford standing side by side with the detective.

"What the fuck?" Mike breathed, pointing at the picture. "Jake's mum was going out with the detective. Maybe he was Jake's dad."

Dani didn't answer.

"You said he never talks about his dad," Mike persisted.

"But why did she move away from here without him then?" Dani said, finally.

"Maybe they just split. It happens doesn't it? Perhaps that was why she left Exham, to get away from *him*. Maybe she didn't want Jake growing up around him."

"So she moves away and then, a few years later, she decides to put

Jake in care. To get rid of him. To wash her hands of him. Then, thirty years later, she kills herself. Why? There's so many loose ends."

"That's why we're here isn't it? To tie those loose ends up?"

Dani nodded.

"It might be harder than I thought it was going to be," she muttered.

"So where do we start?"

She had no answer.

EIGHTY-NINE

Jake Porter had felt pain before but nothing like this.

No amount of physical pain could compare with what he felt as he clambered from the car and walked shakily towards his front door.

At least physical pain could be eased with drugs but what could he take that would help him soothe the hurt he was suffering now? He knew he had failed Lucy, but nothing could have prepared him for her reaction. The anonymous letters had been so vindictive, so spiteful and angry he could never have imagined she hated him so much.

As Jake pushed the key into the lock his hands were shaking.

What did he do next? Confront her? Ignore the whole thing and hope that she learned to cope with her antagonism?

Jake felt dizzy. He stumbled inside, closed the door behind him and blundered through into the sitting room where he slumped into a chair and sat there, tears rolling slowly down his cheeks.

He wanted to be with Lucy now. Wanted to hold her. To tell her he understood her anger. To explain that he didn't feel angry that she'd taken such measures against him. He just wanted his daughter with him. He wanted her back. More than anything in his life he wanted her back.

Jake sat forward slightly, the tears now coming more freely. He didn't try to control them. What good would it do? The pain would still be there. There was no coming back from this was there? He whispered her name two or three times and it seemed to hang in the air.

Again, he wished she was here. He wished he could apologise to her. He wished he could tell her that no matter how much she hated him he would always hate himself more for what he'd put her through. He wanted to say that if there was any way he could give her back the last few years, years that he'd ruined, he would.

For what seemed like an eternity he sat slumped in the chair then, finally he got to his feet and staggered into the kitchen where he dragged a bottle of Jack Daniels from one of the cupboards above a work top. He snatched a mug from the wooden mug tree and poured a large measure of the alcohol into it, swigging it, almost downing the dark fluid in one swallow. It burned its way to his stomach, and he drank more.

And more.

Only when the bottle was almost empty did he finally bang it down on the worktop, his head spinning.

Why wasn't he drunk? Or at least unconscious?

He'd consumed more booze in ten minutes than he'd imbibed in the last six months and yet still he couldn't achieve the oblivion he wanted. Because that was all he desired now. He wanted nothingness. He wanted to escape this pain even for only a short time and he knew that the booze offered the only solution. He didn't want to think this problem through carefully and sensibly. He had no desire to examine it from both sides and offer a considered opinion on how to progress.

Jake Porter wanted to drink until he blacked out.

He dropped onto one of the kitchen chairs, his hand gripping the mug of Jack Daniels, the smell of the liquor filling the air.

It seemed as if he'd lost every woman in his life that he ever cared about. Lucy was just the latest on that list.

His birth mother had abandoned him. His adopted mother had disappeared inside the confines of her own mind. His wife had divorced him. Rhiannon had left him. And now Lucy.

All gone. Or going.

Stop feeling sorry for yourself. You brought it all on yourself.

Jake hurled the mug across the room, seeing it shatter against the far wall. Pieces of porcelain and liquor flew in all directions. He sat there silently, watching as the dark liquid dripped down the wall.

He got to his feet, staggering slightly as he moved across the room.

Inside one of the cupboards there was a small bunch of keys. Jake held them on his palm for a moment then selected the one he needed.

NINETY

"She was old, why bother killing herself? If she'd waited another couple of years, it would have happened anyway."

Mike Quinn's voice sounded loud inside the car

"She wasn't that old, Mike," Dani countered. "Early seventies. That's not old."

"It's old *enough*."

"People who commit suicide usually do it because they're in trouble or have too much pressure on them. Jake's mum seemed as if she was comfortable enough."

"We don't know what was going on in her life. She might have had problems we can't even imagine."

He brought the car to a halt across the road from the main entrance to what had once been Exham Psychiatric Hospital and they both sat gazing in the direction of the gates and the arch that spanned the opening to the driveway.

It was their fourth stop already that day in a route that had already taken them from Margaret Ford's house in Exham to the cemetery where three of the victims of the killer had been buried and then to the offices of what had been the Exham Comet (it was now the headquarters of a design firm). None of the previous locations had yielded anything useful and Dani was beginning to think that the entire trip was little more than a fanciful journey with no hope of success.

However, as she swung herself out of the car, she hoped that a quick inspection of the hospital might offer something. Beyond the gates and the wall, she could see the huge building in the distance. Even in broad daylight it looked menacing and the breeze that had grown stronger during the day shook the iron gates occasionally, the rattling sound filling the air.

Mike joined her and they walked across the street towards the towering wall that surrounded the grounds.

"It's a wonder someone hasn't knocked this down and built a housing estate on it," Mike murmured as they walked slowly along next to the wall, finally reaching the gates.

"What exactly are you expecting to find here?" he wanted to know.

"I don't know," Dani said, exasperatedly. "How do I know what we're going to find when I'm not even sure what we're looking for?"

She moved closer to the gates, gripped one of the metal bars and tugged it. The gates rattled.

"There must have been loads of people in there," Mike said, nodding towards the huge building. "It's massive."

"I wonder what it looks like inside?" Dani mused.

"Only one way to find out," Mike told her. "My toolbox is in the car." He turned and hurried back to the car, returning a moment later with a claw hammer.

Dani watched as he pushed the prongs between the two gates, using it as a lever to force them further apart. The metal, weakened by the passage of time and ravaged by rust, gave way easily and one of the gates moved a foot or so. Mike put his shoulder against it and forced it wider, the whole thing swinging back on its hinge.

He looked at Dani and smiled then he turned and hurried off to fetch the car, pulling up beside her.

She clambered into the passenger seat and Mike drove slowly through the open gate and along the wide driveway, the massive edifice of the hospital looming larger as they closed in on it. He pulled up close to the main entrance and they both looked up at the dark stone construction towering above them.

"What happened to the patients when they closed it down?" Mike wanted to know.

"Some were moved to other hospitals, the ones who weren't considered dangerous were just released into the community," Dani told him. "Jake's mum was one of the psychiatrists who decided which ones were released."

"And one of them was a murderer? Maybe that's why she topped herself. Perhaps she couldn't stand the guilt."

"Why wait until forty years later before doing it?"

Mike shrugged.

"How many did he kill?" he wanted to know.

"Five that they knew of, maybe more."

"And they found him inside this place?"

"Him and the remains of his victims. The heads mostly."

"Sick fuck."

"The man who committed the murders used to be a Porter at a hospital in a town nearby," Dani informed him. "Supposedly he was dangerously disturbed. One of his jobs at the hospital was to burn aborted foetuses but he didn't do it. He buried them in a grave behind the hospital instead."

"Jesus," Mike gasped, his face contorted. "And he was one of Maggie Ford's patients?"

Dani nodded.

"It's all in the scrapbooks," she said, quietly. "Copies of her reports, her notes on their conversations. She was trying to help him."

Again, Mike shook his head. He pushed open the car door and climbed out, walking across the gravel of the driveway towards the short flight of stone steps that led up to the main entrance of the building. Dani hesitated a moment then joined him.

The huge black doors were locked as they'd expected but Mike returned to the car and retrieved his tool kit, working expertly on the large doors, removing the lock completely. He pushed the doors and they swung open, revealing a darkened hallway beyond.

Dani glanced into the darkness within, surprised at how dull it was inside the building despite the daylight outside. It was as if the weak sunlight couldn't penetrate the shadows. She felt her heart beating a little faster. Dani looked at Mike and nodded. They stepped across the threshold into the enveloping gloom.

NINETY-ONE

There was a thick layer of dust covering the floor that rose several inches into the air as they walked through it.

It reminded Dani of mist, but it was more dense, almost organic as it rose and swirled around them.

The entrance of the hospital opened out into a wide tiled area with several closed doors leading off from it. At the far end of the hallway was a wide stone staircase.

"There'll be nothing here after all these years," Mike murmured, looking around.

"There might be some records, some files somewhere," Dani offered.

"They'd have taken them all away when they closed it down," he mused, heading towards the first of the closed doors.

Dani followed him but moved towards one of the other doors, opening it and peering inside the darkened room. Apart from a couple of old metal chairs it was completely empty. Even the blinds that had once hung at the windows had been taken down (Dani could still see the runners at the top of the window frames). She stepped back out of the room and went to join Mike.

The room he'd investigated was also empty. Bare and unwanted now. The other rooms on the ground floor were the same. Everything it seemed had been removed when the facility closed. They walked down corridors that had once been patients' quarters, surprised that so many of the rooms were unlocked.

"No need to lock them any more," Dani mused, pushing one of the doors, looking into the small room beyond.

"I wonder where the murderer lived," Mike said, a slight smile on his face. "I wonder where he kept his severed heads."

Dani didn't share the joke. She wandered off towards another door at the end of the corridor, pushing it open and looking into a stairwell.

"Let's look upstairs," she said, quietly.

"Oh, come on, Dani, this is a waste of time," Mike sighed.

But she had already begun to climb the steps, her footfalls echoing inside the stairwell. Mike hesitated for a moment then followed her up the stone stairs. When they reached the first floor, they made their way out into another complex of corridors to be confronted by more closed doors. One by one they went into the rooms finding little or nothing to show that the building had ever housed patients or carers. All that remained was dust and dirt. Neglect personified.

Dani crossed to one of the windows and looked out over what had been the grounds to the rear of the hospital. The lawns and flower beds were overgrown and full of weeds. Everything about the building and the area around it felt as if it belonged to another time.

"There must have been hundreds of patients here," Dani mused. "I wonder how many of them were looked after by Jake's mum?"

Mike merely shook his head and shrugged, heading towards the next room. He pushed open the door and peered inside.

"Dani."

She heard her name and spun around, hurrying out of the room to join Mike.

The room he was standing in was larger than most of those they'd discovered so far.

The floor, visible even through the accumulated dust and grime, was grey and seemed to be made of rubberised material. There were two wooden benches and a gurney in the room too. Dani walked across towards the equipment that stood against one wall. There was a machine with several electrical leads dangling from it like plastic intestines from an eviscerated body. Several paddles that looked like those normally associated with a defibrillator. Another smaller machine that seemed to consist purely of dials and buttons.

"What the hell is it?" Mike wanted to know.

"It's what they used to do ECT with," she told him, glancing at the machinery warily. "Electric Convulsive Treatment. Electric Shock Therapy. They stopped doing it years ago. That must be why they left the equipment here when they shut down."

"They gave people electric shocks?"

"To their brains. People thought it cured all kinds of psychological problems like depression, mania, and catatonia. My mum's sister had it when she was about eighteen.

"Fuck that," Mike breathed, "Do you think Jake's mum used to do it to patients?"

Dani could only shake her head by way of reply, running her hand over a kidney bowl that was standing on top of one of the machines. There was a rubber mouth guard lying in the dish.

"They used to give them that to stop them biting their tongues when the shock was given," Dani murmured, pointing at the mouth guard.

Mike frowned. He looked around the room once again and then walked back towards the doorway.

"Let's get out of here," he said.

Dani nodded.

She was about to join him when she heard movement.

She wasn't sure where it came from. It sounded like footsteps. Mike heard it too and raised his hand to alert her, pointing in the direction from which the noises were coming. The realization hit them both at the same time.

There was someone else inside the building.

NINETY-TWO

He felt as if someone inside his skull was trying to batter their way out using a pneumatic drill.

Jake sat up slightly, groaned from the effort and slumped back, both hands pressed to his temples as if he feared that removing them might cause his head to split in two. He sucked in a deep breath and held it then exhaled almost painfully, putting out a hand to steady himself. Beneath his fingertips he felt bare brickwork and it took him another second to realize where he was.

The cellar was large, stretching under most of the house. Like most people's spare rooms in most households, it had been used mainly for storing unwanted items. The detritus of a life. There were piles of boxes and crates in the subterranean room, many of them still crammed with things Jake couldn't even remember he had. Obviously, if they were still in boxes below ground, he reasoned, then they weren't useful. There were several wooden shelves attached to the bare bricks. Some gardening tools were hanging from a rack. A hoe, a spade, a rake, and a couple of yard brushes. There were even some old-fashioned metal filing cabinets shoved up against one of the walls.

He got to his feet, keeping one hand against the rough brickwork as if he feared that to remove it would cause him to topple over. Each step made his head pound, but he knew he had to walk. Had to leave this underground chamber. There was only one entrance and it led out into the garden. A wooden hatch that was sealed by a padlock. He had the key on the small bunch in his pocket. The keys he now pulled free. There were about half a dozen of them. Chrome or brass that glinted in the light of the overhead fluorescents. One of the strip lights was fading and it flickered intermittently, buzzing like some recalcitrant blue bottle every now and then.

Jake glanced around the cellar again, blinking hard to clear his vision.

Many of the houses in the area had cellars that had been used to store coal in the days when everyone had a coal fire but, as time had passed, less and less households had needed such space to store fuel and the underground rooms had been converted into everything from store rooms to home offices, play rooms, dens and even spare bedrooms. Many had just had them bricked up and forgotten about them. Jake had chosen to use his as a storeroom for all the things he didn't need any more but couldn't be bothered to sort through. Had he done so he would probably have realized that it would have been simpler to just throw the boxes and their contents away.

The cellar. Like the one your birth mother kept you in.

He swallowed hard and continued his slow amble around the subterranean room.

What kind of mother does that to her child?

He ran his fingertips over the lid of a box that contained some of Lucy's toys he'd kept from her childhood.

Lucy.

Even the thought of her name brought tears to his eyes.

The daughter who hates you so much she sends you abusive letters.

Jake closed his eyes, trying to force the thoughts from his mind.

Towards the far end of the cellar there was a boiler that regulated the central heating and two meters that governed electrical and gas usage. Beside them stood more storage boxes. More crates. Two old chest freezers had also been pushed against another wall. Behind them was an archway leading through into where coal had been stored most recently, probably in the sixties and seventies when many households still used solid fuel.

Jake turned away and glanced down again at the bunch of keys he was holding.

He needed a shower and some headache tablets but, as he climbed the steps out of the cellar, one thing bothered him more than most. From the time that he'd left Claire Conlan's house the previous night, he had no recollection of anything at all. No clue why he'd entered the subterranean room or what he'd been looking for down there.

And no idea why the taste in his mouth reminded him of blood.

NINETY-THREE

"It might be an animal."

Mike Quinn tried to control his breathing, ensuring too that his voice was nothing more than a whisper when he spoke.

"It might be a fox or something," he went on.

"An animal isn't going to come in here," Dani snapped, her own voice wavering and breathy.

Below them they could hear the sounds more clearly now. Footsteps. Moving across the wide hallway towards the stairs.

Whoever was making the sounds was coming up the wide steps.

There were plenty of rooms to hide in but nothing to offer any cover once that simple act was achieved. Nothing to crouch down behind. Nothing to shelter them from the intruder.

"Who the fuck could it be?" Mike whispered. "Did someone see us come in here?"

"Who could have seen us?" breathed Dani. "There's no one for miles around here."

"Perhaps whoever it is was already in here," Mike offered, his breath rasping in his throat.

Dani had no answer, but she realized that their only hope was to get out of the building without being seen.

"We can use the stairs we came up," she said, softly. "Get out that way."

Mike nodded and they both hurried out of the room, turning right, back towards the other stairway, away from the main staircase where the intruder was now climbing. The footfalls on the wide steps were unmistakeable.

They both moved as quickly as they could, both unaccountably frightened by the fact that someone other than themselves was in the deserted building. They didn't stop to consider the possible identity of the newcomer. All that concerned them was getting out of the building as quickly as they could. Getting away from this place.

They hurried down the narrow staircase, Mike occasionally looking behind him to ensure they weren't being followed.

As they reached the bottom of the steps Dani paused, straining her ears to hear through the silence, trying to detect any other movement from nearby. Only silence greeted her.

"We can get out of a window," Mike suggested, and Dani nodded, pushing open the first door they came to, hurrying across to the sash window there. She dug her fingers beneath it, trying to slide it open but it wouldn't budge.

"They leave the doors open but lock the fucking windows," Mike hissed, realizing why they couldn't get the casement to move. They both turned away from the locked opening, moving back towards the door again.

The sounds of movement came from above them now.

They both looked up towards the sounds as if expecting to see the source of the noise hovering overhead.

"If they're up there then we can get out of the main door," Dani whispered hopefully. "Come on." She grabbed Mike's arm and almost dragged him into the corridor beyond. They made their way stealthily along the narrow walkway towards the main hall and entryway.

Above them, more movement.

Dani eased the door ahead of them open a fraction and peered out into the wide hallway. There was no sign of anyone and, that coupled with more footsteps from above them, encouraged her. She beckoned to Mike and they both moved furtively out into the area beyond the door, quickening their pace when they saw that the hallway was empty.

As she ran, she saw that there were fresh footprints in the thick dust that carpeted the hall. Large prints too.

Dani hurtled through the main doors and out into the dull light of the day then she and Mike both bolted for the car, aware that there was another vehicle parked close by now.

They saw the figure emerge from behind an overgrown bush onto the driveway before they heard the shout.

"Stop," the voice bellowed but the sound came from behind them this time. Powerful and insistent. "Stand still."

They both froze.

NINETY-FOUR

Jake stood beneath the shower spray, eyes closed, head tipped forward. All he was aware of was the sound of the sputtering water and the feel of the jets on his skin. Every now and then he would reach out and lower the temperature a few degrees hoping that the colder water might shock him out of his lethargy.

When it became too cold to endure much longer, he shut off the spray and stepped out, drying himself quickly. He cleaned his teeth, looking at his haggard reflection in the mirror.

You look like shit.

Splashing his face with cold water did little to help. If a prolonged spell beneath the jets of the shower hadn't helped, how effective would a few handfuls of cold water be? Jake looked in the medicine cabinet and found a strip of Paracetamol, two of which he took, swallowing them with some water he scooped into his hand from the tap. He'd taken two more earlier and he hoped they would all start to kick in.

He wandered into the bedroom where he'd already laid out some clothes for his trip to the conference. An overnight bag would be enough he'd reasoned. It was only two days. Jake sat down on the edge of the bed beside the shirts, ties, t-shirts, trousers, socks, and underwear.

You shouldn't be going to the conference; you should be talking to Lucy.

He sighed. What good would talking do? The damage was done now, wasn't it?

You'll lose her forever. You're clinging on by your fingernails now but any more of this and she'll be gone.

Jake looked across to one side of the room where there were a couple of framed photographs of Lucy. One was a school photo, taken when she was about five. His daughter in her little blue uniform, smiling happily for the camera.

Those days are long gone.

Another of himself and Lucy together. She was about ten in that one. Standing beside him and smiling, looking at him lovingly.

That was when she didn't hate you. When she looked up to you. That time will never come again.

There were so many other things she could have done he reasoned. Anything but those notes. She could have confronted him about her feelings. It might not have been easy or comfortable to deal with, but it would have been preferable to the spite and anger contained within those short and scathing missives. Because those words had been written with real passion and feeling. The words she used against him were barbed. It took real rage to go to those lengths.

And you never even saw it coming.

Jake exhaled and put a hand to his forehead. The pain killers he'd taken earlier had helped his throbbing head; the only thing now was that he felt so tired. Drained.

He glanced at his watch and noticed that he had a couple of hours before he had to leave. Maybe there was time for a nap. It might help.

So, what are you going to do? Talk to Lucy when you get back? Tell her why she's wrong?

Jake lay down on the bed, his head propped against a couple of pillows. He wondered if he should tell Dani about his discovery.

Why? She doesn't care one way or the other.

Jake shook his head as if to dismiss his own musings. How would he tell one of his patients to deal with a similar problem? It was always easier giving advice to others than it was taking it yourself he thought. All the facts could be examined, all the pros and cons weighed up but, when it was your own problem, it always seemed insurmountable. If someone else had come to him with the same predicament he would have had alternatives lined up, ready to impart. Platitudes on tap.

Again, he shook his head, glancing at his phone.

No messages from Dani.

He wasn't even sure where she was. She'd said she had to see a friend. That the same friend was having problems (she hadn't said what kind of problems and he hadn't pressed her). He thought about calling her but then decided against it. He'd do that when he checked into his hotel before the conference started.

It wasn't like her. She would normally have sent a message to say she'd arrived, just so he didn't worry. She knew he worried. He told himself she was too busy, to engrossed with solving the problems of others. He assured himself that the message would come. She'd probably phone him later. She knew he was leaving for the conference today she would probably want to talk to him before it all got into full swing.

Wouldn't she?

He stretched, a couple of joints cracking in protest.

It's your age.

Jake took a few deep breaths, wondering if his stumbling attempts at meditation might also help to ease the headache. He smiled as he wondered what his patients would say if they could see him now. Not much of an example, was he?

He glanced again at his watch and thought it was almost time to get ready. The journey would take a couple of hours at least. He looked once more at the photos of Lucy, tears welling up in his eyes.

"I'm sorry," he whispered.

NINETY-FIVE

Dani watched as the younger of the two policemen walked towards them. She saw him say something into his radio then he continued towards her and Mike, both of whom were standing rigid at the bottom of the steps leading into the hospital.

The other uniformed man was a sergeant in his fifties, and he made his way down the stairs until he was standing beside them.

"What were you doing in there?" he wanted to know.

"I'm sorry," Dani said. "We were just looking around."

"Why?" the older policeman asked. "You broke in."

"We knew the hospital was closed," Mike offered.

"It's still private property," the younger constable told him. "You're trespassing. You have no right to be here. Not on these grounds and certainly not inside that building."

The sergeant pulled a notebook from one of the many pockets he possessed, wrote down the time then the location. He scribbled trespassing and unlawful entry as possible offences then looked at Dani and Mike more closely.

"Could I have your names please?" he asked.

They complied and he wrote those down too.

"Are we under arrest?" Dani asked, her face pale. "We didn't mean any harm. We just wanted to look around."

"What exactly were you looking for?" the younger constable asked.

"Is that your car?" the senior man enquired, nodding towards Mike's vehicle.

Mike nodded and the younger man hurried off to the police car to check the details.

"It's not stolen is it?" the sergeant said. "If it is, my colleague will soon find out."

"It's mine," Mike told him.

"So, my colleague asked, and I'll ask again, what were you looking for in there?" the uniformed man enquired, pointing at the building behind them.

Dani sucked in a deep breath, aware that whatever she was about to say was probably going to sound either ridiculous or unbelievable and probably both.

"We were trying to find out information about someone who used to work at the hospital," she said. "She was a psychiatrist there."

"And what are you? Family?"

"Sort of," Dani told him smiling. "The woman who worked there was the mother of a friend of mine."

"So, you're *not* family then?" the policeman grunted.

"Her name was Margaret Ford," Mike announced. "She worked here in the eighties."

"You've left it a bit late to look for her, haven't you? This place has been closed for more than thirty years."

"Can you remember it when it was open?" Mike enquired.

"Yes, I can but I don't think that's relevant is it?" the older man said. "All that seems to matter is that you two broke into this building and we caught you."

"We told you we didn't steal anything," Dani insisted. "There's nothing in there to steal anyway."

The sergeant smiled thinly, turning as he heard his colleague approaching.

"Everything checks out," the younger man began. "The car isn't stolen."

"So, we're only dealing with trespassing and a couple of other offences then," the sergeant murmured, his gaze fixed on Dani.

"You said you could remember this place thirty years ago," she interjected. "Can you remember the murders too?"

The older man looked a little shaken.

"Murders?" the other policeman echoed, similarly surprised by Dani's words.

"Yes," the senior man said. "I can remember them. I thought you were interested in someone who used to work here though. Not in the murders."

"We think there might be a link," Mike told him.

"So, you're detectives as well as burglars?" announced the sergeant, smiling.

"Margaret Ford, the woman we were trying to find out about, worked here," Dani explained. "The guy who did the murders used to be one of her patients."

"And she went out with the detective who was in charge of the investigation," Mike added.

"Inspector Randall," the older man said, nodding.

"Did you know him?" Dani asked, excitedly.

"Lou Randall," murmured the sergeant. "He was a good copper. Dedicated. We all liked him." He looked more closely at them. "How do you know all this?"

"I can show you," she announced, walking towards the car. The sergeant joined her, watching as she took two or three of the scrapbooks from the back seat, opening the first at a page she felt was relevant.

The older policeman looked closely, his gaze flicking over the articles there. He turned the pages, his expression darkening.

"What happened to Randall?" Dani enquired. "He caught the killer, didn't he?" she went on. "He caught him inside this place." She gestured towards the building.

"Yes, he did," murmured the older man. "He nearly died himself though."

"What happened?" Dani wanted to know.

"He was badly injured that night and it affected him in other ways too," said the senior policeman.

"What do you mean?" Mike asked.

"He had a complete mental breakdown after that night. The only one who really knows what happened inside this place that night is Lou Randall," said the sergeant, quietly.

"Is there any way we could speak to him?" Dani asked, excitedly.

"You'll be lucky," the sergeant said. "He hasn't spoken a word since that night."

NINETY-SIX

The darkness was total.

So impenetrable that at first, Jake Porter thought he'd gone blind.

He turned his head from one side to the other, blinking hard then rubbing his eyes as he sought even the tiniest glint of light in such enveloping blackness but there was none forthcoming. Nothing. Only the dark.

He sat up, gently pushing out a hand to his right to support him. Beneath his fingers he felt cold stone wall and recoiled slightly but then he extended his hand again, feeling the rough surface, the same way a blind person would read Braille.

What he was laying on was soft and it smelled freshly washed. A pleasing lavender scent that filled his nostrils when he moved. As he swung his legs to one side, he realized that the mattress was indeed laid on a wooden bed frame. Jake got slowly to his feet, using the frame as support and he took a couple of cautious steps across the floor, feeling the cold stone beneath his feet.

The room stretched away before him in all directions, hidden by the darkness. Jake put out his hands to ensure he didn't bump into anything and this time he felt his fingers brush against something close by. He ran the probing digits over it and realized that it was a pile of books. There were more of them stacked up a little further on, he could smell the fusty odour of the pages.

He moved on; his arms still extended before him. And now, as he felt more stonework to his left and right, he realized that the area he was in was becoming narrower. When he moved his foot, it connected with something hard that Jake realized was a stone step.

Supporting himself against the walls on either side he began to climb the stairs, tripping occasionally on them as he rose higher.

When he reached to top, he put out his hands to each wall and found a panel of light switches that he hurriedly and gratefully pressed.

Cold white light suddenly bathed the area all around him and Jake turned to look at his surroundings.

He was in a narrow stairwell that fell away before him into a large room. A room he didn't recognise. Jake made his way cautiously back down the steps, peering around at the expanse before him. He could see the bed he'd risen from and there was also a table, a couple of wooden chairs, a wash basin and a chemical toilet that could be closed off behind some thin plastic curtains attached to a frame connected to the ceiling.

It took Jake only a moment longer to realize that what he was standing in was a cellar. An underground room. He waited a second longer then turned back towards the flight of steps he'd begun to ascend earlier.

At the top of the steps there was a thick wooden door and as Jake closed his fingers around the handle, he expected it to be locked.

He was surprised when it wasn't.

He pulled the door open, stepping out into a large kitchen.

There was a dark-haired woman standing at the sink and, as he took a step towards him, she turned. She grabbed for a towel, wiping her hands as best she could. She looked almost embarrassed that he had interrupted her.

She put down the knife.

The man seated at the table said nothing. He merely sat there, bolt upright, his head tilted slightly backwards. Jake looked at him expressionlessly for a moment then took a step towards him.

"What are you doing?" the woman asked, her face pale, her expression fearful. "You have to stay down there. Just for now."

Jake shifted his attention from the immobile man at the table to the woman. She moved towards him, trying to usher him back towards the cellar door.

Jake stood there silently, wanting to tell her didn't want to go back down there. He wanted to stay with her.

With his mother.

But she shook her head and put both hands on his shoulders, turning him around and almost pushing him back towards the open door.

Again, he tried to tell her he didn't want to go down the steps and he glanced again at the man seated at the table realizing that there was a steadily growing puddle of dark fluid spreading out around him as he sat there. Jake realized that it was blood and assumed it was coming from the deep gash across his throat, the slit that looked like the crimson choked gills of a fish.

"You have to, trust me," she said and this time there was a note of tenderness in her voice. "I have to keep you safe."

Jake allowed her to guide him back down the steps and across to the bed where she encouraged him to lay down again.

He wanted to tell her he didn't feel tired. He didn't want to sleep.

"You can come out later," she said, managing a weak smile. "When I know it's safe." She touched his face with her long fingers, stroking the soft skin there. "Just be patient. This will be over soon. But for now, no one must know."

She leaned forward and kissed him gently on the forehead then she moved away from him, turning again when she reached the bottom of the stairs, waving to him before retreating up the steps. When she reached the top Jake heard the door close and then the metallic click as she locked it, sealing him inside once again.

He called to her, told her he didn't want to stay down here in this room, but it was too late, she was gone.

He was alone again.

NINETY-SEVEN

Jake Porter sat up gasping. The last vestiges of the dream fading as he did. He looked around him, trying to regain his wits. Attempting to re-orientate himself.

It took a moment for him to realize that he was laying on his bed. A second more to discover he'd been asleep for over three hours.

"Oh, Christ," Jake murmured, dragging himself off the bed.

Time had flown since he'd fallen asleep, and now he hurried to get dressed before stuffing his clothes into his overnight bag, hoping he wasn't going to miss the train he'd planned to catch.

The nap he'd planned had turned into much more and he was surprised at how heavily he'd slept.

Surprised too at the intensity and vividness of his dream.

It had been different to the others that had plagued him. Never before had he dreamed about the house in Walmsley. Never before had he seen his mother in his subconscious outings. Perhaps, he reasoned, this latest episode had been triggered by visiting the place. But why did the visions come so starkly in his dreams but not when he was awake?

Jake made a mental note to talk to some of his colleagues about his problem (parts of it at any rate) when he finally made it to the conference. If he ever did. He snatched up his phone and called a taxi to take him to the station. Taking the train would be less stressful than driving he reasoned.

Be careful you don't fall asleep on the train.

Jake inspected his reflection once more in the mirror, adjusting his tie slightly then he picked up his overnight bag and made his way down the stairs to wait for the taxi.

As he stood in the living room, he sent another message to Dani to remind her he was away for a day or two.

There was no answer and Jake sighed.

Where the hell was she?

He sent another message.

What was she doing that was so important she couldn't take five seconds to send a reply? The phone was never out of her hand normally.

He looked at the device for a moment longer then slid it back into his pocket, noticing that the taxi had just pulled up outside.

Jake hurried out and clambered in.

As the cab pulled away, he had no idea Ted Brady was watching furtively from behind the curtains of his sitting room.

Jake settled himself into the passenger seat for the short journey to the station. Once he got there, he got his ticket and wandered down onto the platform, checking his watch and hoping that the train arrived soon. A cold breeze had sprung up and it was whipping across the platform strongly enough to make him seek shelter inside the small cafe there.

It was warm and welcoming inside there and the scent of coffee was strong in the air. Jake stepped back to allow someone to pass him, nodding affably at them as they moved away carrying their cappuccino. The short haired woman behind the counter looked at him and smiled as he approached.

"Tea please," Jake said, fumbling for some change. "Just ordinary bog-standard English breakfast."

The young woman behind the counter smiled.

"I thought I'd better be specific," Jake went on, nodding towards the large menu that displayed the different teas available.

The young woman syphoned boiling water from a large aluminium container onto a tea bag she'd dropped in one of the Styrofoam cups stacked up on the counter. She asked Jake if he wanted milk and sugar and added them accordingly. He pushed some money towards her, thanking her.

As his hand brushed against hers, he drew it back suddenly, glancing down at his fingers to inspect the damage as if he'd just stroked a red-hot skillet.

The young woman looked at him with a puzzled expression on her face, wondering why he was staring so fixedly at her.

"Are you okay?" she wanted to know.

Jake nodded slowly, still looking at her.

"When did you have it done?" he murmured.

"What?" she enquired.

"The abortion," he breathed. "When did you have it done?"

"What are you talking about?" she gaped, the colour draining from her cheeks.

"You had an abortion recently," he went on. "Why?"

"That's none of your business."

"You did have one?"

"Yes, but how the hell did *you* know?"

Jake turned away suddenly, heading towards the door.

"I asked how you knew," the young woman called after him.

Jake made his way back out onto the platform, gripping his tea in one hand, holding the cup so tightly he almost crushed it. He walked to the far end of the platform, the wind whipping around him now.

He looked around and he could see the young woman inside the cafe gazing out of the window towards him.

From the other direction there was a low rumbling and he realized the train was approaching. It pulled in and Jake climbed into the first carriage, glancing again towards the young woman in the cafe. He was still looking when the train moved off.

NINETY-EIGHT

"Maybe he was just winding us up."

Mike Quinn brought the car to a halt and switched off the engine, glancing up at the block of flats away to his right.

"Why would he do that?" Dani wanted to know. "He could have arrested us."

She too was gazing in the direction of the flats.

"Bit of a coincidence wasn't it?" Mike murmured. "The policeman who caught us breaking into that hospital just happened to know where Lou Randall lived?"

"I prefer to call it a happy accident," Dani said, smiling. "You know what small towns are like, everyone knows everyone else. Besides, you heard what the sergeant said, he liked Randall. I think he's pleased to know someone might be able to help him after all these years."

Mike nodded almost imperceptibly.

"Does dragging up his past count as helping?" he mused.

"There's only one way to find out," Dani said.

"Why would Randall talk to us? Why would he talk to *anyone* about what happened all those years ago? Anyway, according to that copper he doesn't talk *at all*."

"We've got to try."

"I wonder what Jake would say if he knew what we were doing," Mike chuckled.

Dani ignored him and swung herself out of the car, reaching for one of the scrapbooks as she did so. Mike waited a moment then joined her, the two of them making their way across the open area of tarmac leading to the main entrance of the flats.

It was a red brick building, only three storeys and there were several window boxes and potted plants on display on the various balconies bringing a little more colour to the dour looking edifice. There was a panel outside the main door with spaces available where the names of the residents of the block could be displayed but there was only one name there.

"Perhaps it's empty," Mike offered.

Dani tried the main door, surprised when it was unlocked. She pushed it open, stepping into the hallway.

There were three ground floor flats leading off from the entryway and she suspected that the other two floors were the same. Followed by Mike, she began to climb the steps.

"If he hasn't spoken for over thirty years what's the point of this?" he grumbled.

"We've come this far, we've got to see him at least," Dani announced.

A door to their left opened and a woman in her sixties popped her head out, trying to discover who was walking past her front door. Mike turned and smiled at her, but she merely looked blankly at them both then closed her door again.

"I hope Randall is friendlier than that," Mike said, smiling.

They continued up the stairs, moving higher, seeking the flat they wanted. When they finally reached the door of number nine Dani paused beside it, glancing at the black painted woodwork. There were pot plants on either side of the door, both of which looked as if they were badly in need of watering. Some leaflets from a local take away were laying on the matt before the door.

"I bet he's not in," Mike whispered.

Dani waited a moment longer then knocked on the door.

There was no answer.

"Told you," Mike said.

Dani knocked again and, this time, they heard sounds of movement from the other side of the door. She wondered if Randall was using the spyhole in the door to check out his visitors. She tapped again lightly.

From the other side of the door, they heard the rattling of a chain then the door being unlocked. It opened an inch or two and a pale, wrinkled face peered out at them.

"Mr Randall?" Dani asked. "Are you Lou Randall?"

The older man held her gaze for a moment then nodded, glancing at Mike too.

"My name is Dani, this is my friend, Mike. I was wondering if we could talk to you."

Randall shook his head.

"It's about something that happened a long time ago," Dani went on. "At Exham psychiatric hospital. Do you know what I'm talking about, Mr Randall? We were hoping you might help us."

Again, Randall shook his head but this time he tried to push the door closed as well. Mike shot out a hand and attempted to stop him, but Randall looked angrily at him and put more weight behind the door, slamming it and almost trapping Mike's fingers between it and the frame.

Dani gazed exasperatedly at the wooden partition then she knocked again.

"Mr Randall it's important," she said. "We need your help."

There was a rustling sound from the other side of the door and then Dani looked down to see a small piece of paper emerge from the bottom of the wooden partition. She saw some words scrawled on it as she picked it up.

GO AWAY.

The words were written in black biro.

"Mr Randall," she said, leaning closer to the door. "A former colleague of yours said you might talk to us. A sergeant Willis. Can you remember him?"

Another piece of paper appeared beneath the door and Dani picked that up too and read what had been written there;

LEAVE ME ALONE.

"We want to talk to you about someone you knew," Dani said, her face pressed against the black painted wood. Mike frowned. "You knew Maggie Ford, didn't you?"

Mike's frowned deepened and he shrugged. Dani waved a hand at him and tried again.

"She was a psychiatrist at Exham Psychiatric Hospital," Dani persisted. "Can you remember? You two were close. We need to talk to you about her. We want to help."

The door opened again.

Randall looked first at Dani, then Mike then returned his attention to Dani.

He was a tall man with snow white hair and sunken eyes, one of which was half covered by an eyelid that looked as if it had been weighted and was hanging down further than it should have done. He was quivering slightly, and Dani wondered if it was early onset Parkinson's.

"You did know Maggie Ford, didn't you?" she said, softly.

Randall nodded, watching as Dani dug a hand into her pocket. She pulled out a photograph that she'd removed from one of the scrapbooks.

Randall and Margaret Ford standing together side by side.

She offered the picture to Randall who took it and looked at the image. The beginnings of a smile touched his lips and he gently ran his fingers over the photograph. When he lifted his head again there were tears in his eyes.

"Can we come in?" Dani asked.

Randall stepped aside, ushering them into the flat.

NINETY-NINE

As the train pulled into the small station, Jake got to his feet and moved towards the nearest exit doors.

Signs on the platform informed all newcomers that the town of Camworth (about twenty miles East of London) was one of the first garden cities. Places designed and built in the 1920's that had been intended as overspill communities for people from big cities like London and Birmingham. The theory that every home should have a garden and every street, lane and avenue should have trees and flowers lining it had been a popular one with politicians and other concerned groups at that time in history so Camworth had become the embodiment of the cliché about a green oasis.

Jake stepped off the train and made his way over the footbridge between platforms, heading outside towards the small taxi rank where a couple of cabs were waiting.

Camworth was well within commuter range but he had sensibly missed the rush hour and it was relatively quiet in and around the station.

Jake climbed into the back of the first waiting cab, placing his overnight bag beside him. He quickly consulted the letter he had in his jacket, checking the address and location of the conference.

"The Park Hotel, please," he told the driver who nodded.

"Nice place," the driver said. "Is it business or pleasure?"

"Mostly business," Jake told him hoping the man wasn't going to be *too* talkative.

"My son works there, he's a barman in The Horse Shoe Bar," the driver announced with the requisite amount of pride in his voice. "They call it that because there used to be a blacksmiths across the road in the old days."

"But not any more?" Jake mused.

"Not for about eighty years," the driver chuckled.

"You live in the town obviously?"

"Just outside. Lovely place. Better than the city for bringing up kids. Have you got any kids?"

"A daughter," Jake told him, a pang of regret filling him.

"I bet she's a real daddy's girl," the driver joked.

Jake managed to smile but that was about it. In the dull light of the rear seat it was impossible to see his expression clearly which was probably just as well.

"You said your trip was for business," the driver went on. "What kind of business? If you don't mind me asking?"

"I'm a psychiatrist," Jake told him. "There's a conference, a convention at the hotel."

"I'd better be careful what I say then. You'll be analysing everything and looking for the hidden meanings."

"It doesn't really work like that," Jake reassured him. "You're quite safe."

"I don't want you knowing all my deep, dark secrets by the end of the journey, do I?"

"Have you got many then?"

"Everyone's got secrets, haven't they?" the driver laughed.

Jake nodded slowly.

If only you knew.

The taxi moved along the tree lined streets of Camworth until the driver finally turned into a large driveway about half a mile from the town centre. Jake glanced out of the side window as the cab passed ornamental gardens and expanses of lawn, glancing ahead to catch sight of a whitewashed building that loomed out of the growing gloom. It was covered by ivy that looked as if it was trying to choke the life from the building and some of the windows at the front seemed as if they'd been covered by the creeping vine. Jake was still musing that the hotel looked as if it had been used as a location in Day of the Triffids when the driver brought the cab to a halt.

Jake thanked him and paid him and made his way towards the ornate entrance of the hotel. Like much of the exterior of the building, the porch way entrance was also covered in ivy and Jake was beginning to wonder if the climbing plant was the only thing keeping the whole edifice up.

He walked across reception and checked in, also picking up a couple of laminates and lanyards that were being issued to other attendees of the conference. There were a few other guests displaying the same kind of id and Jake nodded affably at them as he passed them on his way to the elevator. Away to his right there were signs directing himself and others to the various talks and discussions that would begin the next day. He'd also been given an itinerary when he checked in, so he glanced at it to see exactly what was in store while he was at the conference.

The elevator doors slid open and Jake prepared to get in, almost colliding with the person who was leaving the lift car.

They looked at each other for long seconds.

"Jake?" said the other person.

He nodded; his gaze fixed on the newcomer.

ONE HUNDRED

Dani wasn't sure what she'd been expecting but as she walked into the sitting room of Lou Randall's flat she looked around and thought how welcoming it seemed. It was spotlessly clean, immaculately decorated and furnished and the room looked as if it had been lifted from a furniture warehouse. There was nothing out of place.

The walls were lined with shelves mostly covered by books, CD's or DVD's and a large television hooked up to a Sky TV box, a DVD player and a Games Console dominated the sitting room. The room smelled pleasantly of lavender air freshener.

There was a small notepad on the coffee table on the lowest of the bookshelves and on one of the chairs.

Randall obviously liked to keep himself busy, Dani thought as he motioned to the high-backed sofa. He himself took a seat opposite, regarding the two newcomers with a look he might normally have reserved for someone who had just shit on his doorstep.

"We really appreciate this, Mr Randall," Dani began. "Thanks for letting us talk to you."

He picked up the writing pad, slipped the biro from it and wrote swiftly on the paper;

WHAT DO YOU WANT?

"We're trying to find out some information about a friend of mine," Dani told him. "About his family. His background. His name is Jake Porter."

Randall shook his head dismissively and reached for his pad. He scribbled something on it and held it up for them to see.

HOW DO YOU KNOW MAGGIE FORD?

Dani glanced at the pad as Randall displayed it.

"Through a friend of mine," she began. "She was his mother."

Randall looked quizzical then he shook his head, sneering slightly.

Dani frowned.

"She died recently," Mike added.

Randall's expression darkened.

"She committed suicide," Dani added.

The former policeman drew in a deep breath.

WHY?

Randall scribbled the word hurriedly, his hand shaking slightly as he held up the pad.

"We don't know," Dani told him. "Was she a depressive kind of person when you knew her?"

Randall shook his head.

"Did you know her well?" Dani wanted to know.

Randall nodded.

"She worked at Exham Psychiatric Hospital, didn't she?" Dani went on.

Randall gripped the arms of his chair tightly. It was as if the seat had suddenly begun to shake and he needed to keep himself steady in it. The colour drained from his cheeks and he gritted his teeth.

"Mr Randall," Dani persisted, seeing Randall's reaction. "Are you all right?"

The former policeman didn't answer but merely sat stiffly in his chair, his eyes lowered.

"We know something happened at the hospital," Dani went on. "Something to do with a murderer. You caught a murderer there, didn't you?"

Randall nodded but still didn't look at Dani.

"Was Maggie Ford there that night?" Mike interjected. "Was she there when you caught the killer?"

Dani leaned forward in her seat slightly, her voice low when she spoke.

"What happened?" she breathed.

Randall looked at her, his gaze suddenly fixed on her. She thought it must be how a predator looks at its prey just before it strikes. Then he grabbed his pad and wrote something down, holding the page up for them to read;

GET OUT.

Dani felt suddenly deflated. Why was he suddenly so hostile again?

"We need to find out what happened," she insisted. "It's important. For us and for my friend. He needs to know about his mother."

Randall wrote again, the pen moving across the paper furiously.

NOT HIS MOTHER.

Dani frowned.

"What do you mean?" she asked, peering at the words on the pad and then at Randall himself.

SHE HAD NO KIDS.

Randall wrote the words and displayed the pad with a sense of finality.

"My friend is her son," Dani went on.

The former policeman stood up, shaking his head.

Dani flipped open the scrapbook, found a photograph of Maggie Ford and Jake taken in the garden of the house at Walmsley and pushed it towards Randall.

"That's her and her son," Dani told him.

Again, Randall shook his head as he peered at the picture.

"She put him up for adoption when he was ten," Dani continued.

The former policeman continued to shake his head furiously, his gaze now fixed on the picture.

"He's her son," Dani told him.

"That's impossible."

Randall spoke the words effortlessly.

Dani and Mike both gazed at him, surprised by the fact that he was talking.

"You can speak?" Mike murmured. "They told us you couldn't speak. That you hadn't said a word since that night in the hospital."

"I can speak," Randall said, quietly. "It's just that I've chosen *not* to."

"So, speak now," Dani insisted. "Why do you think this isn't Maggie's son?"

Randall glared at her again. When he spoke, his words were slow and measured.

"She had cervical cancer when she was in her early twenties," the former policeman murmured. "They operated and removed it but there were complications. They had to do a hysterectomy. Whoever that boy is in the picture with her, he couldn't be her son. Maggie Ford couldn't have kids."

ONE HUNDRED AND ONE

The bar was crowded but Jake and his companion had found a quiet spot at one end of the long, polished wood counter.

Surrounded by horse brasses, old farming implements and framed photographs and paintings of village life through the years, they sat undisturbed sipping their drinks. The steady burble of conversation from the other drinkers provided a pleasing back drop, as Jake and his companion ordered another round for themselves and continued the conversation they'd begun about two hours before.

Much small talk had passed under the bridge in order for them to re-acquaint themselves with each other.

Phillip Mason was in his fifties. A tall man with a bald head and glasses so large Jake thought that he resembled an owl. Mason had a slight tint to his skin that made it look as if he'd just returned from some prolonged and exotic holiday. Either that or he'd been using too much fake tan, Jake reasoned, smiling to himself. Whatever his thoughts he had been glad to bump into Mason (almost literally) and the two men had immediately retired to the bar of the hotel to talk.

That talk had consisted of their studies (they had both attended the same university), their first forays into psychiatry, the foibles of various patients (probably unethical but what the hell) and their personal lives. As the evening had progressed and the drink had flowed more plentifully, Jake had relaxed more and now, as they drank their newly arrived drinks, he was actually beginning to enjoy himself. Mason was good company. A warm, amusing man who seemed only too happy to chat about himself and his family.

Jake was slightly envious.

"Do you do many of these conventions?" Mason asked, sipping his drink.

"No," Jake told him. "I suppose I should go to more. Circulate. Get to know some more of my colleagues."

They both laughed.

"I suppose you're too busy," Mason went on. "What with being a writer too." He grinned. "I read your last book you know."

"Ah, *you* were the one," Jake chuckled. "What did you think? If you liked it tell me. If you hated it…lie."

They both laughed.

"Very good," Mason told him. "Will there be more?"

"I'm working on one now." Jake thought about mentioning the promotional tour and the possible TV work but decided against it. It felt like showing off to him and he also thought it might be best to keep quiet about that particular adventure until something was arranged. Best not to tempt fate.

As a young waitress passed them, Mason glanced in her direction. Something noticed by Jake who smiled.

"Stop looking," he said. "You're a married man. And she's too young for you anyway."

"Just because you've bought the goods doesn't stop you window shopping does it?" Mason chuckled. "And that's rich coming from you. How old did you say your current *paramour* is? Twenty-nine?" He raised his glass in salute.

"I do feel guilty about the age gap sometimes," Jake admitted. "And I'm sure having a relationship with a former patient must convene all sorts of ethical codes."

"What were you treating her for?"

"Depression. Her GP suggested some form of CBT and she came to see me a couple of times a week."

"She must have been impressed with your technique," Mason offered, smiling.

"Any photographs you'd like to share?"

Jake smiled and reached for his phone, finding some pictures of Dani, and showing them to his colleague who nodded approvingly.

"If she was waiting at home for me, I would *not* be spending two days with a load of crusty fellow psychiatrists," Mason said as Jake scrolled through some more photos.

As he reached one of Lucy, he withdrew the phone.

"Who's that?" Mason wanted to know.

"My daughter," Jake told him, a note of sadness in his voice.

"How does she get on with your…er…young companion? I understand it can be difficult in those situations sometimes."

"There's…friction," Jake told him, wanting to change the subject.

"What about *that* one?" Mason suddenly said, pointing at another photograph just before Jake put the phone down. "Who's that? You certainly know how to pick them, Jake." He laughed.

It was a shot of Rhiannon Morton.

Jake merely shook his head, grabbed the phone, and put it in his pocket. He took another sip of his drink then looked at Mason again. "So, what do you think about what I told you earlier," he went on, hurriedly. "About my lack of memory. About my nightmares?"

"It's difficult, Jake. I can understand your frustration but if your mind has shut down the way it has then there must be a reason. Whatever is locked away is locked away because to release it might harm you in some way. It might be best to keep it hidden."

Jake shook his head.

"No," he muttered. "I'm sick of not knowing."

"And you think I can help?"

"You use hypnotherapy on your patients. You can use it on me. One psychiatrist to another. Look on it as research."

Mason raised his eyebrows and took a deep breath.

"You know the dangers," he said.

"Yes."

"One more drink first?" Mason suggested.

Jake smiled and nodded.

ONE HUNDRED AND TWO

Lou Randall walked across to his window and looked out.

Dani and Mike watched him for a moment then it was Mike who spoke.

"So, if it isn't her son who is it in the picture with Margaret Ford?" he asked.

"I don't know," Randall snapped. "But I'm telling you it couldn't be *her* kid because she couldn't *have* kids."

"I live with her son," Dani protested. "He's been trying to find out about her. About himself. There are lots of photographs of the two of them when he was growing up. Why would she lie? Why would anyone fake that?"

"Look, I don't know what was going through her mind I'm just telling you what I know," Randall informed them.

"Why was she at the hospital that night?" Mike wanted to know. "It was already abandoned wasn't it?"

"We had a series of leads that made us think the killer was hiding out in the old hospital," Randall said. "It was the only home he'd ever known when he was growing up. It was logical that he'd go back. Maggie was with me when I drove there. I went inside to look around." His face lost its colour and he sat down. "The murderer was inside."

"What happened?" Dani asked.

"He tried to kill me. We fought. He fell down some stairs. Broke his neck," Randall explained.

"Did Maggie see that?" enquired Dani.

"No," said Randall. "She was upstairs in another room. With...with..." His voice trailed away, and he lowered his head, placing one hand over his mouth. "I'm not even sure what you'd call them."

Dani felt the hairs on the back of her neck rise. The look on Randall's face as he recalled that night was a mixture of horror and revulsion. She moved closer to the former policeman, reaching for his hand, and squeezing it, wanting to comfort him but also wanting him to finish the story.

"What did you see?" she whispered, gazing at him.

"Something I've been trying to forget ever since," Randall confessed, a twisted smile flickering briefly on his lips. "The killer, a man called Harold Pierce, he'd worked at a hospital when he was first released from the asylum. One of his duties at the hospital was to dispose of aborted foetuses. He was supposed to burn them in a furnace. Incinerate them. That was how they did that in those days." Randall paused for a moment; his mouth dry. "Pierce couldn't do it. His younger brother had died in a fire when he was a kid, I suppose it brought back too many memories. He couldn't burn them, so he buried them instead in a shallow grave behind the hospital. Then, when he lost his job there, he...he took them to the abandoned asylum with him, three of them." Randall put a hand to his mouth again, his breathing increasing in pace and strength.

Dani saw tears forming in his eyes.

"When I found them...they...they were alive," he said, his voice cracking.

"Alive?" Mike gaped. "That's impossible. You said they'd been aborted. How the fuck could they be alive?"

Randall rounded on him, his eyes fixing on Mike.

"How do I know?" he hissed. "I'm telling you what I saw. I don't understand how they were alive. And they were growing. Perhaps it's because Pierce had been feeding them."

"Feeding them?" Dani asked, her stomach tightening.

"He was killing people so he could feed their brains to those...those things whatever the fuck they were," Randall announced.

"Oh, God," Dani grunted.

"Maggie found them," the former policeman went on. "She told me they had telepathic powers. Thought projection. Mind control. She said they could read minds."

"Bullshit," Mike murmured, trying not to smile.

"That's what I thought," Randall continued. "But I *saw* them. Three of them. They looked like ordinary children." He tried to swallow. "Apart from their eyes. There was nothing there. No pupils. No iris. It was just black where their eyes should have been." He looked to the far side of the room as if seeing what he described there. The memory and the vision were obviously as fresh now as it had been when it happened.

"And they killed the mothers who had them aborted," Randall

went on. "Killed them telepathically. They caused the symptoms of ectopic pregnancy in those women. All the women that had them aborted died as if they'd suffered ectopic pregnancies. But they didn't. Those...things killed them."

Mike looked incredulously at Dani only to see that she was still looking fixedly at the former policeman.

"What did you do?" Dani wanted to know.

"I killed them," Randall told her. "Stabbed them to death. Cut them up. What the fuck did you expect me to do? I killed two of them. We never found the third one but with no one left to look after it, it would have died. Crawled away somewhere like animals do before they die."

"And it was after that you stopped talking?" Mike observed.

"Do you blame me?" grunted Randall. "Maggie left Exham soon after that. Not long after I got out of hospital. I never saw her again. Never heard from her. She disappeared from my life." He looked at Dani. "Until now. And now, after all this time, you turn up to tell me she killed herself."

"I'm sorry," Dani breathed.

"Why did she leave here?" Mike asked. "Why did she leave *you*? I thought you were in love with each other."

"She said she had to get away. Start again," Randall explained. "And that was it. She was gone before I had a chance to stop her or persuade her not to leave. I don't know where she went."

"She went to live in a place called Walmsley," Dani told him. "That's where she raised her son until she put him up for adoption."

"She didn't have a son," Randall interrupted angrily. "How many times do I have to tell you that? She *couldn't* have a child."

Dani pushed the photograph of Maggie and Jake towards him again.

"Then who is that?" she said, tapping the picture. "Who is that boy?"

"How the hell do I know?" Randall rasped. He looked first at Mike and then at Dani. "Now can you go? I've got nothing more to say."

They hesitated but Randall motioned towards the door.

"Go on," he snapped. "Get out. I should never have let you in here in the first place."

"We were trying to help," Dani protested.

"Yeah, help yourselves," Randall growled. "Now get out." He

pushed Mike towards the door. Dani followed reluctantly, allowing herself to be guided towards the door. She and Mike stumbled out, back into the hallway beyond. They saw Randall glaring at them both for a moment then he slammed the door behind them, the sound reverberating inside the building.

ONE HUNDRED AND TWO

The room was in darkness but for the dull light from one of the bed side lamps and some more cold white illumination coming from behind the half open bathroom door.

Jake was seated in a chair close to the bed, his head lolling forward slightly, his arms by his sides. Deep breathing, guided by Phillip Mason, had induced a mild hypnotic state.

He'd been under for the last ten minutes.

Mason knelt beside him looking into his face, watching for his reactions.

"If you experience any discomfort at any time tell me and I'll bring you out," Mason told him. "Do you understand?"

"Yes," Jake murmured.

Mason perched on the edge of the bed; his gaze fixed on his colleague.

"I want you to relax," he said, quietly. "Allow yourself to drift further back. Imagine your mind is like a flight of steps, you're on the bottom step now but the higher you go, the younger you are. The bottom of the steps is now. The top of the steps is your birth. Do you understand?"

"Yes," grunted Jake.

"Climb those steps slowly. Keep climbing until you come to your twentieth birthday."

Jake shifted slightly in the chair.

"Can you see yourself when you were twenty?" Mason asked.

"Yes," Jake told him.

"Go higher, go back. See yourself when you were fifteen."

Jake nodded almost imperceptibly.

"Is it a happy time?" Mason enquired.

"Yes."

"Who else can you see?"

"Friends. School friends. It's a party. My birthday party."

"Go back."

Jake's head sank a little lower on his chest.

"Go back to your tenth birthday," Mason said. "Who can you see this time?"

Jake grunted and his body quivered slightly in the seat.

"I can see a house," he breathed.

"People?"

Jake didn't answer.

"Who can you see, Jake?" Mason insisted.

"My mother," Jake murmured. "My birth mother."

"What else?"

"Sand. A beach. The sea. I'm walking on the beach with my mother. I want to hold her hand, but she won't let me."

"Does that upset you?"

"Yes."

"Go back," Mason told him. "Go back to when you were five."

Jake's breathing increased slightly then he settled back into his usual rhythmic inhalations and exhalations.

"It's dark," he whispered. "It's always dark."

"Can you see where you are?"

"A house. A cellar."

"Why are you in a cellar?"

"I don't know."

"Are you alone?"

"No. My mother...my mother is there."

"Go back, Jake. Go back as far as you can. It's the day after your birth."

Jake suddenly let out a low gasp.

Mason leaned closer and saw that Jake's eyes were still closed but behind his heavy lids they were moving rapidly.

"What do you see?" Mason asked.

"A man," Jake told him. "He's holding me. Looking down at me."

"Who is he?"

"I don't know."

"Are you alone with the man?"

"No. There are others."

"Who are they?"

"I don't know."

"Can you describe where you are, Jake?"

"A big room. Dark. There's another man."

"Who is he?"

"I don't know."

"What else can you see?"

"Blood. Lots of blood."

Mason frowned and moved closer, placing one hand lightly on Jake's arm.

"I can taste it," Jake murmured.

Mason's frown deepened.

"Describe what you're seeing," he insisted. "In as much detail as you can."

Fifteen minutes later, Jake was still speaking.

ONE HUNDRED AND THREE

Dani and Mike drove in silence for most of the early part of their journey.

It wasn't so much that they had nothing to say it was more a case of not knowing where the hell to start.

They'd left Exham an hour ago and were heading along the dual carriageway that took them out of the town, the rain falling heavily.

Dani had one of the scrapbooks open before her and she was looking through it as Mike drove, muttering under his breath about the weather conditions, forced to slow down on a couple of occasions because, even on double speed, the wipers were struggling to clear the rain from the windscreen.

"We should have stayed overnight," he grunted. "It's going to take us longer to get back in this bloody weather."

Dani didn't answer but continued to gaze at the scrapbook.

"Do you think he was crazy?" Mike went on. "Randall. Do you think he was senile or something?"

"What makes you say that?" she demanded.

"Some of the things he was saying. Did you believe him?"

"Why would he lie? What's he got to gain by lying to us?"

"Oh, come on. Aborted foetuses brought to life, fed on brains, and killing the women who had them aborted? Give me a break. He's fucking mental."

Dani didn't answer.

"And how does any of that shit help *us*?" Mike wanted to know. "We came here to find information about Jake. To find information he'd want to know. Information he'd pay for. You think he's going to pay to hear the sort of bullshit Randall was coming out with?"

"Did you see how frightened he was when he was talking about what happened?" Dani mused. "How do you cope with memories like that? All that happened more than thirty years ago, and it must seem like yesterday to him."

"I still think he's a nutter," Mike grunted. He looked briefly at Dani. "Are you telling me you believed him?"

"If he's making it up then he's got a pretty good imagination and, like I said, what is he going to gain by lying? And we know what he said actually happened because there are details here." She tapped the scrapbook. "There was a murderer. People were killed. Randall found that murderer. Maggie Ford was there the night it happened."

"All right, I understand that but it's the other stuff he was going on about I can't get my head around."

"The foetuses."

Mike nodded.

"He said there were three, but they only found two of them," Dani murmured.

"So, what happened to the other one?"

Dani could only shake her head.

"But they'd have been tiny, wouldn't they?" Mike insisted. "A foetus is small. You only have to look at scan pictures when women are pregnant. How could something that small kill someone?"

"Randall said they'd been growing."

"And Jake's mum saw them too?"

"She must have."

Mike drove on in silence for a moment then he glanced at Dani briefly.

"All right then, how do you explain the business of her not being able to have kids?" Mike demanded, finally. "Jake thinks that she was his real mother and yet Randall says she couldn't have kids. What the fuck is that all about?"

"If she'd had a hysterectomy when she was younger then there was no way she could have kids."

She exhaled deeply, gazing out into the darkness beyond.

"It's like the more we find out, the less we know," Mike went on.

They drove on in silence then Mike spoke again.

"How could they grow?" he muttered. "And how could they kill the women who had them aborted?"

"He said they had some kind of mind control. Telepathic powers. Thought projection."

"What's that?"

"When someone can make other people see things that aren't really there."

"No wonder Jake's so fucked up," Mike observed. "I almost feel sorry for him."

"I *do* feel sorry for him," Dani murmured. "I wish we could have helped him."

"Don't start going soft on me now. If we're going to get some money out of him, I don't want you feeling sorry for him. You've got to think about our futures."

Dani nodded and continued to leaf slowly through the scrapbook.

ONE HUNDRED AND FOUR

"Are you okay?"

Jake rested one hand on Phillip Mason's shoulder and pushed the glass of water towards him again.

Mason nodded and sucked in a deep breath, taking the water from Jake, and swallowing some of it.

"I can get you some more," Jake insisted but Mason shook his head.

"No, I'll be all right," the other man grunted, his breathing harsh and laboured.

He looked at Jake warily. "Can you remember what you were saying? Can you remember what you told me?"

"Not all of it," Jake confessed. "I remember you bringing me out of the hypnotic state and seeing you trying not to be sick. That's about it. What was I saying that made you feel so bad?"

"You can't remember anything you were describing?"

Jake shook his head.

"That's probably just as well," Mason told him.

"It's not usual to remember dreams is it?" he muttered.

"You're right. But those dreams are stored in the subconscious even if you can't actually recall them. That's why some people have recurring nightmares. Those same thoughts are always there, always with them. They just disappear periodically. It's like they slip back inside the subconscious."

"What puzzles me with my dreams is that they're so linear," Jake announced. "You know that dreams normally have no chronological sense. They don't happen in sequence or any discernible order. Thoughts are random. In my nightmares, everything happens in order. I know that sounds impossible but that's how I see them. In all my nightmares about my past, the events happen as if I'm seeing them from outside myself."

"That is unusual. How long have you been having these nightmares?"

"For years and they're always the same. The same places, the same incidents."

"The killings?"

Jake nodded.

"Sometimes I'm watching them," he breathed. "Other times I'm participating but they never vary and they're always in chronological order. It's like watching a film that someone's shot."

"And you've never investigated them before now?"

"I've spoken to colleagues about them over the years but never anything like this."

Mason nodded.

"It's also unusual for anyone to relay the details of a dream as accurately as you did," he said. "You described things in such minute detail. It's unheard of for anyone to remember so much from a subconscious experience. Usually, as you know, small details begin to fade as soon as the subject is awake. That's why we mostly can't remember nightmares because the brain wants to shut those details out again as soon as the dream is over. It's like getting the poison out of an abscess."

"But my brain is preserving those nightmares? Processing them? Using them over and over again?"

"I've never encountered anyone who can remember dreams with such clarity," Mason told him.

"Lucky me," Jake said, sarcastically.

"Usually the most vivid dreams are related to trauma of some description," Mason continued. "An accident. Childhood abuse. Something like that. Anything where the subject has suffered either mentally or physically or both. But in *your* nightmares, you're not the one who is undergoing the suffering. It's someone else. You're *observing* that pain and suffering."

Mason sipped at his water.

Jake got to his feet and walked across to the window, glancing out into the floodlit, ornate gardens of the hotel.

"So," he smiled. "Do you think I'm crazy?"

"Let's put it this way," Mason told him. "I wouldn't want to be inside your head."

"But why can I only remember things *after* my tenth birthday?" Jake enquired. "No human can recall much from their early years anyway," Mason said. "As you know the hippocampus, the part of the brain that helps in the creation of memories, doesn't mature until later in life so it can't store long lasting memories that can be recalled in adulthood. Not until the subject is older anyway."

"Everything before I was ten is...is...a black hole, I don't know how else to describe it. Is that suggesting everything after my tenth birthday was devoid of trauma?"

"Trauma makes more of a mark on the mind than good things, you know that. Most human minds recall unpleasant and damaging memories far more easily than they do benevolent ones."

"But these are dreams. Nightmares."

Mason raised his eyebrows.

"What do you know about a woman called Elizabeth Loftus?" he asked.

"I've heard the name," Jake told him.

"She's an American cognitive psychologist. She's most famous for her work on memory distortion and false memories. She's done significant investigation on memory implantation too. She's written a number of books about it."

"Memory implantation?"

"Some subjects can be convinced that they suffered trauma as a child even if they didn't. People can be talked into believing they were abused when they were young even if that abuse never happened. Loftus calls it 'the malleability of human memory'. The idea that the subconscious can be manipulated into believing something it's told even if those events never really occurred. Memories can be altered by things we're told. Perceptions can be changed by the introduction of certain information. Memories can be tampered with."

"So, are you saying that these nightmares have been induced by someone in my childhood? By something I experienced but that my subconscious won't allow me to remember. Something suggested to me by someone else?"

"No," Mason sighed. "What I'm trying to say is that what you've described, what you've seen, what you've experienced in your nightmares, it's so vivid. So detailed. So linear. I don't think that what you're seeing are nightmares. I think what you're describing are *memories*. I think what you see in your nightmares are things that actually happened to you."

ONE HUNDRED AND FIVE

Ted Brady printed fifteen of the photographs he'd taken, watching as each one slid from the printer. He held each image up and inspected it carefully. Several of them he ran his index finger over slowly, tracing the outline of Dani's face, hair, and body.

She was, he reminded himself, a very sexy girl. The long blonde hair so heavily dyed it was almost white. The high cheekbones and pointed chin. The wide eyes and thin lips. Her skin was pale and unblemished apart from on her arms where she sported several intricate tattoos. Ordinarily Brady would have found the designs tacky and unnecessary but, on Dani, they looked exciting. They complemented her he decided. He ran appraising eyes over the pictures of her legs and feet that he'd taken too and, as he looked, he felt a stirring between his legs.

Brady nodded slowly, a gesture of approval. He printed more pictures of her legs and feet.

There was one shot of her sitting back on the bed, slender legs stretched out before her, slightly parted. He studied the contours and the muscularity of her legs the way an archaeologist would pore over a valuable fossil. He wondered how smooth her skin was. Did it become even more supple and silky the further up those legs he went? Did her thighs feel even better than her feet and calves?

It was about time he found out he decided, smiling. Brady shifted position slightly, his erection growing.

He glanced out of his window in the direction of Jake Porter's house. It was still in darkness as it had been for the last day. Brady had no idea where either Jake or Dani were. He'd seen them both leave at various times and all he knew was that they hadn't left together.

Dani had left with that young guy she was seeing. The one he had the video of, he thought. For a fleeting moment he wondered what Jake would do if he actually did see the video. If he actually did discover that his young lover (the word sounded incongruous) was cheating on him how would he react? Would he throw her out? Brady wondered if he'd have to find out or would she continue to cooperate with him?

He looked down at some more of the photos of her and wondered if he had a chance of getting some shots of her and the young guy together. He'd always fancied himself as a director he grinned. Tell them what to do and then join in. As long as he had that video in his possession, they were in no position to refuse, were they?

Brady looked at the pictures of Dani in her knickers and t-shirt and his breathing became a little heavier. He studied the flat stomach. The material of the panties clinging to her mound.

Very nice. Shaved or unshaved?

Beneath that cool cotton was she smooth and hairless or did she have a triangular tangle of curly hair? He knew that lots of girls her age shaved down there and the thought of seeing that silky hairless flesh excited him more than he could imagine. What did she smell like down there? What did she taste like? Her sexy little feet were well looked after, he guessed other parts of her were too.

Well maintained.

Brady shifted position slightly, his lips parted, his tongue flicking over them occasionally.

He selected a photo of her feet and sat down on the edge of the bed, his gaze taking in every contour of the shapely appendages. He was still gazing raptly at the picture when he heard a car pull up outside.

Brady pulled back the curtain slightly, peering out in the direction of the sound. A smile spread across his face as he saw that the car had pulled up outside Jake Porter's house. He watched as Dani climbed out of the passenger side of the vehicle, joined a moment later by Mike Quinn. Brady quickly snapped off the lamp so they couldn't see that he was watching. Hidden by the gloom he watched.

They both walked towards the house, disappearing inside when Dani found her front door key.

Brady watched until they went inside the house, remaining at the window. He saw a couple of lights flash into life within the adjacent building. One downstairs, one upstairs.

He wondered where they'd been. Wherever it was he was confident that Jake Porter knew nothing about it. Brady smiled to himself. She was running him a merry dance, wasn't she? Little slut. Brady glanced down at some more of the pictures of Dani.

Who'd have thought it. A right little whore.
He grinned.

Brady saw the downstairs light go off and guessed that they were making their way up to the bedroom. They probably couldn't keep their hands off each other, he reasoned. And he didn't blame them. He wished he had some way of seeing into the bedroom. Some way of seeing *them*.

Brady reached for his phone and took some photos of Mike's car.

Just in case.

He had enough leverage already but every little helped and there were things he wanted to do with Dani that would take a little more persuasion.

Brady was surprised to see that the front door had opened again, and that Mike was walking back towards his waiting car.

Leaving her alone? Idiot.

Brady watched as the car pulled away, disappearing into the night. He waited a moment longer then reached for his phone again. He found Dani's number immediately and stood gazing at it, glancing from the number to the photos of her that he had strewn across the bed.

Leave it until the morning. There's no rush. Everything comes to he who waits.

Brady smiled and clicked off the light.

ONE HUNDRED AND SIX

Jake looked at his itinerary then at the board before him where each topic had been painstakingly spelled out with individual plastic letters.
POSITIVE PSYCHOLOGY AND MINDFULNESS
APPLIED PSYCHOLOGY AND BEHAVIORAL MEDICINE
MINDFULNESS AND STRESS MANAGEMENT.

He looked at the subject of each lecture or symposium carefully but, no matter how long he looked, none of them seemed to catch is eye.

His mind was elsewhere.

"What do you fancy then?" Phillip Mason asked, also glancing at the menu of subjects.
ADDICTION MEDICINE AND ADDICTION THERAPY.
PSYCHOTHERAPY
PSYCHOSOMATIC MEDICINE

"I'm not sure I fancy any of it at the moment," Jake said, smiling.

"Me neither," Mason echoed. "Shall we get some lunch instead?"

"That sounds like a good idea to me," Jake told him. "Most of those talks don't start until later in the afternoon anyway."

The two men turned away and headed through the hotel foyer towards the dining room. Mason waved happily to three or four of his colleagues as he trudged along beside Jake. He was wearing a different pair of glasses, Jake noticed, the lenses darker than the previous night.

"Hangover?" Jake mused, pointing at the glasses.

"I'm not a big drinker at the best of times," Mason explained as they found a table, leaving their notes and welcome packs on the chairs to signify that the table was taken. Having done that, they made their way to the buffet where others were already busily filling their plates with food.

"Who pays for all this I wonder?" Jake mused, glancing at the array of victuals on display. "Not the RCP surely?"

"Of course," Mason chuckled, selecting some food, and placing it carefully on his plate. "They want to make sure all their members are well looked after."

Jake raised his eyebrows, collected some food for himself and followed Mason back to the table.

"I really should come to more of these, like I said last night," Jake offered as they began their meal.

"It's finding the time," Mason told him.

The two men ate in silence for a moment then Mason looked at his companion more closely.

"Did you manage to sleep last night?" he wanted to know.

"Like a log," Jake told him. "That's unusual for me. I usually find it hard to sleep in hotels."

"I think I got about two hours," Mason sighed.

"You should try some of your own hypnotherapy techniques on yourself," Jake said, smiling.

"Did you manage to speak to your...your...to Dani?" Mason wanted to know.

"No. She wasn't answering."

"There could be a problem with her phone."

"Could be but it's not like her. She's normally got the phone with her twenty-four hours a day. It's like another limb for her."

"That's youngsters for you."

Mason looked instantly embarrassed by his remark, but Jake merely smiled.

"I didn't mean...she...I wasn't trying to say she was that much younger," he blundered on.

"I know what you mean," Jake said. "You don't have to apologise. Normally she sends me messages just to tell me what she's up to or where she is but if she's with one of her friends then they're probably talking."

"Probably discussing *you*."

"I doubt it. I think she's got more interesting things to talk about with her friends."

"Call her now," Mason offered.

"After lunch," Jake told him.

"But before the talk about Addiction Therapy," Mason added, grinning. "You don't want anything to distract you."

Jake nodded, also smiling.

"It's a pity there isn't a symposium on dreams and nightmares," Mason went on. "You could ask them some questions about yours."

"According to you they're not dreams, they're recollections and if I shared any of those with anyone, I dare say all they'd recommend would be locking me up."

"They were disturbing, I'll give you that."

"If I was your patient what would you recommend?"

"If you really want to find out the origin and meaning of your...dreams then I'd recommend more hypnotherapy. But it's going to take time. There could be things hidden inside there," he pointed towards Jake's head. "Things you don't necessarily *want* uncovered."

ONE HUNDRED AND SEVEN

Cheeky cunt.
Cheeky fucking cunt.
Dani glared at the message on her phone and it took all her self-control to stop from hurling the device across the room.
Sick, fucking, twisted, weird cunt.
For long moments she looked at the message as if mesmerised.
SEE YOU LATER. WEAR SOMETHING SEXY.
It was from Ted Brady and it had arrived about an hour earlier as she'd been sitting in the kitchen eating.
Now she looked at the message once again, this time seated on the sofa in the sitting room surrounded by the scrapbooks. However, the contents of those tomes seemed insignificant compared to her current situation. How the hell was she going to get Brady off her back? As long as he had that video of Mike then she had no choice but to do what he wanted. And she knew that the further she went, the more outrageous his demands would become.
He would never delete that video and he would never destroy the photos of her that he'd already taken. She got to her feet and stalked across to the window, glancing out in the direction of Brady's house.
He's waiting for you.
She wondered what he'd want her to do tonight. What other perverted games did he have lined up?
You know what he wants.
Dani chewed nervously on one thumbnail.
He won't let up until he's fucked you.
She swallowed hard.
And even then, he won't stop. He's a problem that isn't going to go away.
She wondered what would happen if she called his bluff. What if she refused to do as he said and left him to show the video to Jake? How would Jake react? Would his first reaction be to throw her out? She couldn't be sure and that was the problem. She could say Brady threatened her, tell Jake that he tried to rape her but, she couldn't explain away why Mike had been climbing out of the bedroom

window that morning.

You brought it on yourself. It's Karma. That's what you get for cheating on Jake.

Dani clenched her teeth until her jaws ached, her gaze still fixed on Brady's house.

You've got no choice. You'll have to go along with what he wants for now.

She was still considering her limited options when her phone vibrated again. She checked the id of the message sender and saw that it was Jake.

HEY YOU. HOW ARE YOU DOING? I MISS YOU.

The pang she felt was guilt. It was unmistakeable.

She sent a message back hurriedly.

MISS U 2.

They exchanged a couple more messages and then she asked him to ring her later so they could talk.

Dani slid the phone back into her pocket and turned away from the window, pulling the curtains across, shutting out both the darkness and also the view of Ted Brady's home. She wished she could shut out the man next door as easily.

She was still thinking that as she made her way to Brady's house twenty minutes later.

Get it over with.

Her hand was shaking slightly as she reached out to ring the doorbell, but Brady opened the door before she could even push it.

"I saw you coming," he said, smiling. "Come in." He stepped aside to allow her into the hallway.

Dani stepped across the threshold.

ONE HUNDRED AND EIGHT

Dani stood stiffly in the hallway trying not to look at Brady any more than she had to.

"Had a good day?" he enquired, conversationally.

"Let's just cut the bullshit and get this over with, shall we?" Dani told him.

"You should get your boyfriend to analyse you, you know," Brady grinned. "Jake, I mean, not your other boyfriend."

Dani sucked in a weary breath.

"You've got a lot of issues, haven't you?" Brady went on.

"Only with you," she grunted.

He ushered her towards the stairs, walking up slowly and glancing around to ensure that she was following him.

"Where have you been?" he wanted to know. "Anywhere nice? I noticed you'd been away for a couple of days."

"It's none of your business," Dani told him.

"And Jake's away too. That's convenient isn't it?"

He crossed the landing to the door of the spare room and pushed it open, stepping aside to allow Dani access. She walked in, seeing that it was set up the same way it had been the first time she'd entered it. Lights and diffusers arranged around the single bed and the white sheets. As before, the room felt pleasantly warm.

"Where is Jake?" Brady asked.

"He's at some convention. What does it matter to you?"

"I just wanted to make sure we weren't going to be interrupted." Brady reached for one of his cameras, squinting through the viewfinder. "Sit on the bed."

Dani did as she was instructed.

"And take my shoes off?" she asked, already sure of the answer.

Brady smiled. "You're learning," he said, watching as she slipped her shoes off, dropping them on the floor beside the bed. "And the socks."

"Obviously," Dani breathed.

"Obviously," Brady mimicked, watching as she slid the socks off to expose her feet.

"How did you get so obsessed with women's feet?" she wanted to know, not attempting to hide the contempt and disgust in her voice.

"My first girlfriend got me into it."

"You had a girlfriend?" Dani snorted. "Wow, the generosity of women never ceases to amaze me."

"Ha, ha," Brady grunted. "I've had my share over the years."

Dani was at pains to show her disinterest. "So how did that turn you into a fucking foot pervert then?"

"She was frightened of getting pregnant," Brady explained. "So we didn't have sex very often. We were only seventeen. She liked having her feet touched and played with so, when I was ready to...you know...I used to do it on her feet."

"You were always a sick fuck then?"

Brady eyed her impassively, his gaze finally settling on her face.

"You are a really pretty girl, you know," he murmured. "You remind me of that actress in those stupid fucking singing films. What's her name? She's got darker hair than you though. There's her and that big fat Australian bird, stupid bitch. They're in some kind of singing group."

"'*Pitch Perfect*' it's called."

"Yeah, that's it. You look like the main girl in it. Anna Kendrick. That's her name."

"Am I supposed to be flattered?"

"She's fucking gorgeous. And so are you. She's got beautiful feet too."

"And you'd know," Dani sneered.

"I do my research," Brady said, smiling.

Dani moved back on the bed slightly, wanting to be further away from him. She watched as he moved around her, snapping away, checking the images on the camera.

"How much longer is this going to go on for?" she asked, finally. "I mean, you're not going to stop, are you? You're going to keep on getting me to come in here as long as you can."

"We'll have to see."

"No. I mean it," Dani rasped. "What's it going to take to make you stop?"

Brady eyed her warily, aware of the venom in her voice.

"As long as you've got that video on your phone there's nothing I can do is there?" Dani went on. "You could keep this up for months. Years. You could keep on blackmailing me because you know there's nothing I can do about it."

"Well, if you stopped being so hostile then it might be easier." He took more pictures. He ran appraising eyes over her. "Why do you always react so badly to compliments? Would you rather I told you that you were an ugly cunt?"

"Compliments only mean anything if they're coming from a nice person. When they're coming from you, they mean nothing."

"Ouch," Brady said, smiling. "So, if Jake compliments you, then that's all right? Or if your boyfriend tells you you've got a nice arse then that's fine, right?"

Dani sucked in another breath.

"Take the leggings off," Brady breathed.

Dani hesitated.

"What if I don't?" she asked, defiantly.

"Jesus Christ," Brady grunted. "You could make this so much easier for yourself, couldn't you? Stop being so fucking difficult. Get the leggings off. Now."

His tone had darkened considerably, and Dani could see the glint in his eyes, and it convinced her that doing as he said was probably best. She slipped her thumbs into the waistband of her leggings and began to pull them down.

"Slowly," Brady murmured, watching intently.

Shaking slightly, Dani eased the tight-fitting garment off, finally dropping it on the floor too. Brady took more pictures.

"And the top," he whispered.

Dani hesitated then began pulling at her t-shirt, finally dragging it over her head and throwing it to one side.

She sat on the bed in just her bra and knickers, her cheeks flushed and her gaze downcast. She didn't want to look at Brady unless she had to. All she heard was several low grunts of approval.

"You should be a model," he told her, snapping more pictures. "Get on all fours."

Dani thought about protesting but then thought better of it. Moving awkwardly, she manoeuvred herself onto her hands and knees, her head still down, her gaze still aimed anywhere but at Brady.

"Arch your back," he said, his breathing becoming heavier. "Like you do when you cum." He moved a little closer and Dani gritted her teeth. "I bet your boyfriend fucks you from behind doesn't he?"

Dani closed her eyes for a second, her hands clenching into fists on the white duvet. She wished she could use those fists to rain blows down on his smirking face. To punch him until she broke his crooked nose. She could hear the shutter clicking constantly now.

"I wish I could have got Jake's last girlfriend in here like this," Brady said. "That little eighteen-year-old. He's a dirty fucker, isn't he? He does love the young ones."

Dani arched her back a little more, her heart beating fast.

"The two of you together would have been even better," he muttered. "Now, lay on your stomach. Lay down and bring your feet up behind you."

Dani followed his instructions feeling suddenly cold despite the warmth in the room.

"Beautiful," Brady purred. "Now take off the bra."

"No way," Dani gasped. "No."

"Take it off," Brady persisted, pulling at his growing erection with one hand.

Dani shook her head and moved back slightly.

"Take the fucking bra off," Brady snarled, looming over her.

"You want to fuck me, don't you?" she said, her voice cracking. "Is that what you want? If I do that will you stop all this? Will you delete that video? Will you stop? Please." There was a note of pleading and desperation in her voice that Brady wasn't slow to pick up.

He was gazing so intently at her he didn't see the movement beyond the door as the figure moved across the landing.

ONE HUNDRED AND NINE

From where she was sitting on the bed, Dani saw the movement behind Brady.

She glanced in that direction swiftly, not wanting the other man to realize that they were no longer alone.

"That *is* what you want isn't it?" she repeated a little more loudly. "You want to fuck me?"

Brady squeezed his erection through his trousers and swallowed.

"Would you let me?" he grunted.

"If that's what it takes to make you stop."

The door of the bedroom opened slightly, the floorboards creaking beneath the new weight that was placed upon them.

Even if Brady had realized what was happening it was unlikely he'd have been able to prevent it.

Mike Quinn barged into the room and glared at Brady. The colour drained from the older man's face and it was his turn to wear a puzzled and frightened expression.

"Who the fuck are you?" he gasped.

"You should know," Mike snarled. "You've got me on that fucking video on your phone, haven't you?"

He lunged towards Brady, grabbing him by the throat, slamming him up against the wall with such force that the older man sagged momentarily, his knees almost giving way.

"First you blackmail her and then you try and rape my girlfriend," Mike hissed, furiously. "You fucking bastard." Again, he slammed Brady against the wall, holding him there, gazing deep into his eyes.

"What do you want?" Brady asked, plaintively. "I haven't got any money."

"We don't want your money," Mike told him, glancing briefly in Dani's direction. She was already scrolling through the photographs and videos on Brady's phone, desperately trying to find the one she sought.

"Leave that alone," Brady snapped.

"Shut your fucking mouth," Mike told him, banging him again into the wall. "You don't get to speak unless I say so."

Dani smiled and Mike guessed she'd found what she was looking for. She deleted the video and held up the phone as if it was a trophy.

"Done it," she said.

"Don't hurt me," Brady implored.

"I should fucking batter you after what you did to her," Mike snapped, nodding in Dani's direction.

"I didn't do anything," Brady protested.

"You humiliated me, you sick fucking bastard," Dani snarled, her face inches from the older man's.

"And what more would you have done, you fucking sicko?" Mike demanded. "Raped her?"

"No, never," Brady said, his voice thin and reedy. "Please just let me go."

"You delete all those fucking pictures you took first," Mike went on, slamming the older man against the wall once again.

As he held Brady there, Dani began hurriedly pulling on her clothes again, anxious to cover herself. When she was dressed once more, she stepped closer to the older man again.

"Just go," Brady gasped, and Dani could see he was close to tears. "Please."

"After what you did?" Mike sneered. "We should call the police and tell them that you raped her."

"But I didn't."

"You were going to," Mike roared. "It's our word against yours. You'll go down for ten fucking years, you dirty old cunt."

"Come on," Dani said, pulling at Mike's arm. "Leave him."

"Why?" Mike snarled. "We should go through the rest of the pictures on his phone and in here. Fuck knows what he's got. Pictures of little kids probably."

Mike picked up the phone and, as he did, Brady lunged at him, but the younger man saw the attack coming and moved to one side, pushing Brady as he lurched forward. The older man tripped, his arms pin wheeling for a second before he pitched forward heavily. As he rose, he grabbed at one of the lights, his fingers closing around the metal legs supporting the bulb. He swung the implement like a club and caught Mike across the face with it.

The blow was enough to open a gash just below Mike's hairline.

The younger man staggered backwards, raising an arm to defend himself as Brady attacked again.

"You fucking scum," Brady hissed.

His swing this time was wild, and Mike ducked beneath it, bringing a foot up hard into the older man's groin. The impact was savage, and Brady doubled up as white-hot pain enveloped his testicles. Mike shoved him hard, watching as he toppled backwards, crashing into some of the storage cases that were piled up on the other side of the room.

He slammed his temple against the corner of a flight case, groaned and flopped over on his back, blood streaming from a cut on his head.

Mike looked down and smiled.

"Stupid old bastard," he said, dismissively, wincing as he touched the cut on his own head. "He could have killed me."

Dani took a step towards the older man, noticing that he hadn't moved since he hit the ground.

The cut on his head wasn't that deep but it was bleeding profusely, spreading out in a dark puddle around his head and neck.

"Oh, God," Dani whispered.

"He's just unconscious," Mike snapped.

"Then why are his eyes still open?" Dani blurted, kneeling beside the older man. She fumbled for a pulse, digging her fingers savagely into the flesh of first his wrists and then his neck, wanting desperately to feel the steady thud of his blood rushing through his veins.

She could feel nothing.

She looked up, her face pale.

"Mike," she murmured. "I think he's dead."

ONE HUNDRED AND TEN

Mike froze, his gaze fixed on the motionless body of Ted Brady.

"He can't be," he gaped. "He only banged his head."

"There's no fucking pulse," Dani snapped, trying once again to find one.

Mike dropped to his knees beside her, grabbing for the older man's other arm. He too tried to find a pulse, rubbing first his thumb and then his forefinger over the wrists.

"He *can't* be dead," Mike breathed.

"Oh, God," Dani said, breathlessly.

"Let's get out of here," Mike suggested.

"And just leave him like this?"

"What the fuck are we supposed to do?"

"We can call an ambulance."

"What for? If he's dead they're not going to revive him, are they?" His voice fell in both volume and intensity. "We call the police and tell them what happened. Tell them he was going to rape you."

"It doesn't matter what he was going to do, Mike. You killed him."

"It was an accident."

"So, we get ten years for manslaughter instead of life for murder? Not much of a choice is it? He's fucking dead." She pointed at the older man, her hand shaking.

"It was self-defence," Mike persisted. "He attacked me." He pointed to the cut on his forehead. "The police will be able to see that."

"He's dead, Mike," Dani went on. "He's dead because of us. The Police won't care how. All they'll see is his body and they'll find the pictures he took, and they'll think we killed him because of those."

"We delete them. They'll never know. If there's no evidence, they..."

"No evidence? What about our DNA all over the body? All over the house?"

"We could clean it up."

"With what?"

"Bleach or something. That's what they use on TV."

"This isn't TV, Mike," Dani shouted. "This is real. Look at him." She pointed again at Brady's body and the blood that had spread out around his head. "We killed him."

Mike stared helplessly at the body for a moment longer then he put a hand to his head, touching the cut there and then inspecting the blood on his fingertips.

"You might need stitches," Dani told him.

"No. I'm not going to hospital," he said. "And all that matters at the moment is getting rid of that." He jabbed a finger in Brady's direction.

"What shall we do? Cut him into pieces, wrap him in plastic bags and dump him in a river?"

Mike caught the sarcasm in her tone and looked angrily at her. They sat in silence for a moment, both gazing at the body of Ted Brady.

"We've got to hide his body," Dani said, flatly. "Get him out of the way long enough to give us time to...cover ourselves or get away."

"I agree, but where do we hide him? And like you said, our DNA will be everywhere."

"We *could* clean the room, clean the house," Dani told him, her expression darkening. "At least enough to give us some time."

"But what if someone calls on him?"

"I don't think he's got any family who visit him."

"Friends?"

"I doubt it."

Dani got to her feet and began pacing the room as if that simple act might trigger some revelatory thoughts.

"Are we sure he's dead?" Mike wanted to know.

"No pulse, no heartbeat and no breathing. I'd say so," Dani murmured.

"But he only banged his head."

Dani stopped pacing for a moment and put a hand to her mouth.

"Jake hates this guy, doesn't he?" Mike announced suddenly, a gleam in his eye.

"So?"

"People would believe that *he* killed him," Mike went on as if he was describing a cancer cure, he'd just perfected.

"You mean we frame him?" Dani breathed. "First you want to blackmail him and now you want to frame him for murder?"

"Do you want to go down for this?" Mike snarled. "Because I don't. Better him than us and he's got the motive."

Dani sucked in a breath, considering the suggestion.

"Frame Jake for it?" she murmured.

"It's him or us."

"No, it isn't," she snapped. "If we hide Brady's body then it might never be found. No one need ever know what happened."

"Oh, come on, someone will find it eventually."

"Not if we hide it well enough."

Dani wasn't sure if she was trying to convince Mike or herself of the validity of this plan. She began pacing again, her heart thudding hard against her ribs. She finally turned towards the bedroom door.

"Where are you going?" Mike wanted to know.

"Stay here," she told him.

And she was gone.

"Dani," he called after her.

There was no answer except her footfalls on the stairs.

ONE HUNDRED AND ELEVEN

Jake paced slowly up and down the platform as he waited for the train to arrive.

The taxi ride from the hotel in Camworth had taken about half an hour because of some roadworks on one of the narrow roads leading into the town but now his footsteps echoed across the wide concrete area as he walked. Large wooden containers filled with beautifully kept displays of flowers and shrubs were dotted all along the platform as were equally well-maintained hanging baskets. Jake could smell the scent of the blooms as he walked past.

There were several posters on the station advertising a garden festival that was due in a couple of months and one of the pictures was of the station. A constant reminder of Camworth's heritage as one of the first Garden Cities, Jake assumed.

He'd said his goodbyes to Phillip Mason, thanked him for his help and the two of them had exchanged phone numbers and business cards.

Jake thought it was unlikely that he'd keep in contact with his colleague, but Mason had impressed him, and he was the sort of person whose company Jake wouldn't have minded sharing again. Even if it was only every six months. He smiled to himself.

There was another conference in Birmingham in six months' time and the two men had decided they would attend. Jake nodded at the recollection. He felt he had re-connected with a friend and it was a good feeling. Perhaps, he thought, his new book and his possible TV appearances would also be in evidence. It was an exciting time for him.

He checked his phone but there were no messages.

The thought of getting back to Dani was a pleasing one too and he had already determined to try and build some bridges with Lucy if that was possible. Nothing was impossible he'd decided. He could understand her feelings and the fact that she couldn't cope with those feelings so well. The discovery had hurt him more than he could have imagined but he had to find a way of putting things right between them. Whatever he lost in his life he couldn't lose his daughter.

There was a vending machine beneath the footbridge that spanned the tracks and Jake walked towards it, fumbling in his pocket for some change.

He'd eaten at the hotel before leaving but the sight of the chocolate bars in the machine had created a craving he needed to satisfy. Smiling he fed coins in, selected a Mars bar, and pushed the relevant button.

The machine finally pushed the chocolate out and Jake picked it up and unwrapped it, biting off a large chunk.

He chewed a couple of times then realized that the chocolate was way past its sell by date. It was like chalk in his mouth and he hurriedly spat it out, throwing the remains of the bar into a nearby waste bin.

Jake wiped his mouth with the back of his hand and sighed.

There was no one else in sight on the station apart from a man in a high-vis jacket who was doing something at the far end of the platform where it sloped down towards the track. Every now and then he would stop what he was doing and glance in Jake's direction before returning to his labours.

Jake glanced at his watch a couple of times hoping the train would soon arrive. There was a cold breeze whipping across the platform and Jake pulled up his collar against it, shivering slightly.

He glanced down the track and was delighted to see the bright headlights of the approaching train. It drew closer, the sound of its engine and churning wheels filling the evening air. Jake looked down at the tracks and saw them vibrating beneath the weight of the approaching train. Beneath the platform opposite a mouse turned and hurried back into a pipe, away from the oncoming behemoth. Jake smiled as he watched it peering from the mouth of the pipe, its whiskers twitching quizzically.

As the train arrived, the mouse retreated out of sight.

Jake stepped away from the platform edge as the train glided into the station, noticing that the carriages nearest the engine were almost empty. Jake made for those and climbed in, seating himself in the warm carriage. Someone had placed a sticker on the window that proclaimed;

VOTE NO TO ABORTION.

Jake considered the sticker for a moment longer then decided to sit on the other side of the aisle. He re-settled himself in a window seat and gazed out at the ever-darkening sky.

As the train pulled away, he checked his phone again. No messages from Dani but it didn't matter, he would be seeing her very soon. They could talk when he got home. He scrolled through his photos, pausing at the ones of Dani. He'd missed her more than he'd anticipated, and he hoped she'd felt the same about him.

Returning early from his conference would be a surprise for both of them he thought as the train picked up speed. It passed through a long tunnel, plunging the carriage into a deep darkness broken only by the cold white light from the overhead bulbs set along the carriage ceiling.

On both sides of the speeding train he could see the dark countryside speeding past and, occasionally the lights of towns and villages. Not far now.

Jake settled down, dug his ear pieces from his pocket and selected some music on his phone, losing himself in the tunes as the train rumbled along.

He checked his watch once more and smiled. Not long now.

ONE HUNDRED AND TWELVE

The smell of bleach was so powerful it made Mike's eyes water.

He put one hand to his nose to try and cut out the odour, watching as Dani lifted a cloth from the water and rung it out. She looked up at Mike then back towards the body of Ted Brady.

The blood that had pooled around the older man's head had begun to congeal, thickening beneath his motionless cranium. In places it had begun to turn darker in colour and the extremities of the puddle were already sticky and blackening. The longer it was left without cleaning, the harder it would be to remove the traces of his life fluid.

They looked at each other for a moment longer then Mike moved closer, sliding his hands beneath the armpits of the corpse, half pulling and half lifting it away from where it had fallen.

There was a soft sucking sound and Brady's mouth opened, a small breath escaping his dead lips.

Mike pulled his arms away, shocked by the sound and the body dropped heavily to the floor once more.

"Did you hear that?" he gasped, staring at the corpse.

Dani nodded.

"Just air escaping from his lungs," she said, swallowing hard.

"Are you *sure* he's dead?" Mike went on.

Dani nodded.

She wished he wasn't. If she'd believed in God, she would have prayed that the older man was not deceased but merely in a coma. Anything was preferable to the situation they now found themselves in. She watched as Mike hooked his arms once more beneath those of the older man, dragging his upper body free of the floor. Brady's head rubbed against Mike's jeans and t-shirt smearing them with blood and Mike wrinkled his nose in disgust but held onto the body this time.

Dani followed behind the body using the cloth to wipe up the droplets of blood. She then went back into the room and scrubbed the flight case that Brady had smashed his head on, ringing out the cloth into the bleach filled bowl, watching the water change from clear to pink and then red as she continued with her task.

It took a good twenty minutes to clean up the puddle of blood on the floor, ringing out the cloths and then scouring the floor again, in an effort to remove all trace of the stains made by the older man's life fluid.

Dani stopped a couple of times, her stomach somersaulting but the necessity of her task drove her on even though there was a vague sense of desperation and hopelessness about her as she cleaned.

You're kidding yourself if you think you can get away with this.

By the time she'd finished in the room the fluid in the bowl was dark red.

Mike dragged the body out onto the landing and Dani followed, watching for any tell-tale drips of blood.

She hurried into the bathroom, poured the bloodied contents of the bowl away and re-filled the receptacle with fresh hot water and bleach before using another cloth to cleanse the sink itself.

That done she returned to the landing where Mike was standing at the head of the stairs looking down at Brady's body.

"We could push him down," Mike suggested. "Say he fell."

Dani shook her head.

"They'll find the cut on his head where he fell on the flight case," she said.

"But he could have cut his head falling down the stairs," Mike protested.

"Just get him down the stairs, Mike. We've got to get him out of this house."

Mike sighed and stepped down the first of the stairs, dragging Brady with him. The older man's feet thumped down each step as Mike pulled, sweat now soaking into his clothes from his exertions. He wiped his forehead with the back of one hand, wincing when he accidentally brushed the cut on his own head.

"This is bullshit," he snarled, letting go of the body.

It fell down the remainder of the stairs, tumbling down until it landed with a loud thud in the hallway.

"What are you doing?" Dani snarled, looking down at the corpse.

"He's fucking dead," Mike shouted. "It's not like he's going to complain is it?"

"Pick him up and get him out of here," Dani hissed, angrily. "How many times do I have to tell you?"

Mike shot her a furious glance.

"Stop giving me orders," he snapped.

"Shall I just ring the fucking police and get *them* to move him?"

Mike walked down the steps and stood over the body while Dani used the cloth to wipe away more droplets of blood that had splashed onto the wall beside the steps. There was also some of the crimson fluid on the bannister and stair carpet. She rubbed each mark and blemish frenziedly, in an attempt to remove it.

"How can we be sure we've cleaned everything?" Mike asked, wearily.

"If he's not in his house then people will just think he's gone away," Dani said, still scrubbing. "No one will suspect. Why should they? But we've got to hide his body."

Mike nodded.

"When we've got rid of him, we'll come back in here and go over everything again," Dani told him. "Every inch of floor. Every wall. Everything we might have touched."

Again, Mike nodded. He took a deep breath then slid his arms once again beneath Brady's armpits, dragging the body up and pulling it across the floor towards the kitchen. Dani followed, continuing with her ablutions, desperate to obliterate all signs that anything had ever happened in the house. As Mike hauled the body away, she walked up and down the stairs wiping the bannister again, occasionally ducking low to look at the polished wood at eye level in the hope of spotting something she hadn't seen before.

She reached into her pocket and pulled out the keyring she'd retrieved from Jake's house when she retreated there earlier to fetch the bleach and the bowl.

Below her she heard Mike muttering to himself and saw that he had put down Brady's body once again.

"What are you doing?" she demanded.

"I think I've pulled something," he told her, massaging the small of his back with one hand.

"Keep going," she urged, noting that there were more droplets of blood in the hallway. "We can't stop now."

Mike nodded.

As he looked down, he saw that Brady's eyes were still open. They stared up glassily at him and Mike was convinced that the dead man's lips were slightly upturned as if he was smiling.

Mocking.

ONE HUNDRED AND THIRTEEN

Dani looked out into the garden, peering at the houses nearby, watching for any signs of movement or any lights that might still be on.

Fortunately, Brady's back garden, like Jake's was enclosed by high privet hedges so was effectively masked from the prying gaze of neighbours but, as she stepped out of the back door her heart was still thudding hard and fast.

She beckoned to Mike who dragged the dead man across the small patio towards the hedge that separated the rear of Brady's property from the rear of Jake's.

There was a small wooden gate that connected the two and Dani hurried towards this, opening it, and allowing Mike to drag the corpse through and towards the back of Jake's house.

There were several small plant pots arranged around the patio of Brady's house and, as Mike pulled the dead man across the paved area, his left foot caught one of the pots and knocked it over.

The small receptacle toppled over, the sound echoing in the stillness.

Dani spun around, looking towards the source of the noise.

Mike froze.

For interminable seconds he stood there, holding Brady's body, the breath frozen in his throat.

Further down the garden there was movement. Slow, furtive movement.

Had someone passing by heard the sound of the falling flowerpot and decided to investigate, Mike wondered? He turned his head slowly towards the sound of the movement.

The cat emerged from beneath the hedge, looked around quizzically for a second then simply walked on.

Mike let out a long breath and then continued hauling Brady towards the gate.

Through the gap in the hedge, he could see Dani hunched over something to the rear of Jake Porter's house. It took him a second to realize that she was trying to unlock the padlock that secured the cellar entrance.

He laid the body down close to the hedge and bent forward, trying to get a second wind. The effort of lugging Brady's corpse all the way from the upstairs bedroom had been considerable. Mike was sheathed with sweat and his muscles, particularly those in his back and shoulders, felt as if they were seizing up. He looked down at the body and felt a sudden surge of hatred for this older man laying at his feet. When the time came to pick the corpse up once again, Mike dug his fingers savagely into the soft flesh, jerking the body upright so he could drag it a little more easily.

Dani beckoned to him again and he managed to move Brady across the expanse of open lawn that separated the hedge from the cellar entrance.

She opened the door, exposing the flight of stone steps that led down into the subterranean room beyond.

Dani led the way, pulling her lighter from her pocket and using the weak yellowish flame to illuminate her way until she finally found the panel of switches at the bottom of the steps. She flicked them all on and cold white light bathed the cellar.

Mike followed, dragging Brady with him as if he was a piece of unwanted and ungainly luggage.

Dani looked around the cellar and thought how much it reminded her of the underground area back at the house in Walmsley.

The cellar where Jake had spent so much of his early life.

Had he retained this room beneath his own house because that time was so ingrained within his mind? She suddenly felt a stab of sympathy for Jake, but it faded rapidly as she glanced around at Mike and the body of Ted Brady.

"Have you been down here before?" Mike asked, keeping his voice low.

Dani shook her head. "Jake hardly uses it," she said.

He just keeps it as a reminder of his childhood.

"That's why there's only that one entrance from the garden," she went on. "He had the other one blocked off. If we leave Brady down here, at least he's out of the way. No one's going to think to look for him down here, are they?"

"But won't he start to...you know...rot?" Mike murmured.

"We can wrap the body in something," Dani offered.

"Like what?"

They both looked around and it was Dani who spotted a pile of black plastic bags jammed on top of one of the shelves fixed to a wall at the far end of the cellar.

She hurried over and grabbed a handful of the bags, shaking them, coughing when dust fell thickly from the surfaces. Motes of it turned in the air, causing her to cover her mouth and nose momentarily.

Dani shook one of the bags again, pulling it open. She advanced towards Brady's body and swiftly slipped the bag over his head.

"There's some gaffer tape in the kitchen," she noted. "I'll go and get that so we can seal it."

As Mike wrapped more of the bags around Brady's corpse, Dani hurried back up the stairs to retrieve the tape. Mike stopped momentarily to touch his fingertips to the cut on his own head, feeling the dried and crusted blood there then he continued with his task, relieved when Dani returned with the large roll of grey tape.

They wound it around the body, securing the bags in place and transforming Brady's corpse until it resembled a large black chrysalis.

"Now what?" Mike gasped, breathlessly, sitting on the cold stone floor.

Dani didn't answer him but merely gazed around the cellar once more. She looked at the piles of boxes, the old chest freezers, the bags full of unwanted rubbish. If they hid Brady carefully beneath some of that detritus, then there was no reason he would be found was there? Jake barely used the cellar.

She walked to the far end of the subterranean room, towards the archway that had once led into the area where coal was dumped.

There was a door beyond it.

Dani frowned and moved towards it.

There were two or three cardboard boxes piled in front of the door, but they only held some old paperbacks and a couple of empty lever arch files. There was no weight in them, and Dani pulled them aside effortlessly to expose the door more fully.

Like the cellar entrance, it was secured by a padlock and Dani glanced down at the key ring, selecting the implement she thought most likely to unlock it. Hiding Brady in the secondary room beyond this door would be perfect, she thought, sliding the key into the lock.

She turned it but nothing happened.

She selected another key and tried again.

ONE HUNDRED AND FOURTEEN

As Dani fumbled with the keys, she realized that her hands were shaking slightly.

Could she and Mike actually get away with this?

If the body was hidden well enough, she couldn't see why not.

The body.

Dani swallowed hard.

Yes. The body. You killed a man.

She tried another of the keys, twisting it in the lock but it wouldn't budge.

"Come on," Mike murmured, appearing beside her.

She spun around angrily.

"I'm trying," she snapped. "I've got to find the right key."

He watched as she slid another into the lock. And another.

"What if the key isn't here?" she panted.

"It must be," Mike insisted, reaching forward to try and pull the bunch from her hand.

"I can do it," Dani hissed, tugging them away from him.

Mike stepped back slightly, watching as she pushed another key into the lock and turned it. The result was once more fruitless.

"Jesus, how many fucking keys do we have to try?" he hissed.

The next one worked.

Dani smiled thinly as she felt the lock give. She pulled it away from the door and turned the handle gently, reaching inside the room beyond for a light switch. Her fingers brushed against something soft and pliant. It felt like cotton. It took her a second to realize that it was covering something thicker. Something that felt like padding.

She turned slightly, her head inclined towards Mike, her fingers still reaching for a light switch beyond the new threshold.

"We'll put him in here," Dani said, and Mike retreated into the main cellar to retrieve the body. Dani could hear him dragging it across the bare floor.

Her fingers finally connected with a light switch and she flicked it on. Light flooded the room and Dani stepped over the threshold.

Unlike the rest of the cellar, the floor wasn't just bare concrete here. It was covered by thin mats and pieces of carpet. Close to the door there was a washbasin. Beyond it some drawers. A chemical toilet. Even a bed.

Dani sucked in a deep breath, but it turned into a gasp as she realized there was someone sitting on the bed.

It was a young woman. Early twenties. Long blonde hair. Angular features. Small framed. She was dressed in jeans and a black hoodie.

It took Dani another second to realize she was gagged.

And one more moment to realize that she knew this girl's face.

She was gazing at the frightened visage of Rhiannon Morton.

Dani tried to speak but couldn't force out the words. Rhiannon got to her feet and tried to walk towards Dani, but she could only take a couple of steps before the metal manacles around her ankles stopped her. A chain ran from those manacles to the wall where it was secured. The metal gleamed in the bright light.

Rhiannon put out her hands imploringly, reaching towards Dani.

It was at that moment Mike also entered the room. He saw Rhiannon and froze.

"What the fuck," he murmured.

For long seconds it was as if time had stopped. All three of them were caught in some monstrous tableau, captured on film, and made immobile by a frozen frame.

And then that film was rolling again.

Dani moved towards the younger girl, reaching for the gag, trying to pull it free. She fumbled with the straps that held it in place while Rhiannon whimpered softly and tried to keep her head still.

"Sit down," Dani said, soothingly and Rhiannon perched on the edge of the bed while Dani continued to loosen the gag. It finally came free and she tossed it to one side.

"Oh God," Rhiannon gasped. "Thank you. Where's Jake?" Her eyes were wide and filled with tears. She looked terrified.

"He's not here," Dani told her.

"Please get me out," the younger girl panted. "Before he comes."

"Where are the keys?" Dani wanted to know, pulling at the manacles around Rhiannon's ankles.

"Jake's got them," said Rhiannon.

"I bet they're on that key ring," Mike offered, moving further into the room, looking around. Like Dani, he was stunned by what he saw.

Taken aback by the situation and the surroundings. His head was spinning.

Dani grabbed the key ring and began looking for a key that seemed likely to unlock the manacles.

So many keys. So many locks. So many secrets.

Mike suddenly pulled Dani towards him, ushering her out of the small room.

"If we let her out, she'll see Brady's body," he said. "She'll know what we've done."

"We can't just leave her in there," Dani protested.

"Please get me out," Rhiannon wailed from inside the room.

"We've got to let her go," Dani insisted.

"How the fuck has he kept her hidden?" Mike said. "How did you not know?"

"The room is sound proofed," Dani snapped. "How the fuck was I supposed to know he'd got her down here?"

Mike held Dani's arm for a moment longer then allowed her to pull free. She walked back into the smaller room and began trying keys in the manacle lock, desperate to find the one that would release the younger girl.

"Don't worry," she told Rhiannon, reassuringly. "I'll get you out."

The blonde girl smiled thinly.

Mike stood at the threshold watching, occasionally glancing back into the main cellar towards the body of Ted Brady.

"How long has Jake kept you in here?" Dani asked as she continued to fumble with the lock.

"A long time," Rhiannon told her, her voice cracking. She began to cry softly, and Dani put one comforting hand on her shoulder then on her cheek.

"I'll get you out," she breathed. "I promise."

Again, Rhiannon nodded, tears still coursing down her cheeks.

At last Dani found the right key and turned it sharply in the lock. The manacles sprung open. Rhiannon pulled her feet free and stood up, looking in Mike's direction and as she did, her eyes widened in terror.

Mike took a step back but never heard the sound from behind him. He never saw what hit him.

Jake Porter swung the shovel with incredible force and accuracy, the metal blade catching Mike across the base of the skull. The impact caused a loud clang that filled the subterranean room, ringing in the ears of those there.

Mike dropped like a stone, blood jetting from the huge gash that had been opened in his cranium.

Dani screamed, stumbling away from his fallen form, looking up to see Jake standing there the shovel gripped in his hands, crimson liquid dripping from it.

"What are you doing?" he hissed, glaring at Dani.

"What am *I* doing?" she gaped. "What the fuck is *this*?" She gestured wildly around her.

"I told you I couldn't let her go," Jake murmured, glancing at Rhiannon and smiling. "I loved her. I always did. I still do."

Dani backed away.

"No one understood," Jake went on. "No one. I couldn't let him take her away from me."

"Who?" Dani gasped.

"Her father," Jake went on. "He tried to take her away."

"Is that why you killed him?" Rhiannon shouted, angrily.

Jake looked at the younger girl and pressed one index finger to his lips gently, a gesture designed to quieten her. She stood motionless glaring at him.

Dani felt as if she was going to be sick. She glanced at Mike who was lying immobile in the doorway of the room, blood spurting wildly from the huge gash in his head.

"You're insane," Dani whimpered, softly, her own tears now spilling down her face.

Again, Jake raised his index finger to his lips.

"We need to talk," he murmured.

"No," Dani gasped, backing away from him until she was standing next to Rhiannon.

"There are things I have to tell you," Jake said, softly and, as he spoke, he looked directly at her.

Dani felt as if her legs were giving way, all the strength draining from them but, as she stumbled, she could not tear her gaze away from Jake's face. From his eyes.

Or where his eyes should have been.

It was as if the bulging orbs had rolled upwards in the sockets, the whites and iris replaced with pure black, gleaming tissue that glistened in the cold, white light.

It was like looking at two polished pool balls.

No whites. No coloured area. Just glistening black. And somewhere in the back of her mind Lou Randall's words suddenly surfaced.

'They looked like ordinary children, apart from their eyes. There was nothing there. No pupils. No iris. It was just black where their eyes should have been.'

Dani felt her knees buckling.

She could see herself reflected in those blank, black, emotionless orbs that Jake had fixed on her.

Darkness hurtled in from all sides. She went down heavily, Rhiannon's screams echoing in her ears.

Jake stood watching; his face impassive.

ONE HUNDRED AND FIFTEEN

At first she thought she was blind.

Dani opened her eyes but could see nothing except darkness.

It took a second or two before she realized that she'd been blindfolded, she could feel the material against her eyelids and face now.

She tried to move but her hands and feet had been bound with something that felt like cable ties. Dani struggled against them for a moment, but they wouldn't give. She grunted irritably.

"I'll untie you soon."

The words filtered through the darkness. Startled, she turned sharply in their direction.

"I just need you to listen to me," the voice went on. "I don't want you...losing control."

Dani tried to swallow but found it impossible. She knew the words had been spoken by Jake Porter and now, as he walked unhurriedly back and forth in front of her, she blinked hard inside her blindfold and tried to focus on his position.

"Why, Jake?" she croaked. "Why have you done this?"

"I had to protect myself," he told her, his voice again coming to her through the black.

Once more she turned towards the source of the words, aware that he was still pacing slowly back and forth in front of her.

"I don't understand what's going on," she whispered, her voice shaking.

"I'm not even sure I do," Jake told her, a lightness to his tone that seemed even more incongruous now. "I suppose it's called self-preservation. That's been a big part of my life as you can imagine. That's why I killed Rhiannon's father. That's why I killed your...friend, whoever he was."

"Mike's dead?" she whimpered.

"Massive skull fracture," Jake added, conversationally. "He would have been dead almost before he hit the ground."

Dani murmured something unintelligible, her words dissolving into sobs.

"But I had no choice," Jake continued. "You *gave* me no choice. Why did you betray me, Dani? Why did you have to cheat on me with him? I thought you were different. I should have known though, shouldn't I? My mother always warned me not to trust anyone."

"Your mother? Which one?"

"My *real* mother. The one who looked after me. The one who freed me."

"Freed you?"

"From that hospital. At the beginning. She took me out of there. She saved me. Kept me safe. But the burden of that ate away at her through her life. She never really learned to accept what she'd done. That was why she killed herself. The guilt. She just couldn't cope. She was weak."

Dani shook her head gently, her mind reeling.

"And Rhiannon? What did she do to you that you had to lock her up in your cellar?" The last few words were shouted.

"I told you," Jake murmured. "I didn't want to lose her. Her father would have taken her away. I couldn't allow that."

"So, you kept her locked in your fucking cellar for two years?" Dani blurted. "Was that her punishment?" Her voice finally began calming slightly. "You said you loved her. Is that how you treat someone you love?" She sucked in a deep breath. "And what about me? What's my punishment going to be?"

"Punishment for what? For betraying me or for killing your child?"

Dani felt herself quivering slightly.

"What are you talking about?" she breathed.

"You killed your child," he said, flatly. "The child you should have had when you were twenty. You had an abortion, didn't you?"

"How do you know?" Dani gasped. "I never told you."

"It's one of my...gifts," Jake chuckled. "I can see *that* kind of betrayal too. I've seen it before in my life, too many times."

"I had no choice," she told him. "I couldn't have raised a child at that age. I would never have coped."

"So, you killed it?"

"You killed Mike," Dani whimpered.

"And you killed Ted Brady."

"It was an accident."

"Does it really matter now?"

Dani tried to stand up but the ties around her ankles prevented that action. She slumped backwards helplessly. As she did, she felt the first searing pains tear across her abdomen. The flesh of her stomach seemed to tighten suddenly but the agony was much deeper than just the skin. It felt as if her internal organs were on fire and she groaned loudly. She felt a wave of nausea hit her.

"What have you done to me?" she groaned.

"You brought it on yourself," Jake told her, flatly. "It'll be over soon. Once your fallopian tubes rupture there'll be so much internal bleeding, you'll be dead in ten minutes."

"Jake," Dani implored. "Please."

But he had already turned towards the door of the room, preparing to leave. There was no point standing watching her die. He knew it was going to happen. It couldn't be stopped now.

"Jake," she wailed again, the sound dissolving into a scream of agony.

He stepped out of the room, closing the door behind him.

Her screams and entreaties fell in volume and then ceased completely after five or six minutes but Jake didn't go back inside the room. There was plenty of time for that later. He'd dispose of her when he disposed of Mike Quinn and Ted Brady.

No hurry.

He'd wait until later, until the small hours so the night could hide him. Over the years he'd learned to welcome the hours of shadows and gloom. They were like friends to him. His mother had taught him that amongst so many other things. All designed to protect him.

For now, he needed to rest. There was a lot to do.

Jake smiled.

"It is absolutely necessary, for the peace and safety of mankind, that some of earth's dark, dead corners and unplumbed depths be left alone; lest sleeping abnormalities wake to resurgent life..."

H.P. Lovecraft,
At the Mountains of Madness and Other Tales of Terror